I0831525

ORCHID ON FIRE

THE PATH BETWEEN REALMS
BOOK 1

L. R. MIRELLE

Orchid on Fire

Published by LR Mirelle, LLC

lrmirelle.com

For my incredible husband, who believed in me from the very beginning, who carved out time and space so I could chase this dream, and who gave me the freedom to create wildly without judgment.

For my children, who gave me purpose before I knew I needed it.

And for this universe I have conjured from the ashes and the stars, a place that has set my soul ablaze.

This book is for every girl who was told to be quiet or to stay small. For every dreamer who was underestimated. For the ones who sat in the silence, let themselves be bored, and out of that boredom built entire worlds.

1

HIDDEN HEIR

Ellandria's heart thundered in her ribs, too loud for a night that demanded silence. She crouched in the shadow of a crumbling archway, her breath rising in soft clouds before her face. Stone walls climbed in jagged outlines around her, barely visible through the mist that clung like ghosts to the ancient streets of Dravaryn. Beyond them, the castle loomed, unknowable and untouched by any map she had ever seen, its foundations guarded by wards older than language.

Gods. The relic had better be here.

She swore under her breath and pressed a hand to her side where the skin was torn from the night before. Her muscles ached, her knee was slick with blood, and yet there was no time to measure the damage. It had taken her years to make it this far into Dravaryn, and she would not falter now. The stronghold was myth wrapped in granite, and everything beyond the city borders was rumored to be impenetrable, the castle most of all.

She had clawed her way across two kingdoms and countless miles of enemy territory. Rewired the very essence of herself to survive. And now, finally, here she was outside the castle they said no foreigner could reach. The castle that held secrets even the most powerful refused to speak aloud.

And she had no gods-damned plan for what came next.

All she knew was that the flame inside her, that deadly quiet truth she had nursed for years, was growing harder to contain. The unfurling heat was not only her nerves fraying but her magic igniting. Her hand flew to her collarbone, just beneath her cloak, where her tattoo curled like a thorn across her chest. She had waited for the mark, trained for it, longed for the day her fire would awaken, as was tradition among her people. Among Orchid's royal line, the ink was a symbol of pride, control, and power.

Now it pulsed beneath her fingers, warm and untamed, wrong in a way that unsettled her bones. She swore louder this time and yanked the cloak tighter.

No, not here. Not this far from home.

Magic belonged to the soil that birthed it, each kingdom's unique abilities woven into its land. Beyond those borders, her flame power should have gone quiet. Stranger still was her mark, the tattooed sigil on her chest that should have been dormant so far from Orchid. She should not feel the thrum of magic this deep in Dravaryn territory, familiar yet volatile, echoing the way it had before she learned to harness it. Before she became dangerous in all the wrong ways. Perhaps she was unraveling.

Ella forced herself to focus, to make a plan. She pressed a trembling hand to the stone at her back, the cold seeping into her bones.

Don't think. Don't remember.

But her memories clawed upward anyway: orchid fields

bathed in moonlight, the scent of her mother's hair as she bent to kiss her forehead, a voice soft and amused,

"Ellandria, darling, if you don't get those bare feet back inside, you'll catch your death in the dew. And try to eat something more than air and pride, just once, to ease your mother's heart."

The memory caught in her chest, tainted with guilt for leaving without saying goodbye. She had always been a mother first and a queen second to Ella, which she loved. Her father had been the opposite, King Eryndor of Orchid before all else, duty before family, which she respected.

But growing up with a king instead of a father had left its cracks. She'd learned early that needing someone was a weakness no royal could afford, so she stopped needing anyone at all.

She longed for the simpler ache of her mother fussing over bare feet and forgotten meals. She missed the girl she had been then.

That warmth flashed and was gone.

Pride no longer drove her forward; now it was purpose.

Leaving Orchid had always been inevitable.

Living with the guilt of it was the part she hadn't prepared for.

Staying would have cost more than her life. It would have endangered her people, her bloodline, her future. She had left in pursuit of a prophecy she had stumbled upon by accident, one that warned of the Veil sealing the realms now beginning to fracture. Her parents, the Queen and King of Orchid, had never spoken of the prophecy, nor had any member of the royal council. Perhaps they had not known. Or perhaps they had chosen silence, defying the fates to protect her. Either way, they had not realized what Ellandria had discovered, words that altered her very being, until it was too late to stop their only daughter from leaving.

She had waited for a signal, a sign that time was running out. It came to her in a dream she barely remembered, save for one word, one name that lingered. *Octavia.*

The pull of the prophecy had been undeniable, and she knew then that she must go. So she left. She changed her name. She buried her power so deep that she forgot how it felt to let it breathe.

So far from the soil of Orchid, her strength had waned; she had not felt it spark or seen her sigil stir upon her chest in so long.

Until now.

Until this cursed kingdom began to wake a wild, old, and eager magic within her.

Her mark pulsed beneath the tattered fabric of her cloak. Once, the tattoo that curved like thorns over her collarbone had glowed softly with ancestral magic. Now it burned low and strange, and she gritted her teeth as she looked down. Still invisible, yet it felt wrong, as though her sigil knew this soil, as though it remembered this land in ways she did not.

This kingdom should not recognize me.

The power inside her, fractured and feral, scraped against the edges of her mind, clawing to be free. Her control was slipping, her identity dissolving.

I am Ella. Just Ella. A nobody in this kingdom. Not Ellandria, Princess of Orchid. Not the flame-bound heir to a bloodline buried in burden and legacy.

She strangled the thoughts before they could take root. She had to forget the prophecy, the sealing of the realms, the banishment of the Fae.

This was not the time. She could not afford to think too loudly, not in a kingdom like this.

Because if anyone in Dravaryn was an Echobinder, they would seize the shape of her thoughts, and she would be ruined. She wasn't a Shield. She had no defenses, no way to guard her mind. Ella had only been gifted with offensive power, and since her kingdom had banned the Claiming ritual for more than five hundred years, there was no chance of her ever gaining new abilities.

If the wrong person drew too close they would hear everything: the truth, the prophecy, and worse still, her name. War between kingdoms would ignite before she ever set foot inside the Dravaryn castle. Her parents had dedicated their lives to preventing another war, and though Ella had already abandoned them, she refused to fail them as well. Not that she had much control over what could yet go wrong. The Veil between realms was thinning, and magic itself was becoming unpredictable.

Taking a steadying breath, Ella swore that once she stepped beyond this barrier she would not think of her parents or Orchid again. It was too dangerous, and besides, she didn't even know if they still lived or what her kingdom had become in her absence. The Dravaryns did not speak of Orchid and scraps of truth were rare, but she carried inside her what mattered. An unforgettable purpose bound to the aching hope that she might see them again when this quest was completed was all that kept her moving. Ella's thoughts were never quiet, never still, and Dravaryn itself felt as though it were listening.

She shifted her weight, and pain exploded through her thigh, shooting down to her knee until she bit back a curse. Her body was a map of wounds, each line etched in half-healed cuts, bruised joints, and skin stitched back together by luck alone, and still, she could not afford to stop moving. The breach into Dravaryn's capital had drained nearly everything she had left, and survival had demanded a web of lies, her quick charm, and a little violence. Necessary, of course.

Exhaling through her nose, she pressed a hand to the

archway behind her, grounding herself once more in its cold, unyielding presence.

The castle loomed ahead, massive and shrouded in myth. Ella had to get inside, fast. There was no time left to mend her wounds or allow her body to heal. Though she stepped into complete darkness, she was certain something waited within the castle, a relic tied to the prophecy, and she could not afford to leave it buried. She didn't know what would happen once she found it, only that the red sun the prophecy spoke of was drawing near. Weeks, at best. Whatever the relic was, she needed to reach it first, and give herself time to understand how it could save the mortal realm before that day arrived.

She closed her eyes and stilled her breath, and in the silence, the city itself possessed a heartbeat, steady and ancient, echoing beneath her skin.

Don't stop now.

A whisper of prayer to the gods she wasn't sure still existed, and she moved, quiet as snowfall, swift as the bite of a blade.

Ella reached the outer perimeter. The wards were supposed to begin farther in, yet here stood a tower, its dark frame rising high into the fog, vanishing into mist as though even the sky had grown weary. At its base, a figure kept watch, posture loose and almost careless, as if no one had ever come this far. And if the myths were true, no one had. She drew in the cold, the air biting her lungs.

If there was only one guard posted at the outer gate, then either the fates were showing her mercy, or it was a trap. Ella froze, her breath fogging in the mist, clothes clinging wet with blood, fabric torn from clawing her way across the icy waste of a kingdom. Every step she took seemed to scream of a foreigner, a trespasser, and it would only take one glimpse of her in this state and any Dravaryn would raise the alarm.

The guard shifted, lantern glow catching on the hard line of his jaw. He appeared muscular, medium build, and the uniform would fit her better than the ruins she wore. But she didn't know what magic thrummed in his veins, what oath burned behind his eyes.

She had seconds to decide: kill him now and slip inside or hesitate and risk him striking first.

Her hand slid to the hilt at her thigh. When it came to battle, she would never let a man make the first choice.

Ella moved, and steel flashed. A breath, a gasp, and his lantern fell from his hand. The flame guttered out midair, and he was already falling by the time it struck the ground.

She caught his cloak before it hit the stone, heavy and lined with the Dravaryn crest, proof that she had crossed into the heart of the enemy at last.

She didn't enjoy killing, but survival had no patience for hesitation, and he had the prophecy to blame for his death.

2

BENEATH THE FLESH

Ella reached the wards at last, and the barrier did not break her. It let her in. She took a step and there wasn't a sound exactly, not a scream of magic tearing the night apart, but something quieter, a hum that curled beneath her skin like smoke.

The ancient wards were meant to repel her, to fling her back, to shatter her mind or burn her from the inside out. That was the legend, the only warning she had gathered from the townsfolk during her time on the outskirts of Dravaryn's capital, Draethmar, but instead, the wards seemed to part for her. There was barely a shimmer in the air, no fanfare, no flash, only a pull, as if the land itself had inhaled and recognized her, opening one eye to let her pass.

She was several steps beyond the barrier when her ears rang, like a bell struck too close, the pressure stabbing behind her eyes. She pressed her palms hard against her skull, fighting the spin of vertigo until the ache dulled enough to breathe. When she dropped into a crouch, her heart pounded loud enough to drown the whisper of wind across the courtyard.

She had expected alarms, shouts, anything but the silence that followed, which was somehow worse because it felt intentional.

Cocky Dravaryns.

Her fingers pressed against the cloth above her collarbone, making certain her mark was still hidden. It was, but the unease that tightened her chest made it feel as though the truth lay bare.

The air within the outer perimeter was thicker, laced with residual magic that tasted bitter on her tongue. The ground emanated power as she looked across the courtyard, sliced into clean, symmetrical divisions: sparring dummies slumped against their stakes, runic circles scorched into the dirt, weapons racks gleaming faintly in the moonlight, each blade waiting for war. This was where Dravaryn trained its elite, her first glimpse into the mystery of their secrets and the powers their warriors might wield.

She drank it in, storing every detail for later. The air smelled of steel, sweat, and old ash, echoes of countless battles never meant for her to witness. The field was lined with polished obsidian that shimmered like oil in the low light, veins of old enchantments winding through the flagstones.

Beyond the training yard, the castle rose, a vast silhouette carved against the mist, its towers serrated like knives and merciless as if they had been hewn from the very bones of the mountain. Moonlight caught on its ramparts, turning stone to silver, but there was nothing soft in the sight. It stood like a sentence waiting to be carried out. One misstep, and this place would be her ruin.

Even the courtyard carried that same austerity. Between the wide sections of onyx-laced stone stretched neat squares of frost-covered grass, trimmed and manicured as meticulously as the divisions of the yard itself. It was a kingdom built on symmetry, on discipline, on cold order that left no room for warmth. Every line of it reminded her of what awaited inside: power, reckoning, and the chance to prove she could survive them both to find the relic.

To the west, a group of guards stood gathered in loose formation, too far to see her but too close to risk.

Ella moved, swift and silent. She dipped low, hugging the shadows where torchlight failed to reach, each movement measured.

Until it wasn't.

Halfway across the training grounds, her boot struck a groove in the stone, sending her staggering into a crouch, ribs flaring with the crackle of bruised bone. She bit back a cry, forced her breath to even, and propelled herself forward.

The cloak dragged behind her like dead weight, its hem dark and sodden from crossing the courtyard. Ahead, the neatly sectioned grounds narrowed into a corridor flanked by towering columns of the castle, their carvings twisted into snarling beasts.

She had nearly made it.

The clatter of steel drifted up ahead, followed by low voices. Three guards rounded the far edge of the courtyard, half-laughing, relaxed, and unaware of her. Ella slid behind a pillar, lungs straining as she stilled her breath.

She didn't want to kill them if she didn't have to. But if they saw her Orchid mark flare... The cloak might hide her face if she pulled it tight, but the combination of her royal mark and her eyes might betray her. Ella had always known she looked too much like her mother, Queen Serenya, especially with her ocean-blue eyes, and these were not mere townsfolk that she could charm or distract. She wasn't sure what powers they possessed beyond brute force, and unfortunately for her, the men were massive, towering figures. Ella cursed under her breath.

The men slowed, turned, and then stopped. One of the guards shifted, his gaze sweeping the shadows. For one breath too long, his gaze lingered on the pillar where she crouched, and the weight of it settled against her skin. Her hand tightened on the dagger at her thigh, ready to strike if he took one step closer. But then he snorted, turned back to his companions, and the moment broke.

A bead of sweat traced a cold line down her neck to the collar of her cloak.

One guard shoved his arm out to halt the others. "High alert, boys." His chin lifted toward the tower where a crimson flag had been raised, its fabric catching the torchlight. A silent signal, meant to spread warning without stirring panic. "Weapons ready."

Clever.

Perhaps she had underestimated their castle defenses.

The second scoffed, low and mocking. "Probably just a trainee setting off the outer ring again."

The first snapped back, voice clipped. "They wouldn't raise the flag for that."

"What then? One of the outer wards?" The second sneered. "Impossible. No one crosses those. Not unless they've got Dravaryn blood. Or they're summoned by Jakobav." His voice dropped. "And *someone's* been doing a lot of summoning lately."

A beat of silence, and then came a third voice, dry and biting. "Careful how you talk about the prince."

"Just saying," the second guard replied, shifting his weight. "He seems to be running things. And no one's told us different."

"The king is handling trade agreements with Velmire," the third shot back.

Their voices faded as the men drifted on, oblivious, but Ella had gone still, a knot tightening low in her stomach.

Dravaryn blood.

Summoned by Prince Jakobav.

The words coiled like venom through her chest, and though she cursed silently, it was not the name alone that made her stomach twist. She knew who he was, not the boy prince from faded war tales, but the blade behind Dravaryn's resurgence. The one whispered about in border towns, rumored to look more beast than man, forged in blood and shadow like the kingdom itself. She had been too young to remember the devastation his father had brought, but the stories lingered everywhere. The Dravaryn king had been brutal during the war with Orchid, and Jakobav would be catastrophic if another conflict ever began.

She had no intention of crossing paths with the prince, not while the prophecy still pulled her deeper into enemy territory, toward something she prayed to the gods was an artifact, a key, something tangible and easy to steal. Especially if she had any hope of making it out alive. And she did. High hopes, as a matter of fact, because if she didn't, she'd already be dead.

She waited, counted to three, and then ran, her steps silent across the stone. When she passed the last column and reached the inner corridor, the spaces between the pillars narrowed into tighter passageways lit with torchlight and banners bearing the Dravaryn crest. She would not be getting out unscathed. It was too far away, with far too many torches burning to cross unseen.

That strange magic stirred again, humming from the hidden sigil in her chest, raw and unfamiliar, flaring as if it wanted to be seen. Her vision pulsed at the edges, hands slick with sweat and blood that wasn't hers. Or maybe it was. Hard to tell anymore.

The practiced smile of a princess, the mask she had perfected and wielded like a weapon more times than she could count, would serve no purpose here, not covered in filth like this. There was no gown to disarm them, no crown to draw their gaze, no honeyed laughter to turn danger into a dance. That mask had fooled generals, courtiers, and even more than one would-be suitor into underestimating her. But here, in a corridor of steel and stone, there was nothing left to hide behind but knives and blood.

The first soldier saw her just as she threw the knife. The blade found its mark, buried to the hilt in his throat, and he dropped with a wet gurgle.

There was no time to hesitate. Another guard had already turned, shouting for reinforcements, and four more surged into the hall. Three were men, and one a woman whose white-blonde hair caught the torchlight as insignia glinted on their armor. Ella had spent enough time in Dravaryn now to recognize the more intricate designs that marked them as higher rank than the previous guards.

Ella's hand closed on her second blade. Longer and curved, it was better for tearing. She dropped low, momentum carrying her through a sweeping kick that took his feet out from under him and sent him crashing to the ground. She was already on him, blade slicing through the leather gap beneath his chin.

Hot blood gushed, steaming in the cold.

Ella turned just in time to catch the shaft of a spear across her ribs, and pain splintered through her torso. She staggered, then pivoted, grabbing the wooden shaft and twisting it hard. The soldier grunted as she slammed the blunt end into his temple: once, twice, *crack*, and he slumped to the floor.

The third man didn't hesitate; his axe arced through the air in a brutal, two-handed swing. She dove backward, landed badly, something popping in her shoulder, but still rolled to her feet, panting and weaponless.

The axe came again as she side-stepped, kicked him square in the knee, and when he dropped an inch, she lunged, snatched up the fallen spear, and rammed it through his gut before yanking it sideways. His scream echoed off the stone, loud enough to summon more footsteps thundering from behind.

"Shit," she muttered.

Two more. No...four. All armored, all bigger than her. One carried a sword the length of her leg, and another hefted a black-glass warhammer that was unmistakably Dravaryn-forged.

Ella was out of weapons, so she used the walls. She sprang off the stone and, using the narrow corridor for momentum, grabbed a hanging torch mid-jump. Pain carved through her shoulder as she hurled the torch at the nearest enemy. The flame caught on his leather, and he screamed, dropping his blade. She was already ducking beneath his flailing limbs to snatch his dagger, driving it into the thigh of the next man.

The woman with white-blonde hair stood at the edge of the fray, insignia gleaming sharper and higher than the rest. She didn't rush in like the others. Instead she leaned against the stone archway, one boot propped lazily over the other, arms folded, watching the fight with a cocky smirk, as though Ella's desperate clash for survival was little more than entertainment.

Ella cut down another guard, steel slicing through the narrow gap of his armor. The clang echoed in the corridor, blood pooling black in the torchlight. Still, the woman didn't move, her gaze locked and assessing, piercing enough that Ella felt stripped bare beneath it.

"Savina! A little help over here?" one of the higher-ranked soldiers barked, straining to hold Ella back.

The woman finally pushed off the wall, rolling her shoulders with a predator's ease. "Fine," Savina drawled, her smirk widening. Then she lunged.

Steel clashed again, Ella twisting, parrying, gasping as pain seared through her injured shoulder and battered ribs. The woman's strikes were brutal, faster than the men's had been, as though she was the real test all along. And for a moment, Ella faltered. The woman snarled, grabbed Ella by the hair, yanked, and then the air around her flared as her hidden mark thrummed beneath her collarbone, alive, desperate to break free.

The woman's gaze flicked down, and for the barest heartbeat her smirk faltered, curiosity flashing in her eyes before they hardened again. That single hesitation was all Ella needed. She twisted and drove her blade across the woman's stomach. Not as deep as she'd aimed, her exhausted body resisting, agony folding through her bones. Still, the blood pooled fast, and the warrior staggered, teeth bared, a snarl tearing from her throat as she crumpled to the ground.

A shout rang out, and the others rushed toward them. Breathing hard and coated in crimson, Ella pushed her body to straighten and willed her expression neutral instead of pained. She was not victorious, just alive. And barely that.

Her hand trembled against the wall, not from fear, but from surviving when she hadn't expected to.

The silence returned, but it wasn't empty anymore. It was watching her. Ella searched for the source of the silence that felt like it was screaming to her, but she could not see past the group of guards that had her surrounded and were closing in.

Fuck. There's no way this is going to end well. I've failed.

The quiver that had begun with her hands had now spread to the rest of her body, shaking violently, likely from blood loss. Then the torchlight flickered, and a voice, deep and velvet-dark, echoed through the hall.

"Stand. Down."

He didn't need to shout. He was the kind of man who could break bones with a whisper.

He emerged from the shadows like smoke made flesh: massive, coiled, dominant, carved from stone with harsh lines and brutal grace. Muscles bulged beneath worn fabric that showcased his tattoos. Black ink, curling down from his neck to the veins of his hands, seemed to shimmer in the torchlight but not with ancestral magic. Either war marks or a warning, likely both.

Razor-sharp jaw and lips too full for a man forged for killing. His dark eyes locked onto her like a predator studying a wounded animal he didn't quite want to kill yet.

She froze as something primal moved between them.

Behind her, a soldier raised his blade.

The man didn't blink. "I said *stand down.*"

The sword lowered.

Ellandria swayed, and he took one step closer, towering, imposing, and yet eerily quiet.

His presence bent the air around him, and his gaze pinned her in place without lifting a single finger. He stared at her like he already knew why she was here, which was impossible.

Her grip on reality faltered, heat surging at her collarbone as darkness pressed at the edges of her vision.

He reached forward, but she was already slipping under. And with a single breath, the world shattered around her.

3

KEY OF DRAVARYN

She awoke to silence. Not the gentle quiet of safety but the heavy kind that lingered in places where blood had been spilled, the strange hush that followed after a battlefield emptied. Her breath came shallow, each pull threaded with the phantom taste of smoke and iron.

Fuck. Don't panic.

Pain had rooted itself deep in her body, pounding behind her eyes and winding through her limbs like thorns beneath the skin. When she tried to shift, regret seared through her ribs until it stole her breath. Her arm refused to obey, her body trembling as something hot and wet spread slowly beneath rough bandages.

Bandages. Gods. She forced herself to stop and think. She wasn't dead. Not yet.

Her name whispered faintly on the fringe of her mind, not the one she was born with but the one she needed to cling to.

Just Ella.

Ellandria of Orchid was a ghost she could not afford to

awaken, not now, perhaps not ever, especially not if she kept bleeding like this.

She dragged her focus outward. The air carried the scent of ashwood and amber, undercut by the mineral bite of winter stone and something harsher still. For a heartbeat, she thought she smelled someone smoking wraith-leaf, that bitter, cloying scent she'd learned to avoid in the border towns of Dravaryn, and her stomach lurched. But no, this was different. Less illicit, more medicinal. That should have been reassuring, but it only unsettled her more.

Where in the hell am I?

Nearby, a fire crackled, its warmth crawling across her frozen skin. Her vision cleared enough to shape the outlines of the space around her: stone walls, a timber ceiling heavy with shadow, weapons mounted in grim display. Blades. Axes. A shield that could have doubled as a door. Not a healer's quarters, then.

A soldier's. And that was worse.

The thought barely had time to settle before a shadow moved across the firelight. A voice followed, low and velvet-dark, carrying an authority that was impossible to mistake, a command sharpened into every syllable.

"You're awake."

She snapped her head toward the sound, and pain lanced through her skull, forcing her to wince.

He stood several paces away, colossal in size, filling the room more completely than the weapons on the walls ever could. His dark brown hair fell unbound past his jaw, framing a face carved in shadowed lines, all sharp planes and unforgiving strength. His arms were folded across his chest, a faint scar tracing the line of his temple, and his eyes, dark and watchful, carried no cruelty yet offered no comfort either. They held restraint, the controlled patience of a predator that had learned to keep its teeth hidden, though everything about him suggested that composure would not last.

He did not ask her name, and he did not offer his. But she knew who he was.

The Prince.

No one else could have commanded soldiers to stand down with nothing more than two words.

Ella had heard many rumors about the Prince of Dravaryn, each more impossible than the last. They spoke of the mystery of his power, of how he could shatter minds with nothing but a glance, that meeting his eyes meant losing yourself entirely. Others claimed he had once silenced a battlefield with a single breath, bodies twisting to his will and leveling an army before they ever reached him.

She did not believe every tale, but she believed enough.

And of one thing she was certain: he was her enemy. One of *them.* Dravaryn-born and heir to the kingdom she had just delivered herself into. His reputation was woven into whispers that spread across the continent, ruthless and unforgiving, the future king of a land where mercy was weakness and silence was tradition. And silence, Ella knew, was how secrets survived.

Her heart stuttered hard against her ribs, and her hand flew instinctively to the mark at her collarbone. It was still gone, thank the gods, because if he were to see it, there would be no hesitation. She found his gaze again.

"You're in my home," he said at last, his expression unreadable, his voice cutting through the air.

For one reckless moment, she glanced toward the door, the iron handle and solid oak frame no more than ten or twelve steps away, though even that small distance felt impossible. She forced her focus back to him, the idea of escape unraveling quickly.

"Do not try to run. You won't make it far."

Her pulse betrayed her, a frantic stammer against her ribs. The steadiness of his stance told her she wouldn't make it past three steps.

"Well, I'm certainly not going to stay," she rasped, measuring her surroundings. She pushed against her elbows and nearly collapsed back, stars bursting across her vision before she swallowed them down. "Take me to your king. I don't want his shadow."

Something flickered across his face, the faintest ghost of a dangerous amusement. "You don't look like someone fit for an audience," he said, his gaze dragging slowly over her.

A shiver trailed her spine. Was he about to kill her, or was there something darker that lingered in the way he looked at her?

"You don't look like a prince," she shot back, her teeth flashing with a razor-edged smile that never reached her eyes.

One dark brow rose. "Disappointed?"

Ella's throat burned with a cough, but she let her mouth curve sharper. "Very."

A full smile broke across his face, like he was amused by her defiance, but it vanished as quickly as it came. His expression darkened. "What do you want with my father?"

She held her silence.

"Trust me." His voice dropped lower. "You don't want him anywhere near your blood when it's spilling like that."

He moved closer.

She couldn't respond, couldn't even keep her eyes open long enough to try, but even as the dark dragged at her, she swore to prove him wrong.

I don't need the king. I need a way out. I didn't come this far to break before the prophecy could be fulfilled.

Before her mind slipped fully into blackness, she fought to

hold his stare. He looked back, head tilting slightly, eyes narrowing as though she were a puzzle he could unravel by sight alone. His gaze was not entirely hostile. It gleamed with the curiosity of a predator deciding what to do with prey that had nowhere left to go.

Then, almost to himself, he murmured, "I have a feeling you don't belong here...for more reasons than one."

4

ENEMY'S TOUCH

Ella immediately noticed warmth, then the stillness of solitude. Her eyes opened slowly, and the same chamber greeted her. The fire in the hearth had burned low, casting shadows that danced like ghost-light across the room.

She blinked and sat up with a wince. Her muscles howled, but her mind moved faster now, more alert. Ella replayed her conversation with the prince, unable to understand why she wasn't chained and tortured, though the pain tearing through her body was certainly a form of torment.

But this was not a dungeon, and unless Dravaryn had suddenly developed a flair for understated luxury, she'd woken up in the exact opposite of a prison. He'd said she was in his home. Ella couldn't make sense of the bloodthirsty prince speaking of the castle with anything resembling reverence.

Dravaryn was rumored to be the most violent of the continent's four kingdoms, so this fate-cursed palace had to have an entire wing dedicated to healing injuries. Because if the rumors were true, and the gods knew most of them probably were,

Dravaryn's military churned through blood and bone like fire through kindling, brutal and unrelenting. Soldiers dropped, and healers mended. That cycle likely repeated daily. She had now seen firsthand how fierce and unrestrained the guards were, even the female soldiers. She despised nearly everything about Dravaryn, but the sight of a woman so highly ranked in their military was one thing she begrudgingly respected. In Orchid, women rarely trained for battle unless they were nobles or wielded flame potent enough to turn the tide of battle.

The woman she'd stabbed in the abdomen upon arrival was named Savina. Hopefully she had survived. Not just because death felt like too high a price to pay, but because anyone who could take a blade like that and still nearly cut her down deserved another chance at life.

Why wasn't she lying in the infirmary among the bleeding masses, or rotting in some dungeon awaiting judgment and execution? Especially after stabbing a high-ranking member of their military. Why was she here? In a chamber far too quiet, and that felt far too personal. The bed beneath her was deathly soft, the sheets exquisite, woven of dark green linen and edged in a thread that gleamed like gold.

She glanced around, heart ticking up a beat. The walls were carved with long, vertical grooves. Were these Dravaryn etchings ceremonial or decorative? A Dravaryn crest was displayed proudly above the mantle.

Something tugged at her memory. When she'd first woken, the walls had bristled with weapons. Now the racks hung empty, stripped bare.

Every last blade gone.

Shit.

She tore her gaze from the now bare walls. Heavy boots were positioned by the door, and on the far table, a silver ring glinted beside a leather wristband and a folded tunic. This wasn't a guest room, and it certainly wasn't a cell.

This was someone's private chamber.

Ella's breath caught.

Fuck. This is his room.

She'd been far too disoriented when she woke the first time to recognize it, but now the truth pressed against her with undeniable weight. The thought struck before she could stop it.

Had she slept with the enemy in his bed?

She prayed to the gods he had been sleeping on the floor. Without realizing it, she'd been lying in the prince's bed, her body surrendering to the enemy's sheets. She swallowed hard, the thought bitter in her throat. Surely he would not have lain beside her, but the possibility sent a chill skittering across her spine that wasn't fear exactly but an awareness that throbbed beneath her skin.

Why had he let her sleep in his chambers—and worse, in his bed? Ella stirred beneath the blankets. Her bloodied clothes were gone, likely taken, burned, or both. The act of someone changing her clothes was far too intimate, and she wasn't sure she wanted to know who had dressed her. The attire she wore now was of higher quality, though far too large, the fabric cinched awkwardly at her waist with a belt. Even her boots and weapons were gone. Gods, her weapons. Of course she didn't expect to be allowed to keep them, but their absence left her stripped and vulnerable in a way she despised.

Her collarbone, where the sigil had once glowed openly, now rested beneath fine fabric, silent and unseen. She prayed it would stay that way. Her fingers brushed the mark, and thankfully, it was still invisible, still quiet.

She pushed back the sheets and swung her legs over the edge of the mattress, the fire in the hearth throwing just enough light to reveal the bandages wrapped tightly around her ribs.

She gritted her teeth and forced herself upright as pain exploded through her limbs. Her knees buckled, and she crumpled halfway to the door, the floor rising to meet her before she could stop it.

The freezing stone sent jolts of pain up her arms as her palms slapped against it, catching herself, but barely.

"Do you have a death wish?" Jakobav's voice was low, angry yet somehow gravel-soft.

She flinched, pain snapping along her spine as she jerked toward the sound. "Gods, you scared the shit out of me," she hissed, breath catching. "Is this a Dravaryn punishment—sneak up on me until I tear open my stitches? Do you enjoy watching me suffer, or could you announce yourself next time instead of materializing like a ghost?"

He ignored her and crouched beside her, arms corded with strength as he gathered her up. The motion stole her breath. She hadn't realized how easily he could lift her. As he carried her toward the bed, she saw now it wasn't truly a bed at all but a throne disguised in linen and shadows.

Her pulse thrummed hard against his shoulder. Yet he didn't set her down.

His mouth curved, not quite a smile. "You don't like doing what you're told, do you?" His gaze raked over her face as though memorizing her defiance, his hand lingering at her waist a moment longer than necessary.

"We'll have to work on that," he murmured.

Ella twisted in his grip, ignoring the flare of pain down her spine. "You'll work on nothing," she spat, fury cutting through the haze of pain. "I don't belong to you."

He didn't even flinch, just held her still with effortless

strength. His gaze didn't waver, but sharpened, amusement laced with dark intentions.

Ella stilled in his arms, unwillingly aware of how his breath brushed her temple, warm, far too close. She squirmed against the cage of his grip, but the motion only drew her tighter against him. The heat of him seeped through her skin, unsettling in ways she refused to name.

His hold tightened, frustration breaking through his calm. "Stop fighting me," he snapped, voice filled with command. "Will you follow orders for your own safety, at least until you're healed enough to try running again?"

Her throat burned, but she forced the rasp past it. "Forgive me for not enjoying the mystery of waking up in unknown territory," she choked out, throat dry. "What would you have me do? Wait politely to be executed?"

The air shifted between them as he set her down gently. Ella could have sworn she caught the faintest glimpse of a smirk on his face.

His dark brow barely lifted. "And you thought crawling on the floor would clarify things?"

She didn't answer. Her pride was already bleeding.

"You're not in a cell because I chose not to put you in one," he said, voice low and deliberate. "You're here because I decide what happens to you now. My quarters are the only place where you won't become a problem."

A chill skittered through her, and Ella responded without thinking. "How exactly would *I* be a problem for *you*?"

Jakobav crowded closer, his phantom smile twisting darker. "You'd become a problem if you were seen. A much bigger one if you died."

Her stomach lurched, and her mind barely kept pace. "Where did you sleep?" The question tore free colder than she intended, suspicion dripping from every word.

He didn't answer, but his gaze lingered.

Of course he hadn't answered. This was his bed, his room, his kingdom. She refused to follow the thought to its end, looked away first, and hated that she did.

Jakobav stood near the bed, arms crossed, unreadable again. There was no smugness or overt threat, only the unbearable calm of a man who knew exactly what he was capable of.

He slowly reached toward the bandage on her knee.

Ella pulled her legs back, wrapped the sheets around herself, and whispered, "Do not touch me." It was ironic, she thought, that the only times he had touched her so far had been out of necessity and for her benefit.

He stilled, but not out of offense. He didn't look surprised. If anything, he looked knowing.

"You needed help," he said at last.

But her focus snagged on the way his hands had touched her ribs when she collapsed moments before—gentle, like he'd been afraid of breaking her. It made her hate the way she'd just pulled away from him, instinctively rejecting his attempt to check on her injury.

But she knew why.

Before Dravaryn, back in Orchid, she'd spent her entire life surrounded by men who wanted something from her—an audience with her father, political leverage, her hand in marriage years before she'd even considered the idea. One suitor had even mentioned the mating ceremony before giving her his name. They all saw her as a path, a prize, a piece to claim.

She'd had enough of men who thought they could shape her, steer her, own her.

Those days were over.

And when she finally let someone close, his hands hadn't

been so careful. He was the son of a prominent nobleman on her father's council, someone she'd once trusted. *Caelen.*

A man with laughter on his lips and a truth she hadn't wanted to see. He'd never left scars anyone could see, but they were still there, buried beneath every flinch she tried to hide.

Caelen had taught her exactly what happened when she let someone close.

She wouldn't make that mistake again.

She hadn't fled her kingdom because of him. That came later. She fled because if she stayed...the kingdom would fall, a fact she'd known with marrow-deep certainty. So she ran, but not from him. From what was coming.

Jakobav's command interrupted her thoughts. "You'll stay until you can walk without bleeding," he said, turning to the hearth. He tossed a log into the embers and stirred the fire to life again.

She swallowed, gulping down air that was too thick with the smell of him. Dangerous and masculine, it wrapped around her like a cloak.

Ella had to move, needed to get away from that smell as it clung too close, suffocating her. She pushed to her feet too fast, and heat surged through her skull, the room threatening to spin.

There was no way she was about to face-plant again.

Ella hated looking weak more than anything in the mortal realm.

Jakobav reached out, fast and unrelenting, his arm locking around her waist to steady her. She gasped, and they both froze. Her heart pounded, too loud and too long, as every instinct screamed: Move. Fight. Flee.

But she didn't.

His jaw flexed, voice low, dangerously so. "I've already had you in my arms three times." He said each word slowly. "When you were bleeding out, when you couldn't crawl five steps, and now because you won't *stay down.*"

He looked furious like he might do something violent, then he stepped back, eyes like stormglass.

"Next time, I won't help you."

Her pulse spiked, and she forced the words past her raw throat and spat them like venom.

"You sound like every man who has ever underestimated me. They all bled for it."

A beat passed before he said, "Maybe I want to see what it takes to break you."

Prince Jakobav stared her down.

Ella refused to be the one to break eye contact this time. Finally, he moved first, but instead of leaving, he lingered at her side.

"Stop running," Jakobav demanded, voice deep and uncompromising.

Ella's chin snapped up. "I thought you said I wasn't a prisoner."

Silence. He only stared her down, head tilting the slightest degree, gaze unreadable and unyielding.

"Well then," she shot back, pulse racing, "I guess I'm free to go."

She spun, but his hand closed around her wrist before she could take a step. He swung her back to face him, controlled and unshakable.

"I can't let you do that."

She shoved him, hard, and pain reverberated through her body. Bad idea. He didn't budge. He might as well have been solid granite. His eyes stayed locked on hers, burning.

Her chest heaved, jaw clenching with anger because she didn't actually want to leave yet. She couldn't without finding what she came for. But the way he looked at her like he was daring her to fight, to fail, had every inch of her body itching to defy him.

Jakobav's mouth curved, more threat than smile. "Would you rather rot in my dungeon or stay in my bedchamber?"

Ella stepped toward him, fists clenched. "I don't think you'd like my response, Prince."

He didn't flinch. "Say the word. I'll throw you over my shoulder and carry you to the dungeon."

When she didn't answer, he bent, reaching for her legs as if to make good on the threat.

"Okay!" Her hand shot out, stopping him. She stumbled back a step. "Okay, I prefer your chambers. But only until my body's recovered. Then I'm getting the fuck out of here."

His eyes lingered on her, unreadable, dangerous. Then, softer, darker: "We'll see about that."

Unbelievable.

She had come here to slip through shadows, steal what she needed, and vanish before anyone ever knew she'd been inside the castle. Instead she had woken in the Prince's private chambers, her enemy's bed. He was controlling, sadistic in his demeanor, and unbearably overbearing. The entire situation was outrageous...and maybe, if she played it carefully, useful. If she could win even a sliver of his trust, perhaps it would give her the chance to search for the relic she had risked everything to find.

Ella's lips lifted in spite of herself, a little hum escaping.

"Hmm."

Jakobav's eyes narrowed. "What now?"

"I want to know the rules," she said. "Where I'm allowed to go. What I'm allowed to do." Her jaw tightened. "Not that I'm agreeing to be held captive."

That earned a smirk from Jakobav.

She braced, praying he'd say something like *I've never held anyone captive before.*

His voice dropped. "This arrangement is a first for me as well. I've never had anyone sleep in my chambers before."

Ella arched a brow. "You're telling me you've never had a woman in your bed?"

His mouth turned darker. "Not one that mattered. And I said sleep in my chambers." He leaned in, voice a razor-edged tease. "There has never been any sleeping."

She refused to give him the satisfaction of a reply, but her flushed skin gave her away, warmth blooming where his eyes lingered.

5

BLOOD REVEALS

JAKOBAV

Maybe he should have killed her. She had broken into his fortress and crossed the wards, knowing she would probably meet her doom. He would not have hesitated with any other intruder.

She'd asked how she could possibly be a problem for him. Oh, how little she knew. She had just become the problem he could not stop circling. Yes, the Claiming should have been at the front of his mind. The solstice drew nearer, bringing with it the rising strength of the sacred pool.

Dravaryn bloodlines were expected to face its waters and emerge marked with the gift of a second power, if the realm deemed them worthy. And yet, not all who entered surfaced again.

For a prince, there was no choice. The rite had to be endured while the king still lived. Only then could the throne be passed without fracture.

But it was not the thought of the ceremony that consumed him tonight. It was her. The way she refused to break in front of him made him want to drag her down to nothing, only to build her back up inch by inch. Every time she spat her venom, her eyes sparked with hate, and her bottom lip trembled as if she meant every fucking word. He longed to sink his teeth into that lip.

She had asked why his chambers, why his bed.

He couldn't keep her anywhere else in this castle. No way in hell he would've allowed that. It would've been even more of a distraction than she already was. Even now, he was itching to check on her—craving the certainty that no man laid eyes on her while she was injured.

From what he'd gathered about her, she'd fucking hate that. Being checked on like that. Possessive. Jealous. Overbearing.

Not that he would call her fragile. She had more grit than most men he had bled beside.

Fuck, she was under his skin.

So far under he'd almost punched the stone wall when she glared at him with that sharp tongue ready to cut. He told himself the reason he'd kept her alive was to protect Dravaryn, to find out what she was doing here and what she knew.

Did she know the truth of the king's failing state? Did she know what Jakobav was covering, hiding, protecting? Was she an enemy spy sent from another kingdom? Those were the reasons he repeated to himself, but none of them explained why he couldn't stop toying with her.

Jakobav watched the girl sleep, breath shallow, brow damp with the kind of fever that burned too hot to survive. But her chest still rose, and her fingers twitched faintly beneath the blanket he had pulled over her ribs.

Gods, he shouldn't have been watching over her at all; he should've been the one to take her out, to slit her throat, instead of ordering his soldiers to stand down.

Maybe the fever would do it for him.

The First Guard, the highest-ranking soldiers in his army, had seen him hesitate, and he fucking despised that.

By dawn, the corridor was scrubbed and the reports sealed. Another mess erased, another secret buried. Too often Soren and Thane had to clean up what should've never reached their hands, but Jakobav told himself it was the price of command, though it grated all the same.

Still, his friends hadn't let it go easily.

Thane was the first to push him. "You drag an intruder out of a blood-soaked hallway and vanish for half a day? You've got to tell us if she's a spy, a witch, or your long-lost conscience."

Jakobav had only grunted, which only encouraged him.

"Don't play stoic," Thane pressed, smirking. "If she's dead, say so. If she's not, tell us what sort of miracle she pulled to get through the wards alive. Unless..." His grin widened.

"You've gone soft for a trespasser."

Soren, quieter but far more dangerous in his curiosity, had only leaned back in his chair. "If you won't tell us, I'll find out myself. Maybe I'll pay our guest a visit."

That had earned him a look sharp enough to cut glass and a low warning growl that Jakobav failed to suppress before it escaped.

In the end, Jakobav told them nothing. Only Soren had pried loose one sliver of truth when Jakobav's restraint cracked. He had confessed his theories about what she might be. Even then, he had left more unsaid than spoken.

He never thought he'd be grateful for a member of his First Guard to be confined to the infirmary, but thank the gods Savina was occupied. Otherwise, she would have questioned him until his ears bled about why the woman was not already dead or locked in the dungeons. That conversation was coming. So was the one with Maeren, his second-in-command.

Jakobav guessed she would be tracking him down for answers any day now.

And yet, they had all seen it. Thane's grin said it. Soren's silence confirmed it. The prince of Dravaryn, the man who commanded armies without blinking, had finally found something in his carefully planned existence that did not fit neatly within his control.

A few other members of his First Guard had witnessed him take the girl after she collapsed, but no one else had inquired about her state since. In their minds, she was already gone, lost to the dungeon or to execution and ash. That was the Dravaryn way.

No one breached the wards and lived, and anyone foolish enough to try was disintegrated where they stood, their body unmade by the ancient spellwork. The only exceptions were those carried through by blood or invited by oath. That was the law of the wards, older than language itself.

So to them, she was a fluke. Either luck or a ripple in old magic that was easily explained away and dismissed, not something to unravel or someone to worry about.

But he wasn't so sure.

Wrong uniform.

That blood-drenched cloak she'd worn bore the Dravaryn crest, but it was too large for her slim frame. Had to have been a stolen soldier's cloak, not hers.

Wrong blood.

He hadn't meant to use his ability.

She had been drenched in it, her own and his guard's. There was too much blood for anyone but him to tell which belonged to whom. When a drop landed on his lips during the chaos, he could smell at once that it wasn't Dravaryn, even without tasting. But resisting had been impossible.

A single drop, and he gave in.

He had tasted it not to steal power, not to plunder her mind, but to know her bloodline. How else had she crossed the wards?

He'd felt it the instant the wards shuddered. The air had thickened, and magic twisted against itself. Something had crossed the threshold, and yet he hadn't said it aloud, not to Maeren or the Guard, not even to Bryn. He'd never heard of anyone being able to sense the barrier, but Jakobav could hear its hum, feel the way its power pressed in.

Once, as a boy, he had dared to mention it to his father, and the king's reply had been a flat warning. *Keep that to yourself, son.*

So when she breached the wards, it had resonated through him like a struck chord. Arguably more concerning was that only someone with blood older than Dravaryn could've passed the wards in such a manner, and yet she looked no older than her late twenties.

Even fevered, pale, and slick with sweat, she was striking, her long dark hair spilling across the pillow in stark contrast to skin that carried both fragility and defiance. And those blue eyes, bright and too large for her face, haunted him, the kind of eyes that had already told him to go to hell more times than he could count.

To anyone else, she might've looked like a half-dead girl who had stumbled too far into the wrong kingdom, but to him, she looked like danger wrapped in something deceptively delicate. And if her sharp tongue didn't kill him first, those fucking icy blue eyes just might.

Unconscious now, barely stitched back together, her presence still felt loud.

Jakobav stood motionless at first, then stepped closer, each movement deliberate, the way one might approach a creature too wild to touch. Gods, she smelled of petals and smoke, like fragile sweetness laced with cold ash, a contradiction that lodged itself under his skin.

His fingers twitched before he gave in, brushing a stray lock of hair from her temple. It was damp with sweat, tangled from the fight. He shouldn't have touched her, yet his hand lingered, thumb grazing the edge of her jaw. He told himself it was to check for fever.

He told himself many things.

Her pulse beat faintly at her throat. He found himself counting each rise, each flutter of breath.

He exhaled, slow, and reached again, combing his fingers through her hair until it fanned neatly against the linen. It looked wrong, disorderly, to leave it matted with blood.

He told himself to leave it.

It was beneath him, indulgent. But the sight gnawed at him, the crimson threaded through strands that had been stained in his hall. For reasons he refused to name, he couldn't look at it any longer.

He crossed to the hearth, poured water from the pitcher into a shallow basin, and dipped the corner of a cloth until it dripped between his fingers. Sitting beside her again, he gathered her hair carefully and began to clean it. The cloth slid through the strands, lifting away blood and ash, each pass slower than it needed to be. The scent of her deepened as the water darkened. He should have stopped, but he didn't. He smoothed her hair back against the pillow when he was done, as if discipline might help make sense of what he'd done.

When he drew his hand away, her eyes fluttered. He froze. For a heartbeat, he was certain she'd seen him.

Fuck. He'd crossed a line.

His body went perfectly still, breath locked in his chest. But she only turned her face deeper into the pillow, lips parting around a whisper he couldn't quite catch.

His fingers curled loosely at his side.

Why did he feel so drawn to her? Who was she, truly?

Whatever she was, she'd tasted like fire magic, which was impossible.

No one from Orchid had stepped foot in this castle, unchallenged and uninvited, in hundreds of years. The protections made sure of that. And if she were truly Orchid-born, she couldn't be royal or military because she bore no mark of rank, no tattooed crest of noble birth. And even if someone had slipped through, they wouldn't have made it this far, not alive at least.

He reached for the table where his armor lay, running a thumb over the scratches still crusted with her blood. It was dry now, flaking red against blackened steel. The sight turned his stomach more than it should have.

She was alive. Blood still moved beneath her skin, proof enough.

He hadn't planned to taste it, only to stop the bleeding and keep the intrusion quiet before the wrong people noticed. Yet she had been fading fast, even after holding her own in a fight that should've killed her. No one crossed blades with Savina and lived to tell the tale. She had been half-conscious when he intervened, crumpled at the feet of his guards, drawing far too much attention.

He moved toward the window, the cold night spilling in through the stone lattice. He looked out toward the courtyard, remembering the sight of her drenched in the color red.

It really wasn't his fault that a drop landed in his mouth, there was so much of it, and even a trace was enough.

Jakobav never flinched from what he was. His highest-ranked guards knew; the inner circle trusted it. Some even respected it. Blood-Scenting, they whispered in hushed tones when his gift was first discovered. It came with intrusive access to others' powers along with blood memory, letting him taste truth and borrow a shadow of power, though not everything and not entire minds, only fragments carried by the blood.

The gift had caused havoc amongst Dravaryn nobility because most people believed Blood-Scenting had died with the Fae, and some royals wanted to keep it that way. But he had never been ashamed to use it, yet this time, he had hesitated.

His hesitation was not from guilt, but from the fear of invading her mind. Thoughts rarely came whole, unless they were screaming to be heard, but more often, he caught impressions, shards of fear, a flash of rage, or a memory half-formed.

Most people felt fear or despair before an execution, but she had sparked with defiance, like the last thought she carried was a vow: *I will not break.* It had struck him harder than any blade, and no way he was letting a guard finish her, much less lay a fucking hand on her.

He turned back toward the bed, the firelight catching on her throat as she breathed. Another impression had slammed into him while her blood was still on his tongue that was as intriguing as it was concerning. His skull was pounded with a name as if she had shouted it like a brand: *I am Ella. Just Ella.*

Her mind screamed it so loudly that the words had echoed in his skull for days afterward. He hadn't meant to take it, in fact, a name was not usually what blood gave him. But hers had forced it, raw and unbidden.

She was an intrusion he couldn't shake.

The taste of her blood was still infecting him, festering. It had been sweet, unsettlingly so, and he'd never tasted anything like it. He'd known soldiers, rebels, priests, and spies. He'd tasted steel, ash, and madness. Jakobav siphoned their magic when needed, able to wield it for minutes, sometimes hours, depending on the toll. Each person's blood held its own taste: some bitter, some flat, but never sweet.

He lifted the basin of dirty water, watching faint red swirls cloud the surface, and his mouth turned dry. Her blood was sweet. This girl, Ella, tasted of fire and a forbidden flower, like old promises buried in bone. And gods help him, it had called to him, maybe in hunger or warning. Though he'd tasted the fire, he couldn't wield it. The power had denied him.

A strange warning, indeed.

Suddenly, she shifted in her sleep, murmuring in a tongue he recognized, and his jaw tensed.

Maybe she wasn't from Orchid at all.

He pushed off the window frame and crossed the room again.

Kneeling beside the bed again, he watched the candlelight reflect across her features. Her lips parted, and the words spilled out softer this time, each syllable laced with melody.

He thought back to that first night in the castle, when she'd bled across his floors and Bryn had worked over her with his endless chatter. The healer had muttered more than once that her wounds should've killed her, that she had no business still drawing breath.

Jakobav had stayed until dawn, silent, watching her chest rise and fall as if by her willpower alone. He could've sworn she'd mumbled in her sleep, words that carried a cadence unlike any tongue of the mortal realm. The sound scraped at memory, at childhood lessons whispered in secret corridors.

Jakobav had been taught the old language since boyhood, many royals had. They spoke it in secret, even those who publicly declared the Fae would never return. The four kingdoms of the mortal realm did not agree on much, but all had outlawed the tongue of the Fae.

Jakobav had never cared for laws written in fear.

He was still kneeling at her side, staring at her, studying every inch of her skin, as if it would reveal what was beneath.

But a kingdom waited for him, and the Claiming crept closer. He needed to prepare.

At last he stood and turned away before she could wake and catch him watching.

Some truths revealed themselves without asking.

Others, he would drag from her, drop by drop.

6

SCENT OF TRUTH

It was her second night in Dravaryn territory, and still she was alive, though she hardly knew how. Rising came easier this time. Her body ached but was no longer broken, the kind of strain that could be endured. She crossed the room without collapsing, fingers brushing the wall for balance, and eased the door open.

The corridor beyond was nearly empty, the air hushed in those hours before dawn. Torches guttered low in their sconces, bleeding dim light across the stone like fading embers. She passed over a stretch of floor scorched black, the remnants of some long-ago spell or battle. Of course Dravaryn wouldn't bother to scrub scars like that away. They wore their history like a warning.

Barefoot, careful, she moved slowly, each step a small prayer to remain unseen. Yet for all her caution, she was not quick enough.

"Impressive. You almost made it down the hall without collapsing." Jakobav's voice rolled from the shadows. He leaned against the far wall with one boot crossed casually over the other, as if he had been waiting for her all along.

Oh gods, there was that cedar and amber scent again.

"I thought princes preferred feather beds to midnight patrols," she said with a smirk. "Or do you just like watching?"

"I don't sleep much." His reply was quiet but deadly serious.

She blinked, thrown off for the briefest moment.

In this light, he looked different—not softer, but less cruel. The danger hadn't dimmed, but the mask of disinterest had slipped.

"I could've slid right past you if you weren't brooding in the corridor. You do love to lurk, don't you?"

A breath escaped him, rough enough that it might have been a laugh.

"You can barely stand upright, but yes, keep telling yourself you could outrun me."

"Still," she countered, chin lifting in defiance, "I'd find a way. I always do."

His head tilted, gaze dragging over her with slow intensity. "I believe you."

The way he said it burrowed beneath her skin, deep and unsettling, enough to draw a shiver from her bones. She steadied herself with several slow breaths, but it did little to quell the unease.

Jakobav pushed away from the wall and inched closer, his voice lowering. "It's hard to sleep when you've seen what crawls in the dark. Easier to face it awake...and end it."

Ella's stomach knotted as his words sank in. Was he speaking of her, the intruder who had bled her way into his fortress? Or did he know of the breaches in the Veil, the whispers of shadows sneaking into the world that did not belong to it?

In Orchid, the warnings had begun as rumors, quietly dismissed as nothing more than superstition, yet Ella had known better. She'd seen too much already: creatures that smelled of rot and carried no name, threads of magic stretched too thin and fraying at the edges.

Her kingdom had once fought to deny the truth, but the dark cared little for secrets. It leaked regardless, slow and hungry, no matter how tightly it was caged. Could Jakobav sense it in her, the same wrongness, the same crack running through the seams? Perhaps she was not meant for this world at all.

She had always felt there was something different about her, and it was becoming more evident with each passing day, something she could not keep hidden forever.

When his gaze landed on her again, something in it made her skin prickle. He stepped closer, his voice dipping.

"Whatever power you carry, I'm guessing it does not belong here."

He let the silence bleed out, watching her as though he expected the truth to break loose on its own.

Before she could even draw a breath, he moved. Faster than she could anticipate, his hand closed around her wrist, and he spun her, pressing her back into the hard stone, steel grazing beneath her chin, cool against the delicate skin of her throat.

She glanced down at the knife handle gleaming in the torchlight. Panic coated her tongue and quickened her pulse. The air felt as though it was thinning, each inhale dragging across the line of his blade. The knife point was resting where one swallow could cut her open and angled so the smallest movement from either would spill blood.

"I don't mind silence," he murmured, voice low enough to scrape along her bones. "Keep your secrets if you like. But don't ever lie to me."

Her muscles screamed in protest, but she forced herself to remain standing, if only to prove she could. He pulled the blade away from her throat, just an inch, not fully releasing her. She shifted along the wall a single step, creating distance between them.

Her body barely held, still propped against the wall, but he had let her move beyond his grasp, and that was something.

She didn't know how long she could survive here, but if she waited until her full strength returned before she sought answers, she might never find them. And though she couldn't tell if this prince meant to kill her or protect her, the prophecy pulled her onward, as if she'd been brought here for something more than survival.

Steadying herself against the wall, she didn't retreat any farther.

Jakobav's gaze narrowed. "I didn't cut you with my blade, yet you're bleeding Orchid magic like it's seeping from your bones."

Relief sparked low in her chest. Maybe he hadn't been speaking of the deeper darkness haunting her dreams and clawing through the Veil. Was he able to detect Orchid magic on her? It was, after all, a truth she knew she couldn't hide forever. Or was he still testing her to see what she would reveal?

"Maybe it's not magic at all. Maybe I'm allergic to arrogance," she said, deadpan.

He didn't smile. He only leaned in.

"Then let's hope it doesn't kill you first."

Ella's curiosity piqued, and she pushed him—just a little.

"For a man so sure of himself, your instincts are surprisingly dull."

He only watched her, head tilting with that predatory stillness, and then he closed the space between them, his hand sliding slowly down the curve of her arm before catching her wrist against the stone, neither tight nor gentle, a reminder of how easily he could darken the moment.

"I told you not to lie to me," Jakobav murmured, the words skimming her skin like the edge of a blade and sending her pulse into a stuttering, traitorous rhythm, every nerve pulled toward him rather than away.

He leaned in, eyes catching the torchlight. "Then explain why your magic reeks of flame and flowers every time you breathe, as if it were stitched into your blood."

Her stomach clenched. She didn't answer, didn't dare move.

Jakobav shoved off the wall with the certainty of a wolf that had driven its prey into a corner. "You don't have to say anything yet. But keep lying, and you will die before you find what you came for."

She swallowed hard and refused to give him the satisfaction of fear. "Why haven't you turned me in?" she asked instead.

Silence held, then he stepped closer, so near that his gaze seemed to cut straight through her, and when he spoke at last, his voice fell low enough to feel like a vow. "Because something in you tastes like it was written into my blood, and I always claim what's mine."

He left, his boots echoing, the cedar-and-amber scent hanging in the corridor.

Ella pressed back against the rough stone, pulse still racing as she let him have this moment. He had dominated the space, twisted her wrist, pressed steel to her skin, and stripped her down to silence, but that did not make her prey.

At full strength, she could have taken ten men twice his size, and one cocky prince was not going to break her. He might move as if circling a wounded animal, but she'd come here with teeth bared and a plan. She had not entered Dravaryn by accident. She'd expected a dungeon, torture, and having to claw her way out to find whatever relic the fates had promised.

Instead she had a prince who seemed far too interested, and a body that refused to cooperate, but he didn't know the truth. He didn't suspect Orchid's lost heir stood before him, didn't know the prophecy had already wound her path into his fortress.

His ignorance was now her advantage.

Ella straightened, fury cooling into focus. Although he might think of her as a secret to unravel, she was the one holding the match, waiting, patient and ready to strike.

7

LOCKED EYES

Later that day, the healer arrived like a storm wearing boots. The heavy oak doors groaned open, spilling him into the chamber in a whirl of clinking vials and swaying fabric, as if the fates had personally summoned him, or perhaps simply because he had sniffed out an audience.

The wide-brimmed hat went first, feather flashing violet as it caught the torchlight, and then the scent followed close behind: juniper, cloves, and something stranger, wafting into the air like mischief.

"Well, well, well," the man said, his grin belonging more to a trickster god than a medic. "If it isn't the Prince of Gloom and his mystery guest. Didn't know you were collecting strays again, Jakobav."

She hadn't noticed when Jakobav returned. He was simply there again—silent as a shadow—and gods, it set her teeth on edge.

He stood near the hearth with his arms crossed, his expression a dam holding back something dangerous.

"She's still injured, Bryn," Jakobav said flatly.

"I know that, princeling," Bryn replied cheerfully, dropping a basket that rattled like a box of knives. "I'd like to think my healing is aging like fine Fae wine, because I've never been more certain someone was about to die. But you insisted I save her anyway. And look, I did."

Jakobav's jaw flexed, a muscle ticking as though the healer had revealed more than he had intended to be known.

"Oh, forgive me," Bryn said, sketching a mocking little bow. "Did I trample all over your grand amusement? Ah well. You know what they say about best-laid plans..." His grin turned feral, teeth catching the firelight. "They rot faster than corpses."

Jakobav's gaze cut to him, cold enough to still blood in the vein. It would have flattened a lesser man. Bryn only hummed, unfazed, and set about unpacking his basket.

"She's not one of ours. You can smell the southern dirt on her." Bryn sniffed the air, eyes glinting. "Or is that blood? Hard to tell with foreigners."

Ella stiffened, refusing to flinch beneath his inspection. The healer had already saved her life and was likely the one who had stripped away her blood-soaked clothes that first night, then dressed her in something clean.

Unless it had been Jakobav, the thought slid cold through her veins, grating like ice against bone. Jakobav's face was stone-hard, all severity, not a shred of compassion, still scowling at Bryn. There was no way in hell that brute had been the one to drag her into clean linen. Surely it was done by the healer and for the sake of preventing infection.

Bryn was older, but there was nothing soft about him. He looked strong but spry, with sharp gray eyes that gleamed like moonlit steel, like he could recite a sacred rite or punch someone in the throat, and you'd never know which was coming first.

What had he meant about collecting strays? Was that truly how Jakobav saw her, nothing more than a wounded animal dragged into his keep, another broken thing he had decided to cage? The thought was ridiculous because a man like him didn't waste his time on shattered creatures, certainly not on an intruder who'd spilled his guard's blood and defied the wards.

No, whatever Jakobav was doing with her was not pity. It was colder, far more ruthless.

He stood there silent, shadow carved deep along the lines of his jaw, his presence unreadable as obsidian, his attention never wavering from her.

Her thoughts tangled, threatening to betray her resolve, and she fought to breathe. It must be Bryn's herbs clouding her judgment, but perhaps it was not the healer's smoke or tinctures at all, but Jakobav himself.

"I'm Bryn," the healer finally said, casting a judgmental glance in her direction. "Don't worry, dear. I'm not one to pry. Unless I'm bored. Which, unfortunately for you, I am. Deeply."

Jakobav took the basket without looking away from Ella. "Go home, Bryn." His voice was flat and quiet, but the promise threaded through it made the torchlight shiver.

"Not until I see the wounds," Bryn sing-songed.

Ella tried to sit straighter. "I don't need help. I can handle myself."

"Oh, I don't doubt that," Bryn replied, rolling up his sleeves. "But if you start glowing, I'd like to be forewarned. I've got a salve for that. Smells like burnt socks. Works wonders."

He flicked a hand at Jakobav. "You heard me, Your Highness. Out. Shoo. If you're not bleeding or useful, you're in my way. Door's that way."

Jakobav muttered something under his breath and stalked

out of the room. He didn't slam the door, but he might as well have.

To Ella's surprise, satisfaction sparked in her chest.

The brooding prince didn't like being dismissed. Good.

Some small part of her lifted at that. Maybe she could start to like the quirky healer. It was a thought she never expected to have about anyone from Dravaryn.

The moment the door closed behind him, Bryn's demeanor shifted, only slightly, but enough.

His tone remained light, but his gray eyes sharpened as he crouched beside her. "Let's see what damage the grumpy one missed."

He began to carefully examine the multitude of her injuries, his eyes softening just slightly. "He's always like that, you know... Tragic. Handsome. Useless at parties."

Ella rolled her eyes but smiled a little despite herself.

He unwound the wraps at her ribs, clicking his tongue when he saw the work beneath. "I should have known better when Jake said he was tending you at night. Swapping bandages in the dark like an apprentice."

Ella froze.

He's been...what?

Heat surged before she could stop it, a flush rising under her skin.

Jakobav, the merciless, scowling Prince of Dravaryn, had been playing healer in the night while she slept in his bed?

Her heart thudded hard against her ribs, breath hitching despite herself.

Gods, she was sweating.

She flattened her expression, biting down on the betrayal of her own body. No way would she let Bryn see her unravel.

"Saints alive," he muttered. "Jake did this? A blindfolded

toddler with kitchen twine would have done better. He should've fetched me sooner."

Ella managed a weak shrug, though she found it darkly amusing to hear Jakobav likened to a blindfolded toddler, so she gave Bryn a half-smile.

Bryn kept going. "Honestly, I've seen better wrappings on roast poultry. At least those get basted."

His touch was surprisingly meticulous for all his chaos, and he worked quickly, muttering to himself as he applied pungent salves and unstoppered a bottle of something that smelled like lightning.

"Jakobav wouldn't say," Bryn remarked as he stitched a gash with swift, practiced hands, "but I assume you're the reason the First Guard is still surrounding the castle."

Ella flinched, and not from pain.

His eyes lingered too long at her collarbone, locked on the spot where the tattoo should have been. It was hidden, yet under his gaze she felt exposed, as if he could see straight through to the mark she carried.

"Don't move," Bryn murmured.

Ella held her breath as he closed the stitching and covered the wound.

Then he leaned in, voice pitched low. "Not that it's any of my business, but whatever you are, you've got the Prince rattled. And believe me, that's rarer than a sober Fae."

He studied her, eyes glinting with amusement rather than malice. "You planning on breaking him?"

She narrowed her eyes. "What in the hell are you talking about?"

Bryn winked. "Good. Keep him guessing."

She exhaled in a rush, too drained to laugh but too honest to hide the hint of humor. "You're deranged."

"Your injuries are just starting to heal. Try not to get gutted like a goat at a solstice sacrifice," Bryn said briskly, already shifting to her leg. "Or at least do it somewhere less tedious for me to sew shut."

Her eyes fluttered shut as the salve burned, then cooled, her limbs sinking until her mind grew too foggy to resist the pull of sleep.

Bryn's voice followed her down into the dark. "Rest now. You'll need strength. To survive your enemies...and allies."

He rose, brushing a sprig of something that had to be illegal in all four kingdoms from his sleeve. "Dravaryn has never been short on either."

8

SECRETS KEPT

Ella sank under, time tilting strange as voices rose and fell around her like waves against rock. She blinked once, and Jakobav was back, thunder riding his shoulders as he stood too close to Bryn's basket of vials, his presence glorious in its fury, the kind that promised violence but not for her. And Ella didn't quite know how to explain that. In fact, she wasn't at all sure how to explain what she was feeling.

Bryn pinched the cork back into the small glass vial of pale liquid, shaking it once like it was no more remarkable than water. "Kethramin. Common in these parts. Medicinal, mostly. Pain relief, helps with muscle repair, keeps your lungs steady instead of making you gasp for air. Kicks in fast, too. Like a hammer through the skull, if you're not used to it."

Jakobav's head snapped up, his voice edged sharp enough to cut. "You gave her Kethramin?"

"Yes," Bryn replied, unbothered as always. "Would you rather she kept bleeding through your nice floors and fancy gold-trimmed sheets?"

"That's not the point." Jakobav stepped forward, his hand

closing around the vial, lifting it against the light where the liquid caught a faint green shimmer. His jaw clenched. "This isn't just medicine. Soldiers pass this around bonfires on long campaigns. It's a distraction. A poison for the mind."

Ella blinked, forcing herself half upright on the pallet, her body still heavy, stitched together with fever and threadbare strength. "Why?" Her voice rasped. "What does it do?"

Before Jakobav could answer, Bryn leaned in with that crooked grin, the kind that might have won Ella's trust outright if not for the spark of genuine thrill at the thought of her experiencing whatever madness he'd just poured into her veins. "Sends them walking through their own skulls, that's what. A little trip of the mind. Quite fun, actually, if you're ever interested. But that would take a higher dose. I only gave you the battlefield standard."

Jakobav's head whipped toward him, all fury and disbelief. "The battlefield dose? You gave her all of this? Bryn, that much would drop a grown Dravaryn-born who's had tinctures of Kethramin since he was teething."

"Correct," Bryn chirped, then froze, his brows lifting as if he'd only just realized he'd handed a dagger to a child. "Oh, fiddlesticks in the mix, I've overdone the fix." He winced, then leaned conspiratorially close to Ella, lowering his voice. "Well, my dear, I do hope you're interested in that trip...because I'm afraid you're about to go on one."

Drugged in an enemy stronghold and about to start hallucinating. Perfect.

Bryn cleared his throat and shuffled toward the door, already gesturing as if he had somewhere else to be. "I'll, ah—yes, I have others I need to attend to. Best be going." And just like that, he disappeared, humming to himself as his voice trailed down the hall.

Jakobav's gaze followed him with the edge of a blade.

"We'll have words," he muttered, too tightly wound to hide his anger.

Ella stiffened, her chest suddenly light, as though the air itself was both too much and not enough. Bryn's cheerful farewell still hung in the corridor like a curse, while Jakobav remained planted at her side, every inch of him radiating irritation at the healer's mistake.

He didn't speak, but his silence was louder than any shout; she could see the strain of his jaw, could feel the storm rolling off him, could picture him dragging Bryn back into the room just to make him choke on his own herbs.

Finally, Jakobav broke the quiet, his voice low. "How are you feeling?"

Ella gave him a slow blink, her lips parting into something that might have been a smile. "Like the ceiling is plotting against me."

He ignored her, turned on his heel, and vanished, only to return moments later with a cup of water glinting in his hand. He thrust it toward her. "Drink."

She eyed it as if it might bite. Her words dragged slowly from her tongue. "That's commanding...you overbearing commander." She shook her head as though she could shake away the fog. "What if I don't want your water?"

His jaw flexed. "You'll drink."

"No." She pushed herself upright, swaying with the effort, stubbornness threading through her unsteady limbs. "You don't get to order me about in your...oversized dungeon bedroom."

His gaze darkened with outrage, and for a moment, he closed his eyes as if in prayer for patience. When he spoke again, his voice was harder, every syllable pressed with authority. "As commander of the Dravaryn military, I've had more practice with Kethramin than you could ever imagine. Now listen and drink. I won't ask again."

Her hand rose, unsteady but defiant, and she jabbed a finger into his chest. "Do." Another poke, sharper. "Not." A third, lingering. "Command." The final poke pressed hard enough to feel the warmth of him through the leather. "Me."

He didn't flinch. He only watched her, brooding, weighing every reckless syllable.

And when that last poke lingered too long, he caught her hand before she could pull away, his fingers warm and unyielding as they closed around hers. He lifted it slowly, deliberately, bringing that pointed finger close to his mouth, his eyes locking on hers, black fire simmering there.

"Do you know what happens to people who touch me?" His voice was quiet, lethal, the sound of a blade sliding from its sheath, and as he spoke he brushed the pad of her finger against his lips, almost a kiss, undeniably a threat. "Most beg for mercy. The rest forget their own names by the time I am finished with them."

Her breath stuttered, heat flashing under her skin until every nerve was alive, and she swore it was only the Kethramin making her pulse stumble, only the drug that made her imagine the taste of his mouth and the promise buried inside his words. But her mind betrayed her, spinning instead to Jakobav himself. Jakobav with his impossible shoulders, carved for war. Who smelled of burnt amber and stormfire, a scent she had no business finding intoxicating, and whose touch had branded her as surely as ink.

He lowered her hand inch by inch, still holding it even as the words sank in, and when he finally let go, it felt like mercy, though deep down, she knew it was nothing of the sort.

"Go," Ella rasped, the single syllable tripping over her

tongue, and she forced it out because she had to get him away before he saw what effect he was having on her.

Jakobav's eyes narrowed, a promise of refusal written in the black fire of his gaze.

She tried again, softer this time, desperation slipping through. "Please. I don't want anyone to see me like this."

That word seemed to still him. Please. His breath left him in one harsh exhale, and then he leaned closer, so close her skin prickled from the heat of him. "I'll be back soon. Don't think you're rid of me." He gestured to the cup by her bed, his tone hard enough to strike sparks. "Drink some godsdamned water before I pour it down your throat myself."

When he finally left, the room shifted around her. The walls seemed to breathe, the ceiling tilted overhead, and Ella pulled the blanket over her face and laughed into the linen because gods, she was floating, every nerve alight, every breath dipped in sunlight, and still he would not leave her thoughts.

She wondered what those hands would feel like if they weren't gripping a blade, if they slid slowly down her spine, if they cupped her hips and claimed her throat while pushing her up against a castle wall. She imagined his mouth, lips too soft for a voice so cruel, tracing her neck, her chest, lower still, and heat flared through her until she choked out a single word.

"Fuck."

She wasn't even sure if she'd said it aloud. Did she want him?

In ways that made no sense, in ways that would end her? Maybe it was only the Kethramin.

The sheet slipped from her face, and she grinned like an idiot, cheeks flushed and fever-warm. "Two Dravaryns," she muttered, staring up at the ceiling beams that swam like shifting constellations. "A prince and a healer...and neither of them has tried to kill me. Yet."

And still, her traitor of a mind circled back to one of them, the wrong one.

His voice, gravel-low when he promised to return. His eyes, dark and dangerous, when he had all but threatened Bryn for gifting her this beautiful herb. Gods, Jakobav was probably terrifying even in sleep. Did he sleep? Or did he just lie awake sharpening swords and glaring at the ceiling? The thought made her snort, a laugh bubbling despite herself. The healer had definitely overdone the dose.

And then her brain betrayed her entirely, tossing up a thought that was as outrageous as it was undeniable. Jakobav would look unfairly good shirtless. Absolutely, ruinously unfair. And what about pantless?

Her stomach flipped, half with nerves, half with the strange effervescent euphoria coursing through her veins, and she shoved a pillow hard over her face to smother the thought.

Gods, what would her parents say? Her father would have scorched this place from the map without blinking if he had the chance. He used to say, *"Dravaryn-borns are bastards by blood. Show them mercy, and they'll show you your own entrails."*

But Jakobav... This man's words were cold, cut from granite, yet his actions had not been. He had kept her warm and hadn't interrogated her or let her die on a blood-soaked floor. Even that first night, his words had been hard, but his hands had been steady.

And gods help her, he looked carved like a warrior-god dragged from old Fae songs, with that jaw, those forearms, and a growling voice that resonated down to her core.

She was delirious and needed to get it together before she started mapping Jakobav's body like a battleground.

She was here for a reason. She was here to succeed. She was...

Ella's vision ignited like an omen.

She stood in an orchid grove, white petals soft as silk beneath her bare feet, the breeze threading through her hair as if the whole world sighed with her.

Then everything shifted as the petals blackened, the sky bruised violet, and the perfume of orchids curdled into smoke. Flames bloomed like flowers, screams rang like bells, and she ran barefoot through ruin, calling out, crying for help, her voice breaking against the silence that answered with nothing at all.

Suddenly, she was in a familiar castle, standing in the throne room and the walls began to shake. The scent of burning silk filled her lungs. The silence of ruin pressed down on her as she reached for her magic and found nothing. Her hands glowed for a heartbeat, then dimmed. Her mark pulsed once, faint and fading, before it vanished entirely.

In the crumbling threshold of the throne room, a man stood, shadow-cloaked. There was something old about him but not aged, more like ancient, as though time itself curled around his bones. His face blurred in smoke and light, but flashes broke through. A distinct pendant hung against his chest. His hair was black as ink, eyes too green to be human, and ears tipped just barely to points. Not sharp, not dramatic, just enough to make her question whether this was real or some dream-warped memory. But the scent... Gods, the scent made it undeniable. Fresh rain. Jasmine. Impossible, yet familiar enough to pour dread deep into her lungs.

She blinked, and the view sharpened, clearer now. She looked down at a gown of strange fashion draped against her body, foreign and regal, then raised her gaze to him, ready to demand answers, but her throat gave no sound. The man only smiled, cruel yet familiar, which was impossible...and then the vision burned, swallowing everything.

Ella woke with a gasp, heart hammering against her ribs, skin slick with sweat. For one terrible moment, she couldn't breathe. The world seemed to pause, her lungs seized, and then at last, air rushed back into her chest.

Jakobav was already there, crouched beside the bed, silent, watching.

"You're burning up," he said, voice low.

"I'm fine," she lied.

"You're not."

She opened her mouth to protest, but the fight drained away before she could summon the words. Her limbs ached. Her pulse raced unevenly.

"I'll go get Bryn."

"I don't need—"

The growl that escaped him silenced her, his glare lethal enough to cut through her protest.

Ella wanted to argue, gods she wanted to, because helplessness scraped at her like chains, and every part of her itched to claw back control, to sharpen her tongue into a razor that could strip that look off his face. But her head was pounding, and she wasn't sure if the vision was born of fever or drug, and neither answer gave her comfort.

He seemed to read the war behind her eyes. His expression softened, his gaze cutting through armor and cruelty until only raw, quiet honesty remained, something unguarded.

"Ella," he said.

She stiffened. The sound of it, soft and reverent, struck her deep.

It was the first time he'd spoken her name aloud, and she couldn't breathe.

How did he—? She hadn't said her name. Not out loud. Not to him. So how in the hell did he know it?

"You resist everything I tell you to do," Jakobav continued, his voice firm but sincere, as though her spiraling thoughts didn't exist. "So fight me if you must. But do not let this fever devour you. I won't allow it."

His concern hit harder than the drug. It felt...earnest.

She hesitated, jaw tight, breath unsteady, still reeling from the question she wasn't sure she dared to ask.

"Might not be up to you, Prince." The retort was deflection, a shield to buy herself time, to decide whether she would demand answers. She dragged in a breath. "I've managed to survive this long... like something didn't want me to die."

She met his eyes, steady and clear, despite the fever burning in her veins.

"Maybe it was spite," she muttered, the words slipping free before she could catch them. "Or maybe your stupid voice wouldn't let me die."

Jakobav stared at her for a long moment, something unreadable shifting behind his eyes, and then with a sigh and the faintest twitch at his mouth he said, "Bryn's a menace, but he has kept men alive who should've been corpses. Warriors with twice your wounds and half your stubbornness. He can handle you."

Ella squinted at him. "Was that supposed to be funny?"

He did not blink. "It was hilarious."

It wasn't, but it was something.

Prince Jakobav, brutal commander, heir of Dravaryn, had made a joke.

Before she could reply, before she could even roll her eyes, he rose suddenly and stalked for the door.

A heartbeat later, his voice cracked like thunder, shaking the walls.

"Bryn!"

Ella sank into the furs, heat prickling behind her eyes. Most of the haze had worn off, but his mouth, his hands, his voice speaking her name lingered like a brand.

Gods.
She was so fucked.

9

THE FATES' DESIRE

Ella had dreamt of her parents, which was a mercy after the last vision of the man with green eyes and the scent of jasmine clinging to him. Her father's gaze had met hers, creased not with worry but with laughter. Her mother's hand had wrapped around her own, and for a fleeting moment, she'd felt safe and whole, until waking cut it short and left the memory unfinished.

Her pain had dulled to a tolerable ache, but her mind burned bright and restless, circling thoughts too treacherous to ever be spoken aloud. Bryn drifted into those thoughts, and she realized why she'd warmed to him so quickly—because he reminded her of her father, not the king cloaked in duty, but the man behind closed doors who was playful and irreverent, forever pulling her and her mother into laughter. The memory struck and left her steeped in guilt.

They had to understand why she'd left. Surely the fates had made them understand. The rest of Orchid, though, probably thought she'd been captured or was already dead. Either way, they'd likely mourned and moved on.

She'd been gone for years, wandering Dravaryn's wilds without her flame, without her family, without even the comfort of hearing her own kingdom's name spoken aloud. When she'd first crossed Orchid's border, the pull north had been strong. She'd followed it blindly, and it had taken her less than a week to cross the continent. She'd been certain the prophecy would reveal the relic the moment she arrived in Dravaryn.

It hadn't.

Instead, this kingdom swallowed her whole.

She moved from village to village, surviving off stolen food and luck, learning their customs, imitating their harsh vowels, keeping her head down so no one noticed the foreigner among them. She chased whispers, bartered for rumors, escaped more than one tight corner without the fire she had been born to wield. And still, nothing. No sign of the relic. No hint of what she was meant to find next.

It wasn't until a dream, vivid and violent, that she finally saw the castle. She hadn't recognized it at first—no one did. Dravaryn kept its heart hidden from the world. But she pieced the clues together one by one until she knew exactly where she had to go. Breaking into the fortress had taken months of planning. And it still hadn't gone as planned. She'd nearly died for nothing. No relic. No answers. Just failure and a bed she didn't belong in.

Gods, she missed home. She missed her parents. She missed Nira most of all. Her best friend would have been the first to know how tangled her feelings were about Jakobav—how she didn't trust him, and yet he occupied far too many of her thoughts. Nira would've given the best advice.

She pressed her palms hard against her eyes, knowing wallowing wouldn't bring her answers. The prophecy hadn't dragged her into this cursed fortress simply for her to bleed out on a stranger's bed.

Forcing herself upright, she pushed to her feet. Each step was a dull ache, yet the pain only intensified her resolve. She hadn't survived this long to falter; she had to find the thing the fates had whispered of, whatever it was: relic, omen, or beast.

The words came back to her then, the ones she'd first read beneath the orchids on the night she fled. A bloom had risen from soil where no flower should have grown, pale and trembling as though alive, and when she plucked it, the petals had dissolved into parchment in her hands.

When realms entwined are sealed away,
The path grows dark, the skies turn gray.
A child shall rise through smoke and fire,
She'll find the relic that the fates desire.
She'll breach the wards that none may cross,
And restore what kingdoms thought was lost.

The spot between her collarbone and chest where her sigil usually marked her felt strangely awake, burning as the words pulsed through her skull. Each word seemed elusive, impossible to hold, and yet the prophecy lived in her marrow all the same.

She stepped into the corridor, the door to Jakobav's chamber clicking shut behind her. The stone beneath her bare feet was cold and uneven, the air damp with iron and wet rock, and her skin prickled with the uncanny sense that this castle remembered every secret ever whispered within its walls. She had once imagined the prophecy would point her toward a single object, something she could steal and be gone within days, but now she was beginning to suspect otherwise.

She steadied herself against the wall, fingers brushing a warped mirror that caught her reflection: hair tangled, shoulders drawn tight, blood still seeping faintly through her bandage. A woman frayed but not broken. So she straightened, smoothing her face into something capable.

"You keep doing that," a voice said, smooth and low.

She spun.

Jakobav stood half in shadow, one boot crossed over the other, arms folded as though he had been waiting.

"Doing what?" she snapped.

"Shaking your head. Like you're swatting at ghosts."

"Maybe I am."

"Or maybe you're clearing your thoughts before someone reads them." His head tilted.

She stiffened.

"You think I'd allow an Echobinder in these halls?"

The word cut, but not for the reason he accused.

Actually, she hadn't worried about an Echobinder since the first night she broke in. She couldn't believe she'd been so careless.

Had anyone been inside her thoughts?

Her chin lifted. "Is that how your father has kept control for so long? Spies crawling through minds, stealing secrets no one ever meant to give?"

The idle ease left his face. He stepped closer, shadows bending with him.

"There are no Echobinders in Dravaryn anymore," he said. "Powers like that do not survive here. The soil rejects them. Many share your disdain."

His eyes locked on hers, dark and unyielding. "Although I'm the last person who should ever complain about intrusion."

Ella stilled as his words clung to her, heavier than he seemed to intend, and she wondered whether the soil itself remembered what it had rejected. Laws that once held the world steady were fraying now, powers buckling as the weave beneath them slipped loose.

In Orchid, whispers had curdled into reports. Powers flickered at the margins of spells, heat flared where it shouldn't, and whole fields crisped to ash, while behind closed doors the royal council finally dared name what all four kingdoms had begun to fear: Threadshifting, the slow unraveling of seams and the opening of breaches where none should exist, with rumors that sealed realms were stirring after five centuries of silence.

In other words, Threadshifting meant the Veil was beginning to crumble.

Her pulse quickened as she watched him, unsure whether he was testing her and weighing what she knew or speaking a truth he did not fully grasp.

There are no Echobinders in Dravaryn anymore.

Had they vanished before the realms sealed or because of it? And if Dravaryn denied Threadshifting, were they spared from it or merely hiding it?

She refused the spiral and rebuilt her calm, holding it like a shield. He was only a curious prince and not a predator laying a trap. She steadied her breath and stilled her hands even as she felt his gaze on her, piercing and far too observant.

She turned before he could read the flash in her eyes, unsettled by his quiet certainty that there were no Echobinders left. It hadn't sounded performative or defensive but simply like the truth.

Honestly, that might've been worse.

Her steps slowed at the next turn, and she could feel him behind her now, a shadow that pressed too close.

"Tell me something," Jakobav said, his voice almost casual

though she heard the bite beneath it. "Is anyone coming for you?"

Ella froze, anger sparking as fast as fear. "Why would you ask me that?"

He moved before she could react, closing the distance to catch her wrists to pin them above her head against the cold, unforgiving wall, his gaze burning into hers with unbroken focus. "Just because you should be a prisoner, and there is no dungeon in sight, does not mean I tolerate outsiders walking free in my halls."

Her breath caught, fury clawing at her throat. "Then why am I still breathing, Prince? Why make an exception?"

He leaned closer, his mouth a breath from hers. "Would you not give someone the benefit of the doubt?"

"I would never show mercy to a man who has wronged me."

At first, he didn't move, but then his lips curved into a smile, dark and intrigued. "Merciless," he murmured, tasting the word. "Always leaping to violence." He clicked his tongue softly, mockery and warning woven into the sound, and let her arms fall, his fingers lingering on hers.

"I have to leave the castle for a few hours," he said at last, still close enough that his heat brushed against her.

Her pulse leapt, and she jerked her wrists free, chin lifting. "Where are you going?"

His mouth twitched, almost a smirk. "Curious little intruder."

"Answer me."

Jakobav leaned in until his breath was warm and rough at her ear. "If you think I'll tell you where I go and why, then you're more reckless than I thought."

Her stomach tightened. "Coward," she whispered.

That earned her a low laugh, dark and amused, before he finally stepped back. His gaze dragged over her. "I'll see you tonight, Ella the merciless."

She decided she didn't mind that title at all.

And she had no intention of proving it wrong.

10

ROOTS OF THE FORGOTTEN

She was barely strong enough to run, but she was planning to do it anyway. That last encounter with Jakobav had lit something restless within, a renewed sense of purpose that unsettled her. His presence lingered even after he was gone, and she was beginning to hate him for it.

At least she had a reprieve for now, a brief absence from his incessant and unexpected appearances, thank the gods, but still, curiosity gnawed at her, whispering its poisonous questions. Where had he gone? If Dravaryn was suffering from Threadshifting, was he out dealing with a breach?

She cursed herself for caring at all. Her focus had to remain on saving her own kingdom, on finding the relic, because sitting in his chambers like some obedient guest wouldn't bring her closer to the object that demanded to be found. If anything, it only risked exposing her to too much of him, and already she caught herself questioning the rumors of his ruthlessness and doubting his reputation for cruelty.

And yet those rumors frayed the more she looked at him.

The very fact that he'd kept her alive, that he'd hidden her intrusion, was proof of some concealed mercy.

But why? And what else was Prince Jakobav capable of?

It didn't matter. She couldn't stay here. The scent of scorched amber still clung to the air, filling her lungs like smoke, sharp and suffocating.

Then, without warning, power stirred in her veins. Strange, yet dangerously familiar.

Ella had always been taught that no two gifts were the same, that power was as singular as a fingerprint, stitched into blood and bone, and hers had always been fire, only fire. But this current rolling through her did not feel like the flame she knew.

She was going to try anyway.

She would listen to that power, seize it, bend it to her will. If she could only reach it, maybe she could make progress toward her plan: find the artifact and escape. So she tried her usual routine: focus, anchor her intention, and burn.

But her body didn't listen.

Nothing happened at first, and then her magic surged, reckless and desperate, clawing its way upward as if it might tear her open to save her. Ella gasped and thrust her hand toward the hearth. Heat flared across her palm, but what came was not fire, not in the way she knew it.

For one glorious second, the air around the fireplace rippled.

Not flame, not even heat, but the stone and fire bent like the surface of a pond struck by a falling drop, the image warping as if the world itself had been tugged sideways. Her chest seared over the hidden Orchid sigil, a sudden burn that pulsed in time with the ripple.

Ella froze, heart stuttering, eyes wide as she blinked hard, but the distortion vanished, the fire crackling as though nothing had happened.

"Burn," she whispered anyway, her voice breaking the silence.

The flames flickered, a single hitch in their glow before they dimmed.

"Seriously?" Her voice rasped, raw and furious.

Gods, she missed her fire.

Back in Orchid, she'd been known as the strongest flame-wielder in generations, proud not just for producing fire but for the way she could manipulate any she touched, which was almost unheard of. She had not only commanded her own flames, but could reach for any nearby and make them hers, a secret she and her parents had guarded, saving it for after what would've been her coronation. She could steal, amplify, twist, even smother, and years of practice had made it effortless.

Now, with her gift buried beneath foreign soil, it was like slamming her fists against locked doors—feeling the fire behind them, but never being allowed in. Her magic had always come so easily that the sudden silence felt like a betrayal, and the more she reached for it, the further it slipped. She had expected her flame to die here, knowing fire born of Orchid soil would not burn on Dravaryn ground. But the more her hidden mark pulsed and flared when it shouldn't, the more it felt like a cruel kind of hope—one she couldn't afford.

Ever since she crossed the cursed wards at the castle, the burn would pulse when she least expected it, a throb that felt like it was trying to drag her attention somewhere, whisper something she wasn't ready to hear.

Fuck, this was maddening.

Exhaustion slammed into her, sudden and brutal, leaving her dizzy. Weak. A word she despised.

"Shit." Her vision swam, her fingers twitched, and for a razor-thin heartbeat, the air shivered in the corner of the hearth, as if some unseen door had almost opened before slamming shut again.

"Great," she muttered at the embers. "You're just like the rest of this kingdom. Moody, unhelpful, and full of misplaced superiority."

The shadows stirred, a ripple so slight she might have dismissed it, but then the darkness thickened and something stepped forward.

Ella blinked once, twice, and her blood went cold. A figure stood at the edge of the firelight, solid and undeniable. Not a phantom, not a trick of fever or smoke, but real.

He was tall, close to seven feet if not more, and his presence carried a sense of inevitability, as if he would find her if she hid, catch her if she ran, smother her if she screamed. It was not the brute force of a soldier nor the crude menace of a cutthroat, but something quieter, honed to a lethal grace.

Ella's body locked, her throat closing like a fist. For one frantic heartbeat, she nearly yelled for help, but she didn't know if anyone in this gods-forsaken castle would hear her, and she feared she didn't even have the breath to scream.

She stood there, every muscle frozen, as if she were watching her worst nightmare step out of the shadows and take form.

Her instincts finally broke free, and she stumbled backward. The backs of her knees struck the edge of the bed, and she toppled onto the mattress with a gasp, scrambling until her spine pressed against the headboard, chest heaving as if her lungs could not keep pace with her fear.

Still, he didn't move to follow.

No blade gleamed in his hands—at least none visible—only the unnerving stillness that he wielded like a weapon.

He was dressed in tailored black trousers with a silver buckle, a dark collared shirt open at the throat, its sleeves cuffed neatly at his forearms. The cut was severe yet elegant, the fit impossibly bold, as if he belonged not to one place but every room at once. His style was timeless, imperial, the kind of authority that seemed to have no beginning and no end.

Across his chest, just above the sternum, hung a pendant that caught the firelight like a secret, gleaming with a slow, pulsing shimmer. The pendant itself was an oval of obsidian wrapped protectively around a violet stone that seemed to breathe with its own faint light. The moment she saw it, her chest flared in answer, her hidden sigil burning hot beneath her skin. She couldn't look away.

She remembered that pendant.

Gods, his features were too perfect to be real—square jaw, strong nose, high cheekbones. His hair was clean-cut at the sides, darker than night, the top left just long enough to fall in loose, intentional disorder. A single curl slipped across his forehead, as if the wind had styled it just to please him. His pale skin caught the firelight and glowed gold along the outline of him.

When his eyes met hers, she felt stripped bare, as if every lie she had ever told was peeled back and laid open. He didn't smile, only studied her, his gaze cool and unhurried, as if she were something rare he intended to savor.

Her pulse thrashed, wild and uneven, but reason steadied her. If he'd meant to kill her, he would've done so already. She forced her voice into something that almost sounded like defiance. "Who are you?"

The figure tilted his head, considering her for a moment that felt eternal. Then he spoke, his voice deep and resonant, thunder wrapped in silk.

"Ah," he murmured, amused. "So this time, you speak first."

She swallowed hard. "This time?"

Fuck. She did recognize him, though her mind rebelled against it. Denial coursed through her; she had convinced herself that the vision was only a fever dream, a trick of pain and exhaustion. But the sight of him here in Jakobav's room had shattered that fragile lie.

He stepped forward, slow and unhurried, and the shadows recoiled from him, bending back as though even darkness feared his touch. His gaze swept across the chamber once, and his mouth curled in quiet disdain.

"This place reeks," he said, his tone laced with contempt. His eyes turned to her, darker now, gleaming with something unreadable. "Is this where you've been hiding? In another man's bedchamber?"

Ella's mouth went dry. Her heart stuttered once, twice, before finding a painful rhythm. "What are you?" she managed, her voice a thin thread of defiance.

He closed the distance between them until only a few feet remained, and up close, he was impossibly more beautiful and infinitely more dangerous. The pendant brushed lightly against his chest with each breath, catching the firelight as if it were alive.

His gaze softened, barely, just enough to make her doubt what she saw. "You're asking the wrong question," he murmured, stepping closer. "The question you should fear is not what I am—but what *you* are."

A chill traced the length of her spine, but she swung her legs over the far side of the bed anyway, finding her balance. She rose as smoothly as she could and forced her chin up.

"I know exactly who I am. And I know where I belong. You're the one intruding."

And she did know where she belonged, though not in this room, not in this castle, not in this cursed kingdom. But he didn't need to know that. Who was this man to walk in here and act as if he already understood her?

With a face like his, he was probably used to getting whatever he wanted. That, however, would not do.

His eyes glinted, amused, as though he had plucked the thought straight from her mind. "Do you know where you belong? Or have you only ever been told where to go?"

Her stomach lurched.

The words struck too close, and the blood drained from her face. Because he was right. She had been following the paths others chose for her. First her parents, then the fates, and recently, she'd been obeying the orders of an enemy prince. Every step she'd taken had been for someone else's purpose.

His words had dragged her truth out of the deep, hidden place where she'd buried it, a part of herself she thought no one else could ever touch.

Fuck him.

She clenched her fists to hide the tremor, nails biting into her palms.

The faintest curve touched his lips, not quite a smile but dangerous and satisfied, like he knew he'd struck a nerve.

"Not all roots are buried," he said, his voice softening into something intimate and uncomfortably certain. "Some reach for the surface. Some ache for light. And some are only waiting for you to remember them."

Her stomach twisted so violently, she thought she might retch.

The heat in her chest wavered as her fury fractured, his metaphor about roots leaving her bereft.

His pendant glowed once, briefly, as if answering her. Her Orchid sigil flared in reply, gone before she could even look down, as though calling her out from within, urging her to figure it out.

"What does that even mean?" Ella demanded. She was getting whiplash from this conversation, but gods help her, she couldn't stop herself from wanting answers.

He stepped closer, closing the space with unhurried certainty until the air between them pulled tight like a snare.

"It means you were never meant to kneel for them," he murmured, low and opulent as dusk.

Ella straightened. "You don't even know who I am."

"But I do," he said, his voice more verdict than reply. "You carry her fire. You move between veins. You dream of ash and bloom."

His tongue dragged slowly across his lips, a gesture so intimate it felt like intrusion, and his hand lifted as if to touch her face.

Ella jerked sideways, catching her foot on the rug and nearly stumbling onto the bed, but she refused to fall. Fear clawed at her ribs like talons, but she stood her ground.

And then he vanished.

No sound or motion, only the fire, crackling as if it had never been disturbed, though the air still vibrated with something ancient brushing against her blood. Her gaze locked on the empty space where he had stood, on the echo of his voice, on the phantom violet glow of his pendant seared into her sight.

A ragged sound tore out of her before she could swallow it back. She clutched her temples, digging her nails into her scalp as if she could hold herself together, tether her soul back inside her skin.

What in the gods-forsaken realms was that? Another fever dream born of exhaustion? She wanted to believe that, but her mind whispered otherwise.

It was real.

She was grateful no one else was there to see her like this: stripped bare, rattled to her core, undone by a stranger's words.

11

SILK AND SILENCE

Ella hadn't touched her supper, and the prospect of sleep wasn't promising either. Her body sagged with exhaustion, yet her mind burned with a restlessness that refused to quiet. The flare of violet light replayed behind her eyes, every word the green-eyed stranger had spoken reverberating in her skull, lingering long after he had vanished into nothingness.

The door creaked open, and Jakobav stepped inside. His gaze swept once over her before landing on the untouched tray of food on the table, and his eyes narrowed.

"You've been alone longer than promised," he said at last. "That must've thrilled you."

Ella forced herself upright, ribs protesting, a painful reminder of the wounds Bryn had stitched shut. She'd likely torn half of them open when she'd scrambled away from that man with the slightly pointed ears, crashing into the headboard harder than she'd realized at the time, but she was not about to explain any of that to Jakobav.

"Not nearly as much as you might think," she muttered.

A mistake. The words slipped out, too honest and revealing.

His brow furrowed, and for a long, weighted moment, he studied her face as if searching for the reason she hadn't been thrilled by his absence. And gods, she hated that he looked concerned. Despised it more than the ache in her ribs, because concern was not something she could afford from him. Yet the way he stood there, like he would have kept guard all day if she'd only asked, made her throat tighten.

She didn't need him to protect her from the man in the shadows, or from the way her sigil had answered him. And yet...some traitorous part of her knew that Jakobav would have.

Should she tell him? Admit what had stood in this very room, close enough to touch?

The thought was as reckless as it was dangerous. Jakobav was Dravaryn. She couldn't trust him. But the omission sat heavy on her chest, guilt curling inward like smoke.

Jakobav's frown deepened. "What happened?" His voice was low and steady, but the concern beneath it was plain.

Ella's fingers tightened around the blankets, knuckles whitening as she fixed her eyes on the fire rather than his face. "Nothing."

But her body betrayed her, pulse hammering against her throat, and from the way his gaze sharpened, he'd clearly noticed.

She straightened and scrubbed at her eyes, but when she risked a glance at him, his attention wasn't fixed on her face. His eyes lingered instead on the shirt she wore. His shirt, too large on her frame, still carrying the scent of him.

Gods.

Jakobav's posture shifted. He drew a breath, his mouth parting as if he were about to speak.

Footsteps thudded down the corridor, firm and steady, and Jakobav went still.

His gaze snapped to the door, and in the space of a heartbeat, he was no longer across the room; he was on the bed, shoving her down beneath the covers. The movement was quick, controlled, suffocating. He slid toward the middle, using the dinner cart and his own body as a shield to block what would otherwise be a lump beneath the furs.

She was thin, thinner still from days of skipped meals born of spite, but she was not invisible. What in the hell was he doing?

He dragged a pillow across her shoulder, adjusting it to break the outline of her body.

His voice dropped, quiet but urgent, pitched like a command. "Hold still. And try not to breathe."

"What?"

"Do it. Now."

The heavy tread of boots drew closer, each thud of leather on stone rattling her ribs. Ella didn't have time to protest.

He pressed her down into the mattress, his command leaving no room for argument. Furs dropped heavy over her, trapping her in heat and shadow, her body caged against his, as though she were something he meant to shield or smother.

She wished she'd worn more than his oversized shirt.

Pants would have been useful.

The press of his thigh against hers, the breadth of his chest at her back, even the whisper of his arm pinning her close, all of it set her body alight.

The scent of him was everywhere: spiced amber and something rougher, salt-sharp. Sweat. She had never noticed him sweat before, never thought him capable of it, but here it was, threaded through the heat of the furs and the closeness of his skin. She couldn't tell if it was the strain of hiding her, or the situation itself, but it was raw, human, dizzying.

Ella tried not to squirm, but every point of contact burned with awareness, and gods, her body betrayed her. Heat spilled low, damp and insistent, a pulse she couldn't stop. Shame clawed at her throat as sharply as panic.

What if he could tell? What if he could smell it? The Dravaryns were rumored to have senses sharper than any other mortals. Fuck, what if he smelled her arousal and mistook it for consent?

Velvet heat and musk closed around her, and fight or flight tangled in her chest until neither option felt possible. Flight, of course, was no option at all, not with how carefully he'd hidden her and not with his massive frame between her and the door, every inch of him a barricade she could never slip past.

The door swung open.

"Jake?" A woman's voice. Smooth, controlled, and touched with amusement.

Ella clamped down on her breath and eased the fur aside, peering through the narrow strip left open where Jakobav's shoulder angled away, just enough for her to glimpse the door. Through that slit of blankets, she studied what she could see of the woman: polished leather boots catching the firelight, the hem of a dark green cloak shifting just beyond Jakobav's shoulder. As the woman moved farther into the room, Ella caught flashes of her silhouette—dark hair braided into a single rope and the grounded, self-assured stance of a soldier. She ached to shift for a better look, but even the smallest movement risked exposure.

"I was expecting to meet with you tomorrow, Maeren," Jakobav said. His tone was even, his breaths drawn slow, deliberate, as though he were forcing calm into every syllable.

"And that's why I never knock," Maeren replied with a grin audible in her voice. "Far more entertaining to catch you off guard. On the rare occasion anyone can."

"You didn't catch me." Jakobav's answer landed hard. "No one could mistake your gait. Your footsteps are louder than a soldier twice your size. I heard you in the corridor minutes ago."

Her smile faltered, only for a breath, before she recovered and took a few steps closer, then stopped. "There's been another Veil breach. A creature slipped through. We didn't recognize it, and your skills would've helped identify the blood. Savina would've been useful too, if she hadn't been taken out by that fierce little intruder you're still pretending not to know anything about. And yes, I checked the dungeon. No new prisoners."

The woman's brows lifted as her gaze swept over him, widening slightly when she registered how he was positioned on the bed.

"Did I interrupt something? Should I come back later?" The smirk returned, sharper now.

Ella's pulse slammed in her throat.

What does she think she's interrupting?

How can Jakobav identify blood?

She could see more of the woman's face now, and of course she was beautiful. Worse, she was the kind of beautiful that came with strength, with belonging. This was a woman who strode through doors without knocking.

Not half-hidden, half-dressed, and silenced under furs.

Ella hung on every word, but her heartbeat thundered louder than a soldier's march.

Maeren scoffed. "Don't give me that glower. We were practically raised together, Jake. I know all your tells. You're hiding something."

The faint grind of Jakobav's teeth reached Ella's ears.

But Maeren pressed on, undeterred. "The rest of the First Guard is furious. I've been smoothing feathers for days, telling the court you're locked in training for your Claiming. Meanwhile I'm cleaning up wreckage from this mystery guest of yours."

Ella felt Jakobav bristle.

"Oh, don't flinch. I noticed. While I'm busy with that, you've been conveniently absent. And then you slip off with Soren? No report, no details?" She crossed her arms. "So maybe use those gods-gifted abilities of yours and help me track this thing. Or better yet, dust off that charm you've buried under all that brooding and remind your people why they follow you."

Ella winced and hoped Maeren hadn't noticed the bed move. Jakobav shifted beneath the furs. His hand brushed against her breast, grazing her nipple through the thin fabric of his shirt, and a jolt shot through her chest like lightning. She went rigid, every nerve screaming as her nipple hardened, traitorous and unbidden.

His hand froze and then he pulled back, but the heat of him lingered, impossible to forget. Jakobav cleared his throat, his voice rougher now. "Thank you, Maeren. If you're finished rambling, we'll discuss this later."

The woman glared as she turned toward the door, cloak swishing behind her. She paused at the threshold. "Perimeter duty tonight. Thane and Soren are riding out with me. We'll carry extra supplies in case it takes us beyond the borders. I'll send word if anything stirs."

The door shut.

Ella threw the furs off and shoved him hard, pain lancing her side. "What in the hell was that?" she practically shouted, her cheeks burning hot enough to scald.

He raised his hands. "I was trying to protect you."

"By smothering me in your sheets and burying me alive under furs? Gods, Jakobav, if that's your idea of protection, remind me never to see what you call mercy."

"I kept you hidden. Trust me, it's for the best. You're not ready to meet the First Guard."

"Hidden?" Her laugh was sharp enough to cut. "You pinned me, sweated all over me"—her voice wavered, breaking despite her fury—"and then you touched me."

"Ella," he said, rough, almost defensive, "that wasn't my intention."

"I don't care what you meant." She pushed herself upright, fire in her eyes. "You don't get to touch me."

The words came out harsher than she meant, too raw to hide, and heat rushed up her throat as soon as she heard them. The quiet stretched until it became unbearable. His gaze shackled her, cold and unrelenting, as if he were sifting through every layer of her for answers she couldn't afford to give.

Finally, he gritted out, "Trust me. If I had touched you on purpose, your reaction would've been very different."

Ella's retort came quickly. "That's a bold assumption for a man hiding someone under his blankets."

He didn't miss a beat.

"I could feel your curiosity. If not for the scowl on your face, I might have mistaken it for lust. And with that scent"—his mouth curved in the shadow of a smirk—"Maeren probably thought she'd caught me in something far more indecent than hiding a girl in my bed."

Ella's face burned hot enough to rival the firelight.

She knew, gods help her, that some part of him wasn't wrong.

Why was the future king of Dravaryn, her enemy, affecting her this way? She couldn't let him in any further, couldn't let him burrow beneath her defenses, and the need for a subject change clawed at her like desperation.

Ella forced her voice lower, steady despite the tremor running through her veins. "You hid me from your second-in-command. She was giving you a scouting report that revealed more than you wanted me to hear."

Jakobav's jaw clenched. "Yes."

"And what she said about a creature and its blood, what does that mean?"

"She shouldn't have said anything. Not when I was giving her every signal to stop speaking," he ground out, his restraint unraveling.

The words sealed it. Her suspicions weren't wild imaginings. There was more to the centuries-old feud between their kingdoms, more to the whispers about Dravaryns holding onto powers forbidden since the Fae vanished. Proof enough that their traditions dripped with secrets, and that they still practiced the archaic ritual of the Claiming.

To be fair, she did not know what the Claiming ritual truly entailed, only that success granted a new ability and failure exacted a price no one spoke of openly. Nor did she know the real reason it had been outlawed by every kingdom except this one. She suspected it was something barbaric at worst and unsavory at best.

Her thoughts tangled and spun. If the kingdom of Dravaryn still kept so much hidden, what else had been concealed from Orchid? What truths had she been fed as lies? Her parents and tutors had always suspected Dravaryns wielded strength beyond mortal limits: brute force, whispers to stone and steel, maybe even shields no army could break. But what if there was more?

And what if Jakobav was not just a brutal prince sculpted by violence, but something else entirely?

She looked at him then, the man who had saved her from certain death, fed her, threatened her, touched her, and her chest tightened with questions she dared not speak.

Jakobav's gaze caught hers, dark and steady, as if he could strip those questions straight from her bones, his voice dropping to a low murmur, soft as smoke and just as dangerous.

"Careful, Ella. Curiosity can kill faster than any blade."

12

DROWNED IN DISTRACTION

The tension Maeren left behind was suffocating. Ella sat, rigid, on the edge of the bed, her fists knotted tight in the blankets, ribs aching where Jakobav's very large, very solid body had pressed against hers. His scent lingered both in the air and in her thoughts, and no matter how she tried to banish it, it refused to let her go. Gods.

She replayed every word she had thrown at him, each retort pulling more gravity than she cared to admit. She had snapped, cursed, practically spat fire into his face. To be fair, he had shoved her down and pinned her beneath the covers. She should've been furious. It should've been unforgivable. Yet her body had betrayed her all the same, liquid heat pooling low, her breasts tightening at the faintest graze of his touch. She was more concerned that she wasn't angry.

What is wrong with me?

The memory of him clung like a bruise, inescapable to all but time. His breath had scraped her ear, his voice rasping low enough to rake along her spine, every syllable barbed with possession. It hadn't been gentle. It hadn't been invited, but gods, it had lit something within her.

And that was the worst part.

Not that he had forced her down or left her body strung tight with sensation, but that for one wild, blinding instant, jealousy had burned hotter than rage. The woman who had barged into his chambers had spoken to him as if she belonged there, as if she knew him in ways Ella never would. It made no sense. Dravaryns were known for brutality and silence, yet with him, she'd seen something else entirely. Not tenderness, not cruelty, but something in between. The way they spoke to each other was respectful, threaded with the kind of ease and teasing that came from history.

Ella pressed her palms hard against her eyes, as though she could smother the thoughts before they consumed her.

He cleared his throat, a quiet reminder that he was still in the room.

"You have a temper," Jakobav said at last, his voice low.

He leaned against the wall as though nothing had happened and he was still deciding whether to chain her or let her set him on fire.

She squared her shoulders. "You have a boundary problem."

The corner of his mouth lifted. Not a smile. A shadow of one. "Then stay out of my reach."

Her head tilted, her smile sweet as poisoned honey. "You would miss the entertainment."

The words were not as cutting as her usual barbs. This was something else entirely, reckless, born of the way his soft brown waves had fallen loose across his forehead. She had wanted, for one dangerous second, to push them back just to see his face unguarded. Instead, her mouth had betrayed her first.

His eyes darkened, steady and unflinching. "I can think of a few things far more entertaining when it comes to you."

The air thickened, her pulse stumbling into a dangerous rhythm. He looked away, but too late. She had already seen it. Already felt the spark ignite, treacherous and undeniable.

His hands curled tight at his sides, as if holding himself back from closing the distance. He pushed off the wall and stalked toward the bathing chamber. He paused at the door, his voice rougher now. "You think I don't notice every time you pull away. But I do."

Buckets clattered in the adjoining chamber as servants hurried to fill the basin with hot water, steam rising in ribbons that drifted into the room, cooling the moment just enough for her breath to return.

The quiet that followed was almost worse. It left her alone with the turmoil circling her thoughts, always returning to him.

She couldn't afford this. Not his distractions. Not his stares. Not the way he had found a path beneath her skin and refused to leave.

Ella had never been docile, and she was not about to start now. Charm had its uses, but submission had never been part of her arsenal. She prided herself on quick retorts and stubborn fire, yet this infuriating beast of a man seemed determined to drag her under, drowning her in him. Fuck that.

What unnerved her most was the suspicion that he was not even trying. Jakobav seemed to simply exist that way: commanding, relentless, impossible to ignore. People probably lined up to obey him.

He was everything she needed to avoid: powerful, loyal to his kingdom, entirely too perceptive.

And worst of all? He was the kind of dangerously attractive that ruined kingdoms. That angular jaw. Those full, smug lips.

And then, as though her traitorous thoughts had summoned him, he returned. Shirtless.

Fresh from the bath, damp hair sticking to his temples, a towel slung low across his hips, moisture still glistening on his chest. Scars mapped the ridges of his body, stories she didn't know. Tattoos beaded with water droplets shifted across muscle like constellations blurred by stormlight.

Jakobav looked down at her with eyes that burned, teeth grazing his lower lip as though weighing whether to speak or to do something far less sensible.

Ella forgot how to blink.

Which was why Bryn's voice startled her all the more.

"Oh, for the love of the seven sacred herbs," came the exasperated voice from the doorway. "Would it kill you to wear clothes, Jake?"

Jakobav didn't flinch. "You're a healer. You've seen worse."

"Yes, but now I will have to unsee it before lunch."

The old man swept in, basket hooked over one arm, his expression vaguely offended by the sight of Jakobav's chest. He gave Ella a deliberate once-over as he set the basket down with a thunk.

"Still alive, I see," Bryn said cheerfully, breezing into the room as if death was no more troublesome than a stubbed toe. "That's promising."

"She's stable," Jakobav replied, his voice clipped.

Bryn raised a brow. "Stable isn't the word I'd use for someone who threatened to disembowel her rescuer."

"I didn't threaten," Ella said. "I strongly implied."

"Ah." Bryn's eyes glinted with mischief. "Semantics. Now, let's have a look at your wounds, dear. Don't worry, I'm mostly professional. I'll leave the ogling to Jake."

Ella grimaced but lifted her shirt enough for him to inspect the bandage. His hands moved with disarming efficiency, too precise for someone so endlessly distracted by his own running commentary. She almost forgot to flinch, until he paused.

Her breath caught. His eyes were not on the bandage anymore. They were fixed just above it, staring at the place her ancestral mark should have been.

Panic surged. She looked down, desperate to confirm what she already knew: the sigil was still invisible. But his stare made her chest feel exposed all the same, as if he could see the power branded beneath her skin.

Jakobav's gaze flicked toward her at that exact moment, tracking her stillness, and though his expression never shifted, his attention landed heavy, as if he'd filed her reaction away to be examined later.

Bryn's easy smile remained, but for all his quick hands and quicker tongue, there was something in his stillness that unsettled her. Humor made him appear harmless, but his eyes belonged to someone older than he looked. Not in his face, not in the nimbleness of his work, but in the way his gaze fastened on details most would miss, in the way his words sometimes tasted like warnings instead of jokes.

"Hmm."

Ella's head snapped up. "What?"

"Oh, nothing," Bryn said lightly, too lightly. "Just that your skin is looking a little pale. Like someone doused your inner flame with a bucket of ice water."

But he was not looking at her wound when he said it, he was looking straight into her eyes.

And in that gaze, older than his face and keener than his grin, she felt as though he knew far too much.

Her mouth went dry. How much did he suspect, and how much did he already know?

If he'd felt her flame, if he'd glimpsed the invisible sigil, then he knew exactly what she was; only those of royal blood carried the mark of Orchid.

Her stomach turned.

Had he already told Jakobav? Or was he waiting for her to confess it herself?

Either way, that was never going to happen.

"Strange," Bryn mused, tilting his head. "Usually trauma makes it flare brighter, not vanish. Unless..." His grin widened, wickedly pleased. "Something distracting you, sweetheart? Emotional upset? Someone scrambling your internal compass?"

Heat rushed to Ella's face so quickly her ears burned. Jakobav's eyes shot to her, dark and intent, and the awareness of him made her skin prickle.

"Stop talking," she hissed at Bryn.

The insufferable healer only grinned wider. "Say no more."

With an exaggerated flourish, he packed his kit, snapped the latch shut, and rose. "The one marked with secrets appears to be healing beautifully." His wink was all mockery as he glanced toward Jakobav, who was pulling a tunic over his chest. Then Bryn swept out the door looking far too smug for someone who was supposed to be a healer.

Ella stared at the closed door, then dropped her face into her hands. "I hate him."

"No, you don't," Jakobav said, his voice unreadable, his back turned as he adjusted his tunic.

She didn't answer because truthfully, she didn't hate any of this, and that was the problem.

For her, and for the fate of everyone depending on her to succeed.

Her magic remained quiet.

She hadn't come here to be saved, hadn't come for a prince or a healer or the illusion of safety in the heart of the enemy.

She had come for one thing: the object tied to the prophecy, the relic buried beneath this castle, the thing no one was supposed to remember.

And yet here she was, distracted by a man with soft brown curls and that stupid jawline.

Ella closed her eyes, forcing the words through her mind like a mantra. Focus.

The fates had already woven their part, and now it was her turn. Uncover the truth, leave before she grew too entangled to run, and definitely, under no circumstances, would she give another ounce of thought to the man who had walked in dripping from the bath, wearing nothing but a towel, and wrecked her ability to form a coherent thought.

But the fates had a way of tangling threads no blade could cut.

13

STEEL REMEMBERS

JAKOBAV

He found Maeren in the upper corridor, where the evening light cut hard across the stone. She didn't look surprised to see him. She looked irritated.

"You want to tell me why Bryn is acting like he swallowed a secret?" she asked.

Jakobav exhaled once, low.

No point delaying it.

He didn't tell her everything, especially not the way it had felt to have Ella trapped beneath him, her breath catching at his accidental touch, but he told Maeren enough. About why he hadn't sent Ella to the dungeons the very first night when he discovered her. And how he didn't believe locking her up or executing her would yield anything useful.

And he told her what he'd been dreading saying out loud, that something about the girl mattered.

"I don't know what she is yet," he said quietly. "Spy, runaway, something else entirely. But she didn't break into my castle to slit my throat in the night. And whatever she's hiding, I need to know what it is and why."

Maeren stared at him, unimpressed.

"And how long," she said, voice sharp, "were you planning on waiting to tell me this?"

"I was hoping to discover the answers to my earlier questions," Jakobav replied, "before I announced to my most trusted guards and friends that I have been harboring our intruder, convinced Bryn to heal her, and have been feeding her, clothing her, and housing her in secret ever since, when I should be preparing for my Claiming and protecting the kingdom from the breaches."

Maeren huffed, seeming to accept that, but she still complained anyway. "I cannot believe Bryn knew and said nothing."

Jakobav gave her a thin shrug. "In his defense, I told him I would revoke his potion privileges if he said anything to anyone about it. I also implied that I would tell you myself."

"He overestimated you," she snapped.

He didn't bother arguing.

She dragged a hand through her hair, then finally relented with a low growl. "Fine. You owe me two things if you want this forgiven."

"I'm listening."

"Training. Dawn. No excuses."

He nodded.

"And after that," Maeren continued, "you're going to let me give you the full state of the kingdom. Court politics, border tensions, breach reports, everything you've been ignoring while you've been distracted."

He didn't rise to the jab. "You will have my full attention, I promise."

~

Breakfast that morning had been quick but grounding: kiln-baked stonebread brushed with smoked salt, seared riverfish, and a bowl of ember-root broth thick enough to heat the blood. It was fuel for a fight neither of them intended to hold back on.

They stepped into the courtyard just as the first light broke across the ground, the cold biting hard enough to tighten breath and thought alike. Frost clung to the training posts and the archways, glittering like shards of glass beneath the rising sun. The space was empty by Jakobav's order, cleared of trainees and officers so he and Maeren could face each other without distraction, without an audience, without expectation beyond the metal they carried.

The castle was only beginning to wake, distant footsteps muted by cold stone. Jakobav welcomed the chill. It scraped away the noise in his head, clarifying everything that had gone unspoken the night before.

Jakobav's blade cracked against Maeren's, the hiss of steel on steel carried by the bite of morning air. Frost-hardened dirt shifted beneath their boots as they circled, each movement measured in the hush of the empty yard. There were no eager trainees, no curious officers, no prying eyes waiting to catch a slip, only their resolve and the relentless rhythm of battle.

He drove forward, muscles taut, and she met him head-on. Their swords sang, each one testing, demanding, never yielding.

"How's Savina?" he asked between blows, his breath steady as his arm. "Back in form yet? Or is she still snarling at everyone for keeping her sidelined while she heals?"

Maeren closed in, her gaze slicing through every weakness. "Close enough. Training again, but not ready for First Guard."

He inclined his head, measuring her. "Anything else?"

The pause was slight, but it was there, a hitch in her blade before she gave the answer. “Another breach, but it was small and contained quickly. Nothing for you to lose sleep over. You should stay focused.”

His sword faltered mid-strike. Breaches were happening too often, creeping toward a pattern he didn’t like, and Maeren’s hesitation ignited something angry beneath his ribs. He didn’t need protecting. He didn’t need to be handled. The kingdom was his to command, not something to be shielded from.

“Oh, do not look at me like that.” She caught his hesitation and snapped at it. “Your second-in-command doesn’t need to hold your hand to report a problem I already handled.”

His mouth curved, humorless. “Then stop acting like you want to cradle me.”

She moved aside, grin flashing like a knife. “I would. But you are not nearly pretty enough to make it worth the effort.”

A snort broke from him, and in the space it opened, she went low and fast, blade slicing near his ribs. He twisted, barely, muttering, “Relentless.”

“You’re distracted.” Her blade swept for his knees. “That girl is in your head, admit it.”

He slammed his shoulder into her, breaking the rhythm, voice iron. “You speak too much for someone whose lungs should already be pierced.”

“And you brood too much for a man with a Claiming in less than two weeks.”

The words landed and his grip faltered, the moment stretching long enough for her blade to kiss his side.

“Dead,” she said brightly, stepping back with her fox’s grin.

“Shit.” He lowered his weapon, the word half a growl. “Insufferable.”

“Predictable,” she shot back, tipping her head. “Still leading with your left. Still flinching. Forgive me for speaking freely to my commander, but you need to focus. The solstice is almost here."

He almost told her she always spoke too freely, but bit down on the retort.

And he wasn't thinking about Ella this morning—not here, at least.

Maybe yesterday, while bathing, when her scent had still clung to his skin.

And after that, she had stared at him with those wide blue eyes while he stood in nothing but a towel, daring him with that stunned look and parted mouth. He hadn't dried fully, letting the towel sit lower on his hips than necessary, just to see what she'd do.

She rewarded him twice: first, she looked deliciously furious, and then her gaze slid over him, bold enough to eye-fuck him before shame caught up just a heartbeat later.

Gods, he loved seeing her flustered and angry.

Shit, now he was fixating on Ella when training and discipline should have ruled his thoughts. She was a storm battering at his stronghold, and storms were meant to be weathered, not worshipped.

Regardless, Maeren was wrong. All morning his mind had been consumed by the Claiming, with every possible outcome running through him like a drumbeat he couldn't silence. He woke up well before the sun, donned his training leathers, and slipped out of his room without Ella even moving an inch, all to carve out some extra preparation. He had the utmost respect for the ritual, and what his kingdom gained from it.

The rite loomed over every warrior, and the solstice that followed thirteen full years of service was no accident. Whether a warrior stood at twenty-eight or at thirty-three, it was the moment where loyalty met power and the realm chose whether to claim them. For Jakobav, it would draw attention as all royal rites did, but this one felt heavier. Reports stacked higher every day, whispers of power bending in ways it never had, the Veil twitching like a nerve ready to snap.

Many would show up just hoping to see the King of Dravaryn, his absence felt increasingly by the day. His father had warned him years ago of the signs of Threadshifting, back when it wasn't happening so quickly. Ella had spoken that word in a whisper as though she'd discovered something forbidden, not realizing he already carried the knowledge like a scar that wouldn't heal.

Gods, maybe he should stop watching her sleep, letting her spill secrets into the dark like prayers. But he knew there would be no stopping.

And Threadshifting was not the only truth she'd let slip.

He'd known about it for some time, and the First Guard had done everything in their power to keep the kingdom from suffering. Yet the Claiming was no ceremonial pageant. If he failed, he would gain nothing—no new ability, no strength to wield against what bled through the breaches—and Dravaryn would not stand behind an heir who faltered at the rite that defined them. They were already fighting to survive the cracks in the Veil. Without the power they expected him to claim, Threadshifting would spread like a sickness until Dravaryn itself cracked open.

No fucking pressure.

"Eyes up," Maeren barked, her voice cracking across the ring like a whip in the cold.

Their rhythm resumed, blades colliding in a relentless cadence that sent a deep vibration through his arm and reverberated across the frost-hardened stone. Strike followed strike, the tempo ingrained into him by years of training, until she feinted left and drove the hilt hard into his ribs. The impact surged through him like a bruise spreading outward, raw and punishing, and his control faltered.

Something inside him slipped, and the frost along the ring cracked like shattered glass, hairline fractures webbing outward from his boots. The courtyard wall, veined with obsidian, shuddered as though it had a pulse of its own, dark veins twitching in time with his heartbeat.

Maeren stilled. Her eyes, bright and unblinking, swept over the fractures, catching every tremor. “Jake,” she said quietly, and there was no humor in it. “This is getting worse.”

Her mouth pressed thin. “Listen to me.” She stepped forward, blade lowered now, voice flat but edged with an urgency he didn’t like. “You’re not the only one losing control. Half the kingdom is misfiring, and the High Vexari has already held two services in the Cathedral. She’s preaching that the land is warning us. That the Veil is thinning. That Dravaryn must prepare.”

Jakobav’s jaw locked. “The High Vexari enjoys the sound of her own prophecy.”

“She enjoys influence,” Maeren shot back. “And she’s using it. People are scared. They look to her because they haven’t heard a word from you or your father.”

That was a low blow and he had a feeling she knew it.

Her gaze flicked to the cracks, still visible beneath the settling frost. “You will need to meet with her soon.”

“I do not answer to the Cathedral.”

“No, you answer to the kingdom,” she said, tone like flint striking. “And they need to hear from you, not from a woman stirring panic with every sermon.”

A long exhale bled from him, white in the cold air.

Maeren lifted her sword again, not with challenge, but with resolve. “Now,” she said. “Again.”

He reined it in with effort, forcing the hum to collapse back into silence. Frost resettled across the ring, shards catching the light like coal dust at his feet. He rolled his shoulder as though the motion alone could erase what had just surged from him. "Again."

Her mouth pressed thin, the humor gone from it. She stepped forward without a grin, blade lifted, her voice flat. "You need to get ahead of it."

"I am ahead of it."

"Then stop cracking the yard."

"Press," he growled, the word both command and warning, as much need as challenge.

Their blades blurred together, faster and harder, until for a fleeting instant it felt as it once had: clean, focused, every strike a note in the rhythm of battle that steadied his pulse. But then Ella's face rose unbidden, and his grip faltered.

Maeren's blade slid past his guard and lifted beneath his chin, the point steady. "Dead again," she said, lower now, though her eyes did not soften with it.

He shoved her weapon aside and stalked toward the rope line, chest tight with the failure.

"Do you want to talk about it?" Maeren asked, her voice even, unreadable.

"No."

She didn't pry. That was Maeren's gift: she knew when to cut and when to retreat. She reached into her coat and tossed him a bundle wrapped in cloth. "Scouts brought that back at dawn. The other thing you are avoiding talking about."

He caught it. The cloth was warm against his palm despite the cold. Inside lay an obsidian shard no larger than his hand, edges smooth as water, a faint ash-scent curling from it. Its surface was not dead black. Instead, it rippled like ink over oil.

He set the shard back onto the cloth and closed it carefully, the fabric swallowing its shifting dark. "Where?"

"North copse," Maeren said. Her tone was stripped of inflection, the way she spoke when the details disturbed even her. "Burned trees still standing like bones, ash falling like snow, and shards arranged in symbols again, tighter this time. There was a smell I could not place." She paused, her gaze locking on him, weighing the lines of his face the way she might judge a blade for flaws.

He wiped his palm against his sleeve, but the sensation clung like static, a faint hum that refused to leave his skin. "What else?"

"Tracks that began and ended in the same place, and there was ash that burned through the soles of a boot." Her eyes flicked toward the cracked ground beneath his feet, unflinching. "Ash that burns, Jake. That is not natural. Neither was whatever you just did to the grass."

"I have it handled."

Her mouth curved in a smile that held no warmth, quick and biting. "Tell that to the groundskeepers who have to restore the courtyard's manicured squares."

He almost left it there, but something had been gnawing at him.

He wanted to keep denying how distracted he was, wanted to let the words lock behind his teeth where they belonged, but instead he heard himself say, voice low and raw, "I tasted her blood."

The air thickened between them, silence settling heavy.

Maeren went utterly still, then snapped her blade higher, the point kissing the hollow of his throat so close that he felt the cold metal through his collar, and her eyes blazed fury. Then, as quickly as it came, the violence smoothed into a scowl, her voice cutting. "Tell me you're not that reckless. Tell me you didn't."

He held her stare until he could taste iron at the back of his tongue. "I did. And worse...it didn't match any known line. Floral on the surface, but underneath, a fire that wanted to be something else. I couldn't access her abilities. It locked me out."

"That's not possible," she said, the words flat and cold.

"I assure you, it happened." His tone left no room for doubt.

He pushed his unbound hair back from his brow, dark waves clinging, damp with sweat, beading on his skin from both sparring and from his confession. "You've seen me borrow many different powers over the years, stolen with a drop of blood: Windcrafters, Waterweavers, Metalbinders. A taste of their blood and their gift is mine for minutes, sometimes hours. But with Ella, I took nothing. And not that I was trying to, but it was like the pathway for access wasn't even there."

The point of her blade dipped until it hovered over the dirt between them. "Then she's not Dravaryn. And whatever she is...her blood breaks rules it should not break."

The floral note in her blood had been a lie painted pretty. With most people, even a whiff of their blood opened doors, but Ella had locked each one and set the whole hall burning, and the longer she kept her truth buried, the more hunger and suspicion twisted tight beneath his ribs.

Maeren began to circle him, boots whispering over frost as her gaze stayed fixed on his face. When she spoke again, her command was hard and controlled. "Jake, do not taste her again."

He didn't respond.

He knew better than to lie to Maeren, although he'd already lied by omission.

Still, she would hold him to any word he gave her, and this was not a promise he could keep.

Her blood still haunted his tongue, intoxicating and deceptively sweet. He wanted to soak up the way her body had betrayed her under his sheets, even as her voice spewed venom and denial.

Fuck, she had a traitorous body, the way her scent had thickened, leaving no question of how wet she'd been for him. It had pulled at him like a lure, something primal and unforgiving. He could have fed on it—fucking drowned in it. The contrast to her usual defiance only left him wanting to uncover every contradiction she carried, to have every lie and every revelation carved into him. She held countless secrets, and she revealed hardly any truths.

Thank the gods for the furs that night. If she'd seen what she did to him, the way his cock had hardened at the sight of her in his shirt and her arousal flooding the air, she would've known exactly how far she'd unraveled him.

But she was a trespasser in his head, just as she had trespassed in his castle, and he knew a threat when he saw one. He could harden for her and still slit her throat if she threatened his kingdom. The two truths did not erase one another.

"Jake," Maeren snapped, "are you even listening to me?"

"Yes, of course," he heard himself say.

Shit, he was not.

Maeren's face tightened. Something like apology flickered through her features before she smothered it, her voice steadying into cold iron. "I'm not saying you can't control yourself," she said, no trace of mockery left. "But if the court hears, they'll use her. And you may be hiding her now, but I can already see it—you won't be able to stifle what you'd unleash if harm found her."

His teeth ground together. "I won't let that happen. I'm focused on two things only: Dravaryn and my Claiming Rite."

The words tasted like ash. Since when did he lie to Maeren?

Maeren shook her head like she didn't believe him and sheathed her sword, eyes locking on him. "My brother thought he could outrun the Claiming. He hid his fear and his questions. It killed him. I push you because I will not bury another fool I love."

For once he had no retort ready.

He held her eyes, her loyalty grating against his secrets. "I hear you. I'm sorry, Maeren."

She nodded once.

Maeren was right. He should've been preparing for the Rite, yet he was distracted. He knew his reputation; people usually screamed and ran from him, though he rarely let it get that far. Ella didn't run from him—not really. She bit back at him.

Fuck. The best kind of distraction.

"Jake, listen to me. You will regain your focus," Maeren said.

He sheathed his blade. "I have it."

"You do not," she said, not unkindly. "But you will, or this kingdom will fall."

He walked to the bundle Maeren had tossed to him earlier and lifted it. The shard's hum rose at his touch.

"Anything else from the north copse?" he asked.

She shook her head.

Jakobav tied the cloth shut. "Keep the perimeter tight. I want Thane and Soren on the north watch again. Rotate the younger pairs through the inner gates. No one rides alone."

Maeren nodded. "And the girl."

He looked at the wall instead of her face. "I will handle Ella."

Maeren's mouth tilted, not quite a smile. "Try handling

yourself first." She lifted her blade again. "And Jake, if she has you this rattled, she must be something fierce. I would like to meet her. Why should Bryn get to have all the fun?"

Feeling guilty for lying to her, he agreed to let her meet Ella soon, dismissing her from training. Maeren returned to the Guards' quarters, and he stayed alone in the training ring, staring down at the broken ice. His reflection gathered itself in the shattered pieces, the face of a man the court would soon either worship or fear. And if he failed the Claiming, they would abandon him just as quickly.

That was if he made it to his ceremony. The Veil had been twitching faster, and more breaches were opening by the day, and Ella's arrival had landed too neatly in the center of it all to be a harmless coincidence.

If she'd come to his kingdom as ruin, he would see it first and make the choice the realm required. Better to bleed her secrets until nothing remained than let her carve weakness into him or his people.

Ella carried secrets like hidden knives. If she aimed them at his throat, she would learn that lust and desire cut as clean as any blade, and with her, he would be oh so fucking willing to wield his sword.

14

ECHOES OF THE PAST

She waited until the castle quieted, until footsteps faded and torches dimmed. Tonight, she would finally begin her search.

Ella slipped silently through the corridor, guided by instinct, a tug beneath her ribs. Somewhere in these ancient halls, the answer lay buried: the artifact promised by the prophecy, strong enough to tear the Veil between worlds. And maybe something that could explain the unfamiliar power stirring inside her, just beyond her grasp.

She'd finally met one of Jakobav's attendants earlier that day. The woman seemed a decade older—beautiful, patient, and carrying the kind of brazen confidence Ella found immediately endearing. Ella had peppered her with questions. Who had changed her clothes while she was unconscious? And was she allowed to make wardrobe requests?

Kalenya, as the attendant introduced herself, arched a brow at Ella's relentless chatter. "What would you prefer, then? High-heeled battle boots to match your demands?"

Ella snapped back without hesitation. "I've never liked

shoes of any sort. I fight best barefoot. But if I must wear something, regular boots will do."

A flicker of amusement crossed Kalenya's face, though Ella caught the hint of calculation in her eyes.

Ella pushed further. "And I'll take a dress. Everyone wants a warrior to fight in pants. No one expects blades strapped at both calves and thighs."

"You want a gown for combat," Kalenya said, the disbelief plain in her tone.

"You asked." Ella lifted a brow and shrugged. She was tired of wearing drab, oversized garb. "Pretty and lethal are not mutually exclusive."

That earned her the ghost of a reluctant smile.

"So that's why they kept you from me," Kalenya muttered. "Fierce little thing. No wonder half the castle's already nervous."

Ella wondered how long it would take for word of her being there to spread. In Orchid, gossip like that would have raced through court like wildfire.

By the time Kalenya returned with the boots and her dress, suspicion had softened into a guarded respect. Ella noticed the quick work of the woman's needle: pockets stitched into the black fabric, the hem shortened above the knee to free her legs. The leather puzzled her. From a distance, it looked like silk, but up close, it shimmered like obsidian veined with starlight.

Now, as she moved down the torchlit hall, Ella was grateful for it. The strange Dravaryn leather flexed easily with her movement, whispering against her skin, catching the light in fractured gleams and reminding her of the castle itself: beauty that was unexpected and alive.

She wound her way through narrow turns until she came upon four guards standing in full armor blocking a wide hallway that opened into a larger chamber. There would be no skirting past them, but she would fight her way through if she had to, even if she'd rather not draw that kind of attention.

Time to find out which way this place leans. Prisoner...or free to roam.

The scrape of steel echoed as every hand went to a hilt. Torchlight struck polished armor, casting an ominous gleam across their helms. Boots shifted. Shoulders squared.

Ella froze. Her palms dampened against her thighs, grateful for the pockets Kalenya had stitched into the dress. One hid the small knife she'd swiped from Jakobav's chamber. It was nothing ornate, just a soldier's blade—one forgotten when his room was purged of weapons.

But it would cut, and it was hers. That was enough. He probably hadn't missed it yet. Or it was a test, and he'd noticed the moment it vanished, deciding to let her keep it—the kind of man who would wait until the moment it amused him to make her pay.

For a moment, the corridor held its breath.

Then, as though a silent command passed among them, the guards let their hands fall back into place. The rasp of metal dulled. The tension bled from the air, but not completely.

The shortest of them lifted his chin, just barely, in acknowledgment.

Ella swallowed, forced her legs to move, and kept walking.

Well, that settled it.

Her muscles only loosened once the guards were behind her, and it became clear Jakobav was the one running things here. No one had mentioned the king since her arrival, and even before that, the townspeople in the small villages outside Dravaryn's capital, Draethmar, had whispered that the crown was hidden from sight.

Officially, foreign delegations were to blame.

Unofficially, rumor spoke of a devastating illness the royal family refused to admit.

Why did Dravaryn keep so many secrets?

The thought lingered as her gaze drifted along the hall, and she realized the castle no longer looked the same.

It had changed, or maybe she had.

She'd been in the castle less than a week, yet it felt as though she was only now seeing it. Compared to the warmth and opulence of Jakobav's chambers, everywhere else had felt cold and hollow. Now, the floors no longer chilled her feet, and the walls weren't slick with mildew. The castle's beauty was almost discreet, drawing her to look closer.

The walls weren't lifeless stone but ranged from charcoal to glassy black, reflecting light like a gem cracked open too violently. The air smelled different now too, less smoke and iron, more spice. Although she should've been afraid, she felt seen instead.

As much as Ella wanted to linger, she knew she likely was on borrowed time and continued her search.

A shadowed corridor revealed a cracked window.

Of course the windows weren't locked.

Dravaryns were proud at best, and overconfident to the point of delusion.

Ella rolled her eyes and moved toward it.

Jakobav might've given her freedom to wander for now, but she had no idea how far that freedom stretched. Certainly not far enough to test the front gates. Better to slip out a window than assume she was welcome to walk out the foyer doors.

She ducked through without hesitation.

The window was barely a story above the ground, an easy drop she could make without twisting an ankle, if luck was on her side. But if anyone saw her outside the castle walls at this hour, she might lose any illusion of freedom Jakobav had given her.

The ledge was slick with climbing ivy, and her foot slipped once, catching on a knot of vines, but she steadied herself with practiced ease. Orchid's palace had trained her well in the art of sneaking out unseen.

It didn't matter how much a child loved their parents, or how steady a life they'd built. Curiosity came calling, even for the content.

Dravaryn vines, however, were thicker, their tendrils coiling like ropes. She forced her way through, leaves whispering against her skin, until the wall released her into open air. From there, the ground sloped downward, leading her to the faint glow she had felt pulling at her ribs. By the time she pushed past a tangle of hedges, the path had already chosen her.

The air outside hit her like warm silk, castle towering behind her, spires jutting against the stars. But here, on its quiet western edge, something else waited.

A garden. No...*the* garden.

Shadow-laced hedges curled in wild spirals, glowing faintly in the moonlight. She followed a narrow path that wound through humming trees until it spilled into a clearing.

And there they were.

Thousands of black roses. Ella stopped cold.

The roses shimmered with a starlit darkness, black but never flat, layered and opulent, with thorn-covered vines seeming almost alive. But as she took a closer look, she realized they weren't just black. Plum, charcoal, and violet glints winked in the petals like secrets. Each bloom unfurled as if painted with midnight, grief, and sorcery.

She reached out and brushed a petal, and it vibrated, warm beneath her fingers.

Breathtaking.

The greenery was so stunning it felt wrong, too vibrant, too intricate, as if painted by a hand that had never seen daylight.

Leaves gleamed a green too delicate to be real. Their texture caught her eye and looked like the skin of a snake, ridged and damp, a chill woven into every vein. She imagined stroking the vine with her fingertip, and she swore she would feel a clammy pulse, wet and dry at once, adrenaline sparking as if the thorns would swivel and bite. Droplets of dew clung to the surface, glittering though there were no clouds and no rain had fallen.

For some gods-forsaken reason, her eyes welled up.

Absolutely not.

She blinked hard, furious with herself. She couldn't help it.

Awe surged as something like recognition and longing seized control. As if part of her had been waiting to find this place, and now that she had, it still wasn't enough.

Every petal of the shimmering roses seemed to lean toward her, listening, as if the buds knew her name and were watching her as closely as she was watching them. A faint warmth stirred beneath her collarbone, right beneath the Orchid sigil she'd spent years hiding. It answered the roses with a single pulse. Quiet but unmistakable.

She'd only ever seen a black rose carved into Dravaryn's crest. She'd thought it only a symbol or maybe a warning.

But they were real, and they were beautiful.

No gardener had shaped this.

No mortal hand could have coaxed such perfection from soil and shadow.

Why did it feel like the roses whispered to her? And why did it feel as though her blood had whispered back?

It certainly didn't fit the narrative.

This was not the version of Dravaryn she had been raised

to fear. Her parents had lulled her to sleep with stories of war and vengeance, weaving Dravaryn into every nightmare.

The hedge curved again, revealing a stone arch grown over with vines, and as she stepped under it, a warm breeze stirred her hair. This place would have been the perfect spot to bury herself in a delicious novel, but this was Dravaryn, so she was far more likely to find blood than books.

She wanted to weep, or scream, or curl into the earth and never leave.

But the pull was back, that tug even stronger now, dragging her away from the roses and toward the castle. Her hand fell from the rose as she stepped back through the hedge, the scent of spice and velvet clinging to her hair.

She didn't want to leave, yet her feet moved anyway.

The garden watched her go.

She felt it, like eyes between her shoulder blades, patient and knowing, as if she would return whether she intended to or not.

She eased through a side entrance, torchlight wavering as though it recognized her, the obsidian in the floor shimmering again. Ella walked for what felt like ages, half-tranced, half-hunting. The halls blurred around her, but she would memorize the turns later. Right now she was following her instincts, which she hoped would lead her straight to the relic.

She turned the next corner and voices caught her ear. A familiar scent wafted toward her, bitter herbs and tinctures filling the air, the same smell that always clung to Bryn's clothes. This had to be the healer's quadrant. She froze just before the archway and melted into the shadows. The door stood ajar, lamplight spilling into the hall, voices threading easily through the gap.

"I've treated plenty of injuries in my time, Jakobav," Bryn said. "But Ella's power, whatever the shit-eating brumblebunnies it is, doesn't feel like anything I've known. Not in decades. Maybe longer."

Jakobav's voice was quieter. "You think she's hiding something?"

"No," Bryn said. "I think something inside her is hiding from her. And that's what worries me."

Ella's breath caught. Her palm flattened against the wall. What in the hell were they talking about?

She wasn't some walking magical time bomb. She had trained, honed, controlled every flame in her until it bent to her will. Just because she couldn't access it now didn't mean it was wrong.

"You don't think she's from the South like I suspected?" Jakobav asked.

"I'm starting to wonder," Bryn admitted. "Maybe she's not from anywhere we've mapped recently."

A long silence stretched between them.

Then Bryn's voice dropped. "Whatever it is...it wasn't Claimed magic. It didn't behave like normal elemental abilities rooted in sacred soil. It was like she had one foot in this realm and the other too far for my gifts to touch."

Ella's throat went dry as she backed away from the door.

One foot here. One foot elsewhere.

The thought gnawed at the hollow beneath her sternum until her breath turned shallow.

She took a step into the corridor, then another.

This was good. She needed to keep moving, because if she stood still, then what she had just overheard would consume her.

The torchlight rolled across the charcoal veins in the wall as if they, too, were listening.

She found herself heading toward the solitude of Jakobav's chambers.

But heat flared beneath her skin, dizzying, and her body remembered before her mind could stop it. Bryn's words had cracked open a memory, and the past surged up to meet her.

Caelen Verelith leaned against the silver-barked tree, golden hair glowing beneath moonlight, watching her with that familiar mix of amusement and envy.

He was beautiful.

That was only part of the problem.

His hands were soft. His smile even softer.

"You've been distant," he said.

"I've been training."

"Training to what? Rule with bruises instead of your charm?"

She said nothing.

"Scare the suitors away?" His grin was teasing, but not cruel. "Ellandria, don't you know that you could simply rule with a smile? You don't need to bleed for your people."

Her eyes stayed on the moonlit orchids crawling up the bark of a tree across the field.

He sat beside her, close enough to touch. "You're different now. You feel...heavier. Like a storm cloud ready to break."

"I've been thinking about the crown. I don't know if I was meant to rule, Caelen. And I'm not sure that I want to," she said.

"Sure you do. Why else would you hide so much of yourself?" he said, voice dipping. "You think I don't see it?"

He moved closer, brushing a speck of invisible dust from his sleeve. "You could have everything, Ellandria. Power. Allegiance. Me. You don't have to make yourself a weapon."

She looked away. "That's not what I want."

"Sure it is. Everyone wants power. And if we were to unite our bloodlines through the mating ceremony, we could force the fractured provinces to fall in line. Bring the rest of the kingdoms to heel. Make the North pay for the siege they started, once and for all—"

"Stop," she said.

He blinked. "What?"

"That's not me. I want to find my fated mate. And besides, that's not what I was taught. The point of power is to protect, not punish. My parents believe—"

"Your parents are cowards."

The air stilled.

Ella turned away from him, but he was already reaching for her hand. He didn't notice her flinch. She pulled away farther.

"Ellandria, it is time to stop being naïve and start thinking about our future." He reached for her hand once more. "I see what you're becoming. You think you're just fire? You think your power stops there? There's more. There's always been more."

She yanked her hand away, with force this time and a matching scowl.

"You're hiding something," he whispered, eyes narrowing. "Maybe you don't even know it. But I feel it. When you walk in, the whole room shifts. Like it's bracing."

Her voice cracked. "Caelen—"

"Come on," he whispered. "Show me."

"Caelen, please drop it. I said no."

"Burn me."

"No!"

His hand closed around her wrist, too tight. Then the magic broke loose. Not with flame or fury, but ripe with instinct.

It knocked them both back. The sound he made was strangled.

Ella stumbled forward, panting, hand on the wall. Not magic this time, but memory. Just as painful. She hadn't meant to hurt him. He'd been right, in his way. She wasn't just fire, maybe she was something else, and it terrified her more than anything Bryn could ever say.

With no other choice but to keep moving, she turned the corner too fast and slammed into someone.

Jakobav didn't flinch.

Of course he didn't.

His hair, usually a fall of soft brown waves around his temples and neck, had been bound back tonight, drawn tight at the nape of his neck. The severe style revealed the full cut of his jaw, leaving nothing softened, nothing hidden. He looked down at her, one brow raised, and that smug little curve touched his lips.

"I was wondering when you'd start sneaking around."

"If I were trying to hide, you wouldn't have found me," she said coolly.

"Mm." His eyes swept over her, assessing.

Without warning, he reached out, and his finger barely grazed her cheek as he brushed a lock of hair behind her ear.

The touch lingered just enough to feel possessive, as though he had a right to move her how he pleased.

Ella's chin lifted, her voice steady despite the jolt it sent through her. "Careful. If I return the favor and stroke your face, I don't promise to be gentle."

Jakobav stilled.

A note of surprise broke through his mask, gone as quickly as it came. His eyes flickered, dark amusement glinting there, but before he could respond—

"What did Bryn mean?" she asked, cutting him off. She needed to take control now. Drag the truth from him before he could twist it. "About my power. About it being different."

He tilted his head, that same assessing look narrowing.

"I think you misheard."

"I didn't."

"Then you misunderstood."

"Unlikely." Ella's voice now had a razor-sharp edge.

Her pulse quickened, patience thinning.

Jakobav leaned just close enough that his breath touched her cheek. "If you're hunting answers," he said, "be very careful you don't stumble into questions you're not ready to ask."

She glared. "That's not an answer."

"No," he said, smiling darkly. "It's a warning."

Her magic stirred in her chest, angry and insistent. She crossed her arms. "You're hiding something."

"Of course I am."

He said it like it was obvious. Like hiding was survival.

"You think this is a game?"

"No, Princess." His voice dropped. "I think this is war. And you don't even know who's holding the sword yet."

His eyes tracked the way the word struck her, a slow, knowing curve pulling at his mouth.

The word split her in two.

Princess.

It hit her like a forbidden sorceress chained to a spire, torch flame pressed to her skin, searing through every layer she'd tried to hide. Her pulse crashed, wild and uneven, and her vision tunneled, the walls narrowing to trap her.

He couldn't know. He couldn't.

Her hand flew beneath her shirt, clutching at the hidden ink as if she could bury the truth. The flush of her cheeks burned hot and traitorous. Her throat closed, and she nearly choked on the secret itself.

Jakobav looked down at her, unrelenting.

He raised his hand toward her quickly, only for his fingers to then slowly drag across the fevered line of her cheekbone. The touch was not for comfort. She was utterly out of control, stripped bare.

Then he stepped past her. "Go back to my room, Ella," he said, his voice colder now. "Before someone starts asking what side you're on."

She had barely even begun the search, and already, she was losing her footing.

15

SECRETS AND SMOKE

Ella paced the narrow span of stone, cloak clutched tight, heart still pounding with the echo of Jakobav's words. Rest was out of the question. From the way his gaze had dropped to her chest, to the way he'd said *Princess* like he was testing the taste of it on his tongue, she knew she was in deeper trouble than she'd ever dared imagine.

There's no way he knows.

And yet there had been no trial or dungeons. No interrogations. Not even a summons from the Dravaryn crown demanding allegiance. There had only been warm food, thick blankets, and a brooding commander who looked at her like he could strip her down to bone and still find something worth savoring.

Ella shivered and pushed the disturbing thought aside.

Why hadn't he turned her in? Ella stopped pacing, breath snagging as the thought looped wild inside her.

He's hiding me.

He's protecting me?

Fuck. He knows.

She pressed her palm to her temple, the weight of it crushing. Maybe it had been obvious from the beginning. Was it her accent or the remnants of her magic that had betrayed her? Maybe Jakobav had smelled it in her blood, and gods, what if that hadn't been a metaphor? What if he had known from the moment she collapsed at his feet?

She thought about Bryn's words. *"It hadn't behaved like claimed magic. It had pushed back, defended her before she even realized she was in danger."*

Her magic had chosen in a feral, instinctive rush, reaching for Jakobav without her command. It had flared in a place where there should've been nothing but silence, smothered within Dravaryn soil.

What is wrong with my magic?

The question swelled until it eclipsed the room, the walls, the night, even the prophecy that had dragged her into the dark and refused to let her go. She'd come for an artifact, a relic buried beneath enemy soil.

Perhaps the relic was never an object, but a path.

A jarring knock split the air, and Ella flinched, her heart leaping into her throat.

Jakobav didn't wait for permission, although to be fair, he never did.

He stepped inside clothed in black leathers, dark hair pulled back in a low tie that once again left his jawline criminally exposed, the kind of jaw sculptors might chase their whole lives and still never capture. His presence devoured the room, towering and composed, every line of him radiating a leather-clad threat.

And his mouth, gods. Full lips, shaped with a kind of impossible artistry, promising either sin or salvation. Tonight, they looked more defined than ever, unbothered and utterly unfair. Ink wound down his arms from beneath his sleeves, dark symbols she hadn't truly seen before. When he shifted, the leather tightened across his forearms, and veins rippled like lightning trapped beneath skin.

"Put on your boots," he said.

"No greeting? No explanation?"

His eyes found hers. "We're leaving."

She straightened, spine stiffening. "And where exactly do you think you're taking me?"

"The southern ridge. A breach just opened outside Velmire's old pass."

She blinked, mind snapping into the training that had been drilled into her since childhood. "That's neutral ground?"

"Was." His voice was clipped. "Now it's a crater. Trees snapped at the roots. Steel melted to slag. Blood...wrong."

Heat surged through her veins, spiked and unsettled. "What is it with you and blood?" The question came out hard, brimming with accusation.

Gods, he was obsessed.

Silence.

"And what do you mean, wrong?" she demanded.

He bit his lip. Just barely. Like he was debating whether to answer.

The pause stretched, scraping at her nerves. Ella despised silence more than anything.

"What kind of magic could do that?" she pushed, refusing to back down, tired of unanswered questions.

His eyes locked on hers. "The kind that isn't supposed to exist anymore." His voice was flat, his gaze unreadable. "Not since the realms were sealed."

They stared at each other, cautious and measuring.

He tossed her the cloak, thick and fur lined. She caught it midair without breaking eye contact.

"I know you understand what's happening," she said. "Tell me why you're hiding it from your kingdom."

Jakobav's jaw tensed, but she pressed on.

"I've spent time with your people. No one has said a single word about Threadshifting."

He flinched at the word and didn't answer right away.

But that silence was all the answer she needed.

"You knew," she said quietly.

Jakobav's voice dropped and he looked deadly serious. "It's being dealt with."

She folded the cloak in her arms. "Then why haven't you warned Dravaryn?"

His gaze deepened. "I suspect you already know the answer to that, Princess."

"Fuck." She swallowed.

He knows.

Jakobav stared into her eyes, then stepped closer.

Ella's breath caught, and she braced herself.

If there was ever a moment to destroy her, this was it. He loomed over her, massive and unrelenting, his strength obvious in the set of his shoulders. She was weaponless and unprepared, but she drew herself as tall as she could and met him with narrowed eyes, unflinching.

He leaned in slowly, deliberately, and whispered against her ear.

"I've known since the moment you crossed my wards... breached *my* castle...gutted *my* guard...and bled on *my* sheets."

A shiver raked down her spine.

Jakobav pulled back just enough to meet her gaze. Her heart stuttered. Her breath came in shallow pants. His voice was a low hum of velvet. "You know what they say about keeping your enemies closer..."

His mouth curved into a slow, menacing smile.

"And I've been keeping you in my bed."

16

THREADS AND TEETH

The cloak slipped from her fingers and hit the ground with a soft thud, but the sound might as well have been a war drum. Ella stood frozen, blood roaring in her ears, his words still clinging to the air long after they fell.

He's known since the wards.

He'd said it like a blade unsheathed.

Her heart galloped in her chest from raw exposure, from the unbearable vulnerability of having her most guarded secret called into the light.

Jakobav didn't have to move to dominate the space between them. He stood there watching her with his arms crossed, unrelenting. And that, more than anything, terrified her enough to send her stumbling half a step back.

She discreetly patted her pocket, empty.

Where the fuck did that knife go?

Her gaze darted to the nearest table, panic rising as she found no weapons. Not even a fork. Her hands balled into fists as her breath quickened.

Jakobav's eyes narrowed the moment she shifted. But

before she could so much as pivot, he moved, fast as a whip, silent as snowfall. His fingers wrapped around her wrist, the grip not crushing but absolute. He tugged her forward, a force that drew her against the hard line of his chest until escape became a fading thought.

Pinned in place, she stiffened, muscles locking as though bracing for a blow. Instead, his hold shifted, intentional and unhurried, sliding from her wrist to her jaw to tilt her face upward.

The move should've been tender, but the iron in his touch told another story. His mouth hovered a breath from hers, close enough that if she so much as flinched, their lips might brush. The awareness of it unsettled her balance, as though the floor itself tilted toward him, leaving her nowhere else to stand.

She trembled, words tumbling to her lips before she could stop them.

"If you mean to kill me, do it. Stop circling." The defiance in her voice faltered on the final syllable, half-threat and half-plea.

He didn't answer at first.

His hold on her chin tightened, just enough to remind her that he was in control. When he finally spoke, his voice slid against her temple in a low, dangerous murmur.

"Do not make me your villain."

His breath taunted her skin, strength coiled beneath his stillness. Her pulse hammered on, traitorously loud no matter how she willed it silent.

The word *villain* thrashed around in her mind.

He shifted impossibly closer, lowering his face until his mouth grazed her ear. His voice was barely a whisper.

"But do not mistake me for your friend."

Her chest rattled, heartbeat frantic and trapped, like a

small bird newly caged and still wild. It was his tone that got her. It wasn't cruel this time, but instead, it was threaded with need and full of restraint.

He pulled back just enough to look at her, gaze raking across her face like a challenge. His lips parted slightly, he dragged the tip of his tongue across the lower one, almost in contemplation. She caught a glimpse of hunger before it vanished behind his mask.

Was that a threat? Or an invitation?

Every nerve sparked. Fear and anticipation, both burning hot and unsettled inside her.

Gods.

Jakobav's grip loosened only slightly, enough to let her breathe, just enough to let her think.

Run? Fight?

But the moment fractured when she found her voice again, biting and familiar.

"Who else knows?" she asked, chin lifting. She tried to stand taller, shoulders squaring. "I know I'm far from the only secret you're holding captive."

"No one else," he said. "Not yet."

Ella took a moment to think but held her ground.

"Then why treat me like a guest?" Her voice trembled with fury now. "Why not throw me in chains the second you discovered me?"

His expression didn't change. "Because I wanted to see what you'd do...amongst other reasons." He smiled coldly.

She glared. "And if I refuse to go with you?"

"Then you'll make a scene," Jakobav said evenly. "And I'll have to chain you anyway. Is that what you want?"

Heat bled up her neck, painting her fury in shades of pink. He let go of her wrist and took a slow, methodical step back.

"Pick it up," he said, nodding toward the fallen cloak.

Ella lifted her chin but didn't move.

"I won't ask again." His voice was deep and commanding, rolling through the room, eyes gleaming with cruel satisfaction.

Infuriated by how much he clearly enjoyed this, she let out a scathing sound.

Her next move would be calculated. Instinct told her it was in her best interest to obey.

His face darkened, clearly unwilling to compromise even an inch.

She crouched, then snatched the cloak off the floor, never breaking eye contact, and shoved it toward him like an answered challenge.

He didn't flinch.

"You're coming with me," Jakobav said. "You can do so as a guest."

His eyes hardened, but the side of his mouth twitched as if suppressing a wolfish smirk.

"Or as a prisoner. Either way...you're not staying here."

Ella's jaw locked and chest tightened, anger rising to an unsafe level for enemy territory.

He turned on his heel, already halfway to the door. Didn't even bother to look back.

"We leave at dawn." His voice, low and deep, reflected that his verdict was final.

It was still dark when the knock came.

She hadn't seen him since he left her with that ultimatum.

No midnight footsteps. No dark shadow by the hearth. Not even the brush of his presence outside the door. Wherever he'd gone, whatever preparations he'd made, Jakobav had disappeared into the castle's depths. And now he'd returned with the dawn to collect her.

Ella already stood cloaked, boots laced, every vein drawn tight with restless refusal.

"I'm not coming," she said, the words bitten off like steel between her teeth.

His gaze was black as midnight stone, steady as the floor beneath her. "Then I'll chain you myself," he said, voice a low taunt. "You'll learn how heavy Dravaryn iron feels...how well I use it." His mouth curved, wicked. "I also enjoy biting. So if you're choosing option B, consider that part of the package."

Ella's stomach flipped, heat crawling over her skin before she could stop it.

Gods, her body betrayed her far too easily around him.

She straightened, forcing her voice level. "Then I'll take option A. I'm coming with you, by my choice, but if I'm venturing with you to investigate a breach, I should be armed."

Jakobav's hand slipped in and out of his cloak, metal gleaming between his fingers as he revealed a familiar hilt. "You mean like this one?" His tone was almost amused. "Yes, I noticed when you took it. And yes, it gave me immense satisfaction to take it back."

Ella made a strained, exasperated sound, rolling her eyes, though the air between them seemed to crackle hotter with every word.

He tilted the knife, letting the torchlight catch on the edge. His voice was velvet over steel. "I'm glad you're drawn to this blade. I'm particularly fond of it myself. After all...it's the same one I pressed against your throat the other night."

Ella's jaw went slack.

Then anger snapped through her.

An annoyed sound escaped as she darted forward, hand reaching for the hilt.

Jakobav lifted it easily out of reach, his other hand closing around her throat, fingers firm but unyielding.

The look he gave her was all pressure and intent, like he was daring her to test him.

"Not yet," he murmured. "Come with me willingly, and I'll give it to you. You'll be meeting a few of my First Guard, and if I put this knife back in your hand, I need your promise you won't try to slit any of their throats with it."

Ella pried his hand off her neck, squeezing his wrist harder than necessary, and smiled sweetly enough to be insulting. "I promise." She held out her hand, expectant.

He placed the knife in her palm, his expression doubtful, then gestured for her to walk ahead of him as though the matter were settled.

She slipped the knife into her pocket, then yanked the cloak tighter around her shoulders, masking nerves with a shard of sarcasm. "So thoughtful. Always the gentleman."

His mouth curved faintly, a shadow of a smirk. "Don't get used to it."

When she still didn't move, his smirk thinned. With a sound low in his throat, he turned on his heel and strode toward the door, cloak flaring behind him. He didn't look back, didn't slow, clearly expecting her to follow.

Ella didn't move right away, her mind shouting that she shouldn't go.

The artifact was still here, buried somewhere in this castle, and the prophecy was the reason she'd come, the only reason she'd left.

She'd already given up her name, her safety, her kingdom... all for this mission. And now she was leaving with a man who'd just had his hand around her neck?

But time was slipping through her fingers like dust.

Her stomach twisted, every instinct screaming that this

should feel wrong. And yet...another pull rose in her chest, steadier, quieter. A thread she couldn't name, whispering that this was part of it, not a detour, but a path instead.

Jakobav's voice lingered in her mind: *Do not make me your villain.* She couldn't ignore it, the strange magic that had stirred in her veins since she crossed into Dravaryn. Besides, it would probably be for only a few days, a ride out on a scouting mission, a chance to see how Dravaryns handled Thread-shifting and maybe even learn new techniques to battle the breaches for the benefit of her own kingdom.

Jakobav may have been her enemy but he might also be the key to understanding this strange magic thrumming just below her hidden sigil, and to surviving what was coming.

She tugged the cloak tight around her shoulders.

This was strategy, not surrender.

A shift in the angle of attack.

17

WARDS WE CHOOSE

Morning broke cold and clear, frost turning brittle grass to crystal. The sky bled pale violet, the kind of color that warned of storms, and the wind dragged at her cloak as if even the land disapproved.

The stables waited. Five horses stamped and steamed in the cold, their flanks heaving clouds into the dawn. Jakobav went straight to the largest: black-coated, leather-strapped, power coiled in every line, like a beast waiting for war. He adjusted the bridle with a focus so controlled it hushed the air. Sleeves rolled, ink flowing down his arms in symbols too old for speech, veins drawn tight beneath his skin.

"First Guard...this is Ella. She's coming with us."

Maeren sat already mounted, sleek black braid hanging over her shoulder like a weapon disguised as hair. One hand on her hip, the other twirling a dagger as if boredom might strike harder than metal. Ella recognized her immediately, remembering that brief glimpse from the time she'd been wedged against Jakobav in the furs, when Maeren had delivered her report. Heat pricked Ella's throat at the memory of being pressed against him, the way it made her skin tingle and thoughts tangle.

"Welcome," Maeren said. A subtle glint flickered in her eyes, almost amusement. "Try to keep up," she said, tone cutting.

Ella gave her a single nod in return and took a closer look around the stables. Two men lingered by the tack benches. One was tall and muscular, the other massive, and he gave her a half smile when he noticed her watching.

She could tell Jakobav had already told his Guard about her joining them on this ride by the way that no one seemed surprised to see her.

"Well, well." His voice rumbled low, rich, a sound that seemed to vibrate in the floor. He strode forward with a swagger that bent gravity, each step rolling like distant thunder. "The little fox returns."

Ella blinked. "I'm sorry...have we met?"

He clutched his chest like she'd wounded him. "Thane Ironfell. East wall, gate duty. You slipped past me like a whisper of chaos. A lesser man would've been offended. I was aroused."

"Delighted," Ella said dryly.

"You should be. You humiliated the Guard, gutted Savina, and landed me two positions higher in command for a week. Should've been permanent, if you ask me." He grinned, and the dimple in his cheek threatened to undo her resolve.

Ella bit the inside of her cheek to keep from smiling back. Thane was...dangerous in a different way, all sun-warmed muscle and irreverent grin. Not scored with scars like Jakobav, though he didn't need them. Trouble clung to him like a second skin, or so it seemed. Mischief danced behind his eyes when he spoke, reckless and knowing, as though the world had been built to notice him.

"You're telling me you were guarding the entrance and still let me slip past you?" she asked.

"You floated," he said, deadly serious. "Like a breeze carrying murder. One second the wind stirred, next second, gone. The trees still talk about you."

Maeren snorted. "Ignore him. He offers every girl Fae wine and dramatic compliments. Thinks a decent vocabulary makes him irresistible."

"Hmm, well, I don't trade secrets for booze," Ella replied, arms crossed. "Even if I could use a stiff drink after dealing with your future king."

"Blasphemy," Thane gasped, a grin already tugging at his mouth.

Jakobav walked past and cuffed the back of Thane's head without looking. "Stop flirting."

"Come on now, Jake, I'm not flirting," Thane said with a grin. "Just thanking her for improving morale."

Jakobav didn't respond. He only nodded toward the last man, hooded and cloaked in charcoal, his gloved hands folded in silence.

"This is Soren," Jakobav said. "He sees everything but says almost nothing."

Soren inclined his head slightly, but remained silent, as promised. His eyes, pale gray and unblinking, met Ella's like fog meeting glass.

"Charmed," she said carefully.

He blinked once. Nothing more.

A clatter of hooves snapped her attention as another rider rounded the corner of the stable with feline grace, reined to a stop, and swung down in one liquid motion, leveling Ella with a gaze sharp enough to cut.

Fuck. Savina.

Ella's breath lodged in her throat. She hadn't seen the

woman clearly the night she'd broken into the castle and opened her stomach with a single slash. Now, in daylight, it was impossible to look anywhere else.

Savina was ruin made flesh.

White-blonde curls spilled down her back like coiled lightning, wild and unforgiving. Her armor hugged a body built for war, for speed, for beauty that promised lethal consequences and dared you to crave them anyway.

Ella's stomach twisted. She remembered the blood, the wound, the devastation she had caused. There was no universe where Savina was fully healed—and guilt punched cold beneath her ribs.

Savina's eyes flicked to hers, bright and unblinking, and in that single look Ella understood one thing with perfect clarity.

She intended to carve that debt back into Ella's skin the first chance she got.

"Well," Savina said coolly, "I didn't expect the girl who gutted me to ride with us. Figured you'd at least look regretful."

Ella opened her mouth, but no words came.

Thane looked far too entertained, his shit-eating grin widening. "Savina, meet Ella. Ella, meet the woman who lost her command for six days and has been threatening revenge every hour since."

Savina's gaze didn't move. "You should've killed me when you had the chance."

"I wasn't trying to kill anyone," Ella said softly.

Savina's eyes narrowed. "Then you failed twice."

Tension filled the air, broken only by Maeren's sigh as she nudged her horse forward.

"Grudges can wait for the ride back," she said. "The Veil won't hold its breath for backhands."

Jakobav mounted, leather creaking under his weight. "Weapons ready. We move fast."

Ella swung into the saddle, hands trembling faintly. The horse shifted beneath her as she adjusted her cloak.

She glanced at everyone around her and noticed the ink, the steel, the strange affection masked as mockery. These weren't just guards. They were constellations in his sky. Fixed, dangerous, burning in their own way. She was pulled into their orbit.

Maeren arched a brow. "Just to be clear, and because our guest here has a habit of stabbing people, if Jakobav dies on this mission, I get command of First Guard. That's what we agreed on, right?"

Jakobav didn't look up. "That was a joke."

"Not to me."

Thane grinned. "She'd hate it. Too many scrolls. Not enough skulls."

"I'm excellent at delegation," Maeren said sweetly. "I haven't personally broken anyone's fingers in weeks."

"Because Jakobav forbade it," Thane muttered.

She beamed. "Exactly. Restraint."

Jakobav didn't join their games. His gaze never left Ella, steady and relentless, like he was memorizing the exact moment she would falter. Whatever game Thane and Maeren played, she knew she was the only opponent Jakobav saw.

Ella exhaled, shaking her head. The First Guard reeked of unhinged madness and loyalty. "Should I be concerned?"

"Oh, absolutely," Maeren said sweetly, sliding the dagger back into its sheath with practiced flair. "But don't worry. There are at least four of us who don't wish to split you open." She smirked and flicked her brows upward. "Right, Commander?"

Jakobav cleared his throat and shot Maeren a warning glare.

Maeren's innuendo landed low, and for one treacherous heartbeat, she didn't hear it as a threat at all. A flush crept, unwanted and shameful.

She locked her face back into defiance.

Jakobav shifted in his saddle, his words a dare delivered with dark amusement. "Rile her at your own peril. She's armed. I gave her the knife."

Thane barked out a belly laugh, delighted. "Gods, I like her even more."

Savina started to speak, but Jakobav cut her off with a single decisive wave of his hand.

"Enough," Jakobav said. "Let's move. We'll reach the outer ridge before dusk."

They rode out together, the forest parting before them like it knew better than to stand in the way. These were Jakobav's most trusted circle of guards, maybe even friends, if that was possible for Dravaryns, and she was riding straight into their fold.

Even as they rode, she couldn't escape her thoughts about the artifact buried within the castle—and the mission that had brought her here. But when the trees opened and the wind cut across her cheeks, Jakobav leading this circle felt inevitable, like the realm itself aligning.

Something deep inside her insisted: *this is the path I'm meant to take.*

18

BREATH OF THE VEIL

They rode hard, the forest blurring around them.

Ella had studied the Dravaryns for years: their speech, their cities, their customs. But now the land felt different, breathing, as though it were revealing itself to her at last.

Golden light filtered through the trees, catching on moss and shards of frost. Jagged cliffs jutted skyward, streaked with veins of obsidian pulsing with buried magic. Wild black roses tangled through the underbrush, smaller and rougher than those in the castle garden, beautiful in their resilience.

The trees whispered as they passed, not with menace but with a secretive hush, the forest keeping watch. Ella kept her hood drawn low, her silence tighter still, though her thoughts refused to quiet. Jakobav's glances settled against her like a thought he meant her to feel, while Maeren watched with the patience of someone waiting for a crack to appear.

Behind them, Savina rode with a deadly poise that made Ella question whether she was brave or simply reckless. Jakobav never once turned to acknowledge her, and that made Ella wonder about their history, because soldiers this loyal didn't simply appear. Savina carried a dangerous sort of beauty, shaped by training and honed by a lifetime of expectation. Whatever bound them was deep, even if it wasn't romantic.

Did any of them suspect who she truly was? What had Jake told them to explain why she was here? Were they blindly loyal to their commander, or did they carry secrets of their own, concealed as carefully as hers?

"Fuck," she muttered, realizing to her horror that she'd called him Jake even in her mind. The name felt too intimate, the kind spoken only by someone he let close. Forcing her attention back to the terrain, she traced every tree and bend in the path, memorizing the route in case she ever needed to escape alone.

They made camp just after dusk, near a crumbling ridge where the wind picked up, cold and biting, carrying the promise of a brutal frost. Everyone else had gone to scout, leaving her alone with Jakobav in the clearing. The fire cracked quietly between them, casting broken shadows across his face.

"Well?" Ella asked, crossing her arms. "Aren't you going to set the wards?"

Jakobav glanced up and let out a low laugh, dark and unsettling.

Her brows snapped together. "What's so funny?"

"You expect me to mutter a few words and conjure a barrier?" His mouth curved faintly. "You think Dravaryn blood works like that?"

Her eyes narrowed, defensiveness flaring. "It's not just me. The whole realm knows the rumors. Dravaryn royalty is supposed to raise protective barriers in their sleep."

"Sorry to disappoint you and your rumors," Jakobav said smoothly, "but neither I nor anyone in my family has that ability."

Ella frowned. "But how? The wards around your castle are strong. I felt them."

For the first time, his composure cracked. His eyes widened, shock flashing raw across his face, and he studied her as though she had just spoken something impossible. With what seemed to be deliberate effort, the mask slid back into place.

"The wards around the castle were there long before us," he said evenly, "and they'll be there long after."

Then what had she felt? If not Dravaryn magic...then whose?

Irritation burned in her chest—she hated being wrong. She leaned forward, her words aimed to wound. "Unless Thread-shifting spreads and the Veil shatters. Then your ancient wards would crumble, and your family would fall along with them."

The fire popped, sparks spinning into the dark.

Jakobav's smirk vanished, gaze fixed on her, taking one step closer, then another, until his shadow swallowed her. Then, in one sudden motion, he dropped down and planted a hand on the log beside her knee, the other on the far side, caging her in. He leaned close, his grip tightening until the bark cracked beneath his palms. His jaw was set tight, the ruthless determination in his eyes promising her words had struck deep.

Ella's heartbeat spiked, and she cursed herself for it, not from fear, but because part of her thrilled at the danger.

She'd wanted to unsettle him.

She hadn't anticipated how the strike would rebound.

His hand flexed against the cracked wood like he might touch her. Her body leaned forward before her mind could stop it, then jerked back as if remembering who she was provoking. "You overstepped, and now you're hesitating," he said, his voice low and unforgiving.

Ella forced her chin up, covering the slip. "I'm allowed to think."

"Then think quieter." His expression was scathing, but he backed away just enough that she was no longer caged.

She huffed as she pushed off the log to stand, folded her arms, and looked down at him with as much confidence as she could muster. "You really know how to make a guest feel welcome." The word lingered like a dare, guest, not prisoner.

Jakobav's eyes held hers too long, unreadable.

The fire painted his face in warped light and shadow, and she had the distinct sense he was deciding what she was worth: an ally, an enemy, or something far more threatening.

Without a word, he rose and took one step, closing the distance again. Close enough that only her ragged breath existed in the space between them.

His gaze intensified, as though she'd just offered him a new game he intended to win.

"You keep saying guest," he said at last, voice barely above a murmur. "As if the word itself makes it true. As if you're testing me...waiting to see if I'll reveal what my Guard already knows. You're wondering if I'm hiding the truth from them or if I've revealed who you really are."

The words struck like a slap.

"I didn't say that."

She shivered, though she wasn't sure if it was the wind biting her skin or the way he kept prying.

"You didn't have to." His head tilted slightly, predatory.

Her jaw tightened. "Aren't you?"

His eyes didn't waver. "Would it matter?"

Yes. It would change her entire plan. But she couldn't make herself say it.

Instead she replied, "If you are...I'd like to know why."

Jakobav didn't blink. He reached out, slow and deliberate,

and pulled her tunic back over her shoulder. She hadn't realized it had slipped, and his fingers grazed her collarbone, rough and calloused, warm from the fire, his thumb tracing slow circles that tested every boundary she tried to hold.

Air snagged in her throat, but she didn't move, refusing him the gratification of seeing her react to his touch.

"You're asking for truth when you've given little of it yourself," he said. His voice was low, private, as though the fire itself had spun a cocoon around them. His hand stayed on her shoulder, warm and unyielding, a reminder that he had no intention of stepping back.

"Fine. You want honesty? I'm not hiding you." His voice hit with the weight of a verdict. "I'm protecting you. I know who you are. I may not know what you're hiding, but I intend to fucking find out."

His gaze locked with hers, waiting, watching, hunting for the truth.

"But something about you..."

He leaned in, not close enough to kiss but close enough that the heat of his mouth ghosted her cheek. His grip tightened on her shoulder.

"...feels like the edge of a blade."

Ella stilled. Jakobav's mouth twitched, half grimace and half something darker. His thumb dragged slowly from her collarbone to the column of her throat in a smooth stroke.

"One wrong move," he murmured, "and you'd slice a man clean through."

His thumb paused beneath her jaw where her pulse thundered, tilting her head toward him. Not painfully, but not gently either.

"Cutting," he added. "Delicate yet deadly."

Ella's breath caught, loud in the hush.

"Fuck." She hadn't meant to say it aloud. Her cheeks

flushed, shame rising hot and fast. She swallowed hard, the sound impossibly loud.

He didn't move or smirk, only watched her.

The moment stretched, taut as a drawn bowstring.

Ella was growing tired of the game, flustered by the endless dance between them. She was about to demand answers, drawn to him in a way she feared would make her reveal more than she ever intended.

Before she could speak, a howl rose in the trees, hollow and wrong. It echoed from every direction at once, and the entire camp stilled. She hadn't even noticed the others return, too lost in the Commander's godsdamned words.

Jakobav moved before she did, his hand already on his sword as the fire cracked behind him.

"Eyes up," he said, voice like steel. "We've got company."

"Not from this realm," Maeren said, already unstrapping her blade. "That noise went straight through my skull."

Thane grunted in agreement.

Ella turned to the others, pulse spiking, her hands tingling with rising heat that wasn't her fire nor was it fear. It was something older, something deeper, and she got the sense that it had been waiting.

The howl came again, low and guttural, but this time, it didn't fade. It lingered. The sound clawed through the trees like it was searching, testing for weakness. Then...silence that was full, heavy, waiting.

Ella held her breath, the forest doing the same. No one moved, but their weapons were drawn and holding steady, eyes scanning the shadows.

They waited, but nothing stirred, like it had completely vanished.

"Jake, stop staring at her and give the orders." Savina snapped.

He leveled her with a look that would have made any other soldier falter. Savina held her ground, but Jakobav stepped fully into command, his voice slicing through the clearing as he issued orders.

The First Guard moved instantly, training snapping into place. Soren was already in motion before his name left Jakobav's mouth. Ella would ask about his magic later. She hoped the answer wasn't worse than the way he moved. Thane gave her a pat and a wink as he disappeared into the trees.

"Maeren, stay with her," Jakobav said, voice clipped.

He didn't even glance at Ella, which only made it worse. She bristled, but Maeren just rolled her eyes and dropped her pack beside the fire.

"Aye, commander," she said, biting off the title with irritation. Then muttered, "As if I planned to wander off and let her die."

Jakobav didn't look back, the last to march off toward the ridge.

Silence settled behind him, thick and watchful, broken only by the low hiss of the fire and the rustle of leaves.

Ella shifted, unsure what to do with herself.

Maeren gave her a quick sideways look and snorted. "You don't exactly need babysitting, from what I've heard."

Ella stood awkwardly until Maeren tossed her a bundle of twine.

"We're not going to stand here like statues," Maeren said. "Help me secure the supplies and stoke the fire."

Ella arched a brow. "Aren't we supposed to be keeping watch?"

"Can't stand around watching while I'm this tense," Maeren muttered as she drove a stake into the earth. "And you look like you'll combust if you stand still any longer."

Ella didn't argue.

Together they worked in silence, stoking the fire, tying down the supplies, unrolling bedrolls in a wide circle around the blaze until the rhythm of motion steadied her hands. Then, as if it were the most natural thing in the world, Maeren pulled a slender green bottle with an iridescent sheen from her pack.

"You just...carry wine around?" Ella asked.

"Fae wine. Worth the extra weight." She grinned. "Don't tell Jake. Or do. He could use some."

She filled two small tin cups and handed one over. "Maeren," she said simply. "In case you didn't catch it the first time."

Ella hesitated, then accepted.

Maeren grinned and then tipped her cup toward Ella's with a wink. "Or the second."

Ella choked on her first sip, coughing against the burn of Fae wine. "What's that supposed to mean?"

Maeren's grin faded. "Jake told me about hiding you. I was furious at first. Doesn't look good for the future king to be tucking away the castle's intruder." She shrugged. "He explained why he didn't want anyone finding out yet."

Ella's eyes widened slightly, heat rising to her cheeks.

"But I'm glad he told us," Maeren went on, her tone softening. "And I'm glad I got to meet you. Couldn't resist meeting the woman who bested Savina before she had time to call on her power. Godsdamned impressive."

A reluctant smile tugged at Ella's mouth. "I'm not sure I deserve that compliment. I feel bad about hurting her. But desperate times and all that."

Maeren smiled. "Deadly and humble. I'll cheers to that."

They clinked their metal cups. The wine burned, but not unpleasantly, warmth blooming in her chest, unraveling a memory she hadn't expected.

"My father used to share his Fae wine with me," she said

quietly. "Not often. But on rare nights, he'd pour us each a glass in secret, always in the garden. And I'd beg him to train me."

Maeren blinked. "To fight?"

"He was a warrior once. Fierce, before he gave it up for politics and peace treaties. I was already learning to fight, but nothing matched the lessons of someone who'd seen actual combat. I think part of him missed the life he'd given up," she said softly. "But he would only talk about it after a glass or two. He'd say things...that peace doesn't happen by accident. That someone always pays for it."

Ella smiled faintly, the ache of missing home tight in her ribs.

"Some of my best sparring happened slightly tipsy. Probably not safe, but it made us laugh."

Maeren chuckled low. "Sounds like you'd fit right in with this deranged lot."

"I'm starting to think so," Ella admitted, her cheeks flushing from honesty...or the wine.

They emptied their cups.

Maeren grabbed a bedroll and tossed it hard to the far side of the camp. "That one's Savina's. You're welcome." She smirked.

Ella grinned. "Thanks. Make sure it's far enough. Maybe beyond the trees."

"I could pitch it outside the kingdom borders," she said dryly. "And it still wouldn't be far enough. Sav's wrath knows no bounds."

Ella laughed, and for a moment, the tension lifted. "Should we be drinking wine on watch?"

Maeren shrugged. "We're fine. They'd be back already if they found anything."

She looked around the camp, at the way firelight danced

over the leaves, making them shift, or maybe that was the wine. She was already getting too comfortable with this group. It was hard not to with the way they all teased and laughed at one another.

Their nicknames came easily, spoken with the kind of comfort that only years could build. She'd already heard Maeren say Sav and Jake, and she was certain they had some filthy nickname for Thane, maybe even one for Soren. They weren't just the highest ranked in Dravaryn's First Guard, they were a close unit.

Ella wondered what it would feel like to belong to something like that.

The thought surprised her with the hope held within it.

She missed her friends in Orchid, especially Nira and Demetrius, and couldn't help but wonder if they would also have such a tightly knit group if she hadn't left. She let the moment swallow her before she buried it.

They had unpacked everything, kindled the fire, and there was nothing more to be done. Her gaze drifted around the campsite and snagged on something. She counted the bedrolls again. Wait. There were only four, plus the one Maeren had hurled to the edge of camp.

Ella froze, and at that exact moment, Jakobav stepped from the trees, cloak slung over one shoulder, sword sheathed but ready. He glanced at Maeren and nodded once.

"Coast is clear. No signs of the creature or the opening it came through."

"There are only five bedrolls," Ella snapped. "Did you forget how to count?"

Jakobav raised a brow.

"Do I look like I was in charge of packing?" The question landed more like a warning than an excuse. Then his gaze slid past her to Thane.

Thane groaned, throwing up his hands. "Godsdammit. I didn't think Savina would make it! She took a blade to the gut, I figured she'd be healing, not riding out beside our small but mighty war sprite."

He nodded toward Ella.

"War sprite?" she hissed.

"In the best way," he added with a wink. "Those tiny things tend to be terrifying."

Before she could retort, Savina strode into camp like she owned the ground.

"I ran a full perimeter. No ripples. No tracks. Nothing breathing that shouldn't be. But it's not over. That sound wasn't natural. If it vanished, it could return."

Everyone went still.

Jakobav nodded once. "We sleep in a defensive pattern. Weapons close."

Then he turned to Ella.

"You're with me tonight."

Ella blinked. "What? Excuse me? The hell I am."

"We're short a bedroll," he said, the faintest curve at his mouth. "You'll share mine."

He delivered it like a tactical order, already moving to check the others.

Ella's lungs stuttered and her vision narrowed, too many emotions rising at once.

It was one thing to sleep in his bed, in the secrecy of his chambers. But here, in front of his fiercest warriors? Absolutely not. It wasn't just the situation, it was his tone, and the way he said it. Not a question or an invitation, but as a command. Her heart lurched before pride caught it mid-fall.

19

BURNING POINT

Ella surged forward. "I'm not sharing a bedroll with anyone." She was breathless now. "I'd rather—"

A hand closed gently around her wrist. Thane's.

"Hey. Please." His voice, for the first time since she met him, carried no trace of humor. "Take it out on me. I packed too fast. I'm sorry. Just...go easy on him."

She stared at him, thrown by the gravity in his tone.

"We've been dealing with these Veil breaches for a while," he went on, steady now. "But this one's different. The realm is more unstable now. The solstice is almost here, which means his Claiming is days away. He's trying to carry an entire kingdom on his shoulders...and still protect all of us. And you."

Something in his eyes, earnest and almost pleading, hit her harder than she expected. Thane did not seem like the type to ever be serious. Ella let out a slow breath and nodded, her jaw set, bristling at the heaviness. She found herself grasping for levity, eager to fracture the silence.

"So I shouldn't skewer anyone from gut to gullet over a missing bedroll?" she asked lightly.

Thane's brows arched, amusement flashing. "That was oddly specific."

"Maybe I was channeling my inner *war sprite*?"

The grin returned, smug and pleased with himself, before he dropped onto his own mat.

Jakobav was arranging camp, pretending not to listen, but Ella caught the twitch of his hand, and the way his shoulders loosened only once she had finally relented. He dragged their shared bedroll to the far side of the fire, half shielded by saddles and packs, then turned to address the group.

"If anything slips through the trees, it will come from this direction," he said, tone clipped. "I'm taking first watch. If my eyes start to get heavy, I'll wake one of you."

Thane arched a brow but didn't argue. The others nodded, then scattered toward their own sleeping mats on the opposite side of the fire, embers popping softly as the camp settled.

Jakobav remained standing, one hand near his sword, his gaze fixed on the dark beyond the circle of light.

Ella cleared her throat. He turned slowly, lifting a brow as if to ask what trouble she planned to start now.

"Of course you volunteer for guard duty," she said.

"Watching people sleep seems to be a favorite pastime of yours."

He paused at that, the jab hanging between them. Then he stepped close, hooked two fingers beneath her chin, and lifted it in a brief, silent tilt, his eyes unreadable.

A soft *tsk* slipped from him, something like amusement or a warning—she couldn't tell—and he shook his head once before releasing her and walking away without a word.

Ella exhaled through her nose, heat prickling the back of her neck. She lowered herself into what would be their shared bedroll and tugged the blanket into place.

It wasn't long before Jakobav returned from his final sweep

along the perimeter. He lowered himself beside her, settling on the edge of the mat, his body angled toward the trees in a posture that was both rest and vigilance.

Ella wasn't sure what unsettled her more: the thought of sharing a bedroll with him, or the way her body betrayed her by welcoming his warmth. The night had turned bone-cold, a bitter wind threading through every seam of her cloak before gathering at the back of her neck and sending a shiver through her. Her breath misted in the air as she tucked herself closer, trying not to notice the slow, steady rhythm of Jakobav's breathing inches away.

They weren't touching. Not really. Yet the bedroll was narrow, and the heat radiating from him seemed to bleed into her, infuriating in its persistence, though perhaps the heat was her own. Her skin felt tight and fevered, as though something deep within her was pushing against the cold, straining to break free, humming in the dark.

She closed her eyes and willed herself toward sleep, but it refused to come. Her thoughts spun too loudly, and his presence was louder still, each shift of muscle beneath his shirt pulling her attention, every piece of him impossible to ignore.

And then it happened. Ella's eyes snapped open as heat bloomed, not a gentle warmth but a small searing fire, a sudden blaze rising from within her. Flames crawled across her skin as a quiet hiss split the air. She looked down in horror to see the fabric of her shirt blackening, burning away in slow strips until each thread shriveled, and vanished into ash, exposing more of her with every frantic heartbeat.

"Oh shit," she breathed.

She reached for the fur cover...only then realizing it had been kicked halfway down the bedroll sometime in her sleep. Her fingers scrambled for it, but she was too slow, too shocked, too bare.

Beside her, Jakobav jerked upright with a harsh inhale.

A thin wisp of smoke rose from a single scorched line along the edge of the bedroll, then the fire was nothing more. The small flame had died as if an unseen hand had pinched it out, leaving only that faint mark behind.

Her fire had never done that.

It had always spared her skin, but before she learned control, it devoured anything close—rope, cloth, bedding, whatever happened to be near her.

Tonight was different. Tonight the flames had chosen. Only her clothes had burned, cleanly and completely, while the rest had barely been touched. It had to be the breach. Her magic was misfiring, burning in ways that were selective and unpredictable.

"What the—" Jakobav's hand shot out and grasped her shoulder before he hissed and wrenched back like her skin was scorching hot to the touch. And now nothing hid what the flames had taken.

She was naked. Exposed. Vulnerable. To the cold. To him. And gods, to the quiet camp surrounding them.

Her heart slammed against her ribs, breath shattering in her chest. If Maeren turned over or if Thane sat up, if Savina opened her eyes for even a moment... Panic knifed through her.

Her voice came out in a sharp whisper. "Do not say a word."

"Wasn't going to," he whispered back, voice hoarse and rough. "Not with my First Guard. Right. There." His voice had turned to pure threat, like he would personally murder anyone who even thought about lifting their head to look at her. "Ella. Do not move. Do not scream."

His gaze dragged over her bare skin again, slow and tortured, his jaw clenching as if the sight physically hurt him.

Ash drifted between them in fragile flakes, catching in the firelight.

"I didn't do this on purpose," she whispered, arms folding tight across her chest.

"I know." He kept his voice quiet, still looking furious, as though the very idea of one of his warriors waking and seeing what he saw was unacceptable.

The air quivered with more than tension, threads of magic shifting in the silence, alive and waiting, as if it had chosen this moment, her most vulnerable, her most unguarded.

Jakobav's hand twitched at his side. Restraint was carved into the hard set of his jaw, in the way his eyes kept burning hotter each time they dragged back to hers, heat answering heat.

"I can feel it," he murmured, barely louder than the wind.

"What?" she whispered back.

"Your power." His gaze locked on hers, unwavering. "It's awake."

Ella's breath stuttered, shallow and thin.

"Do you feel it?" he asked softly.

She blinked, disbelief spilling faster than her words. "I feel naked, Jakobav."

His mouth twitched, the ghost of a smirk threatening and then dying before it formed. His gaze dropped openly now, tracing the bare line of her collarbone, the curve of her breasts, the vulnerable length of skin she hadn't managed to hide. When he spoke, his voice was low, roughened into something close to a growl. "That too."

The answering pull low in her belly was immediate. Treacherous. Her hands drifted lower, hovering near her thighs, fingers curling as she fought the instinct to hide the place that ached most and the equally reckless urge to do nothing at all.

The realm itself seemed to stir, a faint echo threading through the forest beyond their circle of firelight, as if even the trees leaned closer to watch.

Her skin was still searing against the night air as Jakobav scanned the shadows for a threat, every muscle coiled, every line of his body honed into lethal intent.

Her skin tightened, drawn too taut over her frame.

"I'm going to ask you something," he whispered, his gaze fixed on the dark beyond the fire. "And I need you to tell me the truth."

Her throat was dry. "What?" she whispered back.

"Is your magic doing this because of me...or because of the breach?" His words stayed low, barely more than breath.

Ella blinked, stunned.

"I can handle either," he went on, his gaze snapping back to hers, voice steady and almost frightening in its calm. "But I need to know which one is about to kill me first." His tone remained hushed, every word guarded.

Gods, he couldn't possibly be serious, and yet he looked at her with the focus of a man facing war.

His gaze dipped lower again, and in that motion, she saw hunger—not for her power, but for her, raw and unmasked. Ache surged through her, enough that her nipples tightened against the cold air.

Ella followed the path of his eyes to the space between her thighs, where his gaze lingered, darkening. His throat worked once in a harsh swallow, and when his eyes lifted to hers again, the restraint there was brutal, almost savage.

She couldn't look away. But the question still burned in the silence. Him, or the breach? Her body answered before her mind could; her back arched, need spilling from her skin in restless waves.

Jakobav leaned in close enough that she felt his warmth

roll over hers and that one breath too deep would have brought his mouth to hers. The air thickened, swollen with magic and lust, tangled tight between them.

A rustle of fabric past the fire pulled them out of the moment, and Jakobav's head whipped toward the sound, predator-quick. The sound was heavy, likely Thane turning in his sleep. They both held their breath, waiting to see if he would sit up, speak, or stir again. He didn't.

The camp settled back into stillness.

As if suddenly remembering she was still naked—and that anyone could wake and see her—he shot forward, one hand seizing the fur thrown near her feet, the other bracing against her hip for leverage. He tugged the covering upward in a single pull.

The fur snagged on her pack, and he yanked it free with a rough jerk. His bracing hand slipped, knuckles brushing the inside of her leg before his fingers slid suddenly between her thighs, pressed into a slick warmth that answered more than she wanted him to know.

Ella's breath fractured. Sensation crashed over her in a raw, helpless wave.

Jakobav froze. He dropped the fur; it landed across her chest. But his other hand remained a heartbeat too long, still cupped against the most sensitive part of her before he finally tore it back.

"Fuck," he whispered, wrecked. "Ella."

Her stomach flipped, and she struggled to breathe.

For several suspended seconds, neither of them moved. The space between them felt stretched thin, humming with everything his touch had ignited. A tingling sensation still lingered on her skin where his hand had been, a phantom imprint that refused to fade, and the shock of it held her frozen.

Then his shoulders locked, the soldier settling back into place.

He turned away from her with a quick, controlled movement, rolling onto his side as though she had burned him.

Which, in truth, she might have.

The heat of his body withdrew at once, leaving her bare skin exposed to the icy air. The sudden cold hit like a blade. Her magic retreated with it, draining fast, leaving her muscles trembling around the absence.

The shivering began quietly, almost imperceptible at first, a tremor in her legs that spread to her arms until her whole body shook, teeth chattering as her limbs went rigid against the chill.

Jakobav's head turned, his body shifted, and with a low exhale, he reached for her. He didn't speak or ask, simply drew her toward him. Her body curled instinctively into his, dwarfed by the breadth of him, and the fit was too perfect to be anything but maddening. She should pull away, should protest, but she was frozen through, bone-deep tired, and the heat of him felt like salvation.

His chest was unyielding behind her, the planes of his body hard as stone. His arm settled firmly around her middle, strong but careful. She tried not to notice the stillness inside her, the strange calm, how safe she felt in the shelter of his hold.

"I understand the concept of huddling for warmth," she muttered, her voice rough, "but I don't think I'm wearing enough for this to count."

Behind her, Jakobav let out a low, amused sound. "Maybe I'm wearing too much?"

Ella's eyes flew open, her thoughts tangling into chaos. Was he teasing? Was he offering? Or was she losing her mind for even wondering?

Before she could combust, Jakobav shifted, pulling off his outermost layer and handing it to her without a word.

Then he reached into one of the packs and drew out a pair of pants. He didn't look at her as he passed them over, only said, "Might be Maeren's."

Gods, please let them be Maeren's. Anyone's but Savina's. She had already taken her out of commission for days; she didn't need to steal her pants too.

She muttered something incoherent as she tugged them on with a huff. They were slightly too large, and smelled faintly of leather and smoke.

Jakobav lay back down without another word, his arm returning to her waist and hauling her more firmly against him. She sucked in a breath as the hard length of him pressed against her lower back, hot and insistent even through the fabric.

She told herself it was nothing, a reflex, an accident of proximity, but her flesh refused to believe the lie. Every muscle in her frame went taut, awareness sparking everywhere his body touched hers.

He didn't shift away; if anything, his grip tightened. And gods help her, she didn't move either.

She knew she didn't get a single moment of true sleep, though she had pretended to. Dawn hovered close, perhaps an hour, perhaps minutes away. She only knew she had to steady herself before morning light revealed everything they hadn't dared to name in the dark. The light would be here soon, and with it, the truth.

20

BLOOD BETWEEN REALMS

She had survived the night, and as the sun crested the ridge in a slow bloom of gold, the truth seemed to rise with it—certain and inescapable.

Ella had lost track of how many times she had tried and failed to summon her fire over the past week, yet she felt with unshakable certainty that it was no coincidence her power had flared last night. Not when the mortal realm threatened to split at the seams. Something was stirring, and she couldn't shake the feeling that an older presence had been peeking through the cracks, watching her.

She reminded herself that paranoia was not weakness. It was something she could harness, turning awareness into preparation.

She pushed herself upright with care, her muscles still stiff from the night before. Her body had not forgotten, but the new day demanded her focus, and she needed to stay alert.

The half of the bedroll where Jakobav had been beside her was now empty. She'd felt him untangle his arm from around her shortly before dawn, his warmth long gone.

She looked around and found him standing near the horses at the far side of camp. She watched him check the tack and reins with quiet focus, then move down the line, brushing a hand along a dark flank before offering each horse its feed. Frost steamed faintly from their coats in the cold morning light.

The others still slept, scattered in loose circles around the fire, their weapons lying close at hand, their rest uneasy but unbroken.

She considered calling out to Jakobav, knowing it was probably time for everyone to pack up and keep moving, but the words gathered at the back of her throat. Hesitation held her in place.

The silence didn't feel like absence, but like tension, the entire forest suspended in waiting. It felt charged and brittle, as though she were listening for a note too low for mortal ears, one that hovered just out of reach yet refused to fade.

The wind whipped against her face, cold enough to sting and bitter enough to make her slightly nauseous. She hated how Dravaryn mornings always seemed to turn the air into a punishment.

Suddenly a howl broke through the trees, faint but wrong in a way that crawled beneath her skin. It wasn't simply sound. It was dissonance, like a note bent too far on a string, the kind that unsettled without warning.

Her body reacted before her mind did, every muscle jolting tight, the hair along her arms prickling in answer.

The noise roused the others, steel flashing as they moved with the precision of soldiers who had woken this way too many times before, bodies falling into rhythm without a word. Soren was no longer at the edge of the fire where she'd seen him moments ago; she would have sworn on Orchid's throne that he'd been there, and yet he was gone, vanished so completely she couldn't decide whether she'd actually blinked.

The sound came again, louder now, tearing across the forest in a pitch that was not human, a scream that cracked somewhere between howl and shriek. The tone clawed at her memory, dragging her back to the first time she'd ever heard a mountain lion in Orchid's eastern ranges. Sleek predators, silent in their movements, yet when one screamed, it was high and raw and utterly jarring, like a woman crying out in distress.

She remembered thinking it was obscene, the way the noise betrayed the creature's shape, how the mind refused to reconcile predator with that terrible cry.

This was worse.

The sound in Dravaryn carried that same wrongness but stretched beyond it, a warped echo that did not belong to flesh at all.

Ella turned instinctively toward the noise, as if tugged by the spine.

Shadows moved at the treeline, skittering shapes half-glimpsed and already gone. The horses reared, hooves tearing up soil, ears pinned flat against their skulls as they thrashed in terror, their panic so stark it was almost contagious.

"*Move*!" Jakobav's roar cracked through the clearing and he was already sprinting toward her, sword half-drawn, closing the distance in seconds.

And then the creature came.

It lunged from the forest in a blur of motion, towering over the firelight, easily twice the height of any man. Its frame was hunched but massive, the outline still human enough to suggest it had once been mortal before being twisted into something demonic. Black flesh clung to its body like tar, stretched tight over ridges of bone and sinew that shimmered faintly with glassy threads of light. Its arms were grotesquely long, ending in claws with fingers so extended they looked made for rending, while its taloned toes gouged the earth with every step. A whip-like tail lashed behind it, anchoring the weight of its hulking body with each jagged stride.

There was no face to meet, no eyes or mouth to mark it living, only a smooth, skull-like head split clean down the center, a vertical seam that glowed faintly red, pulsing like a wound that refused to close.

Its movements shifted unnervingly between a predator's fluid grace and the marionette-jerk of something dragged on invisible strings, every twitch a reminder that this was not a beast of flesh but something far older and utterly wrong.

Jakobav met it head-on, his own roar answering, his sword flashing as it sang through the air in a single strike.

Maeren cut left without hesitation, twin blades gleaming as she dipped low to the ground, while Savina mirrored her in the opposite direction, their movements so perfectly aligned it was clear this was not chance but a pattern drilled into their bodies by years of training together, a dance rehearsed a thousand times with blood as its music.

Thane surged forward with far less grace, his curse ripping through the clearing like an oath as he tore twin axes from his belt, his broad shoulders rolling as if eager to split something in two.

Soren, by contrast, made no sound at all. In one heartbeat, he was at the edge of the firelight, cloak drawn close, and in the next, he was gone, swallowed by shadow completely.

The creature shrieked again, and the forest responded in horror. Every leaf curled inward on itself, branches bending as though recoiling from the sound. The very air trembled, brittle as glass about to splinter.

Ella flung out her hands, calling on her fire. Nothing answered.

She tried again, and her power sputtered once, a weak static jolt under her skin, then collapsed in on itself like air punched from her lungs. The creature didn't seem to notice, still entirely focused on Jakobav.

"What the hell is that?" she gasped, her voice torn raw.

"Veil Leach," Jakobav snarled, meeting its bulk head-on, his blade already sinking into its chest with brutal force. Sparks scattered as steel hit bone. "Stay back, and don't let it feed on you!"

Ella tried again, desperation delving deeper than fear.

This time, her palms shuddered with heat, but what came forth was stranger: a shimmer in the air, no light, no flame, just a wrongness that bent the clearing for a single heartbeat before snapping back into place.

A ripple. Small and barely visible, yet undeniable.

The Veil Leach reacted instantly. Its eyeless head jerked toward her, the vertical split along its skull peeling wider with obscene hunger. The scream it unleashed was not sound but force, low and vibrating, a pressure that rolled outward in a wave so dense it buckled Ella's knees.

"Shit!" She stumbled back, legs locking against the ground that seemed to heave beneath her.

It lunged, abandoning all others, limbs snapping wide like broken spears, every line of its misshapen body angled toward her.

Jakobav intercepted in a blur of steel, his blade flashing across its side. "It can't see!" he barked, shoulders braced against the impact. "A Veil Leach senses power and feeds on it! I've never seen one hone in like that—what did you do?"

"I—I tried to access my power...I don't know!" she shouted, and with no other weapon left, she hurled her knife.

The blade flew true, spinning end over end, but when it struck the split in its skull, it vanished as if it had never existed, swallowed whole into that endless wound like a drop into a bottomless well.

The Leach reared back, towering higher, its limbs stretching unnaturally wide, then drove forward again with enough force to crack the ground.

Maeren was faster. She vaulted into its path, blades flashing in an X that raked across its chest, the sound like steel scraping glass. The strike landed, but the creature's counter-blow was brutal. The force hurled her backward, her body slamming into the dirt with a crack that made Ella's stomach lurch.

"Maeren!" Thane roared, tearing toward her, but the creature was already descending, its too-long arms bending at wrong angles as it prepared to finish her with a blow that would cleave her in half.

And then, movement so swift Ella almost missed it. Soren emerged from the treeline as if the shadows themselves had spit him out, his knives already in motion. One blade sliced clean across the Leach's shoulder, while the other buried itself deep into the sinew of its hind limb.

Ella's eyes widened, and she stumbled backward.

The creature screamed again.

Savina struck, erupting from behind Jakobav with the ferocity of a storm breaking its banks, her blade gleaming brutal in the firelight as she drove it deep into the creature's chest. The steel sank straight through the pulsing split in its skull, biting into the core that seemed to shudder in recognition.

The Veil Leach seized, its limbs locking in place, then it exploded, flesh and blackness spraying out. The clearing convulsed as a shockwave burst from its core, not wind but something visible and tangible, bending the fabric of the world around them.

The Veil between realms buckled like glass under a hammer. The blast threw everyone to the ground except Jakobav.

He staggered back, head snapping to the side as a spray of the creature's dark ichor splashed across his mouth.

"No!" Ella's voice tore free, panic raw.

What if a Veil Leach's blood is poisonous?

His body locked, spine arched. His eyes rolled white, then burned black, veins threading with silver light that flickered like molten rivers beneath his skin.

And then he moved, and he was not Jakobav at all.

His movements cut through the clearing with the same unnerving jerking as the Leach, each step too stiff, too fast. And then his gaze snapped to her. Black fire burned in his eyes, silver veins flaring under his skin as though they would tear him apart from the inside.

The sight rooted her where she stood, terror climbing up her spine.

What if he'd just been devoured and remade right in front of her? What if he didn't come back? The thought hit like a blow to her chest, raw and unrelenting.

She shouldn't care this much about him, the Dravaryn warlord who had forced her to come here, yet devastation rose, fierce and choking, a desperate urge to drag him back from whatever that demonic creature's tainted blood had done to him.

But then, slowly, the silver bled away. His body sagged, color rushing back into his skin. Jakobav collapsed to one knee, dragging in ragged breaths as the remains of the Leach dissolved into smoke around him, its ichor hissing into nothing on the ground.

A scream cracked the air. Definitely human this time.

Maeren.

She was down, her leg twisted at a wrong angle that made Ella's stomach pitch. Blood slicked the earth beneath her where she had landed, her face pale but her grip still locked tight around her blades as if she would rise and fight again by sheer will alone.

Savina staggered a few feet away, one hand pressed hard against her side where the creature's thrashing limb had cut deep on its way down. Blood seeped between her fingers, but she stayed on her feet, teeth bared, eyes flashing like she dared the world to try and put her down.

Ella had found herself among a group of people whose stubbornness rivaled her own.

Thane was bleeding too, a fresh gash running down his arm where one of the Leach's claws had raked him in the chaos. He swore under his breath, flexing his fingers around the haft of his axe.

Soren crouched beside Maeren, his knives dripping with ichor that hissed as it burned into the soil.

"Shit," Soren muttered. "Her leg. We need Bryn."

Jakobav was already on his feet, staggering toward them, still unsteady but commanding all the same. "Thane. Take Maeren. Now."

Thane crouched and gathered Maeren up with surprising care, his usual grin gone, jaw tight. She hissed but did not protest, only drew her blades closer to her chest, as if she refused to let even her weapons leave the fight.

Soren rose smoothly at his side, eyes like knives themselves.

Jakobav turned to Savina. "Do you need to be carried?"

Her head snapped toward him, eyes blazing. "Touch me and die."

Even bloodied, she stood tall, defiance burning through every line of her body.

Thane's grin flickered back, crooked despite the blood running down his arm. "Gods, Sav, I almost believe you'd kill me before the Leach could."

She shot him a look. "Almost?"

"Get them to Bryn," Jakobav said, his voice leaving no room for argument. "There's something else needing my attention, I'll be back at the castle as soon as it's handled."

Thane shifted Maeren's weight and turned his head toward Ella. "You coming with us, little fox?"

Ella took stock of the minor scrapes and bruises on her body from fighting off the Leach, realizing with a small sense of pride that for once she wasn't the one in dire need of medical attention. She wouldn't mind paying Bryn a visit, maybe she could interrogate him and obtain something useful to uncover the relic.

But before she could tell Thane she would return with them to the castle, she was interrupted.

"She stays," Jakobav answered, his tone cold enough to silence even Thane.

Thane's brow rose and he turned to her. "You sure?"

"I said she stays."

Ella's spine stiffened. "Excuse me?"

"You'll be safer with me," Jakobav added.

Thane gave a lopsided grin, his gaze bouncing between them. "Oh, come on. You don't trust me with the little fox? I'd keep her warm. Real warm. Give her a proper Dravaryn welcome. Slow. Intense. Memorable."

Jakobav turned his head, and the look he gave him could have frozen fire.

Thane coughed. "Right. Not the time."

Maeren chimed in, looking more annoyed with Thane than

her injured leg, "Set me down first before Jake chooses violence over patience."

Ella rolled her eyes. "Thane, you're insufferable."

Thane chuckled, still cradling Maeren. "You wound me, Princess."

Ella's stomach dropped.

Jakobav's jaw flexed.

The air went still.

Thane's face paled slightly. "I mean, not princess like Princess, obviously. I just meant, like, regal. You know. Elegant. Mysterious. Secretive. Not that we...uh..."

He trailed off.

Jakobav raised a brow, slow and lethal.

"...shit," Thane muttered. "We're not supposed to say that, are we?"

Ella's eyes snapped to Jakobav. "You told them?!"

Jakobav didn't answer.

Thane, flustered now, adjusted Maeren in his arms again like he could hide behind her.

"Shit. Look, I didn't mean to blow it, alright? We won't tell anyone. I swear. No one will know about your...your little secret. Not a soul. We'll keep you secure. Hidden. No one will —" He glanced at Jakobav's expression. "Fuck."

"Thane," Jakobav said, voice like steel drawn bare, "For once in your life, shut your godsdamned mouth."

"Shutting," Thane said, nodding fast. "Mouth? Closed. Sealed. Buried in the woods."

Ella's pulse hammered, every beat hot with betrayal.

The damage was done.

She looked between them. Jakobav, stone-faced and unreadable. Thane, visibly sweating.

The lie unraveled in the dirt between them.

Jakobav's head turned slowly. His eyes locked on hers.

Her last tether of calm broke. Something inside her snapped, cold fury spilling free.

"You promised," she hissed, voice rising. "You said—"

"I said I hadn't told anyone yet," Jakobav said evenly. "I never said I'd keep secrets from my inner circle."

"Gods, you arrogant..." She stalked toward him, fury blazing hotter with every step. "Do you know what you've done? I've hidden who I am for years. I've bled and run and clawed my way to survive, all to protect Orchid. And in one fucking week, you've blown everything I gave up the crown for!"

Jakobav didn't flinch. "My circle has never betrayed me."

"Good for you," she spat. "Must be nice not to feel betrayed."

His voice was so calm that it was almost cruel. "I told them you were some princess from another kingdom. That I was unsure of your purpose. You just confirmed you're the heir to Orchid's throne."

Ella went ice-cold. Gods, a moment ago she had cared whether this man lived or died, had felt devastation at the thought of losing him. Now?

Fuck. Him.

21

REALM AND REVELATION

The others were gone. The clearing had emptied, and in the hush that followed, there was only him, her, and the truth she had flung into the air where it hovered and refused to fall.

Fury rolled through her in tight, burning waves. How could he guard her like a zealot one breath, then hand her most guarded secret to his inner circle the next, leaving her exposed in the very place where vulnerability could end her?

Yes, she had reached for power in front of them all. Yes, if her flame had answered, they would have known what kingdom claimed her the instant her fire burned, but that was not the fucking point. The choice should have been hers.

"Fuck, Jakobav. I trusted you."

She shoved him hard.

His boots scraped against the dirt as he caught himself, muscles tensing, irritation flashing across his features before he locked it behind that infuriating calm.

As if I'm the one being unreasonable.

Ella's rage surged. She stepped toward him again, fists

clenched, ready to do far more than shove him this time. She wanted him to feel every ounce of the betrayal burning through her. His eyes cut to the glow kindling at her collarbone, and all the breath seemed to leave the world.

Her sigil had woken.

The ink that lay quiet and invisible flared from nothing to black and then to molten gold and crimson, the symbol of Orchid so bright it was as if it were being etched anew from the inside out. Heat raced outward as the light refused to stop at her heart. It leapt like a spark to dry tinder and crossed the fragile bridge of bone to the other side of her chest, unfurling in mirrored strokes across her collarbone, then down the angle of her right arm, where it curled toward her wrist like living fire seeking a path, as if fury itself was bleeding through her skin in streams of ink.

Ella yanked the cloak closed, but the reveal had already happened.

The ink kept moving beneath her palm, expanding, the lines multiplying into elegant constellations, a map written in black with threads of red and gold glinting through as if the stars themselves had taken root beneath her skin. In all the years she had borne the mark, she had never seen the tattoo change, had never even heard of such a thing.

"Fuck," she breathed, staggering back. "No—no, no—"

Jakobav took a step forward, eyes locked on the mark. "How?" he said, voice low. "That breach has been closed for hours now, Ella. Tell me what is happening. The truth this time. Your mark is changing, and you should have no magic here."

"Don't," she hissed. "Don't look at me like that. I don't know."

"Ellandria—" he began.

"Do not call me that." Her voice cracked on the last syllable, like the first fracture in a dam.

But the knowledge was already in his eyes, and could not be unknown. She was not merely Orchid-born and not merely the heir who had slipped a crown for anonymity. She was more dangerous than either title accounted for, and even she did not understand it.

The thought tore her resolve loose. She turned and ran.

She didn't pick a direction so much as fling herself into motion, vaulting onto the nearest horse with a grace born of habit and long hours in the saddle. The stirrup caught, her boot drove down, and the animal surged forward under the command of a heel and a need to be anywhere else but here.

Branches clawed at her hair and stung her cheeks. The wind dragged at her cloak and pride alike until both snapped behind her in a single dark stream. It didn't matter where she was going, only that she was away from his stare and his questions and the strange patience in his voice that made her want to scream.

The world tilted.

A pulse ran through the air as if some invisible string had been plucked too hard and too deep, and the note it made kept ringing, shivering through her bones. The ground quivered under the horse's hooves. The temperature dropped. The wind, which had been at her back, shifted to meet her head-on, and ahead of her, the line of trees did not sway so much as wave, bending as though reality itself were a curtain caught by a draft from a door that should not have been opened.

She blinked, and the sky darkened between one breath and the next. Clouds turned in tight spirals against the wind. Lightning crawled in the wrong direction, streaking down and then sideways, like a thought changing its mind. The leaves on the trees shuddered not with breeze but with recognition, as though something old had brushed the world and they remembered, fluttering their hello.

Her mark answered, brightening like coals. Heat coursed through her veins until the lines already carved across her chest and arm began to writhe. The ink itself undulated beneath her skin, each stroke shifting like a serpent testing its cage, black filigree stitched with threads of gold and ember-red that twisted and reformed as though alive. Her stomach lurched, bile rising as she realized it wasn't just growing, it was *moving*.

"This is a godsdamned nightmare," she rasped, the words shaking out of her as the air thickened with the taste of rain and metal and something she was never meant to see. As if she were walking the edge of a revelation.

Rain fell upward.

Droplets rose to meet her, soaking into her cloak, hot against her skin, proof that whatever she had stepped into was no illusion.

And then it hit her. This wasn't merely her magic flaring and not any storm the sky should make. A seam had opened; a ripple in the Veil had loosened and widened like a mouth learning hunger. For a sliver of time she was between, not wholly in Dravaryn and not wholly anywhere anymore.

Her pulse thundered in her ears as she looked down, and her mind stalled. The creature beneath her still bore the outline of a horse, but the shape fractured, as though the world could not decide what it was. Too many joints bent where the legs should have ended, its eyes burned yellow, glimmering like language, and its hide was no longer hair but a shifting surface of scales that caught the dim light with a sheen suggesting depth rather than texture, as if a creature far older and more dangerous wore the skin of a steed only long enough to carry her through.

"Shit," she whispered, the word slipping soft and low, terrified that speaking too loudly might startle the thing beneath her. The creature did not exist anywhere in the mortal realm, further proving what she already feared. She had slipped the threads and crossed into another realm entirely.

She had Threadwalked.

The word landed on her tongue as if it had been waiting for centuries to be spoken again, myth and curse and truth braided into a single sound. The ability had not existed since the Fae vanished, not since the realms were sealed and the Veil raised to keep creatures like her from moving between places that should remain apart.

Creatures like her.

The realization chilled her more thoroughly than the storm that wasn't.

This was too much. She needed to return.

Desperation clawed through her, and she found herself pleading for Dravaryn soil in a way she would have mocked mere moments ago.

She closed her eyes, gripping the reins not with her hands, but with her mind. She gathered the loose threads of place and pulled, picturing the real trees and the black seam of the obsidian cliffs, calling up the shape of the trail they had ridden that morning and the exact tone of his voice when he had said her name, *Ella*, flinging herself toward that sound as if it were a rope thrown across a chasm.

Something snapped, though there was no sound.

The creature beneath her was only a horse again. The storm vanished as if a curtain had been torn down. The air returned to its ordinary chill, the kind that bit but did not dream of devouring. Her skin was merely skin, and yet she did not trust the word *merely* anymore, not when her hair was still damp at the temples and not when her fingertips still sang with a bright, thin tremble like the echo of lightning that could not find ground.

Her breathing slowed, each inhale steadier than the last, and she forced her heart to match it. She lifted her gaze, scanning the world around her. The trees stood quiet and ordinary, their branches swaying gently in a breeze that carried no threat. The ground was solid beneath her horse's hooves, damp earth and fallen leaves exactly as they should be. Above, the sky was a stretch of clean blue, bright with sunlight, a slight chill in the air but not a cloud in sight. The world looked unchanged, untouched, as if nothing unnatural had bled through its seams.

"Going somewhere, Princess?"

Jakobav stepped directly into her path, blocking the horse with infuriating ease. She yanked the reins, and the animal rocked back before settling.

"You were behind me," she said, voice rough, accusation cutting through the tremor in her breath.

"I was," he answered, stepping closer. "I saw you. And then you were gone." His gaze locked onto hers, unblinking. "You disappeared, Ella."

Her pulse spiked. "For how long?"

"Long enough," he said, his voice even and too calm, "for me to know it wasn't a trick of my eyes. You slipped the Veil." He studied her like he could pin her in place by will alone. "That should not be possible."

Fear and fury tangled in her chest, spilling into her words. "And what, you think hovering over me is going to stop it?"

His reply came low and certain, a growl shaped into language. "Not hovering. Not guarding. I want the truth, and I think I know where we can find it. Come with me."

Her retort caught in her throat. There was fire in his eyes, but not the blaze of anger. It was steadier, darker, as though he'd been bracing for this all along.

She slid from the saddle, folding her arms as if she could hide her fear beneath her skin. "Then where the hell are we going?"

He held her stare in silence long enough for it to bite. "East of the pass," he said finally. "A seer lives there. Never met her, but my family has known of her for generations."

"And why the fuck would I trust that?"

He removed his cloak before answering.

"Because I need to know what you are." He stepped closer, the last light burning in his eyes. "And I think," his voice dropped lower, brushing against her like a touch, "you do too."

Her throat tightened.

"Is that a demand? Chains and all if I say no?" A drop of water slid down her arm, and she wiped it away, her fingers unsteady.

"Here."

He held the cloak out, not quite touching her.

"You're shaking."

She drew a breath and unfastened her own cloak, the fabric heavy and dripping as she slipped it from her shoulders. The cold hit her instantly.

She let her wet cloak fall to the ground. Dramatic, maybe, but right now she didn't care. Only then did she reach for his and take it, her fingers brushing his in a fleeting spark of warmth. She wrapped the dry fabric around herself and dragged the hem across her arms, wiping away the last raindrops clinging to her skin.

His jaw set while he waited, but when he spoke, the words came rougher, almost reluctant. "No. I'm not forcing you to come with me. It's your choice. But if you come, you follow my lead. It will be dangerous."

Ella stepped close enough to feel his breath. "I'll follow what keeps us alive," she murmured, "not orders for the sake of orders."

His mouth curved, less than a smile, but more than a challenge. "I can work with alive."

Alive.

It sounded pleasant enough, and yet in his mouth it was both a promise and a threat.

22

HISTORY THAT HAUNTS

They were down to one horse. Ella had felt awful when hers was set free, but the creature hadn't been the same after crossing the Veil—its eyes too wide and too white, every sound sending it skittering as if the forest was haunted. So now she rode with Jakobav. She was just as unsettled as her horse after Threadwalking, but unlike it, she didn't have the luxury of bolting. Forward was the only option, whether her mind was ready or not.

The trail narrowed through damp undergrowth, the ground slick in places, and the saddle was never meant for two. Her thigh pressed against his, every rise and dip of the terrain sending her back against the solid breadth of his chest.

His hand held the reins steady, guiding the horse with unerring control, but when the animal stumbled over a hidden root, his other hand came to her waist to steady her. His touch lingered longer than it needed to, as though it belonged there.

Perfect. As if she needed another reminder that Jakobav did whatever he wanted.

His possessiveness scraped through her awareness until

she had to clear her throat, willing her thoughts toward anything else.

"How far is this seer, exactly?"

"If the weather holds, we'll reach the village tomorrow." His voice was lower than usual, closer too, as though the narrow space between them swallowed half its strength.

"And she lives where?" Ella asked at last, her voice casual to disguise her curiosity. "In a cave? A tower? One of those cliffs where the wind sounds like whispers?"

"There's a woman in the village who knows how to find the seer. Cathea. We'll go see her first."

Ella blinked, a smirk tugging at her lips. "Cathea? Sounds like someone who brews potions and collects goats."

Jakobav huffed a quiet laugh, the sound warm against her ear. "I wouldn't say that to her face. But she does brew the strongest ale I've ever tasted, and she holds the rare honor of being one of the few people in this realm to have knocked me flat on my ass."

Ella's grin widened. "Now that's a story I want to hear."

"She once threw me out of her tavern for too much ale and a little destruction."

Ella's laughter rose, surprising even herself, and when she tilted her head, he continued, obliging her unspoken demand. "A broken chair after a wrestling match with Thane, which toppled a table, which broke a few mugs. It was fun until the entire tavern broke into a fight, and half the furniture didn't survive."

"And she kicked you out just for that?" Ella asked, delight dancing in her tone.

"To be fair, I did protest," he replied, his voice bone-dry. "I thought it was a bit of an overreaction."

She shook her head, laughter spilling through, half in disbelief that Jakobav had made another joke.

"So the mighty commander of Dravaryn was bested by his own ego and a tavern keeper."

Jakobav's lips curved, utterly unrepentant.

The moment softened, a welcome reprieve from their arguing, and they settled into a comfortable silence.

As the hours dragged on and the trail stretched farther, hunger began to gnaw at her ribs, until at last she broke the quiet. "So," she said, "are we going to resupply, or just flirt with starvation until one of us caves and eats the other?"

"Depends on how tender you are."

She turned her head, meeting his gaze squarely. "If you think I am tender, you have not been paying attention."

"Wrong," he said, voice low, the sound carrying a strange reverence. "I've been paying *very* close attention to you." He dragged his tongue along his bottom lip, a deliberate gesture that hinted at words he wasn't saying, the gleam left behind catching the dying light.

As the trail narrowed again, Jakobav shifted his weight to let her settle against him more comfortably. She didn't resist. She simply rested her head back, the movement unthinking, as though her body had grown tired of fighting every closeness, letting herself ease into the hard ridges of him. The small comfort carried the familiarity of safety, which she wanted and needed more than she was willing to admit after what she'd endured.

Her fingers drifted down almost without thought, brushing the hilt of the blade at her side. It was heavier and sharper than what she'd carried before, stolen from Thane's pack earlier that morning when no one had been watching, fitting far too well within her grip to give it back just yet.

Jakobav's scent wrapped around her like smoke, cedar threaded with that rich amber she could recognize anywhere, lingering like the storm he never quite let loose.

When the late sun reflected across the ink winding his arm, it shimmered faintly, black fire stitched into muscle, and she averted her gaze before memory carried her too far into what she'd just seen those arms and hands do. She should have been alarmed by the brutality and ease with which Jakobav fought the Veil Leach after it had focused its violence on her. Yet, her gut feeling leaned inexplicably toward intrigue.

He held the reins steady in one hand, while the other settled on her thigh, anchoring her as the horse picked up a trot, spooked by something unseen. His touch didn't lift again. She drifted toward sleep not long after, the line between waking and dreaming blurring until she no longer knew whether the tightening of his grip when the horse jolted was real or part of the haze pulling her under.

Ella stirred as they reached a clearing, the sky bleeding from gold into deepening gray. Jakobav swung down first, his boots pressing quietly into moss and stone. Still thick with sleep, she shifted to dismount but swayed, and Jakobav caught her before she slipped, his hands steady at her waist. She blinked up at him, disoriented by the sudden stillness beneath her feet. He didn't speak, only guided her forward toward where they'd make camp for the night.

The spot he'd chosen was a quiet, small hollow tucked beneath an overhang where moss-cloaked boulders leaned close, shielding the space from wind. Ferns bordered the hollow like silent sentinels, and above them, the moon flickered between restless clouds, pale and watchful in the dark.

Jakobav set to work on the fire.

Ella pulled the meager food from the pack and tore free a strip of dried meat, handing it across the fire. Jakobav took it without hesitation, teeth sinking in with the ease of a man long accustomed to rations. He chewed, swallowed, then said evenly, "I've survived on worse," the faint curve of his mouth betraying the closest thing to a smile.

Ella rolled her eyes and claimed a strip for herself, chewing with exaggerated stubbornness as though to prove she was unimpressed by the hardship.

They ate in silence, the fire crackling and spitting in the damp air, its glow licking faintly at stone and skin while the wind threaded through the canopy above, carrying secrets from one branch to the next.

Jakobav finally spoke, his voice low enough that she knew their unspoken truce to avoid serious discussion was over. "Can we talk about what happened? When you vanished."

Ella did not look at him. Her focus stayed fixed on the flames, following the way they flared, how they bent with the wind as though mocking her lack of control. At last she shook her head, her voice flat. "I don't even know what to say."

He nodded once, his reply almost a whisper. "I know what it's like to carry something heavy, waiting, not yet ready to be spoken."

Her head snapped toward him before she could stop herself.

The words were too close, too knowing. But he didn't press her on her secrets. Instead, he laid another log on the fire, each movement extended, as though he understood she was unraveling and was content to wait her out.

"We'll stay here tonight."

Ella wanted to tell him she'd already figured that much out, but she saw the subject change for the mercy it was. So instead, she stayed still, weighing her answer, then sat straighter. "Fine. But if I'm sleeping in the middle of nowhere with you yet again, I get to ask you some questions."

He glanced at her over his shoulder, one brow lifting. "Like what?"

She met his eyes, refusing to soften. "Your friends."

Jakobav's brow arched higher. "Is that what you call us?"

"No," Ella said, certain. "I can tell that's what they are to you. Don't bother pretending they're only soldiers. You trust them with your life, and now with mine."

The firelight danced, casting deep shadows across his face. This time he didn't brush her off. He only kept sharpening his blade, the rasp of stone against steel slow and unhurried, filling the stillness with its steady rhythm.

Ella leaned back on her elbows, her gaze glancing toward Jakobav's face to gauge his mood. He was stoic and unreadable as usual, but she asked her question anyway, her tone relaxed but too measured to convince anyone it was casual. "I want to know about your inner circle, what their abilities are, and about the chain of command. Will you actually answer me?"

He didn't look up right away, but his jaw tightened, a hint of contemplation passing before he finally said, "Depends."

She took that as permission. "Tell me about Thane."

A note of sadness in his expression came and went too quickly for her to question him about it.

"He was born in Velmire," Jakobav said quietly.

Ella blinked. "Wait, really? I thought—"

"Most do," he cut in, his tone flat and unyielding. "His reasons for leaving are his to tell." His eyes darkened, shadows drifting across them. "He hasn't shared them with many. He might share them with you one day. Might not."

A heaviness passed through the air, then eased as he went on. "He escaped when he was ten, found his way to a Dravaryn military camp, lied about his age, and got in. They believed him because of his size. Giant bastard already looked like one of us, then he learned to fight better than the rest of us."

Jakobav's mouth curved, faint but real. "We met as teenagers. The King had heard about him, thought I needed real competition. Hated each other at first. He kept beating me."

Ella grinned. "Bet that went over well."

"Until the day I knocked the smugness off that big head of his. Been thick as thieves ever since."

She laughed under her breath. "What about his abilities? I haven't seen anything magical."

"Because there isn't," Jakobav said as he stopped sharpening his blade. "He doesn't have any, not in Dravaryn at least. Doesn't need them."

He looked at her then, eyes steady and dark. "Don't underestimate him, Ella. He's in my circle for a reason. Best hand-to-hand fighter in the kingdom. Loyal beyond reason, despite not being born on this soil. And he can disarm a tense room with nothing but a dirty joke and that shit-eating grin."

Ella smirked. "So the crass humor is tactical."

"Unfortunately." Jakobav rolled his eyes, the faintest trace of humor tugging at his mouth. "And now he's got you smiling at it. Gods, not you too. Thane doesn't need another fan."

Her cheeks warmed. "I'm just...observing."

"Uh-huh." His tone was light, but his darkened expression told a different story, his brows knitting together as his jaw clenched.

Ella cleared her throat. "What about Maeren?"

Jakobav's gaze went back to the fire, the light painting hard edges across his face. "My second," he said. His voice was lower now, almost careful. "She was born to fight."

He leaned into memory as though the words carried both significance and vulnerability. "She was always strong, even as a child. Stronger and faster than most boys her age. Terrifying compared to the other girls. Every Dravaryn girl trains with a blade, but Maeren was something else."

Ella stayed quiet, listening.

"Her family always held rank, so her Claiming drew attention," he went on. "But it was more than that. Her older brother died during his."

A hush fell as Ella's stomach tightened. She blinked, the hint of shock threading through her voice. "Her brother died during his Claiming ceremony?"

"Yes. It was a tragedy. He faced an arduous path in life, and in many ways, he was reckless. Brilliant, but wild. Funny, in a way that surprised people. Clever enough to invent things from scraps of magic that shouldn't have worked, but they did. If he had stayed focused, he could have made more coin than half the realm. But he drank too much Fae wine. Smoked wraithleaf. Didn't prepare like he should have. And the cost..." Jakobav exhaled. "It gutted her. Scared the hell out of her too."

Ella's chest tightened, but she didn't interrupt.

"There's a rumor," he added, voice softer still, "that she received both their destined powers during her rite. Hers, and his. I don't know if it's true. But I know she only uses one set in public."

Ella blinked. "What does she use?"

Jakobav looked up, firelight catching his eyes. "Maeren is what we call a Stonecaller."

He let it register before continuing. "She doesn't just shift the earth. She speaks to it. Calls, and it answers. I've seen her arm turn to basalt mid-strike. Her fists have splintered shields. I've seen her boots crack the ground like paper. But she doesn't do it often. Says the stone remembers each request."

His fingers flexed, as though the memory still lived in his muscles. "But when she does..." He met Ella's eyes, gleaming in the firelight. "Gods help whoever stands in her way."

Ella glanced down quickly, brushing away the emotion before he saw, and before it had a chance to consume her while already feeling raw. She wanted to hug Maeren the next time she saw her, and tell her how sorry she was for the loss of her brother, but she would wait until Maeren chose to share her story.

"Soren, then."

Jakobav's eyes gleamed faintly. "Ah. I've been waiting for you to ask about him. Peculiar, isn't he?"

"He moves like nothing I've ever seen before. I've watched animals go still around him. I have to know what he is," Ella murmured. "Even birds stop singing. It's disturbing."

"He's an Earth-Vater," Jakobav said. "He can become one with the earth as long as it's dirt of some sort: soil, sand, mud. And not just camouflage. He disintegrates into it, burrowing into the world and coming out somewhere else."

Ella went still. "Like a living tunnel."

"Yes. He once described it as having access to bridges and shortcuts no one else can see. Makes him an exceptional spy. That's why he's in a rank of his own, Commander of Intel."

Ella was captivated, and Jakobav went on. "Once, long before the King got sick, we were sent on a scouting mission to the deserts of Thirelle. A sandstorm rolled in. Bad one. Coated everything in dust. Tents, trees, even the horses looked like ghosts."

His lips twitched. "Soren had a field day. I went to take a piss behind the only half-decent tree I could find, and he Vated right out of the sand-covered trunk next to me, like he'd been hiding there the whole time."

Ella's mouth fell open. "No."

"He looked me dead in the eye and said, 'You were about to piss on my head.' Scared the shit out of me."

Ella burst into laughter, full and unrestrained.

Jakobav's mouth tugged into a reluctant smile. "Haven't trusted a tree since."

"And the animals?" she asked.

Jakobav's mouth twitched again. "They know a predator when they sense one. Soren can feel every creature within a certain radius. When he hunts, he doesn't need weapons. He is the weapon."

A chill slipped down her spine. "Remind me not to upset him."

"Good instinct."

She hesitated. "And Savina? I know she's third in command."

Jakobav's smile vanished. "Pray you never have to see what Savina can do."

He said nothing more, and Ella didn't press. She wasn't sure she wanted to know.

23

BLOOD THAT BINDS

The full moon rode high above the canopy, its silver glow bouncing off the leaves as bright fragments of light peeked through the branches and lit up the clearing. Sleep unraveled around Ella in broken segments, tugged apart by the certainty that something was amiss, the kind of wrong that prickled against the skin long before the ear caught it.

A twig snapped in the distance, sharp and sudden. Another followed, closer.

She jerked upright, lungs tight, but Jakobav was already moving, soundless as a whisper swallowed by night. Imminent violence was written all over his face, visible even in the moonlight. He dropped low beside her, one hand tightly wrapped around the hilt of his sword while the other pressed flat to the ground, as though listening through the earth. His hushed warning cut through the silence. "Do not speak. Do not move. They're already here."

Ella's hand darted beneath the bedroll until her fingers closed on Thane's dagger, and gods, she was grateful she'd stolen it. Three emeralds glimmered along the hilt, deep and polished, each perfectly set in the body of a serpent coiled in eternal strike. Its citrine eyes caught what little light touched them, burning with a predatory gleam. It settled against her palm, the balance unnervingly perfect, as if the blade had been waiting for her hand, the rush of strength that coursed through her veins leaving her both unsteady and unwilling to let go.

Shapes bled out of the trees, one by one, until she counted eight, maybe nine. Their faces were hidden behind cloth masks, only their eyes glinting in the moonlight. As they got closer, she saw that their clothes hung torn and filthy, seams split, fabric stiff with dried blood while fresher streaks darkened their sleeves. They looked like men who'd already been broken elsewhere and had crawled out of ruin in search of easier prey.

They had chosen wrong.

Jakobav rose, his movements slow and intentional, his shoulders squaring as if some ancient inheritance stirred awake inside him. He didn't reach for words. His presence was its own warning.

Ella's gaze swept across the intruders, her voice little more than breath. "They don't look Dravaryn."

Jakobav didn't answer.

His jaw tightened, a small ripple of muscle betraying that he already knew.

She wondered how he could tell—how he always could—as if the truth reached him without sight or sound, sensed in a way that defied explanation. She wanted to demand answers, to ask if it was the same instinct that told him she was from Orchid the night they met.

But this wasn't the moment.

"Stay hidden," he murmured, the command barely a breath.

Before she could respond, he rose from their crouched position behind the boulder and stepped into the clearing with a predator's calm.

One of the masked men moved ahead of the others, shoulders squared, every step carrying the command of authority. The rest held back, a subtle deference that marked him as their leader even before the first trace of sorcery touched the air.

He hesitated, his stance rigid, eyes narrowing beneath the mask as his form wavered—a second figure peeled away from him, and then a third—until three versions of the same man stood in the clearing where only one had been. Each moved with the barest fraction of difference, almost imperceptible, yet enough to set her nerves on edge and tilt the world slightly askew.

Ella's stomach hollowed.

This was illusion magic, the kind spoken of in old war stories, feared because it could turn a battlefield into a labyrinth of ghosts—sound warping, sight betraying, men dying slashing at shadows while the real blade slid unseen across their throats. It was rare, unpredictable, lethal, and now it stood before her, convincing reality to lie.

The clearing erupted.

Steel clanged. Blades glinted. Men grunted from impact. Flesh tore. An attacker gurgled, choking on blood.

Jakobav moved like nothing she'd ever seen before. He wasn't simply trained, he was transformed. Each dodge, pivot, and strike landed with a terrifying force that was somehow also fluid, a grim choreography. Every motion clean, every blow lethal, every arc of his blade unnervingly beautiful.

When one man lunged, Jakobav dropped low and twisted his sword in a sudden curve that sliced into the side of the attacker's thigh, and as the man screamed and staggered back,

Jakobav pressed forward without pause, his momentum as unstoppable as a tide.

And then Ella saw it.

Jakobav sank to one knee beside the bleeding man, his fingers slick with blood. He drew a single drop onto his hand and lifted it to his mouth.

His eyes went black, not the ordinary black of shadow or midnight, but deeper, a darkness threaded with faint veins of silver, an ancient magic that did not belong to this world. His spine straightened, and around the clearing, the illusions wavered before they steadied again, but now, each one bore Jakobav's likeness.

Jakobav stepped forward once, and six perfect copies moved with him, blades gleaming, feet silent, faces as unreadable as his own.

The masked men never stood a chance.

They were overtaken in seconds, Jakobav's figures cutting and feinting and vanishing into the smoke of their own making, striking so swiftly even Ella lost the thread of which one was flesh and which was shadow.

She only knew the truth when the real Jakobav appeared behind the leader and bent to whisper something she couldn't hear before driving his sword cleanly through the man's back.

The illusions collapsed into nothingness.

Ella's lungs seized, her chest refusing air.

He was not merely a warrior. He was power incarnate.

And not just any power. Blood magic. Ancient, forbidden, impossible.

Blood-Scenting was supposed to have been extinct for centuries, ever since the realms were sealed and the Fae had vanished into myth. From behind the boulder, she watched a legend made flesh, alive and breathing, carving through masked men with the kind of lethal grace mortals weren't meant to witness.

Goosebumps rose, and her heart hammered like a drum.

Jakobav hadn't simply tasted a man's blood. He'd taken his magic and made it his own.

It had been too fast, too seamless, too effortless. Which meant the man beside her was something else entirely. Dangerous. Other. And gods, was she not the same, for had she not whispered those very words about herself only the day before?

Jakobav had ordered her to stay hidden, so she'd remained behind the rock, obeying as though she were some trembling novice. She watched him turn the night into a battlefield of fallen men.

Why in all the gods' names am I crouching here like prey?

Movement jarred her attention. Three of the surviving men broke and fled for the trees.

Cowards.

Ella was faster.

Fueled by adrenaline and fury and a motivation darker than either, she surged forward from her cover. She caught the first man by the collar and dragged him back hard, driving Thane's stolen knife into his thigh with such force the scream ripped out of him before he even hit the ground.

She wrenched the blade free, spinning with the same wild momentum, and buried it in the chest of the second man just below his collarbone. He fell gasping, clawing at the steel, but she was already moving again, meeting the third who swung in blind desperation. She ducked beneath his strike, slammed her boot into the back of his knees, and when he dropped, she cracked her fist into his jaw with every ounce of wrath in her veins. He crumpled at her feet.

Panting, wild-eyed, her hands slick with blood, she bent

and ripped the knife free from the man's chest. The hilt was wet, the blade gleaming dark in the faint light, but she held it tightly as she stalked back across the clearing.

Jakobav hadn't moved. There was only one of him now, thank the gods, for even that single figure was more than she could bear right now.

He'd watched every moment of her violence, his sword idle now at his side, his expression unreadable.

She stopped in front of him, chest heaving, her hair plastered to her temples with sweat, and raised her eyes to his. "You just going to stand there and watch?" she taunted, her voice breathless. "Suddenly you're no longer overbearing and overinvolved in everything I do?"

He smirked, a fleeting glimpse of amusement cutting across his mouth. "You had it handled."

Before she could summon a retort, his hand lifted, slow and unhurried, and his thumb brushed a smear of blood from her cheek. She stilled, lips parting, stunned less by the touch than by the certainty in his words, the ruinous truth of him believing in her.

Jakobav's gaze lingered as he dropped his hand, and then, almost lightly, he said, "Thane will be furious when he realizes that knife is gone."

"Is that so?" Ella's lips curved just slightly, the words carrying more anticipation than doubt.

"It's the only thing he brought with him from Velmire. Passed down. It's his favorite."

Ella lifted the heavy, blood-slick blade in the moonlight and arched a brow. "I know the people you keep closest to you are brutal," she said, voice laced with dark amusement. "But this"—she gave the deadly weapon a languid wave—"is a level of family baggage that I don't wish to unpack. I'll give it back as soon as I see him."

Jakobav chuckled, and the sound was like light breaking through stone. She caught herself staring, because for a fleeting heartbeat, he looked lighter, unarmored, almost human again, though the air between them hadn't settled at all.

Her gaze dropped to the blood still staining his fingertips. "So," she said carefully, voice low and measured, "you really do have a thing for blood."

Jakobav's smirk didn't vanish, but it twisted darker.

"You shifted forms," she continued. "I saw it when the Veil Leach exploded and its blood got in your mouth. At first I thought that was just how the creature's blood affects anyone who ingests it. But you moved like the creature itself, borrowed its speed and strength. Tonight, you knew those men weren't Dravaryn before they even raised a blade. Then you took that man's blood and used his illusion magic. And before any of that, you already knew I was Orchid-born. You knew it before my sigil flared." Her tone turned curious, edged with suspicion. "There were rumors, years ago, that your father had a power no Dravaryn was supposed to possess. A foreign, ancient ability that the palace buried fast."

Jakobav didn't answer, making a noise in his throat that might have been a grunt or a caution to tread carefully.

"Jakobav," she said firmly. "I know you have Blood-Scent magic. I saw it."

Instead of answering directly, he tilted his head. "Do you remember your first few days at the castle?"

Of course she remembered. Every warning from her childhood had hissed through her head. But she'd ignored them all in pursuit of the prophecy.

"I knew something was different about you then," Jakobav said quietly. "You shouldn't have made it past the outer wards. No one should. But you bled your way in." His jaw tightened.

"After you collapsed, I carried you. You were unconscious, barely alive. And your blood...the scent was foreign, enticing. I told myself I wouldn't." He hesitated. "But a drop landed on my tongue. By mistake."

Ella's expression darkened, heat flashing in her chest.

"You tasted my blood?"

He raised both hands, defensive. "I swear I didn't mean to. It was instinct. It felt like..." He exhaled. "It felt like I was breaching something sacred. I didn't want to invade. I wanted to earn that right."

The words struck her harder than she expected.

Her laugh came short and disbelieving, edged with anger.

"Earn the right to invade me? Gods, Jakobav." She wanted to be furious, wanted to cut him down with the harshest words she could muster, yet his phrasing unsettled her, caught her off guard in a way she hated.

Jakobav's eyes darkened as he leaned closer.

"Still working on that."

The words sparked between them, tension coiling into something volatile.

He didn't press further, only held her gaze as though daring her to look away. "I knew your fire ability instantly," he said at last. "I could taste the smoke in your blood." His voice dropped lower, husky with something almost reverent. "But I couldn't access it. Couldn't reach it. There was more, Ella. Your blood didn't just hint at power—it was full of patterns, layered and ancient, woven into something I couldn't trace. Sweet, intoxicating, but unreadable. I still don't know what you are. Not fully."

Ella's body clenched without her permission.

Her pulse was racing, heat pounding in her veins as though he had branded her from the inside. Gods, he just kept going, and it should disgust her. It did. Yet the way he described the taste of her blood in such intricate complexities sent a flash of heat pooling low, a wild thought whispering what it might mean to be claimed in that way.

Jakobav stepped closer, placing a hand on each of her shoulders, grounding her, his touch far too calm for the storm she felt rising.

"When that Veil Leach locked onto you, I knew you had abilities you hadn't even touched yet. I thought I saw a ripple when you extended your arms and called to your flame. But I didn't know for sure until you vanished into another realm right before my eyes. That moment… It was how I felt when I first used my blood magic. I knew it was wrong. I knew it shouldn't exist. But in that moment"—he lowered his forehead until it almost rested against hers—"there had never been anything more right."

She went utterly still, as if even the smallest movement might break the fragile thread between them.

He drew back just enough to meet her eyes. His stare held her hostage, daring her to move. To run. But she didn't.

"You tasted my blood without permission," she whispered, her voice softer now, though the storm hadn't entirely left her.

He sighed and gave her a light shove. "I just told you more about my power than I've ever told anyone."

"Really?" Her chest tightened, a shiver racing down her spine.

"Yes." His gaze did not waver. "It's taboo in Dravaryn. We don't talk about blood magic here. My people fear it. What it used to be."

Ella fell quiet, her thoughts twisting because he had just opened up to her about his gift, something forbidden in his own kingdom, something he clearly did not share with anyone outside of his circle.

She didn't know why he'd chosen to tell her, but it was

affecting her more than she'd care to admit. A small part of her argued that she should answer with something of her own, that offering a piece of herself was a good move if she wanted to gain his trust. That was the strategic thing to do, a step in the right direction. But another voice rose beneath it. She didn't want the conversation to end yet, savoring each truth revealed.

"I don't understand how I Threadwalked," she said, the words slipping out before she could second-guess them. "I've never shown any sign of another power besides my flame. Not once. But the moment I crossed your wards, something changed. My royal Orchid mark flared on my chest like it was waking up."

She drew a breath, unsteady but honest. "I told myself it was just the Veil thinning, magic reacting, the world unraveling. But this...this ability to Threadwalk is not tied to any soil magic that I know. No kingdom carries this gift. It doesn't exist anywhere in my family lineage that I know of."

Her voice dropped. "I don't understand how any of this is possible."

Jakobav went still, as if he were memorizing each syllable she dared to give him.

"I know the feeling," he said. "But we can't waste time wondering how. We keep moving." His grip tightened, steadying her in a way that felt like a promise. "We use what we have, even if it shouldn't exist. Neither of us belongs fully to the gifts of our kingdoms. So we make our own path."

He moved his hand, fingers grazing a strand of her dark hair. "And while we hesitate, breaches continue tearing this realm apart. More every day."

She hadn't meant to let the emotion rise, but it did, clawing its way up until she could hardly swallow it back. His words struck true, and she found herself worrying about more than just her own kingdom.

So when he pulled her into his arms, she did not resist.

He held her close, his voice low against her ear. "You won't face this alone. Stop running from me."

Ella was flayed open, hating that his words sank deeper than she wanted to allow, hating most of all that he could make her feel anything. But she couldn't allow herself to read too deep into his words, so she wielded deflection as a weapon.

"Okay, so we push forward. We keep moving. I've revealed enough for one night. I feel naked," she added quickly, "not literally this time. Thank the gods."

Jakobav let out a low sound, more grunt than laugh.

His hand lingered at the base of her spine, both steadying and unsettling. For a long moment, he didn't move, as if reluctant to break the fragile peace that had settled between them. When he finally sighed, it was slow and loaded, filled with something that felt like resolve.

And Ella, despite her instinct to retreat, leaned into it.

24

TAVERN AND TRUTH

They reached the village well past midnight, the narrow lanes deserted, the air thick with the faint tang of peat smoke and stale ale drifting from shuttered windows.

Ella was still dusted in dried blood, dirt clinging to her boots, her hair tangled and matted from the fight. When they'd first entered town, they had passed an inn, and every instinct in her body was screaming to scrub herself clean.

She rubbed her forehead and glanced at Jakobav.

"Do you think we can rent a couple of rooms for the night? I saw an inn earlier, and I desperately need a bath before we find the seer."

Jakobav blinked at her as though she had sprouted wings.

"Of course not," he said. "We're staying at the tavern."

"What?"

"Cathea runs it. She has a loft above the bar. She'd have my head if I stayed anywhere else."

"Oh, perfect," Ella muttered. "Can't wait to meet the woman who literally threw you out of her tavern. And sleep in her loft."

He only huffed and swung down, tugging her with him from the saddle as if eager to make introductions. Jakobav tied the horse outside, then pushed open the tavern door without hesitation, marching in as though the place belonged to him.

The tavern smelled of spiced mead and woodsmoke, its rafters charred dark with age and memory. Bundles of dried herbs dangled from the beams overhead: lavender, sage, and something musty that pricked at Ella's senses. A wide stone hearth crackled low behind the bar, its flames throwing amber light across weather-worn tables and mismatched chairs that looked as though they had been salvaged from a dozen different households, none of them alike, yet somehow belonging together. Symbols had been carved into the lintel above the threshold, old and curling, and though she didn't know their language, power hummed as she passed beneath them.

The tavern noise dipped as they walked by, just slightly, as a few heads turned. A pair of older men nodded once in acknowledgment before pointedly returning to their dice. A barmaid lowered her gaze as she slipped past, quickening her steps. No one dared interrupt, but clearly everyone knew exactly who had walked through their door.

At the center of it all stood Cathea, her presence unmistakable. A glint of obsidian gleamed at her throat, the carved black-rose pendant catching the firelight and holding it fast.

They grabbed a table near the bar, tucked at the edge of warmth and noise. Laughter swelled from the far end of the room where a cluster of men threw dice. A bard plucked at a stringed instrument in the corner, his notes soft enough not to intrude. Tankards clattered, chairs scraped, voices tangled and rose again, and for the first time since the clearing, Ella allowed herself a breath.

Cathea was everything and nothing Ella expected. Tall,

broad-shouldered, her silver-streaked curls framed a weathered face with eyes that missed nothing. Her tunic bore the stains of a long shift, ale-darkened and lived-in, and she moved with the absolute command of someone who had built the place with her own hands and dared the world to try and take it from her.

The moment she spotted Jakobav, her voice cut through the din like a cleaver.

"If you break anything this time, boy, I'll sell your ass to a Thirelle sea circus."

Jakobav grimaced. "Hello to you too, Aunt."

Ella nearly choked on her drink. Aunt? Of course the terrifying tavern-keeper with a voice like a war horn would turn out to be family. Why had a Dravaryn royal chosen a tavern over living at the castle?

Cathea's sharp gaze flicked to Ella, eyes glinting in the firelight.

"And who's this? Pretty and bloody—just like those two women you usually haul through my door. What is it with you bringing me beautiful, half-feral fighters, boy? And I assume you've already roped her into your messes?"

Jakobav stiffened. "Maeren and Savina are not—" His jaw clicked, irritation flashing. "They're soldiers. Respected First Guard. And Ella is..."

He faltered, as if a single accurate word simply did not exist.

Ella cut in smoothly before he could drown in the attempt. "More like dragged," she said, lifting her cup and swallowing hard. "Threatened me with chains, actually."

Jakobav bristled, his jaw tightening as his shoulders twitched, like the words had landed harder than he wanted them to. Ella smiled in quiet triumph. Gods, if he weren't so determined to brood, she could've sworn his cheeks might have flushed.

Cathea barked a laugh that rattled the shelves. She slapped her palm against the bar and shook her head. "Ooo, I like her. About time someone poked holes in your armor, boy."

"And the rest of you, quit staring," she barked toward the tables without turning her head. "This tavern isn't a throne room. He's just Jake here, same as the rest of you sorry bastards."

Jakobav only sighed, the sound long-suffering, as though he had carried Cathea's antics for half his life.

Up close, Ella was drawn to the pendant at Cathea's throat, a carved obsidian rose etched so finely the petals seemed to fold inward on themselves. The sight unsettled her, a faint shiver of something otherworldly crawling beneath her skin.

When she lifted her gaze, Cathea was already watching her, sharp and unhurried, patient as stone. The woman wore the look of someone who knew exactly what Ella had felt and was just waiting for her to catch up. Gods, it was the same way Jakobav acted most of the time. That same watchful, silent knowing sat in both of them like a birthright.

Before Ella could linger on the thought, Cathea's grin curved as she leaned across the table and launched into a story about the night Jakobav had tried to juggle flaming mugs, only to catch his own shirt on fire.

"Nearly singed his princely bits," Cathea said with relish.

Jakobav buried his face in his hands. "Why are you like this?"

Ella's laughter broke loose, wild and unstoppable, tumbling out of her like something that had been waiting too long to be freed. When she finally managed to pull air into her lungs, Jakobav was staring at her, but not with irritation or his usual storm. Just...watching.

"There," he said softly. "That smile is the real one. It suits you."

He leaned in slightly, the shift subtle but intentional. "Second time I've seen it. The first, you were holding my knife you thought you'd gotten away with stealing, which I'm learning is fitting for you."

Ella opened her mouth to reply, but Jakobav lifted a finger, gaze never leaving hers. "Don't ruin it by explaining."

She lost the words completely, caught staring at him, exposed in a way she hadn't braced for.

Unfortunately for her focus, the next image that forced itself into her head was Jakobav half-naked. Not a hazy fantasy or some imagined indulgence, but the very real memory of him walking out of the bathing room, water dripping over his skin, unapologetically bare, as though modesty was a language he'd never learned. She'd only glanced once. Well, maybe twice, but that glimpse had burned the image into her memory.

The ink crawling down his chest like it had a mind of its own. The ridges of muscle shifting with every step. The deep V cut into his hips, leading downward like a map she hadn't meant to memorize yet had clearly imprinted into her subconscious, staging mutiny at the worst possible moment.

She swore under her breath and raised her mug high.

"Another round, please!" she called to the barkeep, maybe louder than she intended.

Then, under her breath, barely a mutter, she added, "Before I start remembering more things I didn't fucking ask for."

Jakobav nearly choked on his drink.

"What?"

Ella flushed. The ale in Dravaryn must have been stronger than anything she was used to.

"What were you just thinking about?" he asked, a wicked smile curving his mouth.

She blinked. Hard.

Fuck.

Maybe she should switch to water.

A smell wafted through the room, pulling her attention across the tavern. In a shadowed corner near the hearth, two cloaked men sat hunched over a low table, smoke seeping from their mouths in slow, iridescent spirals, twisting like serpents toward the rafters. The metallic tang of wraithleaf thickened the air, bitter and sweet all at once, stinging her eyes. One of the men exhaled through his nose, his gaze glassy and unfocused. The other muttered in a language Ella didn't recognize, the words thick and syrupy, each syllable dragging heavy through the air.

Jakobav didn't glance their way, but his posture shifted subtly and his hand drew closer to the hilt of his blade.

Ella forced herself to look away, too exhausted to ask if he'd understood the foreign words, though the echo of them clung in her mind a beat too long. She tipped her mug back and drank again, the ale suddenly tasting bitter, fizzier than before, the swallow harsher than she intended.

When she lowered the cup, Jakobav was watching her.

"You want to head up soon?" His voice had dropped, quiet enough to belong only to her. "We face the seer tomorrow. Best not to be hungover for...whatever that'll be."

She parted her lips to reply, but the conversation at the next table bled into her awareness.

"...Orchid's queen... weeks now..."

"...doors shut... physician from the capital..."

"...collapsed in the hall, I heard..."

"...the girl should be crowned already... what's her name..."

The words fell heavy as stones into water, rippling outward until everything else in the room blurred. Sound thinned, the chatter dimming to a muffled hum, and her hand tightened around the mug until the handle bit into her palm. Heat stung behind her eyes, sharp and useless. She couldn't tell whether her lungs remembered how to expand.

The prophecy had warned her that the queen's death would be the spark, the blaze that would drag her into the light.

Ella's rise was never meant to be born of ambition but of necessity, and now it was the cruelty of the fates that her mother was the tinder destined to ignite it all.

Jakobav didn't turn toward the whispers, didn't betray her with so much as a twitch of recognition. Instead, he set his cup down with quiet care and smoothed his features into stillness, a choice she recognized instantly, and hated how deeply grateful it made her.

He leaned closer, near enough that the warmth of his presence brushed her skin. His gaze went from her mouth to the whitened grip of her hand, before returning to her eyes.

"Ella," he said, her name shaped as both question and vow.

It landed as grave as the prophecy itself.

She couldn't move. She only stared at him, caught in the echo of tavern gossip and the terrible weight of what it implied.

Pity surfaced in the set of his expression, wrought with sorrow, scraping along her nerves, loud and unwelcome.

Ella's breath hitched, her throat tightening until the words tore out of her before she could stop them.

"Don't ever look at me with pity," she whispered, raw and furious.

He didn't bite back, didn't bristle at the anger in her voice. Instead, he reached across the table, fingers brushing the inside of her wrist in a cool, grounding press that quieted the chaos inside her head.

"I understand," he said, voice even, neither resigned nor uncertain but chosen.

His hand lingered before slipping from her wrist. He didn't rise. He eased back into his chair, as if declaring that he would follow her lead and stand wherever she chose to stand, whether she remained at this table with her drink or left for the loft above.

The tavern carried on around them, a low hum of laughter and clinking mugs, and the sound grated against her rawness.

It unsettled her to hear such mirth after the whispers of her mother's illness, even though she'd known for years that the prophecy foretold a sudden sickness that would force her to take the throne.

Knowing hadn't lessened the sting.

She let her gaze roam for distraction, catching the scrape of chairs and the thick curl of smoke still unfurling from the far corner. Her own mug sat empty, and she slid it across the table before pushing to her feet. Without a word to Jakobav, she brushed past him, her steps carrying her toward the bar. She told herself she needed more ale, though perhaps what she needed was a moment of space, and either way, she welcomed the distance.

One of the men who'd been smoking in the shadows all evening shoved his chair back and rose, the wooden legs dragging harshly against the floorboards. He cut across the room with a crooked smile that never touched his eyes.

"You look familiar," he said, his voice slick with drink.

Ella turned, mug in hand, her reply immediate. "No offense, but I really doubt that."

His grin widened, teeth catching the light, a flash too calculating to be friendly. "That's a bold tone for such a pretty girl. Why don't you trade that mug for something stronger?"

He tilted his head toward the smoky corner where his companion lounged in the haze, watching. "Come sit with us."

Ella set her drink down on the counter with a calm that belied the pulse thudding in her throat. "Well, in that case," she said, her voice cutting clean through the noise of the tavern, "I do mean offense. Fuck. Off."

The man's posture shifted at once, his smile vanishing. He leaned closer, the air around him thick with the stench of wraithleaf smoke, the black in his eyes dilating until his gaze was all pupil and malice. "You won't say that to me again."

Ella stepped forward, reckless defiance tightening every line of her body. She gave a mocking smirk as her hand dropped to the dagger strapped against her thigh, fingers brushing the hilt with slow, unmistakable promise. "I wouldn't have," she said, her tone sharp enough to draw blood, "but now I absolutely will."

His hand shot toward her throat, fingers curled like claws —but it never reached her.

Jakobav caught the man's wrist mid-lunge, his grip iron. In one brutal movement, he slammed the man's hand onto the bar, the crack of impact splitting through the tavern like a struck drum, wood groaning beneath the force. The man staggered, his expression twisting with pain as Jakobav's shadow swallowed him whole.

"For someone so familiar with smoke," Jakobav said, his voice low, steady, and colder than steel, "you should know better than to play with fire."

"Relax," he slurred, eyes gleaming with something insidious. "I didn't realize she was spoken for. Maybe you wouldn't mind sharing. Don't princes like to sit back and watch?"

In a single, merciless motion Jakobav shoved the man against the bar, one hand fisted in his hair to hold him down, the other pressing a knife against his throat. The edge caught the light, a glint of promised ruin.

The tavern stilled around them.

The bard stopped playing music, the scrape of chairs ceased along with the shuffle of boots, and the tavern chatter faded into complete silence.

Ella's breath lodged in her chest.

They were making a spectacle, and yet some strange part of herself couldn't look away.

From the smoky corner, the second man rose, his body tense, but he didn't advance. He only watched, like he was weighing the knife's gleam, the predator's stance, the inevitability of what was about to happen.

Jakobav's grip tightened. His voice dropped into something darker, almost ritual. "Hope you've made peace with the old gods." The blade shifted, the moment on a razor's edge.

For a breathless instant, the tavern didn't exist.

There was only Jakobav, the man bent beneath his grip, and the way violence seemed to breathe from him as naturally as air.

Ella should be afraid, tell him to stop before he crossed a line they couldn't uncross, but her body betrayed her and her lips refused to shape the words. The sight of him, all power and absolute command, struck something deep and unfamiliar inside her.

It was terrifying, yes, but it was also magnetic. The part of her that had always bristled against chains now ached at the knowledge that, for once, someone had chosen to wield their fury on her behalf.

"Jake. Stop."

The command came firm and unshaken, and Cathea appeared at the bar with a mountain of a man looming at her side. Her eyes, keen and knowing, fixed on Jakobav.

He didn't release at once. The man beneath him groaned, sweat streaking his temple as the knife pressed a breath too close.

Then the steel kissed flesh. A bead of blood welled at the man's throat, bright against the dull gleam of iron, and rolled slowly down, proof that Jakobav was not bluffing, that the next breath could be his last.

"That's enough," Cathea said, loud and firm, yet calm as still water.

Only then did Jakobav relent, pulling back with agonizing slowness. The man sagged, gasping, and his companion rushed forward to haul him upright.

Together they staggered toward the door, vanishing into the night without a backward glance.

The tavern noise began to stir again, unease humming through the rafters, but Cathea's focus never left Ella. She wiped her hands on her apron, her expression unreadable, and said with pointed politeness, "It was lovely to meet you, dear. But I think it's best if the two of you head upstairs."

Jakobav drew in a deep breath, his gaze fixed on Ella, watching her intensely, as though he expected her to splinter beneath it all. She was not that fragile, only shaken by all that had just collided around her.

"She's right," he said at last, his tone firm but gentle. "We should get some sleep. The sooner we get our answers, the sooner we can return to the castle. I need to check in on how well Bryn has managed to fix up my *friends*."

He was likely trying to distract her by wielding the word she'd used, but she couldn't speak, couldn't even move, still stunned by the revelation of her mother's health.

Jakobav's voice carried her forward.

"Bryn is probably making a mess of the infirmary...and eager to see how we've managed."

She gave a small nod as her body remembered what her voice could not, taking one last look around the tavern.

The fire cracked in the hearth, sparks leaping toward the rafters. Cathea's black-rose pendant caught the glow of torch-light, while the smell of wraithleaf smoke lingered faintly in the air. Ella's eyes followed Jakobav as he turned toward the stairs, his steps unhurried, leaving her thoughts to twist into a knot pulled taut by too many threads at once.

No, this was good. This was the push she needed. She hadn't come here to crumble beneath the news she'd long expected, nor to let herself unravel over the brutal reality of finally hearing it aloud.

She wouldn't linger on why Jakobav seemed to understand instinctively what she needed in that moment, or why he'd defended her so fiercely, nor would she try to untangle the pull between them that only grew tighter with every hour.

And she definitely wouldn't chase the question of why they both carried forbidden gifts, power unblessed by the soil of their birth.

Ella was here for one purpose alone: to fulfill the duty laid before her by the fates. For the crown she had never asked to wear, but would take all the same, because it might save her people, might save the mortal realm itself.

And if the last weeks had taught her anything, it was that the Veil was bleeding, and such a wound would wait for no man.

She would return to Orchid soon.

Even if it broke her.

Even if it meant leaving him behind.

25

WHERE THE PROPHECY LIES

Ella collapsed onto the narrow bed in the loft above the tavern without even tugging off her boots, her body folding into the thin mattress as the past days closed in from every side. The impossible magic she'd provoked into being, Jakobav's brutal display of power, and the whispered news of her mother's illness collided inside her until she could hardly separate one from the next. Not to mention the look of care and concern written on Jakobav's face in the aftermath.

She'd been too distracted, too consumed by Orchid's looming shadow to truly take in the way Jakobav had tempered himself with her. He'd followed her cues, matched her silence, and offered steadiness where she expected command. She loathed how much it unsettled her, that his restraint chipped at her defenses, leaving her more aware of him than she had ever wanted.

The bed shifted beneath her as Jakobav lay down, and her senses went rigid in wary recognition of his nearness. She pressed her eyes shut against the dull ache in her temples, grateful when sleep claimed her quickly. Even in dreams she felt him there, his steady breathing brushing the quiet. Long into the night, she thought she had felt the soft graze of his hand find hers.

Morning came too soon. Ella woke to Jakobav's rough voice cutting through the gray light.

"Up. We need to move."

She blinked against the haze of sleep, eyes adjusting to the muted light spilling through the loft window.

He was already on his feet, dressed and packed, her satchel in hand, as though he'd been waiting for her to stir. Gods, it was infuriating how the morning seemed to conspire with him, chiseling the line of his jaw, highlighting the black ink scrawled across his skin, gilding the darkness of him until he looked devastating despite having slept only a handful of hours.

She felt like ruin, but he looked as though the dawn had been created for him alone, and it was an injustice she couldn't help but notice.

"Ready?" he asked softly, his eyes scanning her face as though searching for fractures she might be hiding.

She rubbed at her eyes and pushed herself upright, nodding as she followed him toward the stairs. "You know, you're annoyingly awake and irritatingly good-looking for someone who drank enough ale last night to knock out a horse."

A slow, dangerous smile spread across his mouth, unhurried and self-assured. "You don't look so bad yourself, Princess, especially considering what we're about to do."

Ella rolled her eyes, though the tug at the corner of her lips betrayed her, a smile threatening to form. "Let's just get this over with. And after that, you and I are going to discuss last night."

A teasing smile curved his lips farther. "Ready when you

are. Unless you're too scared to let me in again." His tone carried both challenge and the faintest glimpse of humor, cutting through the shadow of the night before.

Ella shoulder-checked him as she slipped past, satisfied by the grunt it dragged from him. She took the stairs quickly and entered the morning without a backward glance.

Their horse waited in the chill air, breath misting faintly as it pawed at the ground. Ella swung into the saddle first, and Jakobav mounted behind her with practiced ease. They set off down the narrow road that cut into the trees, the rhythm of hooves steady beneath them. And though she sat straight-backed in the saddle, Ella couldn't quiet the turmoil twisting inside her.

The ride from the tavern was brief, yet it stretched on endlessly for Ella. Mist clung to the trees, their blackened trunks rising like a charred warning of what had once burned here. The forest's stillness pressed close, broken only by the steady rhythm of hooves and the quiet shift of Jakobav's breath behind her.

Her thoughts tangled like brambles.

What if the so-called seer was nothing more than a charlatan and this entire errand a waste? What if it was a trap, and Jakobav had only pretended to soften, care, and help her? Gods, where was her blade?

She steadied her breathing.

Everything will be okay.

Thane's dagger was still strapped to her thigh and ready.

Jakobav had brought her here instead of preparing for his own Claiming ceremony, whatever that entailed, and that had to mean some small part of him cared. He had, after all, kept her alive when he didn't have to. The thought steadied her enough to stay upright in the saddle.

The closer they drew, the more their surroundings seemed watchful.

The seer's home rose from the forest floor as if the trees had bent to her will. Wood and stone twisted together into a small cottage, ivy spilling down its walls in ghostly green cascades. It looked less built than summoned, alive with secret knowledge.

Ella climbed down from the saddle, Jakobav steadying her with one hand, warm at her back. She started toward the door, her fingers brushing the dagger strapped to her thigh, and she lifted her hand to knock. Before her knuckles met wood, the door creaked open on its own.

The seer was waiting in the doorway.

Small, hunched, white hair tumbling like spun silk down her bent shoulders, yet her gaze was knowing. Her lips turned in something between amusement and accusation.

"Well, well. The royalty has finally arrived."

Jakobav's eyes narrowed, his voice wary. "You knew I was coming."

"I wasn't talking about you, Prince." Her voice rasped, dry as parchment dragged over stone. Her head tilted, eyes gleaming with something too perceptive. "Never thought I would get to invite the Queen of Orchid into my home."

Ella froze. "I'm not the queen. I'm—"

"Oh, semantics." The seer waved a clawlike hand. "You're the lost heir who wasn't so lost after all, were you? And it could be any day now, dearie. You'll find yourself taking the throne whether you want it or not."

A shiver lanced down Ella's spine, but the seer only smiled wider, candlelight dancing behind her. "Come in, come in. Close your mouth and hurry along. The creatures in this forest tolerate *my* antics, but they don't know you."

They crossed the threshold, the door closing behind them with a slow groan.

Inside, the air felt heavy, thick with the tang of herbs and smoke. Shadows warped and stretched with every waver of candlelight, and the room looked more like a ritual chamber than a home.

Jakobav stayed close to Ella, watchful and tense, one hand already brushing the hilt at his hip as though he didn't even trust the walls around them.

The seer drifted to the center of the room, her bent frame haloed in trembling light. She tilted her head, her eyes rolling back until only white remained, endless and terrible. The air seemed to lurch, pressing tighter, and before Ella could draw a breath, the seer convulsed violently, then went utterly still. When she spoke, the sound was not her voice at all but something vast and resonant, ancient as the rock beneath their feet.

"When realms entwined by fate's desire,
A child shall rise through smoke and fire.
A queen will fall, her time undone,
The daughter crowned beneath the red sun.
She'll thread the Veil that none may cross,
Restore what kingdoms thought was lost.
But when she seeks what's locked away,
The relic found shall hold no sway.
For what she seeks lies not outside,
But in the blood that realms divide."

Ella stood frozen as the last echoes of the words faded, her heart pounding with a force that seemed to reverberate through her entire body. They struck her like a faultline breaking open beneath her feet, sudden and irrevocable.

She'd never spoken them aloud, never trusted another soul with them, yet here they were, words she'd carried alone for years, pulled into the open as if the seer had stolen them from the compass of her soul.

Nothing in the prophecy had ever frightened her more than hearing it spoken by someone who shouldn't have known it at all.

Beside her, Jakobav stiffened, his gaze glancing between her and the seer with guarded suspicion. It wasn't only Ella's fate he seemed to be measuring, but what those words might mean for his people, for the Claiming that loomed over him, and likely for Dravaryn itself.

A sudden flash pierced her mind as if the seer's voice had cracked through stone, unearthing what she had buried long ago.

A memory surged with startling clarity.

Her parents whispered by firelight when she'd been a child too young to grasp meaning, their voices urgent, their faces shadowed by fear. "Threadwalking," her mother had said in a tone that carried both respect and dread. "Will either mend the realms or break them entirely."

The memory hollowed her. Gods, where in the hell had that come from? She shouldn't have been old enough to understand any of it, much less recall it now.

An ache bloomed in her chest where breath should have been, a fierce, impossible longing to see her parents again, even for a single heartbeat. The floor seemed to tilt beneath her as though that faultline had deepened, her vision blurring until the room dimmed into encroaching darkness.

When her eyes fluttered open again, she was on the floor, cold stone seeping through her clothes while Jakobav held her upright, his hands firm on her shoulders as if anchoring her to the world.

"Ella?" His voice was tight with worry. "You okay?"

She nodded slowly, veins thrumming under his touch, and

he didn't immediately release her. He only eased her to sit, the space between them narrow, his attention fixed on the seer, the focus of a man who measures threats before he acts on them.

He helped her up to stand, then took several steps away, giving her space. "Stay upright this time." The words were quiet, almost an order, the command undercutting the concern.

Yet something had shifted between them, not announced, not spoken, but present in the way his hold lingered past necessity and how he positioned his body so that she was half-sheltered by it, the change no more dramatic than a tide turning and just as impossible to stop. Recognition lodged in her chest, unwelcome and undeniable.

Her thoughts surged in a single, long current rather than in broken pieces. The Threadwalking when she fled the creature had not been an accident. Her mother's failing health had set more than grief in motion. And the seer's words had pried open what she'd tried to keep sealed.

Time was thinning. It could tear with one wrong pull, yet there might be enough left to reach her mother before fate closed its teeth.

The seer twitched violently, the motion cracking the room's stillness, and both of them turned.

Jakobav visibly tensed but said nothing.

Ella flinched. "Um. Are you all right?"

"Oh, just another demon clawing through my skull, dear. Nothing to fuss over. Happens more often than I'd like," the seer replied, airy and unsettlingly calm, and then her gaze cleared as if a film had lifted. She moved with a speed that belonged to a body much younger, leaning in until her breath touched Ella's cheek.

Ella didn't flinch this time, and Jakobav stepped closer in a single controlled shift, his fingers finding her hand and closing around it with a grip that spoke of possession and protection in equal parts. She couldn't tell which he intended; she only knew she was grateful for the steadiness and answered by squeezing back.

"You believe you're still hunting the relic to reopen the realms, don't you?" the seer hissed.

Ella straightened defiantly. "I am—"

"No, silly girl," the seer cut in, sharp as a snapped thread. "You haven't been hunting for that for some time." Her head tilted, her attention sliding to Jakobav with open disdain. "Your heinous Guard is working overtime quelling those breaches rather than curing them, Commander. Quite distasteful, really."

Jakobav shifted a fraction, placing himself half a step more in front of Ella, the line of his jaw set, his grip tightening once at her hand before easing into a looser hold. His voice came out cold. "Careful." The word landed with threat, his stillness radiating menace into the already suffocating air.

Her attention swiveled back, pinning Ella with unnerving focus. "Tell me, Princess, have you felt the call lately? That insatiable pull?"

Ella swallowed hard, her throat suddenly dry.

Her heart jolted painfully as she realized the truth. She hadn't felt it, not for days. The obsession that had once consumed her, the relentless drive to seek the relic had vanished, and the absence hollowed her in ways she couldn't explain.

But how...?

The seer withdrew slowly, her body bending and slithering in movements too unnatural to belong to flesh and bone. "No, dear. Your thread is pulling elsewhere now, isn't it?" Her gaze dropped pointedly to where Ella's fingers were still tangled in Jakobav's grip.

Ella's lungs seized, air catching uselessly in her chest.

Her fingers slipped from his hand as her knees weakened, and she swayed into him before she could stop it. Jakobav's arm came around her waist instantly, anchoring her, as though anticipating the collapse.

Jakobav was the key.

Gods. She'd been so wrong. The magic hadn't been guiding her to an object at all. It had been guiding her to him. He was the match. He was the flame.

Not some ancient artifact.

The revelation struck with the force of an earthquake, rattling through every part of her until she could hardly stand. Heat gathered in her palms, unsteady and barely contained, pressure building behind her ribs in a way she couldn't will away.

The seer turned from them as though bored, drifting deeper into the shadows with her crooked gait.

"No!" Ella cried, desperation cracking through her voice as she reached after her. "The prophecy said relic. Relic means old, ancient. The fates selected that word specifically. How could I have been so far off?"

The old woman paused at the far side of the room, her spine twisting as she turned slowly back toward them.

Her grin spread grotesquely wide. "Perhaps what is within is far older than what is on the outside."

A terrible cackle tore from her throat, rising higher and louder until the rafters seemed to vibrate with it.

"Don't judge the guts by the carcass, dear. They might be the tastiest you've ever eaten."

Jakobav's jaw tightened. His voice cut through the noise, low and final. "Enough. We're done here."

Then she vanished around the corner, her laughter trailing behind like a curse.

Ella's gaze fell to his hand still clutching her arm protectively, his thumb brushing absently across her skin, and for one suspended moment, she clung to the steadiness.

Jakobav let it linger no longer than necessary. His hand squeezed once, and then he pulled her firmly toward the door. "Let's go. Quickly."

They burst outside into the mist, the air colder, more bleak, as if the forest recoiled from the seer's laughter too. The horse reared against the reins, nostrils flaring, hooves striking the earth in protest until Jakobav's deep command steadied it. Ella swung numbly into the saddle, and Jakobav mounted close behind, his chest pressed against her as they urged the horse down the narrow road, the forest reluctant to let them pass.

Shadows clung thick between the trees, branches groaning as though something unseen had stirred them.

They rode in silence for several minutes, the trees hemming them in, until Ella finally found her voice. "I thought your family trusted her."

He appeared as disturbed as she felt and gave her a sidelong look. "Perhaps that trust was slightly exaggerated. Known about her for generations might be more accurate. Tolerated her living on the outskirts of town, with Cathea keeping an eye on her. That woman is a godsdamned lunatic."

Ella should have demanded more explanation, but her mind reeled too fervently to focus. "Agreed. But lunacy doesn't mean she was wrong about everything." Her stomach lurched at the memory of the seer's demented analogy. "Although the carcass comment was...uniquely horrifying."

Jakobav's gaze stayed on the dark road ahead, his voice flat, steady. "Prophecy or madness. Either way, it changes nothing tonight."

He was right.

The seer's laughter still clung to her skin like a film of oil that she couldn't scrub away, yet Jakobav's calm resolve steadied her enough to keep going.

At least she had some answers, even if those answers only opened darker doors. And deep down, Ella couldn't shake the terrible certainty that the worst of her truths still waited ahead.

26

FATE AND VOWS

Ella couldn't sleep, not after what the seer had said and not after what she learned.

The ride back to the castle unspooled beneath a sky the color of ash, hoofbeats striking a steady cadence like a distant drum. When the guards lifted their lanterns, they asked nothing, and she was grateful. She had no strength left for ceremony, only the need to reach a door and be done with the night.

She lay sprawled across the gigantic bed that belonged to the equally massive, infuriating warlord she had just shared a horse with for days. Her hand traced the edge of the luxe furs, the fire crackled low in the hearth, and a smell that was now familiar wrapped around her, grounding and comforting her even as her thoughts spiraled.

She lay very still and let the truth assemble itself piece by piece, as if naming it too quickly might shatter her. Turning her face into the pillow, Ella let the seer's words echo again, softer now but no less potent, hating that a part of her wanted to argue with a woman who could peel truth from blood and bone.

The relic she'd been searching for, chasing across rumors and ruins, through treason and prophecy, wasn't some buried artifact or enchanted object.

It was Jakobav.

It had always been Jakobav.

The revelation moved through her like a tide building beneath the surface for months, not loud or triumphant but vast and undeniable, and with it came the memory of a dozen small moments that now made sense in the wake of the seer's gaze.

The pull in the corridors when she first stepped within these walls, the strange certainty that the castle breathed with her, the way the air seemed to lean when he entered a room and the floor steadied when he spoke, all of it had been him.

She'd told herself it was instinct and hunger and stubbornness, a compass fashioned out of will, but it had never been that at all.

And gods help her, she hadn't even questioned it. She had followed him. Trusted him. Stopped searching for the relic the moment he stood at her side and barely questioned why that felt like enough.

She'd mocked him, fought him, baited him...and somewhere between all of that, she'd started to enjoy it.

Not just with Jakobav and his maddening scowls, but with the ones who bled beside him. Thane's irreverent grin came to mind, followed by Maeren's steady hands, Soren's watchful quiet, Savina's blade-bright rage, and Bryn who laughed at death like an old acquaintance and still had a healer's touch.

Somewhere along this path, she'd begun to care about the people who cared about him, and if that was not a confession, then it was at least a change of weather inside her chest.

A part of her longed to go to them, to see with her own eyes that they were safe, but there was something else she needed first.

She pushed herself upright, the room seeming to press closer, pulsing with the quiet shock of change. It was subtle but undeniable. Somehow this place had started to feel suspiciously like home.

But beneath that warmth, a harder truth existed. If Jakobav was the relic, everything she believed about the prophecy had changed. Whatever object she'd imagined finding in ruins or archives was now a breathing, stubborn, very much alive, and infuriatingly large man.

And if she had any hope of preventing the Veil from shattering, she would need to figure out what it meant to wield a living relic. How his blood, his magic, and his fate fit into the old lines of the prophecy she'd studied most of her life.

Threadshifting was accelerating. The world was changing faster than she could track, and she needed to decipher the rest before it was too late.

The solstice was in two days. Jakobav would walk straight into a magical firestorm, one that might split him open and demand he remain standing, and who knows how he might fare. Especially with the Veil fraying.

The gods, if they listened at all, were not known for mercy. It might kill him, and she hadn't even asked if she'd be allowed to go, to help.

Fuck, she had to fix this.

Her boots waited by the bed. She pulled them on with unsteady hands, tied the straps tight, and told herself that fear was useful when it pointed you in the right direction.

Jakobav was where Kalenya had told her he would be, in the small office overlooking the training grounds.

It smelled faintly of smoke and cedar, the kind of clean,

controlled order that felt unmistakably like him. Shelves lined the stone walls, holding maps weighted with knives and worn tomes with broken spines. The mahogany grain of his desk caught the firelight in deep, rippling lines, polished smooth in the places his hands touched most. The hearth was kept to a thoughtful flame, and the desk pared to little more than a few unread pages and a half-empty mug.

He was still holding one of the pages when she stepped inside, and though he didn't startle, he set it down slowly and leaned back in his chair, a long exhale escaping him as if bracing for a fight.

His brow lifted in silent question.

"I'm not here to argue," she said quickly, and it felt like an opening she had to make with care, the first cut in a knot.

His mouth tipped in the smallest warning of a smile. "Then I'm terrified."

She ignored him, moving to sit opposite. Her fingers traced along the grain of the table instead, restless, unwilling to be still. "I want to know everything about the Claiming."

He set his mug aside with careful hands, as if the table might startle if he moved too fast. "Ella."

"No games," she said, her voice steadier now. "I get that it's dangerous. But I need to know more. And no half-truths this time. Please."

His eyes narrowed, and his silence smoldered deeper than the fire's crackle. "Ella." His voice roughened. "You're relentless. Always pushing. Always prying. And you think you're ready for every truth you demand."

"I can handle it. Tell me." She slammed her palms on the desk, the sound cracking through the room.

A slow breath left him, unbothered by her fury.

"I saw what happened when the seer gave you too much. She peeled you open, word by word."

His expression darkened, his gaze dragging over her like a touch.

"You looked...unsettled by her words. Stripped bare."

He leaned forward, his voice dropping lower still. "I would know. I've seen you naked. It did not unsettle me in the slightest. It settled in all the right places."

Heat struck her cheeks, but she didn't let him deter her. "You're not going to deflect by flirting. Tell me about the Claiming ceremony."

His jaw worked once, resisting, and then his shoulders eased in something close to resignation. "Fine. It begins at dusk," he said at last.

Ella waited, ready to curse his ancestors if he stopped there.

"The day after tomorrow. You'll walk into the arena through the High Cathedral. I'll be there long before the bells toll, preparing. You'll arrive with Maeren and Savina, along with Kalenya and some of the other female attendants. The walk is part of it, meant for the people of Dravaryn, and for the realm itself, to see who stands with me, to measure every soul chosen to witness."

She caught it immediately, the way his words placed her not in the crowd behind him but beside his inner circle, displayed before the entire realm. Ella leaned back in her chair, arms dropping to her sides in a stunned, disbelieving huff. "I'm walking in with your inner circle? Do I get to sit by Maeren and Savina during the ceremony?"

His mouth curved faintly, though his eyes stayed unreadable. "You won't be sitting. But yes. Something like that."

Relief loosened her chest before she could stop it. She'd been worried he'd keep her hidden away, that she'd be set apart as an outsider. The thought of being beside them, of not being alone, settled her more than she wanted to admit. She chose not to press him on "*something like that.*"

Her pulse quickened, but she kept her face steady. "And then?"

"Then I give myself to the ritual," he said, voice low but unflinching. "Every piece of me. If the realm wants me, it answers. If it doesn't, it will take my life instead."

Her throat caught. "Has anyone of royal blood ever died during their Claiming?"

His voice was quiet now. "Yes."

Ella's chest constricted. "Even heirs?"

His eyes did not leave hers. "None recently, but I'm sure at some point, yes."

She swallowed, the sound loud in her throat. "I have to ask...before you heard the words of the seer, before you discovered the role I might play in the fate of our kingdoms...were you just going to vanish into the ceremony and leave me behind?"

His answer came without a blink, dark as the hearthstone. "It may not be for the reasons you think, but even before what I learned yesterday, I would not have let you slip away while I faced the gods. If you tried, I would have dragged you back myself." He narrowed his eyes a bit, the words settling like iron. "So no. If the Claiming takes me, you will be there to witness. And stop looking at me like that."

"Like what?" she asked while bracing for his answer, changing her face into a neutral expression.

"Like I need saving," he said, voice clipped, almost cruel. "Like you're planning to throw yourself between me and the High Vexari, just because you don't like the odds."

Heat flared behind her eyes. She crossed her arms, covering the ache with more spine than sense. "Maybe I just don't like being kept in the dark."

That landed like a strike. He stilled, his jaw working once before his gaze broke from hers and fell to the firelight, and when he finally spoke again, the fight had left his voice. "I know you want to protect your kingdom as much as I do mine, and I'm sure you want to put a stop to Threadshifting. But trust is earned with time. It was never my intention to keep you in the dark."

"Speaking of being kept in the dark, who is the High Vexari?"

His mouth pulled tight, a faint crack in his composure. "She's the spiritual head of Dravaryn. The kingdom listens to her... sometimes a little too much."

"That sounds inconvenient for you," Ella said.

A humorless breath left him. "For my father it was a war. They hated each other openly. The High Cathedral and the Dravaryn Court barely spoke for years." His gaze shifted to the firelight, jaw tightening. "So I took over the ties between the High Vexari and the castle. Someone had to keep the Crown and the Cathedral from tearing the kingdom apart."

"So you trust her?" Ella asked.

"I trust her power. I respect her position."

Ella's fingers tightened around the arm of her chair. "And what about me? Isn't she going to question why I'm walking in with your inner circle? If she realizes I'm an outsider, will that put everything at risk?"

He pinned her with a look of determination. "That's enough questions. I don't need saving, Ella. I need focus. Control. And the last few days haven't exactly consisted of training or preparation for the ceremony."

"Don't blame me. I didn't ask to go on your mission. I can't control the Veil unraveling," she said defensively.

He studied her, and his expression softened. "I'm not," he said. "You're the reason I haven't drowned in it."

"Then let me help," she said at last, the words stripped of all her armor. "I went from your prisoner to your shadow to your guest, apparently. You've just started to let me in, probably more than most, if I had to guess. Don't shut me out."

Doubt shifted in his gaze, and maybe even acceptance, buried so it wouldn't draw notice.

"You weren't all that surprised by the seer's words. I saw it on your face, Jakobav. You've felt the pull too," she pressed. "Don't deny it."

His gaze slid toward the hearth, as if the answer were written in the slow collapse of the charred wood into coal and ash.

"I wouldn't get too attached to that pull. The rite is meant to test what stands before it. Threadshifting fractures that ground. There's no way to know what it will demand of me."

It wasn't everything, but it was enough to reveal he was already planning for a battle inside the Claiming arena that no seer could predict.

A strange sense of calm opened in her chest at the honesty of it.

She leaned forward, elbows on her knees, the air tightening with unspoken thoughts. "You haven't let me out of your sight for more than a few hours, and yet I think you were planning on leaving me behind for the ritual. What if I had decided to run, and you never heard from me again?"

A muscle in his hand twitched.

"Well," she said with a smirk she knew he would taste for what it was, "I suppose I wouldn't have to run. If you'd gone to the ritual and left me behind, then I would have been free to come and go as I please."

He rose then, as if stillness could no longer hold him, and when he looked down at her, his face was composed in that particular way he wore when a choice cost him something.

He stepped close enough that the fire highlighted his cheekbone. "You wouldn't get far," he said, quiet and sure. "Not from me." His gaze held hers. "But if you're truly a guest now, then you deserve a proper tour. And you will take it with me."

She arched her brow. "Is that a royal decree, Commander?"

"If I let you wander alone, you'll cause a riot. Or you'll almost get yourself killed. Again. And I'll have to step in. Again."

"I'd say the risk is mutual. And you're the one who took so long to decide if I was a prisoner or not."

"Your incessant questions have me still on the fence," he said as his mouth curved into that dangerous half-smile that seemed to know too much. "Though no prisoner has ever ended up in my bed."

"Neither should guests who weren't invited."

"Then what are you?"

"A problem. Your favorite one, apparently."

He let out a sound that wasn't quite a laugh, quiet and rough-edged. "Gods help me."

She turned before her smile gave too much away. "Lead the way, host."

Outside, the castle had begun to wake, floors whispering with servants' steps and the far clang of practice steel, the corridors still cool with night and the torches along the inner walk just catching.

The day would come, whether either of them were ready, but for a length of time, in a room gone quiet, they let the morning wait, a new and unspoken agreement forming between them.

27

HISTORY THAT BURNED

The castle by day felt different than it had beneath night and chaos. Sunlight poured through the narrow arched windows and laid long bars across the stone floors, illuminating banners stitched with old magic so that their threads glittered.

As they walked, Jakobav pointed out training halls and war rooms, hidden stairwells and ancestral chambers steeped in history, the tour unfolding like a map of his life and of the kingdom that had made him.

One place remained conspicuously absent, and she felt the omission like a pebble in her shoe. He had not taken her to a throne room. In Orchid, the throne room stood at the center of daily life, a place where business was conducted and pleas were heard, and her childhood had been spent there far more often than she had liked. She would've preferred more time in the dense tropical forest south of the palace, but duty had kept her mostly inside under the weight of a hundred eyes.

Here, in a stronghold that seemed to contain everything else, perhaps they didn't keep a throne at all.

Ella tried not to linger when they passed the courtyard where she'd first fought his soldiers, or the corridor where his fingers had brushed her cheek and threatened to break her, only to find an unwelcome realization tugging at her subconscious. The castle wasn't supposed to claim space inside her, yet the memories clung anyway, unsettling her softly. Traitorously.

"Is this where you drag all your prisoners?" she asked, light on the surface, trying to smooth the flutter in her chest.

He glanced at her with an almost smirk. "Only the pretty ones."

"Oh good. I was worried I was special."

"You are," he said, without an attempt at denial. "Unfortunately."

She pretended not to notice his shoulder brushing hers as he led her onward. A smile formed; she swallowed it down.

"Admit it. You like having me here."

He did not answer at once. "You ruin my plans. Antagonize my people. And you ask far too many questions."

"That's not a no."

His eyes cut to hers, dark and unamused. "It's not a yes."

Her smile sharpened. "Then you're lying to one of us."

For a moment, he said nothing, then exhaled through his teeth. "Maybe I like having you here."

He glanced away, muttering like it tasted bitter. "I should've locked you in the dungeons instead. There. Are you pleased?"

"Almost," she said, sweet as Fae wine disguising the punch beneath. "Now say I am a guest."

"You are a distraction."

"Say it."

He sighed like a man accepting defeat. "Fine. You're a guest."

"And?"

"And I am showing you around like a proper host," he said. "Which brings us to a place no guest ever gets to see."

Her gaze lifted as they entered, and wonder rose like a tide that could not be stopped.

The Dravaryn library was vast and reverent in its quiet. Rows of towering shelves climbed toward a high ceiling, ladders suspended between them like narrow bridges. The scent of old paper lay in the air, threaded with the same cedar scent from his office and a dust that was almost sacred.

She slowed, awe moving through her chest as she took in spines bound in rich hues and worn leather, gilded titles and hand-inked marks from long-dead scribes. These were not only archives on war and history. She saw tomes of ancient magic and of modern, earthbound craft, volumes on soil-derived powers, the land itself a source of strength. A shelf of romances surprised a laugh from her, quickly swallowed when she noticed an entire section given over to volumes long forbidden, their titles speaking plainly of the Fae.

Only a few weeks ago she would have doubted this. She would have sworn Dravaryn-hoarded weapons and erased anything that didn't serve the blade. And yet, here stood a library that refused to forget. Where paintings hung between shelves, and spectacular pieces of art watched the aisles with oil-bright eyes.

The system, if there was one, eluded her. Subjects bled into each other, histories slept beside poems, maps wedged themselves between books. A ridiculous part of her longed to rearrange everything by color and gradient until the stacks glowed like a tapestry. She pushed the thought away with a faint huff and kept walking.

Jakobav moved at her side with his hands clasped behind his back. "Most of this was written before the sealing of the realms. We've tried to preserve it all. Dravaryn does not erase what it has been, no matter how dangerous it becomes."

She turned sharply. "You think Orchid does?"

"Your kingdom doesn't acknowledge the Claiming."

"There are reasons," she said, her temper rising.

Jakobav's brow lifted, unimpressed. "Then tell me. What reasons?"

Ella opened her mouth—and felt her cheeks warm when nothing arrived. "It was decided long ago. And we do not erase history. We are a kingdom of fire magic. Sometimes history burns. A spark in a schoolroom, a lesson that flares too high, a careless moment in training, and shelves can become cinder. We try to avoid it. Most libraries now are fully fireproofed, the same way our garments have to be."

He tipped his head. "It still sounds convenient."

"It's a miracle I haven't set you on fire yet."

"Only because you cannot," he said, a taunt softened by the awareness in his eyes.

"But please, feel free to try. I'll even stop and hold still...let you burn me however you like."

She glared and rounded the corner of the upper gallery. The glare dissolved as the air thinned around her. There, framed in carved obsidian and gilded bronze, hung a portrait unlike any other in the room.

The man within the painting stood tall and poised between light and shadow, as if the painter had trapped a storm at rest. His skin held a pale gold like sun caught on water. His hair was the sheen of a raven wing. Beauty gathered itself in his features until it became something beyond mortal measure, and yet the chill of it came not from perfection but from the way his gaze seemed to know too much. High cheekbones and a strong jaw, eyes slightly slanted and bright even in oil, and an expression that sat calm and calculating, amused without warmth.

Her breath stalled when she saw the chain at his throat. The pendant had a center stone wrapped in dark metal vines and set on a gleaming length of links that looked almost thorn-spun. It was the same shape she had seen in her vision, the same stone that had pulsed violet when he moved close, the same light that had called fire into her sigil like a strike of flint.

She stumbled nearer, heart pounding. “This is him,” she whispered. “The man from my dream.”

Fuck. She really hadn’t meant to say the words out loud.

Jakobav appeared beside her, his posture straightening. “You’ve seen him before?”

“Yes.” She couldn’t look away. “I thought it was a fever. He looked exactly like this, only alive, speaking as if he knew me.”

Jakobav’s voice cooled, each word precise. “That painting predates the Veil. His name is not known. He’s Fae.”

“Fae portraits are banned. Why is this painting here at all?”

“Because we don’t erase what shaped us,” he said.

Ella watched his hand close behind his back, fingers curling into a fist so tight his knuckles cracked. He did not look at the painting again. He only looked at her. But she glanced back at the picture, unable to stop looking at the raven-haired man.

“You sure you spoke with *him*?” His words fell like iron, quiet but scathing. “Tell me *exactly* what was said.”

She barely heard him and didn’t answer, entranced by the painting. Up close, the details multiplied. A high-collared coat tailored with ruthless precision. Midnight trousers pressed into perfect lines. A belt with a silver buckle. Rings on each finger like quiet commands. Nothing about him was accidental. Not like Jakobav, whose power was all fury and scars and strength carved into living muscle.

This man didn’t need to prove anything; he pulled at her

like a different realm's gravity, unfamiliar and impossible to ignore.

Gods, he frightened her.

He felt like a secret her soul already knew.

"I argued with him," she said, voice thin with disbelief. "He told me I was never meant to kneel. He said I move between veins."

A low snarl broke from Jakobav behind her, snapping through the air and sending her pulse stumbling.

She tore her gaze from the portrait, but the image stayed lodged behind her ribs like a blade she couldn't pull free. Heat stirred where her sigil lay hidden beneath her skin. She didn't dare look down to see if the ink had surfaced. The pendant, the words, the certainty in his voice when the Fae man had spoken to her—all of it gathered into a single echo that would not quiet.

Not all roots are buried.

Even now, his words thrummed through her, quiet and relentless, as if something ancient had opened its eyes and was watching her remember.

Jakobav was still looking at her, unyielding. Yet she still sensed the Fae man's gaze following her from the wall, eternal and knowing. Ella felt the weight of both, certain that whichever one she turned from, the other would still be watching.

28

THE BLADE AND THE BOND

JAKOBAV

The moment Ella looked at the painting, something inside him cracked.

She'd gone utterly still, which was unusual for someone so hell-bent on pulling trouble from thin air and dragging it straight to her feet. It was that rare kind of immobility he'd only seen in her a handful of times: once when she was half-dead in his bed, once when she'd accused him of betrayal, and once when the seer had spoken a truth she believed belonged to her alone.

But this was worse.

It wasn't fear that froze her, nor fury, nor even shock. It was awe. Reverence. Something dangerously close to longing.

And he wanted to fucking shatter it.

She looked at that portrait like she was remembering a kiss. Not just anyone's. His.

The Fae staring down from the canvas was polished and infuriatingly well dressed, every line of him was meticulous. His godsdamned clothes were tailored, pressed smooth as if no wrinkle could touch them. Smug bastard. He probably had some servant—or some trick of magic—to keep them flawless.

Jakobav wore nothing like that. He carried blood on his boots, dirt under his nails, and scars scored into skin that he'd never given time to heal soft. He didn't own a single garment that fit like that. Not one piece of silk that gleamed like armor. Or any fucking silk at all.

That pendant, glinting at the man's throat, was likely what had made her sigil respond.

He knew that kind of pendant.

Old magic clung to them. Fae magic. And nothing good ever came from it waking.

He saw the way her breath caught, the small flinch she couldn't disguise, the way her fingers grazed her collarbone as if some hidden part of her had answered his call.

She sees power. Power. Elegance. Mystery.

What does she see when she looks at me?

A brute. A war prince. A creature built for battlefields and blood.

Gods, she kept looking at him.

Fuck that.

She needed something real. Someone who could match her, stand unflinching before the fire she carried, see her as more than a weapon or a symbol. Someone who could bear her fury and her beauty and the innate defiance of her will. The way she never backed down from a challenge, never flinched in the face of danger or allowed herself to be lesser, even here in a fortress surrounded by enemies.

Somehow she'd broken straight through the walls he'd built around himself. A barrier no one else had touched. One he'd trusted to hold against kingdoms. And she demolished it with nothing more than that infuriating, intoxicating smirk.

He shouldn't even be thinking about her, especially not

now, when the whole of Dravaryn would be gathering in the capital by nightfall tomorrow, ready for elevation or devastation, depending on if he survived the rite. Not when his every move should've been weighed against the gods and the realm and the cost of failure. He should've been focused on getting ready for his Claiming. And yet, gods help him, all he wanted was to claim her, more than he had ever wanted anything.

~

He shouldn't have been there.

He should have been in his war room, finalizing security protocols and preparing for the moment the kingdom would fill the arena in black and crimson, waiting to see if their prince would rise or fall. Instead, he stood in the shadow of a stone archway, silent and unseen, watching her as if keeping her in his sights was the only thing that quelled the urge to seize her.

Ella stepped into the infirmary like she owned it, barefoot and tousled and fierce, crossing the room with that purposeful glide he was beginning to recognize, and she'd made it only halfway before she threw the door open again and bellowed into the corridor, "Bryn!"

Jakobav tensed at the sound. A crash answered her, metal clanging hard against stone.

"Gods save me," came the muffled reply.

Moments later, Bryn appeared, glitter-dusted and somehow sticky, a satchel of clinking vials in one hand and a half-eaten pastry in the other. "I'm glad to see you survived," he said at once, brushing crumbs from his coat as if it were an infestation. "More than that, from what I heard. I knew I detected something different about you. Would've been a shame if you died. You're the obsession of the castle right now, and life has been dull for far too long."

Jakobav bristled, the word "obsession" settling in his chest like grit. It was a struggle to remind himself that Bryn had a knack for embellishment.

"I'm glad to see you too, Bryn," Ella said, folding her arms. "But right now, I need answers."

Bryn sighed, bit into the pastry, and chewed with theatrical misery. "By the seven sacred hemorrhoids, Ella, you're always wanting answers."

She laughed, soft and unguarded, and Jakobav's stomach tightened as if the sound had hooked something low inside him and pulled.

"Shut up and tell me the state of everyone's injuries and where they are. I want to see them," she said. "Thane. Maeren. Savina. Soren. All of them. And don't you dare pretend you don't know how they're doing."

Jakobav went still, breath held without meaning to.

Bryn gave her a slow blink. "Excluding Jake, you do realize you just named the four most emotionally unavailable people in the entire kingdom, right?"

"They'll let me in," Ella said, her certainty was absolute. "Where are they?"

Bryn chewed and swallowed, the pause stretching, Jakobav's patience fraying with it.

"You know," Bryn said at last, "people don't usually want to talk to Savina when she's fresh out of a wound."

"I'm not most people."

"No," Bryn muttered, "you're the reason half of them were in the infirmary."

Jakobav flinched. Ella did too, just slightly.

"I didn't ask them to protect me," she said, voice low.

"No," Bryn said, softer now, "but they did anyway."

It sounded like there was more he wasn't saying. Jakobav had known Bryn his entire life and had never heard him this cryptic.

Why in the gods' names was he pushing her so hard?

What did Bryn know that he didn't?

Everything in the infirmary fell silent. Long enough that Jakobav felt it sinking into her, and she had been through enough. He wanted to cut through it, break it open with his hands if he had to.

"Tell me how they are," Ella said finally.

Bryn studied her and then relented. "Savina's already back on guard duty, stubborn as ever. She woke up mid-stitching and threatened to hex me with a blade to the thigh if I touched her boots, then marched out like nothing had happened. Soren barely said a word, which means he's fine. Maeren's got cracked ribs and an injured leg, probably more, and she's pretending it's just tight muscle tension. And Thane..."

Jakobav leaned forward before he could stop himself.

"Thane?" Ella asked, almost too quiet.

"I heard you stole his favorite blade, and I couldn't be more proud."

"Thanks," she said, a ghost of guilt shading the word. "But I do actually feel a little bad about it."

"Then go return it," Bryn said, stepping aside with exaggerated courtesy. "They might still be in the training wing. And try not to make anyone cry, or at least don't tear any stitches open, which would only make more work for me."

Jakobav exhaled slowly.

A vicious and wordless heat stirred in his chest that did not care for reason or duty, only for the sight of her moving away from him and toward the people who had bled for him.

He didn't move, not yet, tracking her as she walked down the corridor. The names she had listed thudded through him like steps on stone. His best soldiers. She cared about their wounds; she wanted to see them.

His people.

Were they now hers too, by some strange twist of fate?

Jakobav slid from the archway and moved like smoke along the wall, keeping to the darker seams of stone as Ella disappeared into the old training wing. He shouldn't have followed, not when dawn would bring the final preparations and dusk would demand everything he was. But she'd named them and claimed them, and that damned blade, the one Thane had carved a kill count into with pride and reckless flair, still hung at her hip like it had always belonged there.

His jaw flexed until it ached.

He wasn't used to this, this merciless kind of wanting that gripped low in his gut just from watching her exist. He'd been angry before, but not like this, not possessive, not with a hunger that didn't give a fuck about the Claiming or the kingdom or the cost. Usually so steady, he had become something mercurial, unpredictable even to himself, pulled into Ella's orbit.

The old training wing lay half-lit, a cathedral of stone and shadow, and Jakobav found the alcove near the southern arch, the same quiet pocket he had used as a boy when spying on older trainees, old habits clinging like older ghosts. He'd arrived first and hid out of sight; it helped that he knew a faster route.

He saw her before she saw Thane.

She stepped into the chamber and stilled. The room was thick with sweat, steel, and years of echoing grunts, yet she moved through it like it recognized her, like this wing of the castle had been waiting for her return.

Thane sat beneath the window, sharpening a long dagger with slow, practiced strokes, the light catching on the blade and along the cut of his jaw. He looked up.

"No cloak this time," Thane said. "I barely recognized you without the dramatics."

"Sorry to disappoint," Ella murmured.

Thane's gaze dragged over her with unhurried weight. "You don't."

Jakobav's fists clenched until the bones protested.

She walked forward slowly and unhooked the blade from her side, turning the weapon once as if considering its balance, then held it out, handle first. "I think this belongs to you."

Jakobav knew that blade better than most men knew their own hands, a Velmirian steel meant for Thane's grip, yet in her hand, it looked different, as if the weapon had chosen her and not him.

He could barely breathe.

But Thane didn't take it. He only stared, not like a soldier reclaiming property but like a man cataloguing something rare. Something dangerous.

"I told Jake he wasn't ready," Thane said quietly, eyes fixed on the blade. "Told him he needed to take his Claiming seriously. That the kingdom couldn't afford a hesitant heir."

Ella said nothing, but her fingers tightened on the hilt, the smallest movement betrayed how the words hit her.

"He's changed," Thane continued, voice even. "Focused. Clear-eyed. More than I've ever seen him."

Jakobav hadn't expected the approval, almost pride, shaping his words.

"And that's because of you."

Jakobav's jaw tightened, the truth landing harder than he would ever admit.

Focused. Clear-eyed. Because of her. He couldn't deny it, not even to himself. She'd been good for him. The past weeks had honed him in ways war had not, in ways council had not, in ways years of training for the

Claiming never had. She'd forced him to look beyond his own walls, beyond the iron weight of expectation, and see more.

And yet not right now.

Right now she was a fucking distraction, keeping him from the training field or in the war room, drilling strategy into his generals, preparing himself for the most important day of his life. Instead, he stood in shadow like some jealous wraith, watching her, wanting her, knowing he would burn everything he had built to the ground just to have her look at him and no one else.

Fucking fates. He couldn't turn away.

Her hair had grown longer since she'd arrived, falling in loose, dark waves that brushed against her lower back, unbound and wild, exactly like her. The dress she wore tonight clung to her in ways that made his blood heat, a soft curve here, a sharp line there, the kind of contrast that seared itself into a man's mind, refusing to let go.

She had no idea the dress was flame resistant, tailored exactly to her, commissioned the moment he realized he didn't want her to leave.

And she didn't need to know.

She looked devastatingly feminine, but Jakobav knew better than to mistake softness for weakness. She radiated power, raw and unapologetic, curling under his skin and promising to strike quickly.

And if she smiled at another man one more fucking time, he might come undone.

He needed to regain control.

Ella opened her mouth, then closed it. Her chin lifted in that stubborn way of hers.

"I didn't—"

"You did," Thane said, cutting her off. "Whether you meant

to or not. You woke something in him that we've all been waiting to see."

Jakobav's jaw ached from clenching. He didn't know if he wanted to put his fist through the wall or storm into the room and kiss her until the stone itself cracked under the force of it.

Then Thane did the unthinkable.

He pushed the blade back toward her.

"Keep it."

"What?"

"You earned it," Thane said. "Besides, I'm due for a new one. Maybe something with less dramatic flair."

Jakobav stared, heat spiking through his veins, a dark surge climbing.

Ella laughed softly, her eyes gleaming, like she'd just been handed a gift more precious than steel, one that Jakobav knew should've been his to give.

"Thank you."

"Just don't die," Thane added, turning back to his whetstone with infuriating calm, and Jakobav wanted to wipe that calm from his face with blood.

"You're the only one who's ever rattled him. That makes you...inconveniently rare."

Jakobav swallowed a curse so vicious it scalded the back of his throat.

Why the fuck is he complimenting her so much?

It should have been him standing there and saying those words—to make her laugh like that, to see her face soften, to feel her look at him as though she might actually stay.

His pulse was a war drum in his ears.

He'd never felt anything like it. The sheer loss of control made him want to grab her, haul her into the shadows, and erase every other man from her mind until she remembered nothing but *his* hands, *his* mouth, and *his fucking name.*

He didn't recognize himself. He didn't want to. Instead, he stood in a hallway full of shadows and teeth, his restraint fraying with every breath.

And then he moved, not because it was wise, not because he had chosen to, but because he couldn't stop himself.

Ella barely had time to react before his arm hooked hard around her waist and hauled her clean off her feet, his stride already devouring the space between them and the exit. Out of the corner of his eye, he caught Thane's reaction in the dim light, a wide grin flashing, a small nod that looked far too approving of the spectacle, and then, gods damn him, a fucking wink.

"Jake—" She gasped, but he didn't answer, didn't even look at her. He carried her forward with relentless purpose, his silence heavier than any threat, his wrath pressing into every step.

He would deal with Thane later.

Right now she was his obsession. His fury. His fucking ruin.

And he would not be letting her go.

29

THE GARDEN AND THE BREACH

JAKOBAV

Through the halls he carried her, past startled guards who looked away quickly as if they had not seen, past torchlight that bent in the rush of his passage, out into the night where the air bit cold against his skin, her breath hitching uneven in his hold.

And then into the black rose garden.

He wasn't sure why his fury had carried him here, only that his feet had chosen before his mind could catch up. His blood had always stirred in this place, the dark blooms gleaming like onyx fire beneath the moon. Out here, among the roses, his power had never once faltered. If he was going to break, if he was going to lose every ounce of restraint he had left, this was as good a place as any.

She twisted once against his grip, but he growled, so low it reverberated in his own bones, and she stilled as though her body understood better than her mind that fighting him would be useless.

The night here was warmer than all the rest of the castle grounds, as if the garden kept its own climate. The roses stood like sentinels, thousands of them spilling beneath the moonlight in spirals and arcs, their dark petals drinking in silver light until it fractured into plum and violet and deep wine, gleaming like shards of obsidian wet with dew. The hedges curled in deliberate patterns, the buds tilting as they passed in a slow, collective lean as if the whole garden recognized them. Even the air thickened, laced with spice and velvet, clinging close around them like a second skin.

But Jakobav barely registered any of it. His grip was iron on her wrist, the furnace in his chest burning hotter with every step. That smile she'd given Thane, the way she'd stood too close, and before that, the look she'd given the painted Fae: not fear, not curiosity, but longing.

The thought scraped raw down his spine, jealousy like he'd never known before, a snarl that made him push harder and walk faster, instinct driving him deeper into the heart of the garden until the scent of the roses drowned the night.

She stumbled when he stopped, and he used the momentum to spin her, pressing her back into the hedge. The roses shifted under her, petals crushed with a hiss, their perfume flooding heavy between them.

"You think I didn't notice?" His voice came low, dangerous, threaded with something feral.

"Notice what?" she shot back, her chin tilting up in defiance.

The sheer gall of her, standing there as if she didn't know she'd dragged a side of him into the light that he'd never seen in himself, scraped at him until his jaw ached and his pulse thundered. Rage and hunger warred in his veins, a violent swell that left him shaking with the need to claim.

"The way you looked at him," Jakobav growled. "At that fucking Fae. And Thane. Like they were worth your eyes."

Her lips curved, not soft but taunting. "Maybe they were."

Heat spiked through him, dark and violent. "Careful, Ella."

"Or what?" she whispered, her pulse fluttering beneath his grip.

He leaned closer, his breath rough against her skin. "I will not share that look with another man," he said, voice low with warning. "Nor that smile. Not even your breath."

His grip tightened.

"The next time you give it, it will be to me."

Her voice was taunting, infuriating. "Fuck, Jakobav, you sound jealous."

"I am," he admitted, his mouth so close to hers he could taste the shape of the word. "And you don't want to know how far that goes."

The way she looked at him, ocean-blue eyes catching in the moonlight. Gods.

They widened just slightly, and she breathed, "Maybe I do." The words left her softer, more ache than defiance.

"Then maybe I should ruin you for every other man who thinks he deserves your gaze," he said, voice low and threatening.

She faltered, her gaze shifting down before locking on him again, her mouth opening then closing.

That hesitation lit something wild in him.

Gods, she wanted to. She wanted him to break past her armor, to push until she bent. He could feel it in her body, in her eyes, in the stubborn silence that was no silence at all. She'd lived her life carrying strength like a blade, forced to be defiant, forced to prove, never allowed to yield.

But here she was begging without words for that weight to be stripped from her shoulders. To fall without fear.

He would be the man to teach her how to give in, to surrender without shame.

He would destroy her and remake her. Piece by piece.

Until she was his in every way.

Right now, he only needed to close the distance, to take whatever she gave, to drown himself in it. Because he would take it like the jealous, greedy bastard she'd turned him into.

Fuck, he wanted her.

His stubborn, relentless, merciless Ella.

He stepped in until space ceased to exist between them, his thigh driving between hers, his hand closing around her jaw in a grip that offered no escape. Her breath caught, but she didn't push him away.

He had meant to demand answers, to drag the truth out of her about what that look at the portrait had meant, but the sight of her lips parted and eyes daring him to show her his dark intentions had every question in his mind burning to ash.

In fact, the whole fucking world could burn. Nothing else mattered except this.

He didn't think. He didn't weigh the consequences.

Jakobav closed the distance, his mouth taking hers in a deep kiss that was pure hunger, the kind of claim that left no room for doubt.

She met him head-on, kissing him back harder, hungrier, her fingers fisting in his hair and pulling him closer with a wildness that was lust incarnate. The taste of her hit him like Fae wine poured straight into his veins, subtly sweet and dangerously addictive.

Fucking delicious.

He broke the kiss only long enough to lean down and drag his hands up the backs of her thighs, lifting her and pulling her against him so fiercely that she let out a half-gasp half-moan, before he claimed her mouth again in an all-consuming kiss.

With her legs wrapped around his waist and arms around his neck, he tightened his grip on her hips, thrusting his hips forward just enough to make her feel exactly what she'd done to him.

The garden swayed around them, thorns and roses leaning close as if eager to witness their ruin.

When she gasped, he swallowed the sound and drove the kiss harder, coaxing giving way to the conquest that burned between them. He kissed her with the full intent to ruin every other taste she'd ever known, to make her remember only him.

Whatever hesitation she'd carried earlier was gone; Ella came alive beneath him, tearing her lips from his and biting the side of his neck before soothing the mark with her tongue. Her devious mouth and those soft lips made him somehow even harder.

The groan that tore from him was raw, guttural, ripping free before he could stop it. He'd never made a sound like that for anyone. Not once.

He lowered her slowly, her body sliding against his, and stepped back—just enough to take in the sight of her. Her dress had ridden up, and the glimpse he caught beneath it slammed straight through him, a need so intense it bordered on pain. He wanted more of her. Wanted to taste beyond her mouth. Wanted to devour every inch she'd let him touch.

He forced himself a few steps back, fighting for air.

"Gods," he breathed, the words torn from him before he could stop them. "You're so fucking beautiful."

Color rose to her cheeks, a soft, blooming pink, her dark hair falling in messy waves around her face. Instead of shying away, she lifted her chin in that stubborn, defiant way of hers, as if daring him to see all of her. His gaze locked with hers, chest heaving, every muscle strung tight with the truth of it: his restraint was gone.

If she pushed him back now, he would stop.

But gods, he prayed she wouldn't.

She didn't. She smirked, parted her lips, sucked in a small breath, and waited.

That was all it took. His control shattered as he closed the distance between them. Jakobav guided her, laying her backward, gently toward the ground, wishing he had a fur blanket to lay beneath her.

As he lowered himself, steel brushed his forearm. Her weapons. Even now, she was armed to the teeth, blades sitting against skin he was about to taste.

His gaze flicked to the Velmirian steel at her waist—Thane's blade—and something dark and territorial snarled through him. He slipped it from the sheath with one hand and tossed it aside, out of anyone else's reach but his.

But the knife strapped to her thigh? He left it. He liked her dangerous.

And gods help anyone who thought of taking even one weapon from her. Except him.

He didn't give her more than a breath before he shoved her dress up farther and lowered himself between her thighs. He hooked her legs over his shoulders and tore her undergarments away with his teeth, the scraps ripping clean before he caught them in one hand and stuffed them into his pocket, a gift he would save for later.

Then his hands were on her again, one palm gripping the curve of her ass, the other circling her clit until her body arched against him. His fingers slid lower, grazing the wetness he had dreamed of, the kind that had haunted him since the first time he discovered it.

"Gods, Ella," he rasped, fingers slick with her arousal as he worked her open. "You're soaked for me."

Her hips lifted helplessly, meeting every stroke of his fingers, her breath breaking apart in soft, desperate sounds he wanted burned into him forever. The scent of her filled the air, sharp and intoxicating, growing heavier with every second he teased her like that.

"Fuck," she whimpered.

Then his mouth was on her, and she tasted like heat and sin.

He stroked her with his tongue, slow and relentless, not just for her pleasure but to savor every drop of wetness, every noise, every gasp, devouring her as though she were the only thing worth worshiping in the realm.

Ella arched, a broken sound punching from her chest, her fingers tangling hard in his hair as if anchoring herself to the only thing keeping her alive. When he pulled back, it was only to watch her wrecked against the grass, her breasts rising and falling, her peaked nipples visible through the thin fabric that clung damp to her skin.

He dragged his mouth up her stomach, rising slowly until he reached her chest where he tore the neckline wider with his teeth until one breast spilled free into the cool garden air, biting the hardened peak before kissing it softly. He freed the next one and gently bit it too before swirling his tongue over it and sucking it into his mouth, eliciting a small gasp.

He pulled back to watch her expression, hoping he would see that exact look on her face when he buried himself inside her, when she shattered around his cock.

"Look at me," he growled, voice rough with command.

Ella's eyes fluttered open, wide and dark, and she met his gaze through the uneven rise of her panting breath. Power surged through his chest at her obedience, a rush that made his veins burn, her scent intensifying as her eyes reflected the same dark desire he recognized within himself. Moonlight caught on her bare skin, accentuating her exquisite curves, begging to be tasted.

He lowered himself again, settling between her thighs, his

tongue relentlessly circling her clit, devouring her as if the sounds she made were the only air he had left to breathe. Moving his attention lower, his tongue dragged down to her entrance, thumb pulsing on the sensitive spot to replace his tongue and keep her writhing with the tension. He pushed in deeper with his tongue, tasting her more intimately, groaning against her as she trembled, the vibration sinking deep.

The garden reacted in waves—roses trembling, petals loosening into the air, the hedge behind her pulsing like something alive.

He savored every tremor he drew from her, and the night itself seemed to bend, the world narrowing to the ragged rhythm of her breath and the dark, desperate devotion in every movement of his mouth. He'd never licked anyone like this, never wanted to. Desperate, rough, like the sight of her melting beneath him and her nails dragging across his skin could sate him for a lifetime. It would never be enough.

Ella's legs trembled against his jaw, rocking her hips against his face. He watched every wave of pleasure hit her, captivated by her blissful surrender, the taste of her slickened core crashing over him like summer lightning—wild, sweet, unmistakably hers. He chased it with the hunger of a starving man who had finally found what he'd been dying for. She arched, crying his name, and he almost spent himself just from the way she gave herself to him in that moment.

"Fuck, Jake. That was—" she whimpered.

Her legs slid down from his shoulders as he dragged his mouth higher, pressing his hardness along her body as he moved, making sure she felt what her undoing had done to him. Their kiss was messy, desperate, and charged with anticipation. Her mouth tasted like his salvation, and it carried the mark she had just left on him, proof that she'd come undone just for him. Only for him.

"You taste so fucking good." He groaned, thrusting his hips toward her. "I need more. Come apart for me again, Ella."

His cock pressed hard against her thigh, aching for release, and his voice came ragged, harsh against her lips. "I want to feel all of you."

She nodded, likely too far gone to form words, and that broke something in him all over again. His breath came in heavy pulls, and he couldn't tell if it was from the fight to hold back or the need to take every last inch of her until she could never forget what he'd done to her body. He kissed down the line of her throat, across her shoulder, biting at her collarbone before claiming her mouth again.

"Fuck," he hissed when he pulled back, realizing too late that he had broken skin. A single drop of blood welled, hot and bright, and when it touched his tongue it was sweet iron, sharp as her. He was too far gone to feel the warning beneath his skin.

The world ripped sideways. The ripple burst with violent force, air splitting like torn cloth, reality shrieking as if it had been wounded. Jakobav recoiled back on his knees, the taste of her blood still searing his tongue.

The Veil flared open in the center of the garden for half a heartbeat, just long enough to see shadow shift and feel raw fury pour through. Roses blackened, petals curling inward as if retreating from what had dared step too close.

Then it snapped shut with a sound like a snarl ripped in half.

Jakobav dropped back down beside Ella, panting, vision reeling, his gaze wild on her as if she were the only thing anchoring him to the ground. Her hand clutched her chest, the Orchid tattoo beneath her collarbone glowing faintly, ink alive.

For a long moment, neither of them moved. The air shivered, charged and wrong, the garden holding its breath with them as if waiting to see if something else would tear free of the dark. Roses crackled softly, their blackened petals flaking. Jakobav's heart hammered in his throat, blood still thrumming with adrenaline.

Some vicious, primal part of him bared its teeth at the thought of anything else reaching for her. She was his to protect, and the idea of another force touching her magic made his vision burn.

If anything had stepped through that tear, he would have torn it apart with his bare hands before he let it lay a finger on her.

"What the hell was that?" she whispered.

"That wasn't me," he rasped, voice hoarse. "That was you."

"No," she shot back, shaking her head hard.

Ella's hands were trembling. She pulled her dress back down, covering herself and adjusting the torn neckline. "I felt you pull my power. You created that ripple."

Fuck, she was right.

But before he could answer, a horn split the night, urgent and too close.

Branches snapped, hedges parting, and Bryn stumbled into the clearing with leaves in his hair and his coat askew. He froze.

"Didn't think you were the gardening type, Jake," Bryn said slowly, eyes sweeping over the wreckage. "Guess I was wrong." He grinned like the bastard he was. "Ten out of ten for spectacle. Two out of ten for the damage you just caused to a five-hundred-year-old sacred garden. And gods"—his nose wrinkled theatrically—"you reek. Like a rotflower tonic left out in the sun."

Jakobav pushed to his feet, breath still uneven from the breach, instinct rising faster than reason.

He reached down and offered his hand. Ella accepted it, and he pulled her steadily to her feet. She smoothed the fabric of her dress with shaking hands, cheeks still slightly flushed, trying to make herself whole again.

Without thinking, he stepped in front of her to give her the space she needed, a moment of dignity in the aftermath.

With his attention locked on Bryn, Jakobav reached back and found her wrist, his fingers closing around her. His thumb brushed over her pulse once, steadying her, telling her what he couldn't voice in front of anyone else. *I've got you.* Then, without looking away from Bryn, he said evenly, "Close your eyes, Bryn."

Bryn arched a brow. "Bit late for modesty, don't you think?"

Another horn blared, closer this time, the sound slicing through the garden's heavy air. Instinct forced Jakobav's attention to the horizon, the hairs along his arms rising in warning.

"Outer ward breach. By the gate," Bryn said, amusement fading into focus, though the leaves still clung to his hair. "And whatever the two of you just did, don't ever make me smell it again."

Ella scoffed. "We'll add it to your growing list of complaints, Bryn." She tugged free of Jakobav's hand and dropped into a crouch, snatching Thane's blade from where it lay in the dirt. In one efficient motion, she strapped it back to her waist.

First the ripple in the garden and now a breach within minutes—too much of a coincidence to ignore.

"Let's move." Jakobav's voice dropped to command, and the three of them ran.

30

THE HUNT AT THE GATE

Bryn had broken off toward the castle, disappearing down a side path without explanation. Ella and Jakobav kept to the route from the roses that cut toward the outer ward, the air humming with a low metallic resonance that did not belong to wind. Jakobav set the pace ahead of her, jaw locked tight, every line of him carved with focus, as if the taste of her wasn't still clinging to his mouth like sin.

Ella matched him step for step, ignoring the sting of his bite and the ache between her thighs, each movement a reminder. There wasn't time to talk about what had happened or make a battle plan; the warning horn pulled them forward. Still, her time in the rose garden had been life-altering, and she felt as though the truth of it was written across her face for anyone to see.

She prayed no one would notice her torn neckline, her scent, or the wild disarray that clung to her like a confession. And under her dress she wore nothing, not even the armor of modesty. She didn't make a habit of running half-clothed into battle, but tonight, her dignity would have to fend for itself.

They cleared the final archway, and torches flared in the courtyard, flames bending as the night wind rushed across the stones.

A small unit of First Guard had already formed a staggered line, shields locked and angled, spears braced like teeth ready to strike. Maeren stood at the point, leather and linen strapped close to her frame, hair braided back tightly, her entire posture radiating vengeance as though the breach had personally insulted her. Thane was beside her, sword propped against his shoulder, smile lazy and sharp-eyed, already watching the darkness like it belonged to him. Soren was nowhere to be seen, and in an instant, he was there, rising soundlessly from the ground just beyond the flagstones, his form condensing into flesh.

Bryn came skidding in from the opposite corridor, his satchel thumping against his side where he'd clearly dashed back into the castle for supplies, purple shoes flashing with every ridiculous step, utterly wrong for battle. Then again, she was barefoot in a torn dress, so who was she to judge?

Bryn grinned despite the chaos and called out, "Oh good, everyone's dressed. That'll save time."

"Report," Jakobav barked.

Bryn's gaze traveled to the far side of the courtyard, his nose wrinkling as though he could already smell the wrongness waiting there. "Something is pressing through the breach, and fast. The ripple is vibrating like fury-eating shit bunnies with a death wish."

Maeren scanned the dark. "Is the Veil holding?"

"Barely," Bryn said. "It's straining like something inside wants to rip the gate off its hinges."

Thane's grin deepened, slow and feral. "Excellent. I was starting to get bored."

Ella kept to Jakobav's right where his sword could sweep

wide without striking her, close enough that the heat radiating from him felt like a shield. The night beyond the gate carried an icy chill that did not belong, colder than the Dravaryn climate this time of year.

Between the moon and the heavy ring of torches at the gate, the courtyard was almost bright as day. The ripple hovered ten paces beyond the gatehouse, a wound in the air that bent and twisted, like glass struggling to remember it had once been water. Its edges folded inward, warping against a wind that did not exist, and black smoke bled steadily from the center, curling downward in patient coils that never touched the cobblestones. The stench was wrong—bitter and metallic. It pressed against her, a pressure that lodged behind her eyes and made her stomach churn.

The guards shifted restlessly, the line faltering by fractions. One lifted the chain at his throat, fingers closing around the Dravaryn crest and pressing it to his lips without ever taking his eyes off the breach.

"Hold," Jakobav commanded, his voice steady.

Maeren's hand flexed once over her weapon, her stance ready. "Holding. Bring on whatever dares to breach this close to the stronghold."

"Do not get cocky," Jakobav said, his gaze never leaving the shimmer at the gate. "I need every one of you alive and standing in that arena tomorrow."

"Who, us?" Thane grinned. "We're the model of restraint."

The breach thrummed louder, smoke funneling through it, thickening into a rising column that began to take form, condensing into limbs, into mass, solidifying as it stepped through.

Humanoid, but wrong. As tall as Thane, broader still across the chest, its body corded with muscle that looked carved too deep, tendons drawn too tight, every movement strained against itself. Its skin gleamed the color of old oiled wood, slick with a sheen that caught torchlight.

Its face could almost have been handsome, if not for the warping: cheekbones cut like razors, a mouth stretched too wide, filled with teeth that shifted and scraped when it opened, sound spilling out like a chorus of broken echoes. The noise vibrated against her bones, uncanny and dissonant, a sonar call that twisted Ella's stomach.

The creature floated just above the cobbles, carried on smoke that puffed at its ankles and dragged upward as if bound by invisible chains. Each time it shifted, the shadows beneath it smeared across stone, gravity bending around it.

Its mouth yawned wider, that echoing shriek rippling through the air. It had no nostrils, yet the noise bent as if it were smelling, hunting. The creature's head snapped and locked onto Jakobav like a predator catching the faintest trace of scent.

The smoke bunched like muscle as it slid forward. Not a run, but a glide, a speed impossible for its size until it was suddenly there, closing half the courtyard in a breath.

Spears met it first. They pierced, biting into the corded flesh, reddish-black fluid spraying hot against the ground, drops fizzling into smoke. The creature didn't slow as Thane's blade ripped across its shoulder, shallow but clean, earning another spill of ooze. The sound it made in answer scraped down Ella's spine.

"On me," Jakobav snapped, pivoting low and driving his sword hard along its ribs where any mortal ribs would have given way. It lunged at him, and black-red fluid hissed against his steel, searing down the blade.

What in the hell is this thing made of...fumes and blood-laced tar?

The creature didn't scream, but it turned its face, mouth

gaping too wide, eyes bleeding smoke, and its gaze locked on Jakobav.

Thane moved to intercept.

It lunged again, gliding past Thane's guard easily, as if he weren't a warrior almost as massive as the creature.

Savina moved next, her blade cutting deep across its thigh —another gush of smoke-thick fluid spilling out—yet it did not falter, its speed belonging to something far beyond flesh. It crashed into Jakobav, claws bared, striking hard enough that the crack of bone rang so loud the courtyard seemed to flinch. He seemed to brace himself before he twisted and slammed the thing back against the wall of the gatehouse, rock booming with the impact.

"Jake!" Thane's voice rang out.

Maeren's hand cut a quick gesture, obsidian spiking from the cobbles to clutch the creature's ankle. It held for a moment, long enough for Jakobav to move away, then it wrenched free with terrifying force, tearing the rock loose as though pulling weeds from soil.

Still it came for Jakobav with unwavering focus.

"Gods, that bastard only wants to fight Jake. I'm offended," Thane growled, blades flashing as the monster nearly clipped Jakobav's arm.

Bryn tossed a vial that burst green fire across its shoulder, the flames sizzling but refusing to catch. He was already digging for another, muttering under his breath, "Well, that's new—and I've seen a lot of weird shit."

The creature paid no heed to Bryn's alchemy nor to Savina's blade. It just shoved through Jakobav's defenses as if built for this single task. The noise from that thing vibrated out in a pulse that made her ribs hum.

Ella hovered at the fringe of the fight, reading every movement, searching for an opening—though none appeared. If the

First Guard couldn't pull its focus, then what in the hell was she supposed to do?

It was locked on Jakobav like a starving animal finding a feast.

Was it because of the ripple he opened in the garden?

The horn had signaled the breach immediately after he'd accidentally cut her and borrowed her Threadwalking ability. Her gut dropped, dread pooling low as the pieces knit together in her mind.

The garden.

The drop of blood he'd taken from her.

Is the creature after my blood?

It couldn't be that. She had more on her than he did. If it were her blood alone, the creature would be coming for her.

But it wasn't.

She tracked its movements, every lunge and recoil, searching for a pattern.

The creature's gaze wasn't on him at all, but fixed on the pocket at his side.

Her breath caught as the truth hit—it was following the scent of her arousal. Her undergarments were covered with it —and currently in his pocket.

What. The. Fuck.

She could only guess, but every instinct screamed: her scent had become a beacon, one the creature had latched onto obsessively, calling to it as it hunted.

Why her? Why in the hell would anyone send such a vile thing after her?

She flinched—not from the creature, but because Jakobav was taking the hits meant for her, and he was getting hurt. Badly.

Guilt and vulnerability tangled in her chest until her breathing thinned.

The courtyard clanged with steel and churned with strange smoke, thick enough to choke on. Ella hovered near the fight, no space to intervene, uselessness clawing at her and feeding the guilt already gnawing inside her.

First Guard pressed in together, years of practice evident in the rhythm of how they fought: Maeren striking with living stone, Thane a force at her side, Savina with her brutal finesse, Soren vanishing from the ground to reappear where he was most needed.

Jakobav was at the center, his sword a shield between the monster's reaching hands and the pocket that betrayed him. Blood darkened his shirt. Too much of it was his, yet his stance never faltered.

Ella's chest cracked open with the sight. The breach still churned behind the creature, its edges fraying wider with every second it lingered here. If this thing had been sent, there might be more, and whoever commanded it was likely watching closely. She moved at the thought, needing to be useful, to help, raising her weapon and lunging into the chaos.

"Ella," Jakobav growled, looking back. "Stay behind me."

"Not a chance," she answered, sliding right, her blade angling to close his blind spot.

The monster struck again and Jakobav parried, but the second hit landed hard against his shoulder. The wet rip of tearing flesh carried across the stone. He grunted but held.

Thane cursed and drove his blade deep, a cut that should have felled any mortal or beast. Savina slashed its hamstring, but the creature spun, backhanding her with a force that sent her skidding bloody across cobbles. She rolled, teeth bared in a smile that promised pain in return. "I'm fine," she spat. "Keep it busy."

Soren vanished, his body dissolving into earth. He rose behind the beast, arms clamping around its throat, trying to drag it down. Smoke bled against his grip, but still the creature strained forward, its red leaking eyes locked unerringly on Jakobav's pocket. Every feint, every strike curved back toward him. Soren's eyes swiveled from Jakobav's pocket and then back to the creature.

"Jake," Soren said, moving to cover him, quiet and calm even in the chaos. "Drop it. Whatever you're guarding is not worth your life."

Soren vanished from its flank and rose beside Jakobav with one hand already outstretched, as if ready to tear the pocket free for drawing death to his commander.

The thing lunged faster than it had moved all night. Soren caught its forearm and twisted, tendons popping under his grip until it gave with a wet crack.

This was her opening. The creature's head cocked again like it was listening, scenting, and she cut in hard from its blind side. Her blade drove up beneath its jaw and punched out near the ear, a clean line of steel that sent a sheet of black and red blood across the cobbles.

It bucked loose from Soren and clawed toward Jakobav, still reaching for that godsdamned pocket even as Thane's cut took both tendons at the back of its knees. Savina followed through without hesitation, her strike slicing through its neck, finishing what she started.

The head toppled, the mouth still stretched too wide, a last ripple of that awful echo spilling out. The body staggered back, smoke still leaching from it, before collapsing.

Shadow unwound from the corpse like breath from a dying fire and twisted back toward the waiting breach.

Silence fell, and then sound returned all at once.

"Jakobav," Maeren said, stepping toward him and stopping only when he swayed.

"I'm good. I'm fine," he answered, though the torchlight

showed him pale and set his soaked shirt to a darker red along the ribs.

Ella moved to help him, and he let her, which was its own small miracle. Or a very bad sign.

She pressed her palm to his side, and heat surged against her skin. She couldn't tell if it was the wound burning or simply the furnace of him whenever she stood too close.

"Stitches," Bryn said briskly from Jakobav's other side, already fishing through his satchel. "Also a fresh rack of ribs, if anyone happens to be carrying a spare."

"Bryn, not now." Ella shot him a glare before turning back toward Jakobav.

"Can you walk?" Maeren asked, eyes on the blood.

Jakobav gave one short nod. "Take the head," he said. "That thing is a Tracker, but nothing like the ones I've seen before. I want it studied." His tone was resolute.

Savina nudged the severed thing with her boot, lip curling. "I would rather lick the sweat from Thane's disgustingly hairy backside than touch that thing ever again."

Ella's gaze had already gone to the breach.

It was still open, thinner now, but open all the same, leaking smoke that curled like beckoning fingers.

She felt the pull distinctly and looked around. It didn't seem to be calling to anyone else—only to her. If another Tracker slipped through, or if something worse stepped out while Bryn had his hands in Jakobav's side, they would all pay for her hesitation.

She moved before caution could catch her.

"Ella," Thane snapped, reading her angle. "No."

She ignored him and stepped to the cusp of the shimmer's threshold, close enough that the fine hairs along her forearms lifted. The air tasted like metal shavings and summer rain as she closed her eyes and reached for the threads.

The first time she Threadwalked she'd slipped by accident. Anger and fear had opened the world under her feet, and she'd clawed her way back with instinct, stubbornness, and a prayer to gods. This time she went looking on purpose.

She pictured the threads as the seer had described them, not a single rope but a thousand strands braided and unbraided by intention. She reached for where they loosened near the breach, slick and writhing like living current. She caught one, and it seared her palm. She caught another and pulled it to the first, forcing them to twist together, and her Orchid tattoo sparked in response, heat blooming under her skin before dimming as though pouring itself into the space between worlds.

The sounds of the courtyard blurred, but she registered faintly that someone had called her name, Jakobav's voice, low and furious, laced with fear. But she held the threads anyway and pulled them tight. The shimmer shoved back, a raw current slamming into her arms until they shook and her knees threatened to buckle. She dragged harder.

"Shut," she hissed through her teeth. "Close."

The seam widened in defiance. She tasted oranges and smoke and something sweet, like Fae wine spilling across her tongue.

She thought of Orchid soil and the way her fire had always come when she called it. She wished she could burn the breach shut with something that belonged only to her, but she didn't have her flame, she had only this.

She steadied. The threads brightened beneath her grip, like they recognized her after all.

Finally, they surrendered.

The breach folded inward like a curtain pulled closed by an unseen hand, smoke vanishing into nothing. The hum in the air cut off so suddenly that the silence rang in its absence.

Ella swayed. The world tilted, despite the ground being solid beneath her boots. She would have gone down if Savina had not caught her forearm in a grip that was pure strength and only a trace of gentleness.

"Easy," Savina said.

Ella blinked up at her. Savina was close, eyes dark, the scar across her cheek pale against flushed skin. She looked the same as ever: furious, unflinching, ready to kill anything stupid enough to breathe near her, but something else glinted beneath it now. Something harder to hide. Respect dragged reluctantly into daylight.

"That was..." Savina's mouth tightened, as if the words themselves resisted her. "Impressive."

Ella stared. "Did you just compliment me?"

Savina's expression soured like she had bitten straight into a lemon. "Do not make me repeat it."

"I wouldn't dream of it," Ella said.

Savina's grip steadied her with a firmness that was almost protective.

"You were ordered to stand down, but you stepped toward the breach instead. No hesitation."

Something raw flashed behind her eyes, brief yet unmistakable.

"You know...I'm starting to think you belong here."

The words seemed painfully honest, and Ella forgot how to speak. The moment stretched too long, both fleeting and endless.

"I hope you decide to stay."

Ella's mouth went dry. She had no clever answer for that, only a breath held tightly, one that she couldn't seem to let go.

Savina cleared her throat as if to erase the softness. "Tomorrow...there are five phases to the Claiming," she said, tone clipped and practical again. "The one being Claimed gets to choose who stands with them in each phase, anchoring the rite. It's tradition and strategy both, and if Jake wakes tonight, you need to ask him to put your name forward. The High Vexari will want it finalized before the first bell."

"What are the five phases?" Ella asked, still catching her breath. Jakobav had changed the subject when Ella asked him questions about the High Vexari so it was unlikely that he would want or let Ella be a part of the ritual, but she didn't say that to Savina, not wanting to shatter the moment.

Savina gave a single nod. "Binding of Stone, Tempering of Mind, Warding of Earth, Anointing of Flesh, Claiming of Truth. Sounds dramatic, doesn't it? Really, it's just blood, dirt, oil, water, and a lot of theatrics." The ghost of a smile touched her mouth and died quickly. "I'm sure Bryn will call the fifth phase something ridiculous like bubbles and bath time. Ignore him."

"Savina," Bryn said from behind them, scandalized. "It does involve a sacred hot spring, and there are indeed bubbles."

"The sacred spring is not something to be downplayed. Or underestimated," Maeren snapped, approaching her and Savina with a pointed glance toward Ella and the place where the breach had been. "Good work."

Thane slung the creature's severed head into a sack with theatrical flourish. "Are we keeping this for décor? I know a spot in the great hall."

"Try your room," Savina said. "It'll pair nicely with the horrors that probably occur there," she muttered, smirking.

Soren's focus was fixed on Ella with unsettling intensity. She met his gaze, and he didn't look away. Instead of speaking, he gave the smallest tilt of his head and shifted his focus to Jakobav.

Shit, Jakobav.

They turned together.

Bryn had already pressed him back against the stone wall, hands moving quickly as he examined the wound. Blood streaked Bryn's fingers to the wrist. Jakobav's face had lost the color it wore when he was winning, and he seemed to be standing only by sheer refusal to do otherwise.

"Stop pretending you're granite," Bryn said flatly. "Granite bleeds less."

"How bad?" Maeren asked.

"Cracked at least," Bryn said without looking up. "Broken. The claws shredded through muscle but missed the lung, because fate has a twisted sense of humor. He needs rest, but please somebody, anybody, take his sword before he stabs me for suggesting it."

"I'll take it," Thane said while reaching out, offering to hold the weapon, but Jakobav's grip did not loosen on the hilt, seeming oblivious to the blood soaking his shirt or to Bryn's hands pressing into his side.

His gaze swept the courtyard until it found Ella. His voice didn't sound as furious as she'd expected. "Are you okay? What did you do?"

"Closed it," she said, and only then did she feel what it had cost, exhaustion and pain coursing through her veins. Still, she was standing, breathing, and that would have to count.

His focus jumped to her collarbone, to where her Orchid mark was now faded, nearly gone, and his mouth drew into a hard, flat line. "This isn't over. You disobeyed a direct order."

"Technically, Thane was the one who protested," she countered.

Shouts rose near the gate before he could answer. "Breach is gone!" a guard called, breathless. "Sealed completely."

The courtyard relaxed, soldiers sagging in relief before straightening again, as if reminded that their Commander still bled. Maeren shouted orders through the night. Torches swung high while one runner bolted toward the healers' quarters, and another sprinted to ring the all clear.

Savina was already barking instructions at the gate captain. Maeren returned and slid beneath Jakobav's arm without hesitation, bearing his weight as if it belonged to her alone. Thane fell in beside them, sack swinging over his shoulder, sword still in hand. Soren moved like a shadow wearing the shape of a man, sticking to the darkness along the wall. Somehow Jakobav kept moving.

Bryn walked backward to keep pace, voice brisk and relentless. "No more heroic lunges. No more frolicking in the gardens or tearing the sky open. Your injuries are questionable at best, so listen to me when I tell you, take shallow breaths and don't even think about sneezing."

Jakobav's jaw flexed, looking irritated by the effort of restraint.

"That's the spirit," Bryn said, utterly unfazed. "Spite heals."

"Spite is not a medical plan," Maeren muttered, bracing him harder when he shifted too quickly.

Thane glanced over his shoulder with a grin. "I don't know about that. Spite has worked for me."

Savina snorted. "You're too stubborn to die. That's not the same thing."

"But it's effective," Thane said cheerfully.

Jakobav didn't respond to any of it, and his eyes stayed forward, every step measured, his weight balanced between Maeren's shoulder and the stone wall. Ella kept close, ready to steady him, though she knew he'd rather bite her than lean on her.

His hand remained locked over that pocket like a man guarding the last secret he owned.

31

WAKE OF THE BLACK ROSE

Ella woke from a shallow, restless sleep to the sound of hurried footsteps rushing past the door. Solstice morning had arrived, and the palace moved with a purpose Ella felt in her bones. Not the quiet shuffle of servants setting about their daily tasks, but a tide of movement with urgency in every stride.

She turned her head and found Jakobav still lying beside her, stretched on his back with one arm cast over the sheet, the other resting protectively against his side where Bryn's stitching had closed the worst of last night's damage. His breathing was steady now, though she hadn't stopped counting each rise and fall through the long hours of night.

Not after the Tracker had stepped from smoke and shadow with its eyes fixed on him in a hunger that haunted her sleep and still tightened her stomach at the memory.

At some point during the night, his hand had found hers. The rough heat of his palm folded over her knuckles like a clasp locking shut, and she hadn't let go. It was the smallest of touches, nothing like the all-consuming lust of the garden, yet it was exquisite in its simplicity. She wasn't certain what they were to each other, but she knew this: Jakobav had carved himself into her life, and the thought of him stepping into the Claiming while injured left her hollow with worry.

The door burst open, and she was swept into motion before she could think. Maeren at one side, Savina at the other, and a cluster of attendants she didn't recognize surrounded her. They moved with choreographed urgency, robes folded and unfurled, braids pulled taut with deft fingers, bowls of shimmering oils set out, pear-sweet and juniper-crisp in the air until the chamber itself felt newly awakened.

Jakobav jolted awake at the commotion just as Thane strode in, followed by the lead attendant, Kalenya. Without hesitation, Thane ripped the covers back and clapped a hand on Jakobav's thigh in a rough, brotherly smack that made him wince. "Easy now," Thane said, grinning like he owned the room. "I've never known you to oversleep your call time. And I've definitely never found anyone else in your bed. Up. Dressed. Before I start making guesses about what you two did in here all night."

Kalenya, sharp-eyed and severe, gave a scandalized cough and fixed Thane with a glare meant to cut stone. He only grinned wider and blew her an unapologetic kiss, which earned him a muttered curse from someone near the braiding bowls.

"Careful, Thane," Ella said. "If you're that curious, I can leave the door open next time."

"How long is that offer good for?" Thane's grin spread into a full beam.

Jakobav's low growl cut the air, enough to still the entire chamber. Heads turned, a few attendants hesitating mid-motion, every eye caught by the exchange.

Her mouth curved, slow and deliberate. "Ask again when Jakobav isn't injured. I'll let him answer."

Jakobav rolled carefully to his feet, slow with pain but steady with will.

An attendant dropped to one knee, lacing his boots while Thane's fidgeting pushed the urgency forward.

Thane walked out. Jakobav stopped at the threshold and turned, his eyes locking on Ella's as though the rest of the chamber had ceased to exist. He only said, low and certain, "I'll see you in a few hours."

He started to leave, then paused. Something crossed his expression, and he glanced at the tray by her side before looking back at her face. His mouth curved with the faintest smirk. "Do not drink too much of that tea." Then he was gone, his shadow swallowed by the hall.

"You look like shit. Couldn't sleep?" Savina observed, her voice teasing as the sweep of her ice-blonde curls caught the light.

Ella gave her a dry smile. "Was I supposed to, after yesterday?"

Bryn drifted in through the open door and strolled toward her, holding a tray of steaming cups, the liquid inside a deep violet. "Ladies," he announced. "Your pre-Claiming tea. Heightens the senses and sharpens the mind. Makes the ceremony about three times as intense."

Ella eyed it warily. "What's in it?"

He shrugged. "Mostly flowers. A few roots. Some ingredients I'll leave unmentioned."

Maeren downed hers in one swallow. "I've survived this long, I'm not dying from ceremonial tea."

The others followed suit, slamming the cups like they were shots of Fae spirits. Ella took hers last, slow sip by slow sip, under Bryn's watchful eye.

"Interesting," he murmured. "The men in prep? Coughed, gagged, one of them even fainted. And you all just...drank it."

Savina smirked. "We're better equipped for most things."

Bryn grinned. "I've been saying that for years."

Warmth unfurled in Ella's chest, liquid sunlight blooming through her veins. The air felt richer, the torchlight more vibrant, every sound edged in silver. A few of the other women were giggling, shoulders bumping as they swayed where they stood. She almost laughed with them. This wasn't the grim, brutal preparation she'd imagined when she'd accused Dravaryns of clinging to barbaric rites.

If anything, there was a strange undercurrent of celebration. And somehow, they'd managed to keep this from the other kingdoms entirely, another secret in a land already famous for keeping them.

LED BY MAEREN, then Savina, the group swept her through the outer courtyard and up the sloped streets of the capital, Draethmar. The roar of the crowd began as a low hum in the distance, growing with each step Ella took.

They walked in comfortable chatter sprinkled with a few giggles from the effects of Bryn's potion-disguised-as-tea until the High Cathedral came into view. It loomed like a mountain's shadow against the dawn, its black spires veined with crimson light. The glass windows, deep garnet, onyx, and quartz, held the light captive, twisting beams of color into blood-tinted patterns. In the largest window above the cathedral's main doors, a black rose shimmered faintly, its petals rimmed in silver light.

Inside, the air was incense-thick, vibrating with the realm's heartbeat. Rows of carved stone benches rose toward balconies lined with blood-red windows, and black roses filled silver bowls along the aisle, their petals impossibly lush and alive.

Ella was fidgeting with her cuticles, nerves rising. Despite the sanctity of the space, she moved closer to Savina and whispered, "How do we get to the arena?"

Savina leaned in as they walked. "This cathedral sits on the ridge. The arena was built into the valley below." Her chin lifted toward the distant roar beneath their feet. "The people of Dravaryn enter through the arena gates. Only participants and those chosen by the royal court come down from here."

Ella's brow arched. Of course this kingdom would build a holy place directly above a battle arena. War and worship weren't separate here. They were two sides of the same spiritual blade.

They moved from the main aisle, past the altar, and out the balcony doors leading to an impressive terrace that was braced by exquisite pillars and arches. Beyond a carved archway, stone steps curved down, carrying them deeper into the ridge's bones. The hum of the crowd grew into a roar, and the air thickened, warmer now, tinged with steam.

They emerged into a sight that stole her breath.

The Grand Arena unfurled beneath the cathedral like a hidden heart, an enormous oval carved directly into the rock, its walls rising high and stands filled with thousands of Dravaryns, eager to observe the Rite.

Ella had expected a filthy training pit, maybe a dueling floor with weapons gleaming, and an audience hungry for blood, but this...this was not that.

The floor was a patchwork of rock and dirt, threaded with veins of glittering black obsidian. The patterns thickened near the center. A towering black tent had been erected there, its panels a heavy, ornate fabric, each corner anchored by iron spikes driven deep into the ground. From her vantage point, the seams were closed tight, but a faint curl of steam slipped out from the bottom edge and vanished into the air.

So this was where the sacred spring was held, hidden and guarded. She imagined what lay beneath that tent, a pool carved into open stone, a ceremonial grotto steaming in the dim light, a place meant for transformation. Whatever it was, the tent felt less like a cover and more like a shrine, guarding something ancient and alive.

Whatever lay inside was the final phase of the Claiming, the part Bryn had joked about until Maeren snapped at him, deadly serious. Dravaryn did not flaunt their rituals. They contained them, protected them, and revealed them only when it was time.

Set directly behind the tent was the Dravaryn crest, carved on a massive slab of dark stone: an ornate black rose in full bloom, a double-edged blade gleaming across its petals, and a winding script in an unfamiliar language.

She lifted her gaze, searching for him, but the crowd blurred into a sea of motion.

Then the roar surged, pulling her focus toward a lone figure near the tent. Jakobav stood there, the applause folding around him like a living thing. She'd heard he was beloved among his people, but seeing it was something else entirely; the sheer force of their devotion was overwhelming, their fervor a heat that brushed her skin. It made sense that Dravaryn adored a brutal prince with dangerous magic. But watching his power and heritage collide was a reckoning, one that shattered every expectation she had carried.

Still, Ella knew with certainty there was far more to him than that.

He was stripped to low-slung ceremonial trousers, every inch of his chest and arms marked in streaks of black ash that traced the ridges of muscle and the breadth of his shoulders.

Even bound and still healing, he looked as if he could tear the mountain apart with his bare hands, like he could hurl her over the peak and still catch her on the other side.

The tea in Ella's veins transformed the world into vivid, perilous color, the blue-white torchlight spilling from the arena walls turning the sheen of sweat on his skin into molten silver, sliding over the thick line of his throat and the cut of his jaw. His hair was loose today, dark waves brushing his shoulders, and the sight of it unbound tightened low in her belly.

Then he saw her. His gaze swept from the braided crown of hair to the shimmer of ritual oil glinting at her collarbone, lingered for a scorching heartbeat at her hips, and then locked with hers.

The crowd roared again, but all she registered was the slow, deliberate heat in his stare. A muscle ticked in his jaw, and his hand flexed at his side. Though the ceremonial trousers were meant for freedom of movement, they did nothing to hide the sudden, unmistakable evidence of how he was looking at her. He didn't seem to care that thousands were watching their future king stare at her like that. She should've been mortified. She wasn't.

Fuck. What is in that tea?

Whatever it was, it had stripped her of every last sense.

He didn't look away when her chin lifted, or when a slow blush crawled up her cheeks. Her pulse tripped so hard that she could feel it in her throat, and the corner of his mouth curved, not quite a smile, but something that told her he was promising things he could not give right now.

Ash clung to the tattoos on his arms and chest, turning the ink into something feral. The crowd might've been here to witness a ritual, but she could barely breathe past the truth that every line of him was built to ruin and remake. Even wounded, he moved like a man born for violence. The bindings across his ribs only emphasized the strength beneath.

And gods help her, if he looked at another woman the way he was looking at her now, she might burn the whole arena to the ground.

Shit. Where is this jealousy coming from?

No doubt Jakobav was to blame.

Maeren's hand closed around her elbow, guiding her through a narrow break in the crowd to a raised platform of stone along the arena's right flank. Thane and Soren were already there, dressed far finer than usual. Thane wore dark formal leathers embroidered in silver. Soren stood beside him in deep forest-green, the tailored coat cutting a clean, severe line across his shoulders.

They stood like sentinels beneath the Dravaryn crest carved high into the stone behind them. From this vantage, the entire arena opened beneath her: the black tent standing at its center, the sea of Dravaryn citizens in the stands, and the cathedral balcony high above.

"This is where we hold," Maeren murmured, her voice pitched low enough to be swallowed by the roar.

Ella glanced between them, realizing she wasn't just standing with his friends. She was in the place reserved for his blood and battle-bound family, the thought making her spine straighten.

Ella swallowed and leaned toward Maeren. "Where's the king?"

Maeren's jaw tightened. "He isn't coming."

Ella opened her mouth, but Maeren shook her head once.

A ripple moved through the crowd as a woman in black robes stepped into view, emerging from the tent's shadow. The hem of her garments whispered along the ground, and her face was marked with dark ink patterns. In her hand, a staff of black Dravaryn glass caught the torchlight. The energy of the crowd shifted, as if acutely aware of the power she carried.

Before Ella could confirm who she was, Maeren leaned in. "The High Vexari. She speaks for the realm."

The Vexari lifted her staff, and the noise of thousands died to a charged silence.

Her gaze swept the arena tiers, solemn as a severed vow.

"By blood, by realm, by rite," her voice rang out, deep and resonant, carrying to every last ear. "We call forth the truth of this mortal realm. Let it rise in the one chosen. Let it burn away falsehood. Let it claim what is his."

But then, instead of turning to Jakobav, she addressed the crowd.

"This is no ordinary Claiming." Her tone was reverent, threaded with iron. "Today, the rightful heir to the Dravaryn Throne stands before you, not just as your future King, but as the commander of the military resurgence keeping this kingdom whole."

A ripple went through the audience, and the High Vexari's staff lowered slightly, as if to punctuate each word.

A sudden chill skated across Ella's skin.

"You've heard the rumors," she continued. "You've felt the strain in your magic. You have seen the signs: breaches in the Veil, the unmaking of our wards. Your Prince and his First Guard are facing these horrors to protect you."

Her voice held a current of fierce pride.

"So it should be no surprise that today's rite carries greater weight than any in living memory. If the ritual succeeds, it may not only bind his power, but it may steady the realm itself, and restore the full strength of your magic. Watch closely, Dravaryn, for you stand witness to history."

The crowd erupted, fists pounding against stone and

weapons striking in rhythm until the sound became thunderous, rolling through the arena.

A realization shot through her, halting her mid-thought.

He hadn't hidden it from them.

Not the breaches. Not his role in stopping them. The entire kingdom knew, and still they cheered for him, not from fear but from vehement, unshaken loyalty.

When she looked at their faces, she saw the truth clearly: they would die for him—and kill for him without hesitation.

She still held far too many secrets for that to be comforting.

32

THE CLAIMING

Her chest tightened. Gods, she was once again forced to confront how wrong she had been. She had been raised to believe Dravaryns were cold and cruel, bound only by blood and fear, yet what she saw in their faces was not so different from the devotion she'd known in Orchid. Passion that burned bright, loyalty given freely, a love for their Prince that no threat could shake.

Jakobav stepped forward then, bare feet on dark stone, eyes fixed on the tent.

Maeren, Savina, Thane, Bryn, and Soren flanked her, standing straight and still, unwavering at their posts like immortal guardians.

An attendant stepped from the tent, carrying a heavy, black-handled mug that steamed in the cool air. She approached the High Vexari and bowed, presenting it with both hands. The Vexari accepted the vessel, lifted it, and turned toward Jakobav.

Even from the raised platform, Ella knew that color—deep

violet, the same tea Bryn had given them earlier. Nothing else in Dravaryn glowed quite like that brew.

Jakobav didn't spare the Vexari a glance when she offered it. His eyes were locked on Ella, steady and unblinking, the roar of the arena thinning beneath the force of that stare.

He took the mug in one hand, lifted it, and drank. The entire thing was gone in a single, unbroken pull. When he lowered the mug, his lips were slick with violet. She forgot how to breathe.

He licked it slowly from his bottom lip, never once breaking eye contact with her. Had he meant to remind her of exactly what that tongue could do, of how he had taken her apart against the garden hedges with nothing but his mouth? Gods, help her. She felt as though they were the only two in the arena, instead of thousands of Dravaryns who had no idea the heir of their rival kingdom stood in their midst.

The way his gaze fixated on her, almost daring her to look away, was indecent in a way no touch could match.

He'd accused her of being a distraction, and right now, she'd never felt more like one, a sick satisfaction twisting inside her. The Jakobav she first met would have belonged only to his people today, to his fate, to the power waiting to choose him.

It shouldn't matter. But it did.

A strange lightness drifted through her limbs, as if her body briefly forgot the simple act of being.

When the Vexari spoke again to announce the first phase, Maeren's boots scraped the ground as she left Ella's side.

"First, the Binding of Stone."

Maeren strode to Jakobav, a blade carved from pale rock in her hand. Without hesitation, she sliced her palm and pressed it to his chest, crimson blooming over the ash painted on his heart. "The stone remembers," she murmured.

The ground hummed, the low vibration sinking deep into the earth.

She returned to Ella's side without a glance, the cut already sealing. Strange.

"Second, the Tempering of Mind."

Savina's silver-mesh gloves caught the light as she crossed the floor. She cupped Jakobav's jaw and temples, her words spilling too fast for Ella to catch. The tang of ozone filled the air, and Jakobav's eyes flared metallic before dimming again.

Savina stepped back, lips twitching faintly, and rejoined her place beside Ella.

"Third, the Warding of Earth."

Soren walked barefoot to Jakobav, his silence somehow louder than the crowd. He held a lump of rich, dark soil. He pressed it to Jakobav's palms. The arena floor groaned, cracks spidering outward, threads of obsidian racing like veins toward the tent.

Without a word, Soren turned and returned to Ella's side. What the hell was that?

"Fourth, the Anointing of Flesh."

Bryn sauntered forward with a shallow silver bowl. Steam curled up, carrying the scent of pear and juniper. He tipped it slowly, oil sliding in gilded rivulets over Jakobav's chest and shoulders. Jakobav's throat worked as Bryn's fingers spread the shimmer over skin and muscle, lingering just long enough to draw whistles from the crowd.

Bryn smirked, patted him twice on the chest, and returned to Ella.

The Vexari's staff struck stone, and the tent shuddered, its seams rippling as a rush of steam escaped into the air.

"Final phase, the Claiming of Truth," she announced. "Hand selected by the Prince, this duty falls to Thane Ironfell—"

"Not today." Jakobav's voice cut through the arena like a blade.

Silence rippled through the stands.

Even Thane's head snapped toward him, brows lifting.

Jakobav never looked away from Ella. "The final Rite will be performed by Ellandria of Orchid."

Ella's heartbeat slammed against her ribs, loud enough she could feel it in her teeth.

Fuck. Did she imagine that, or did he just announce her to his entire kingdom?

Her knees threatened to buckle.

The murmur that swept the crowd was incredulous.

Even the Vexari's inked face stiffened, her dark markings seeming to writhe in the torchlight. "Prince," she said, her voice dripping with distaste, "her name was not submitted for the final phase. You tread outside the Rite."

Jakobav didn't flinch. "She has walked our halls as both guest and prisoner. She has fought beside us, bled for us, and faced the breach when others faltered. I name her before all of Dravaryn, not as an enemy, but as the one I trust with the heart of my Claiming."

The Vexari's gaze lingered on him a heartbeat too long. Then her staff struck the rock, the sound echoing like a warning bell. "So be it," she intoned, her expression darkening. She lowered her voice. "But know this, Prince. When you alter the Rite, it alters you. And the realm will remember."

Gasps broke like waves, and Ella's pulse thudded in her ears. Thane's mouth curved into a smirk as he stalked toward her.

"Since you're stealing my part," he murmured for her ears alone, "I'll at least see you enter it properly. Required to enter the sacred waters."

His hands found the knot at her ceremonial gown. One

smooth pull, and the silk slid from her shoulders to pool at her feet.

The sound the crowd made went from commotion to havoc, ranging from shouting to applause.

She stood naked before them—the thousands of Dravaryns who now knew exactly who she was: Ellandria of Orchid, the lost heir. But it wasn't only her body laid bare. It was everything she'd dragged to this moment: years of self-chosen exile, the bloody path to an enemy stronghold, the prophecy she'd never wanted and couldn't outrun. Now, stripped beneath the eyes of a kingdom, she wasn't merely exposed to Dravaryn—she was exposed to Orchid as well. Word would spread. Her people would learn where she'd gone, what she'd done. And the fallout...gods, she couldn't afford to think about that now.

Jakobav's gaze swept over her, unhurried and certain.

The heat in his eyes burned through her.

"Come," he said, extending his hand. It wasn't a request. It wasn't quite a command. It was possession dressed as an invitation.

Ella placed her hand in his, and the arena blurred as he drew her forward.

The High Vexari's voice rose over the murmuring tiers.

"Clear the shroud. Bare the witness."

At once, attendants rushed forward, black-and-silver robes flaring as they moved in perfect sync. Ropes were loosed, stakes drawn up, and the heavy silk walls of the tent collapsed inward before being pulled away entirely. Steam rolled outward from the hot spring and billowed into the chilled air, curling around Ella's skin and causing her nipples to tighten, but she refused to be ashamed.

She was honored that Jakobav had chosen her.

The spring at the center wasn't just a pool, but more like a living thing, larger than any courtyard fountain yet bottomless at its heart, its surface reflecting molten gold shifting over black petals caught in a current. Heat rolled off in pulsing waves.

From deep below, a low, continuous murmur seemed to rise through the water and seep into her soul. She couldn't quite make out the words, or maybe it was incoherent syllables.

Is it possible for a body of water to murmur? Can anyone else hear that?

She stood at the top of the steps into the hot spring, bare to the air and to the truth of who she was. And though thousands watched, it wasn't shame that rooted her in place; it was destiny.

Jakobav had undressed at the top of the stairs and was already halfway down, steam wrapping around the planes of his chest and shoulders like it couldn't decide whether to caress or consume him. At the last step, with the water licking at his hips, he glanced back over his shoulder.

"Come, Ella," he said, holding out his hand. Not a command she could refuse.

Her bare foot touched the first step, stone warm beneath her sole, and the scent of pear, juniper, and mineral heat wrapped around her as she descended. At first, she could still touch the bottom, her toes gripping smooth rock. But as they moved toward the center, the slope dropped away until the water was holding her entirely.

The inner circle took their places at the edge: Maeren's blade still bloodied from Phase One, Savina's silver-mesh gloves sparking faintly in the steam, Soren barefoot and bent forward with his palm on the arena floor, Thane's eyes fixed on her with a private, unreadable smile, and Bryn grinning like he already knew the outcome.

They stood evenly spaced, forming a living ward around the spring.

The attendant's voice carried to her from across the water. "Guide him. If the fates find him worthy, they will draw him below. Keep one hand beneath his back, the other at his thigh, and lead him to the center. Only there may he be taken."

Ella swallowed. "And if they don't?"

The attendant's expression did not change. "Then he will not rise with new power. Or he may not rise at all. And this day will be remembered for a very different reason."

The water shimmered as Jakobav turned onto his back, muscles shifting under the molten light. "Ready?"

No. Absolutely not.

But she nodded.

Her hand slid beneath the small of his back, the other cupping the solid weight of his thigh, a low current rolling off of him, stirring the water around her fingers. Slowly, she guided him forward.

The hum beneath them deepened.

They reached the center, where the gold gave way to inky black, and nothing happened at first. Then the sacred pool answered and didn't wait for them to be ready.

Its surface split open with a force like a thousand hands and dragged Jakobav beneath. He vanished in a rush of bubbles, his body wrenched down into the black.

The crowd erupted in shouted prayers and gasps.

Ella stayed frozen, chest tight, eyes fixed on where he had gone under. The heat of the hot spring pressed into her head, dizzying, her skin prickling as the steam bubbled. Something ancient stirred beneath the surface, a magic that felt older than the mortal realm, and every instinct she had screamed that this water wasn't ceremonial at all.

She turned and started for the steps, not knowing what else to do.

The gold threads in the water curled toward her wrists like molten bindings.

"Shit."

The spring seized her and dragged her under in a single, merciless motion, her body plunging in after him without her permission.

The pool's golden veins wrapped around her wrists like chains, and the water closed around her head, into her chest, suffocating, turning the world briefly into blackness.

When the water calmed and Ella could see again, she scanned the pool frantically, searching for Jakobav but not knowing which way was up. Finally, she found him caught in the depths, his body bent by the pull, his ribs bound not by Bryn's stitching but by threads of light coiled around his chest like serpents. Each pulsing contraction drove him deeper, forcing the air from his lungs, breaking him piece by piece.

Fuck. Why isn't he fighting more?

He was going to suffocate and drown if he didn't move.

She kicked toward him despite the water's pull rocking her in every direction. The gold threads pulsed, constricting tighter, and she swore she heard them whisper: *Broken. Let him fall.*

Panic cleaved her in two.

No. This can't be happening.

Every nerve in her body sparked as she reached for him. She tore at the golden threads with her bare hands, pain streaking through her palms as if the fire of her Orchid blood was colliding with the sacred magic of the pool. Heat flared under her skin, her tattoo burning so bright it lit the water around them in pale green-gold light. The threads hissed, recoiled, then tangled again, more of them, endless, knotting across his ribs until his chest shuddered once and stilled.

I can't let Maeren lose another to this cursed water—gods, not again.

And if he drowns here, what then?

What of the prophecy? The relic I've chased across kingdoms?

Prophecy be damned—I need him alive.

She sealed her mouth over his, forcing breath into him, the intimate press of lips made fierce and desperate by the certainty that he was slipping from her. He jerked beneath her touch, and his eyes opened, wild and glazed, locking with hers through the water. She fisted his hair floating around him in waves, tugging gently as if it could help force the air into his lungs.

Suddenly, he responded with a bite that was soft but had pierced her skin nonetheless. He'd tasted her, even here, and she felt it...that strange prickle of his Blood-Scent magic brushing across her.

The threads quivered but didn't tighten; instead they seemed to be listening.

Then came the other voice that wasn't Jakobav's, and it wasn't her own; it was the pool itself. The realms, speaking through the current: *Not just him. Take her. We want her. We have not tasted the fireblood of Orchid in centuries. Take her. Take her. TAKE HER.*

The golden threads ripped away from his chest and coiled around hers instead, spearing through the water like a net. They wrapped her wrists, her throat, her ankles, dragging her down with a hunger that was not Dravaryn's, but older, darker, and endless.

Her lungs convulsed, her body twisting as she reached for him, and her only anchor was his fingers still laced with hers.

He was weak, bleeding, broken, but he didn't let her go. His jaw clenched, his lips bared, and then he moved with a savagery that appeared both instinct and choice, tugging their laced fingers close to his face with all the force he seemed to have left. His mouth closed over her wrist, teeth driving deep until blood bloomed in the water like a living flame, seeping outward until the water seemed to burn bright red.

He drank her in, deeper than ever before, and her entire body blazed as though he were siphoning the sun from her veins.

The pool recoiled, and the threads loosened, as if confused, writhing like they were tasting her magic in *his* blood and breaking the pattern they'd sought to weave. Jakobav seized their hesitation and surged upward, pulling her with him, as if reforged in the furnace of her veins.

Her lungs strained, her vision searing at the edges, and with brutal clarity, she understood: if Jakobav faltered, the spring would claim her whole, pulling her into its depths like a prized treasure, never to see the light again. But Jakobav's grip was iron, his arm banded around her waist as he kicked with the strength of a man who refused any fate but his own.

The water churned in their wake, the whispers howling now, a cacophony of rage and desire: *She is ours. She is ours. She is ours.*

The last of her breath spilled from her lips, but then his mouth found hers again, fierce and consuming, giving her the air he had stolen from her just as he had stolen her blood. It was not a kiss, not entirely. It was survival, and yet it singed through her soul, as if it were both.

They broke the surface in a violent rush, gasping into air and steam, her body clinging to his. Above the water, the arena held its breath. Then a single scream split the stillness, answered by another, until the stands roared to life like a storm given voice.

The pool shrieked beneath them, golden light splintering into black before vanishing altogether, leaving only the calm surface and the sound of their ragged breaths. The crowd's roar rose behind it, swelling like a tide.

They had emerged alive. They had emerged together.

And as Jakobav staggered up the steps with Ella in his arms, the world saw what neither of them could deny... His was no ordinary Claiming. It had taken them both.

33

SHIELDING THE FIRE

A plume of vapor surged from the spring's surface and into the cool morning air. The roar of the crowd faltered, caught in the throats of thousands, until an unnatural hush fell over the Grand Arena.

She was on fire.

Not metaphorically.

Flames curled from her hair, danced over her shoulders, wound down her arms to lick the water still dripping from her skin. They burned white-gold, the color of lightning behind closed eyes, shimmering through the rising steam. Her skin was unmarked, her breath steady. This was not the wild, uncontrolled blaze she'd feared for years.

This was all her. Ella's Orchid magic was wholly her own again.

Realization hit all at once. She was naked before them—bare to thousands—the fire crowning every inch of her. A jolt of vulnerability shot through her, instinct sending her toward Jakobav's arms, toward shelter, the flames exposing her in ways nakedness never could.

He caught her without hesitation, hauling her tight against him. The wet heat of her body met the slick coolness of his skin, steadying, comforting, and she forgot about the arena's crowd.

Jakobav had risen from the final phase alive, power singing against hers like steel meeting steel.

The flames answered her need, flaring higher, and she pressed closer without meaning to. The answering pressure of his body met hers, sensual and slow enough to make her breath catch. His arm tightened around her, a low sound catching in his throat that was part growl and part claim, holding her as though clinging to a victory the entire kingdom now witnessed.

She realized he wasn't burning.

The flames spilled over his shoulders, curling down his arms, but left no mark. An unseen power shimmered in the air around him, bending the heat away from his flesh without breaking their hold on each other.

Her breath caught as the flames climbed higher across her bare skin, bright and wild. "My fire," she whispered, hardly daring to believe it, though she could still feel the ghost-touch of the golden strands that had tried to drag her underwater. She'd evaded their grasp, but she couldn't shake the thought that there'd be a cost for her power restored outside Orchid soil.

She said none of it aloud. Instead, she lifted her gaze to him and confessed, quiet and certain, "The sacred water brought it back. It Claimed me."

She watched her flames roll against his skin but leave him untouched, unease sparking in her chest with a fleeting thought. Was her fire broken?

The look on her face must've told him what she didn't say.

He spoke low and steady, his voice carrying the weight of

absolute truth. "You will not burn me," he said. "Not anymore."

Ella blinked at him in disbelief. "What do you mean, not anymore? And—" Her eyes narrowed as she whispered, "Why didn't you tell me you were going to announce who I am?"

His jaw flexed. "It wasn't exactly planned."

"Nothing with you ever is," she countered, though her voice trembled with the shifting weight of the moment. "So what happens now? Jakobav, what—"

"I'll explain everything," he said, low but urgent, leaning in until she could feel the warning in his voice. "But your safety hinges on what happens next. Do exactly as I say."

High above, the High Vexari had started to draw the crowd's gaze, staff in hand, her inked face darkening. Her eyes followed every ember unfurling from Ella's skin to Jakobav's, and in their black depths, calculation gleamed with something deeper than ritual.

Movement at the edge of the spring pulled Ella's focus. Attendants surged forward with arms full of heavy ceremonial robes, hurrying toward the steps, reaching out as if to drape the fabric over both of them.

But the flames hadn't dimmed.

They swept down Ella's arms in a sudden, eager flare, spilling outward.

Maeren stepped closer, her expression etched with something that twisted in Ella's chest—concern and maybe shock. Gods. It had to have been triggering, watching them struggle beneath the water, unsure if they were drowning. Had she been reliving the nightmare of her brother's Claiming?

What is Maeren feeling now?

Her pulse spiked, and with it, her power.

"Ella," Jakobav said, voice low and urgent. "Could you rein it in, please?"

She tried. The fire answered by leaping higher.

Maeren lifted a hand, motioned the attendants back, positioning herself between them and Ella's still-raging flame.

"Maeren, wait—" Ella's cry tore out, panicked, protective.

Too late.

A tendril of fire snapped outward, curling toward Maeren as if it recognized her. The steel at her wrist caught the light a heartbeat before the flame raced higher toward bare skin.

Maeren shouted, reflexively raising her arms to block it. But before the fire could land, Jakobav moved with unnatural speed, his arm locking around Ella's waist and twisting them both until he stood between Maeren and the strike. The shimmer around him surged outward, snapping into a dome that flared bright enough to swallow Maeren from sight.

The flames slammed into it and broke, deflected harmlessly away.

The shield vanished as quickly as it had formed.

Maeren lowered her arm, flexing her reddened hand once, her eyes narrowing as she looked from Ella to Jakobav. "New trick?" she asked, the bite in her tone undercut by the faint tremor in her fingers.

Jakobav's mouth curved, a note of intensity shaping his voice. "I learn quickly when it comes to protecting those I care about."

Attendants approached again, this time with ceremonial robes of rich fabric layered with inked designs. But the moment one brushed Ella's arm, the cloth ignited with a hiss. The attendant jerked back, dropping the robe before the flames could catch their hands, and it crumbled into blackened ash at their feet.

Gasps rippled through the closest rows of spectators.

Jakobav swore under his breath, steadying her as the flames around her surged upward. "Soren," he commanded, jaw tight, “my chambers. Bring one of the garments I had Kalenya make for her—now.”

Soren vanished instantly, Earth-Vating into the stone like a shadow swallowed whole.

Another attendant stepped forward with a robe for Jakobav, but he shook his head once.

Thank the gods. He isn’t leaving me uncovered alone.

The crowd erupted, their voices surging all at once into chaos—cheers, boots hammering against stone. The High Vexari’s voice cut through the noise, cracking like a whip, summoning guards, attendants, and ceremonial stewards with commands that echoed across the arena.

The eruption swelled, deafening, but then faltered, thinning into uneasy murmurs as the crowd seemed to sense a shift. The arena fell silent as mist drifted thicker across the floor, and beneath it, a presence twisted like a shadow taking shape. The High Vexari was no longer above them. She was at the water’s edge, robes whispering against stone, her inked face foreboding in its calm, unreadable expression.

In three soundless strides, she was face to face with them, staff lifted high. With a crack, she drove it into the stone right beside them, leaving it upright and quivering as if rooted there by the realm itself.

She reached for their hands, cutting through Ella’s fire without hesitation, seizing their wrists at once. Ella’s flames, shrunk back at the touch but still kissed her flesh, reddening her fingers.

“Show me,” she hissed.

Her grip was iron, turning their palms up in the same swift motion, exposing skin to light. The High Vexari didn’t flinch, nor did she loosen her hold as her gaze darted between their upturned wrists. The steam gathered on her lashes as her face changed from disbelief to fury. A vein rose at her temple like a cord drawn tight.

"What have you done, Prince?" she asked, almost a whisper.

Ella looked down and saw it only because the Vexari made her see. A small black rose had bloomed on the inside of her wrist, ink dark as midnight, seemingly carved into the skin. Jakobav bore its twin, and the sight of it tilted her world.

It sat exactly where his teeth had closed over her, where his mouth filled with her blood beneath the water. The skin around the rose was raised and hot, as if it had been branded.

Sweat broke along her spine. Her knees almost slipped on the stone.

The High Vexari didn't look at her. She held both wrists like evidence and fixed Jakobav with a gaze that could have split rock.

She'd never seen someone so terrifying in ceremonial robes.

"We have kept outsiders from the sacred waters for five centuries," she said, voice deepening as the cathedral's weight gathered behind it. "This is why. An outsider has been Claimed, Jakobav."

The name struck like a verdict. She released his wrist last, almost with contempt, and her voice rose, cold as iron.

"Two souls should never be Claimed at once. You have broken a law older than your line. You have contaminated the sacred spring." She turned to look at Ella. "And both of you will pay for this."

Ella shuddered, and her flames guttered out at once.

Jakobav adjusted his shoulders, fury leaching from his posture, and his expression was that of a man who would not yield. "Enough," he said, quiet and dangerous. "Mind your place."

She leaned in so close Ella could taste pear and juniper and the scorched-skin scent of her burned hand.

"All of Orchid will pay for this," she murmured. "If they accept you at all. Unlike your kingdom's fickle ink, this mark will never fade. The rose endures. You are bound to it forever... and to all the spring poured into you."

Jakobav stepped between them, the movement so familiar it felt inevitable. "That is enough," he said, and this time, the command carried the room.

He took Ella's hand from her tight grasp and turned, drawing her away, and the inner circle closed around them like a shield.

"Prince." The High Vexari's voice rang after them. "You will meet me in the High Cathedral. Two weeks. Do not make me come find you."

Jakobav didn't look back.

The inner circle moved.

The mist billowing from the sacred pool swallowed the High Vexari's silhouette, as if the spring had taken her in.

Ella barely had time to breathe before the inner circle was herding her out of the arena. Thane cleared a path with his voice raised like rolling thunder, Savina barked orders to the nearest guards, Maeren following close at Ella's heels.

Soren Earth-Vated right into the ground, bypassing the chaos entirely, and reappeared right next to her. "Main gate secured," he said to Jakobav.

They moved together, the six of them folding in tight formation into the shadowed labyrinth beneath the cathedral. The roar of the crowd faded the farther they moved down into the tunnels. The corridors pressed close, their damp walls breathing with the scent of moss and rotted wood. Shadows crawled over the carvings etched into the stone, twisting across ancient scriptwork as torchlight flared against them. The air was heavy, yet cooler than the spring above, each step drawing them deeper into the mountain's veins.

Ella's fire had lit back to a faint smolder, glowing around her wrists and the ends of her hair like stubborn embers, heat radiating off her in restless waves. She should have extinguished it, called the flame back, yet after years of absence, she simply couldn't bring herself to smother it.

Jakobav's arm never left her waist as they moved, his body an unyielding barrier against the crush of attendants and guards trying to fall in step.

Thane strode ahead, his voice cutting through the corridor. "Clear the passage! If you're not First Guard, get out of my sight."

Behind them, Savina's orders rang out. "Seal the upper levels. No one leaves until names and loyalties are confirmed."

And Bryn, of course, walked backward in front of them, as if none of the chaos had touched him. "Not to interrupt this very intimidating march," he said cheerfully, "but in case anyone missed it, that was the single most dramatic Claiming in Dravaryn history, and I've attended seventy-eight."

"Seventy-nine," Maeren corrected dryly, still flexing her reddened hand.

Bryn's eyes glinted. "Yes, but who's counting? This one? This one will be sung about for decades. Possibly with more revelation than ritual." His gaze flicked to Ella.

She kept her chin lifted, unwilling to let emotion rise. "Don't assume all will survive to sing about it, healer."

"That's the spirit," Bryn said brightly, twisting to avoid running into a wood column, as though this were nothing more than a stroll.

Soren emerged from ahead of them, stepping under a torchlight. In his hands was a folded garment, dark and sleek.

Jakobav took it from him with a curt nod and turned to Ella, extending it out to her. "Here. Put this on."

Ella blinked at the thing in his hands. It wasn't a tunic. It wasn't armor. It was...a dress. Fitted. Structured. Meant to move.

"You had a dress made for me?" she asked, breath hitching. "I don't think I should wear it. I'd hate to destroy it like I did the robe."

Jakobav didn't flinch. "Kalenya told me you asked for clothing you could fight in weeks ago. Something you could hide blades beneath." His eyes roamed over her flames, softening for half a heartbeat. "I made some changes to your request. Fireproofed. Reinforced."

Ella stared, struggling to form words. "Fireproofed," she echoed. "So you...anticipated this?"

"Not this," Jakobav said quietly. "But I thought your power might return one day. I knew the fire in your blood wasn't gone. Not really."

Her throat tightened. "So when you said—" Her voice trailed off, hovering between accusation and awe.

Jakobav held the garment out to her, his expression unreadable but his voice steady. "Get dressed, Ella. We need to hurry."

He stepped back just enough to give her space, though his gaze never fully left her. Ella took the dress, half expecting her flames to consume it too, but the material only shimmered in the heat, untouched.

The shimmer caught her breath. She knew that glint.

It was the same strange Dravaryn leather she'd noticed in the first gown Kalenya ever gave her. She'd worn it the night she stumbled into the black rose garden, believing it was a rare hide she'd never seen before.

Understanding unfurled like a slow, startling pulse. She'd worn it before.

That hadn't been ordinary leather at all.

He'd been protecting her, even then.

She slipped into the dress quickly, the leather-like material molding to her skin, protective yet impossibly light, as if made with magic. Only when she was fully covered did Jakobav turn, jaw set, and lead them onward, but her heartbeat didn't settle. Not after that.

They reached the heavy iron doors of the war room. Soren was already waiting there, leaning against the wall like he had known their exact pace. "Perimeter's secure," he said simply, before pushing the door wide. Inside, all noise fell away, leaving only the tense crack of Maeren's knuckles, as though she were readying herself for battle. The long table gleamed beneath a black-iron chandelier, maps and ledgers spread across its surface.

Jakobav didn't leave her side until they crossed the threshold.

When he did, it wasn't abrupt but intentional, as though setting something valuable exactly where it belonged.

In truth, she wasn't entirely sure where she belonged now.

Her Orchid tattoo and the new rose mark pulsed once—two heartbeats out of sync.

34

THE RIPPLE AND THE RIDGE

The war room carried the echo of the spring and the roar of thousands still ringing in her bones, raw and waiting to fracture. She stood very still, one hand braced against the edge of the table, letting her breath return in shallow threads.

Maeren was the first to break it, planting her palms flat against the granite. "The arena will be in chaos for hours. Half the crowd will swear it was a blessing. The other half will think it's the beginning of a war."

"It is," Savina said flatly, pulling the silver mesh gloves from her hands with deliberate movements. "They just don't know which one yet."

Thane leaned back against the wall, folding his arms across his chest. "We need to get ahead of this before Orchid sends an envoy. Or an army."

Ella's palms pressed harder into the table, the cold stone biting into her skin. "They will respond. The question is how. Has there been contact?" She tried to sound casual, but the eagerness in her tone betrayed her.

"I think," Savina replied, eyes narrowing, "that they'll hear about a bare, burning Orchid princess in our capital, standing beside the future King of Dravaryn, and some conclusions might be drawn. Ones that we may not like."

Bryn dropped into a chair, stretching out as if this were no more than a tavern quarrel. "In fairness, those conclusions won't be entirely wrong."

Jakobav's voice was low, a rumble that silenced the room at once. "Enough."

He stepped to Ella's side, his presence grounding her.

"We'll test our new abilities away from the city, and then we worry about the repercussions. Claimed magic is unpredictable at first. My shield held, but I refuse to gamble with any of your lives." His hand brushed hers briefly before his gaze returned to the table. "Maeren, Thane, and Savina, choose a location we can secure. Bryn, you're with us."

Maeren's brows drew together. "And if the High Vexari demands an account while we're gone?"

Jakobav's eyes darkened like polished glass. "Then she'll get one. But not all of it. Soren will assess the risk before I meet with her again."

For a long moment, no one moved. Then, one by one, clipped words replaced silence as they spoke of routes, supplies, and contingencies. The cadence was brisk, but beneath it, disbelief was still heavy in the air. Their words were little more than scaffolding built to contain what none of them fully understood yet: the Claiming and the fallout.

She stayed where she was, warmth swelling in her chest, a strange certainty that whatever had just happened in that spring, whatever the fates had demanded, had bound her to this circle.

By the time they left the war room, the afternoon sun had climbed high enough to set the cathedral's black spires blazing with light. The brightness hit Ella hard after the dim tunnels, forcing her eyes to narrow as Jakobav strode ahead, his pace unrelenting.

The remaining six of them fell into motion behind him. Ella kept step near the middle of the group, the formation tightening every time a passerby turned to look at her.

Jakobav didn't slow as he crossed the courtyards, his stride cutting through attendants and guards until they reached the stables. Their horses were already saddled. Soren must have sent word ahead.

Jakobav mounted in a single motion, reins tight in his fist. "We leave now," he said, his voice carrying a command loud enough for the entire castle to hear. "South Ridge."

Thane frowned as he swung into his saddle, broad shoulders shifting with the motion. "We could test closer to the city."

"Closer means witnesses," Jakobav replied, his tone final, enough to close the subject. "The fewer eyes, the better."

They set out at once, hooves striking sparks from the cobbles.

As they rode through the outskirts of Draethmar, Ella realized that word of the Claiming had already outrun them; the few who hadn't crowded into the arena, travelers and servants bound to their posts, had clearly heard what took place.

From balconies, voices rose in Jakobav's name, fists lifted in fervor, while in the courtyards below others gathered in clusters, whispering behind their hands as their eyes followed Ella's every step. A pair of merchants dropped to one knee when Jakobav passed, while a cloaked woman gasped and staggered back as Ella's shadow stretched across the dust at her feet.

The attention scraped at her nerves.

Bryn gave a low whistle that carried on the morning air. "Well. The kingdom's talking, at least."

"They always talk," Savina muttered, her voice cold as steel. "The trouble starts when they act."

The city of Draethmar soon fell behind them, its rooftops swallowed by distance.

The air grew crisp as the road climbed, the forest thinning into ragged slopes. The ridges rose in stark lines against the horizon, serrated like the spine of some long-dead beast.

Something about the ridge's shape tugged at her memory —the faint glint of scales she'd thought she imagined on the night she first Threadwalked. She had dismissed it then, blaming shock and fear, because flying creatures with scales like that had been vanquished from the mortal realm for more than five centuries. But as sunlight struck the spine of the mountain again, a shiver threaded through her. Maybe their lineage wasn't buried after all. At least...not in every realm.

The farther they pressed on, the stranger the world became. The wind shifted in uneven currents that tugged at their clothes and whispered against their ears like half-heard voices. Light bent oddly in places, shadows stretching longer than they should, crawling across stone outcrops and skeletal trees that clung stubbornly to the slopes.

Bryn was the first to break the silence. "You realize no one comes here on purpose, right?"

"That's exactly why we are going," Jakobav said, gaze fixed forward, unflinching.

"Most avoid it for fear of losing their minds," Bryn continued, still irreverent, though his eyes focused uneasily on the uneven horizon. "The Ridges don't just warp the air, they warp you. Thoughts get twisted, emotions heightened, sometimes for days afterward."

Perfect. Exactly what she needed. More emotions. She was barely holding herself together as it was.

Jakobav's reply was steady, almost too calm. "We'll handle it."

No one argued.

When they reached the wide clearing beyond South Ridge, Jakobav was the first to dismount. The others followed, the motion practiced, wordless. Without needing direction, they spread into formation: Maeren pacing east with her hand on her blade, Savina and Bryn taking the west, Thane and Soren flanking Jakobav like pillars at his back. Ella stepped into place opposite him, the wind pulling loose strands of her hair across her cheek as if to test her composure.

Jakobav's eyes found hers across the clearing. "Out here, the damage is ours alone to bear," he said, voice carrying into the stillness. "What we brought back from the spring is untested. If it breaks loose in the city, we risk more than whispers and rumors."

Ella lifted her chin, though her pulse rattled fast against her ribs. "So you brought me here to burn you again?"

The faintest smirk tugged at his mouth. "If that's what it takes."

She let out a breath that was half a laugh. "Then you should hope the fates are still feeling generous."

The smirk sharpened into provocation.

He lifted his hand, and the air around him distorted, light bending into a translucent shield that spread outward in a soft, opalescent curve. It hummed faintly in the silence. Ella's magic stirred in response, heat pricking along her palms. She lifted them, fire spilling in white-gold arcs that licked toward the barrier.

The flames broke against his shield like surf against a cliff, dissolving into harmless mist. Jakobav's voice cut through the trees, low and commanding. "Again."

Ella drew her fire back, then let it unfurl again. It obeyed instantly, the blaze more controlled, the color deeper. A jolt shot through her. Even at her most skilled in Orchid, her magic had never burned this fiercely. The Claiming had deepened and honed it, as though the spring had reforged her fire.

Jakobav braced against her power, shoulders tight, his shield holding steady although she could see the strain working through the muscles in his jaw. "More," he demanded, and the translucent dome expanded outward, shimmering with that opalescent gleam. The shield swelled larger than before, vibrating across the clearing, and Thane let out a rough, ringing cheer.

"There he is," Thane called, grinning fiercely, his voice rolling like thunder. "That's our future king."

A sense of pride moved through the group.

Even Savina's mouth twitched faintly, though she masked it quickly. Their excitement settled over Ella, her flames feeding on it until she was alight from fingertips to crown, grateful now more than ever for the impressive garment she wore.

She released her fire in one final rush, then drew it back, letting the white-gold arcs gutter and die against the wind drifting through the clearing. Jakobav's shield still hung in the air, bright and suspended like glass, until the surface shuddered.

It pulsed once, faltered, and split with a jagged seam. A shockwave burst outward, splintering the ground in a widening fissure that tore straight toward Soren.

The world narrowed to a single point. Something surged inside her, an instinct so deep it hollowed her chest and bent the air around her. Her body moved before thought could form. She thrust out both hands.

The clearing warped. Light folded inward, and a ripple opened in front of her, thin and gleaming—roughly the height of Thane. Jakobav's power slammed into it and vanished. Not broken. Not destroyed. Simply gone—pulled through to somewhere beyond this realm.

The tear in the Veil snapped shut as fast as it appeared.

Ella staggered. She'd opened it without thinking at all.

The Claiming had awakened her more than she realized.

The hum in her ears deepened, rattling her bones. She stood on the edge of the fissure Jakobav's shield had torn into the ground, the split running jagged toward where Soren had been standing. Its path ended in an abrupt line, the earth severed cleanly at the exact point where the rest of Jakobav's power had been shunted into the tear in the Veil she had created.

The ripple wavered once, the air thinning around its edges before the tear sealed shut. The last trace of it vanished, leaving only the raw scar in the earth. Ella stumbled back, sweat slick on her skin.

When the haze lifted, Soren stood unscathed. He raised one dark brow, his expression flat, though his eyes betrayed a flicker of surprise. "Not bad." His tone was flat, but the respect was unmistakable.

The clearing held its breath. No one moved, no one spoke, the silence ringing louder than a roar. They only stared at her.

Bryn's brows shot up, and for once, his grin was muted. "Remind me never to stand in front of you when you're improvising."

Jakobav clenched his jaw and ignored their comments, his gaze cutting to Ella as he closed the space between them. "What was that?" His voice was low and edged with fury, but fear hid beneath it. "You could've been hit. And by my own shield. Unacceptable."

Ella's temper rose, raw and unchecked, shoving his chest hard enough to force him back a step. "And you could have killed him, Commander." She let the title linger like an insult.

The air throbbed, deeper than anger, intensified by the effects of this place. She understood why no one ever came here.

His face eased for a single breath, something unguarded flashed before he forced it down. "Will you stop hurling yourself toward death before I can reach you?" he asked, the last word breaking rough in a way she'd never heard from him. "Please."

She crossed her arms, refusing to respond.

Jakobav's hand brushed a strand of her hair, fleeting and almost tender, the touch deflating her fury before she could hold onto it.

Maeren stepped forward, her voice ringing like tempered iron. "You ripped his power out of the air, Ella. That wasn't fire. You opened a seam in the Veil. How did you even do that? Was it the Claiming?"

Savina's gaze was cool, assessing, her tone softer but no less direct. "Any other tricks you've been hiding, Princess? If there are, now's the time to speak. You're in this circle. That means no more surprises."

The words tightened within her chest. Being "in this circle" should have felt like safety, but it carried expectation, and the knowledge that she was no longer only responsible for herself. She still held secrets, some Jakobav knew, others she hadn't dared to voice. But for the first time in years, she felt guilty for keeping them.

"I don't even know where to start. The last few weeks have swallowed me whole," she admitted, her voice unsteady. "I'm still catching up to what happened days ago, let alone what happened in that arena."

Their eyes focused on her, questions brimming, especially

in Thane, whose usual grin was absent, his watchfulness turned solemn.

Jakobav stepped between them, his voice snapping the tension in half. “Enough. Ella stepped in front of Soren without hesitation. She’s fought beside you all. Never backing down, even when she should.” He shot her a pointed look before turning back. “She’s earned the time to process. I shouldn't have pushed her.”

His hand brushed her elbow as he moved past, an anchoring touch, before his voice cut across the clearing. “The Ridge twists minds. Heightens what’s already there. Weak spirits fracture. And none of you are weak, so hold steady.”

Savina’s lips parted as though she was about to argue, but before she could speak, Soren’s quiet voice followed, even and sure. “He’s right.”

The effect was immediate—a testament to Soren’s standing within the circle. The last of the tension eased, though questions still lingered like smoke in the air.

Ella wished she had answers for them. The fates may have bound her to Jakobav in the spring, but trust here was still delicate, fragile as spun glass.

The wind shifted, carrying the crisp bite of pine. And beneath it...something else. A presence that hovered over the Ridge, brushing against her like unseen fingers. A sweet scent unfurled—night-blooming jasmine twined with the metallic whisper of rain on pebblestone. It tugged at the back of her throat like recognition, too intimate to be imagined.

By the time she turned to ask the others if they sensed it too, the scent was gone.

35

ASH AND CROWN

Ella knew they must have all felt it the moment the Ridge slipped behind them because oxygen seemed to return, the atmosphere crisp and bright, the noise inside her head quieted as pine gave way to open sky, and the tightness in her chest eased, though only by a degree.

They rode in a loose formation across pale grass. Thane led the line, easy in the saddle, his voice occasionally carrying back in some careless remark. Savina shadowed him to the right, alert and focused. Soren kept to the hardest ground, eyes fixed on the horizon. Bryn hummed something off-key that might have been a drinking song. Maeren lingered at the rear, watchful as always.

Ella should've been furious with Jakobav.

He had stood before thousands and spoken her name, binding her fate to a foreign crown and painting her as both prize and threat.

Dravaryn, the kingdom she'd come to strangely admire with its obsidian-veined stone, shadowed ridges, forests dense as its secrets, and black roses blooming in hidden gardens, now likely saw her as an enemy interloper or, at best, a suspicious guest with political motives.

Worse still, she doubted the Dravaryns themselves had come to a consensus on the spectacle that was Jakobav's Claiming. One successful Rite was cause for celebration. Two emerging from the sacred water, bound together in breath and blood, had shattered precedent, leaving the kingdom wondering what it had meant.

She should've resented him for dragging her into that, for tying her to his future when neither of them had measured the cost.

And yet, when she turned in the saddle to feed that anger, it unraveled. What she wanted...what she hated herself for wanting...was not distance from him. She craved the closeness of just one horse between them and his hands steady at her waist. Silence around them and space enough to speak the words neither of them had dared to say, to finally discuss what happened in the garden.

She drew in a long breath, steadying herself. She could take the high road, let the days soften the rawness, wait until her words were tempered and calm, until she could address the betrayal with composure. That would be the wise choice, the responsible one.

Or she could punch him. That would be cleaner, maybe even more satisfying.

She nudged her mare closer until her knee brushed against his stirrup. "If I hit you," she said, her voice light, "will that fancy shield of yours stop me from bloodying up that annoyingly distracting face of yours?"

His mouth almost curved. "Try it and find out."

"Tempting." Her tone stayed playful, though the frustration beneath it was real. She didn't follow through. If she were to give her anger a voice, if she tore open the knot of fear and fury tangled inside her, she wasn't sure what would come spilling out or if she could even stop it. So she set her jaw and let the moment pass.

Thane did not. "I've never seen you make a mistake like that," he called back without glancing over his shoulder. "Not in training, not in battle. Nearly split Soren in half when your shield didn't hold."

Jakobav's gaze cut forward, voice clipped. "He's fine."

Savina snorted softly. "Only because Ella saved your ass. You're both lucky she acted so quickly and sent Jake's assault into another realm."

Ella bit down a smile because there was no suspicion in Savina's tone, no edge of accusation this time. It almost sounded like pride, like something a sister might say when jumping to defend their own.

Soren spoke and everyone glanced over, his words quiet but steady. "It wasn't only Jake who faltered. When his shield split, I tried to Vate to get away, but the ground refused me, as though it didn't know me. It's never done that before."

Bryn flicked his reins, catching Ella's attention. The gesture was almost careless, though his tone was anything but. "I don't believe that was coincidental. The fates didn't drag two of this realm's most gifted heirs down into the depths of the Sacred Pool for nothing. If the Veil snaps, no one will be left standing."

Her pulse stumbled. Ella's gaze found Jakobav's, and though no words passed between them, worry shadowed his face.

She knew with her whole heart that what happened at the Claiming was somehow tied to the prophecy. But gods, did

Bryn even know how close he was to the truth? Or was he simply too perceptive for her comfort?

Hoofbeats shattered the troubling thought as two riders crested the rise to the south and came hard, scattering dust, urgency in every line of their bodies. Jakobav lifted a hand, bringing them to a halt. The nearer rider kicked free of his stirrup and slid to the ground, dropping to one knee in the grass.

"Kerris," Jakobav said, recognition breaking through the steel in his voice. "Breathe."

The boy, young enough that he still looked startled by his own speed, dragged in air and squared his shoulders. "My Prince, I bring two reports."

Jakobav's entire frame shifted at those words, stilling, every trace of his easy arrogance stripped away. A prickle of dread in her chest warned this news would not be kind.

"Go on, Kerris," Jakobav said, calm and absolute.

"There is unrest in the city. Not a revolt, they are not that foolish, but rumor spreads fast. There have been small breaches, many of them actually, since the Claiming. The Guard was divided to answer them. People are questioning how the Orchid Princess has flame in our capital, and...why she's here." He faltered, gaze moving to Ella before darting away, his throat working. His breath came uneven, and he stammered through the words as if speaking them aloud to the future king unsettled him more than the message itself.

Jakobav turned toward Maeren, a subtle tilt of his chin. Her posture straightened, as though she were preparing to act. Jakobav turned back to Kerris, his tone steady. "You said there were two reports. What is the second?"

Kerris's voice dropped to a whisper, his shoulders folding. "My second report is... she is not the princess anymore." He bowed his head as he extended a parchment toward Ella, the seal dark against his trembling hand. "I am deeply sorry, Princess Ellandria."

And suddenly her world collapsed.

Ella didn't reach for the letter; she didn't need to. The way Kerris spoke was proof enough, and the subtle shift in Jakobav's demeanor was even more damning. She'd known this day would come, had been waiting for it since learning of the prophecy.

"My mother," she said, her voice trembling, betrayed by her sorrow. "Say it."

Kerris cleared his throat as if to steady himself, and when he finally raised his eyes to hers it was not with pity, but with respect and sadness. "Her Majesty, Queen Serenya of Orchid, is dead," he whispered. "The message came through the southern post at dawn."

For a moment, only the wind answered, and then her fingers went slack, the reins dropping from her hands and landing against the saddle with a dull slap.

Her mare flinched at the sudden looseness, sidestepping in a quick, uncertain motion. The disturbance reached Jakobav's stallion. His hand clenched around the reins, leather groaning as the horse jerked in protest. Jakobav reached over to grab her reins.

Probably afraid she might bolt.

But she couldn't move. The guilt of leaving Orchid, of not saying goodbye, of not returning immediately upon discovering her mother's illness, all sunk into her bones, paralyzing her.

She was left hollow.

The world around her blurred, sounds drifting in and out as though carried from a distance she couldn't cross. She folded forward without meaning to, her palm finding the saddle horn only to realize her hand was shaking. A faint pressure built behind her eyes, not yet tears, just the sting of a truth finally realized.

Her mother.

The word formed like a bruise inside her, dark and spreading. She tried to breathe, but her chest refused her.

Jakobav sucked in a deep breath, slowly, and a single word escaped him, harsh and low. "Fuck."

His curse reached her as if through water, and she lifted her head only enough to glimpse his face and see his shoulders lock. The sight nearly undid her, because for the first time since meeting him, she saw grief on his face too, grief for her.

Ella forced her spine straight, awareness threading back into her. She wasn't alone out here, nor was she hidden in the safety of solitude—she was surrounded by Jakobav's circle, watching her, waiting. She gathered what pieces of herself she could and held them tightly.

Maeren stepped forward, stance already set like a drawn blade. "We return to the castle. We hold the lines. We silence rumors before they can grow teeth."

"I will escort her to Orchid," Thane said at once, his voice unflinching. "She should not ride alone into grief."

Bryn's gaze moved between Jakobav and Ella, his humor stripped away. "And the Veil," he said. "What is your answer to a roof that keeps lowering and a floor that keeps sliding?"

Jakobav turned toward Maeren, his tone firm. "Take the city, address the court, and set the story before anyone dares rewrite it. Assign commands and leave no room for busy tongues. Silence the Vexari until I return."

Ella's head turned at that, catching the startled look from Kerris, and the sharp intake of breath from the other messenger, whose name she didn't know.

He didn't say High Vexari.

He'd always spoken of her with a kind of clipped respect,

but this was different; the word he used now was stripped down, dangerous, and everyone had heard it. She wondered how close that command had come to treason against his own beliefs.

His eyes shifted to Savina. “The streets of Draethmar are yours. Soren, the borders. Keep people safe and make it visible.”

Ella swung down from her horse, boots striking the earth. Her body felt strangely untethered, her hands trembling as she smoothed her dress, but she forced herself to stand tall.

Maeren reached her first, hard arms drawing Ella into a soldier’s embrace. “I’m sorry for your loss. Go and see to Orchid’s crown,” she said. “Then come back.” She framed Ella’s face with both hands, her voice resolute. “Alive. Unharmed.”

Savina followed, her hug quick and tight. “Don’t make me come fetch you out of Orchid’s throne room.”

Soren lingered, hovering as though unsure, then patted Ella’s arm once, firm and inelegant. “Thank you,” he said simply. “For earlier.”

Thane turned his horse as though ready, but Jakobav’s command cut him off. “No.” His voice was not harsh, but it was final. “You’re needed in the capital. Restore their faith. Remind them who we are.”

Thane’s mouth twitched before he gave a two-finger salute, his irreverence tempered by the gravity of the moment. “Orders heard.” Without hesitation, he swung down from his saddle, crossed the space in two strides, and swept Ella off her feet in a crushing embrace. The air fled her lungs in a startled gasp, and then he set her back down with a sheepish grin, his hand lingering for a moment as though reluctant to let her go. “Too much?” he asked, giving her a gentle smack between the shoulders as if he could knock the breath back into her.

She managed the faintest shadow of a smile and lifted one shoulder in a quiet shrug. "A little."

"Good, that means you'll remember it," he said, and the humor fell from his face as quickly as it'd come. He tapped the hilt of the emerald serpent blade strapped to her waist, its jeweled glint catching the last slant of fading light. "Take care of my dagger. It's the only thing I carried out of Velmire, and the only piece of my childhood worth a damn."

Bryn jumped down from his horse to stand before her and placed his hands firm and steady on her shoulders, his eyes startling in their sudden kindness. "My dearest Ella, keeper of more secrets than anyone deserves to bear, and soon enough, Queen Ellandria," he said softly, his voice carrying chaos even in a whisper. "Fiery thorn in my side, more like it." He smiled softly, plucking the purple feather from his hat. He pressed it into her palm, curling her fingers around it. "Loved ones are never truly gone, not where it matters most. I am sorry for your loss in this world." He kissed her cheek, brief and warm, before leaning back with that half-smile that always seemed to disarm. "Don't lose Jake on the road. He broods and disappears like it's his only calling."

Jakobav's gaze shifted between Bryn and Ella, his voice full of tension. "Bryn, I heard you—don't think I'm not concerned. We'll speak more when I return. There may yet be something we can do about the Veil."

The words caught in Ella's chest. Was he speaking of the prophecy—of the two of them as the key? Did he truly believe they could steady the Veil before it tore the mortal realm apart?

She looked at Bryn then and understood for the first time why Jakobav trusted him above all others. He was a healer, yes, but he was also far more—his counsel keen, his knowledge vast, and his loyalty carved deep.

Her mind caught on the word loyalty, and with painful

clarity she realized how much she cared for each of them: Maeren's unflinching steel, Savina's ferocity, Thane's reckless warmth, Soren's quiet strength, and Bryn's wry insight. They were Jakobav's family, and against all reason, they'd become hers as well. Leaving them felt wrong.

Jakobav held Bryn's gaze for a beat, something unspoken passing between them, and Bryn inclined his head in silent understanding.

Then Jakobav lifted his chin to the others. "Give her space. All of you. Go."

Thane and Bryn mounted, and one by one, the circle turned their horses toward the city.

Thane twisted in his saddle as he rode, calling back with a grin that didn't quite mask the ache beneath. "If he argues, remember he is taller, not smarter." He winked, then put his heels to the mare and was gone. His soft laughter carried across the quiet, reckless even in parting. Savina, though she didn't laugh, let the corner of her mouth betray her, and Maeren shook her head and urged her mare into a clean canter. Soren never looked back.

Dust rose in their wake and settled again, leaving the hills in silence.

Ella closed her fingers around Bryn's feather and looked at Jakobav. He didn't reach for her, though he seemed to strain toward the impulse, and yet he only waited.

"Jakobav," she said, her voice steady though her chest ached. "You don't have to come with me. I know you need to deal with the unrest in your kingdom, the fallout from the Claiming"—she lifted her wrist, the rose etched there burning like proof—"even if this whole mess is partially your fault."

His gaze glanced at the mark, then back to her face, unwavering. "I'm coming with you. It's not up for debate. As you've seen firsthand, my circle is more than capable of handling it.

And you're not facing Orchid alone, let alone traveling by yourself after everything."

She nodded softly, whether in defeat or acceptance, she couldn't say.

Her eyes drifted south. The road stretched before her, like a willow bowing toward a river, its roots sunk deep in sorrow, its branches bent low beneath the weight of her return.

36

BETWEEN GRIEF AND FLAME

She turned her mare in the direction of her kingdom, and for the first time since the Ridge fell behind them, the future pressed in, unwelcome and bringing with it everything she'd been holding at bay: her mother's death waiting like the sealed letter she hadn't dared to open, an ache for a circle of warriors from an enemy kingdom who had become, impossibly, her own, and the sudden fear of not knowing when she would see them again.

It was all too much. She hadn't been allowed a breath since the Claiming, since Jakobav had spoken her name before thousands, since the black rose had etched itself onto her wrist and into her heart, the world shifting and refusing to stop. Grief and fury and loyalty and longing tangled inside her until the threads refused to separate, and a wave of dizziness swept through her, the whole of her threatening to unravel at once.

Her fingers slackened on the reins, and before she could stop it, her body gave way, toppling as the burden she carried finally broke through, the feather slipping from her hand to be caught by a stray breeze. The ground rose to meet her, and the sky wheeled in a slow green-blue spin. She struck the grass hard enough to drive the air from her. She blinked, disoriented. The feather drifted after her with stubborn grace before settling across her chest.

Jakobav was there before the air returned to her lungs, his hand moving with surprising care as he plucked the feather from where it sat above her heart and slid it inside his cloak. He braced beneath her shoulders with his other hand, lifting her gently. He bent close, his voice full of concern. "Ella. Can you hear me?"

She gave the smallest nod, and at that, he set her upright in his saddle, steadying her with one hand before turning away to gather her things.

He swung her pack over his shoulder, turned to her mare, and smoothed a hand along the warm neck in a gesture that was part farewell and part command. Then he touched his heel lightly to the flank and spoke softly. "Go home, Chestnut." It was the second time he'd sent this poor horse back to the castle without a rider, and yet the mare barely flicked an ear, accepting the order without question, trotting toward the distant line of riders with the confidence of a creature that knew the way.

Jakobav turned back to her. "Drink," he said, pressing a canteen into her hands.

The water was cool and clean, each swallow easing the dry tightness in her throat. Warmth crept back into her cheeks as he mounted behind her, his thighs closing firmly around her hips. His arm circled her waist in an unyielding hold that told her without flourish—she would not fall again.

The ride south passed easily enough, but the hours dragged on, leaving too much room for her thoughts to churn. She adjusted in the saddle a few times, and each time Jakobav's arm hugged her tighter.

The miles turned into days, the kingdoms blurring one into the next. Jakobav was careful to avoid towns except when there was no other way around. When they rode by Velmire's watchtowers, grim and scarred by old wars, the soldiers stared too long at Jakobav but didn't challenge him; his cloak was marked with Dravaryn insignia. Velmire and Dravaryn were long-standing allies, but she couldn't help the sweep of awareness that ran through her while passing through, knowing Orchid remained sworn against them as rivals.

They crossed Thirelle's lowlands, golden fields bending beneath late-season winds, again skirting anyone who might ask questions. Along a narrow dirt road at the edge of a village, the people fell quiet as they passed, every gaze following, watchful with unspoken concern. It wasn't lost on her that he'd taken off his cloak, looking more civilian than soldier.

None of it mattered; the world narrowed to hoofbeats and the ache in her chest.

Jakobav didn't break that quiet, and she found herself grateful for it. His presence was a shield against the emptiness, and though grief hollowed her out, the warmth of him pressed close enough to remind her she hadn't unraveled completely, the air around them softening as the land turned gradually warmer with each mile south.

By the time night settled, they'd reached a rise sheltered from the wind near Orchid's border. Still technically in Thirelle, yet so close to home she could almost taste it, the air was lighter, heavy with the perfume of grass and wild blooms, the kind of sweetness that made her chest ache with memory. Jakobav set about building the fire, sparks striking against the deepening dark, while Ella remained astride for longer than was necessary, letting the fading comfort of the quiet soak into her before she finally slid down.

The journey had been mercifully uneventful, and the gods

knew she'd needed the calm. Even those last few hours had steadied her, bit by bit, sorrow settling into something she could hold without breaking, strength finding its way back, slow and certain.

Jakobav had brought more food this time, dried meat and bread and even a pouch of berries. Another small mercy she thanked the gods for.

At least she wouldn't be starving and grieving at the same time.

They ate without words, the hush broken only by the crackle of flame and the restless hiss of insects in the grass. Jakobav sat close enough that their knees brushed. The touch felt intentional, and though he said nothing, she couldn't help thinking this was his way of trying to comfort her, a silent offering in place of the words he didn't know how to give.

"I don't know how to do this," she said at last, her voice steady though it scraped her throat to admit it. "To go back and face my kingdom. Face my father and have to explain why I left. And to take my mother's crown, when I never truly wanted it in the first place."

A breath shuddered out of her, the words spilling now that she'd begun.

"The crown passes only through Orchid's daughters. It was always going to be mine, whether I wanted it or not, but I have no desire to lead a kingdom. I've only ever wanted to help my people."

"You'll do it," Jakobav replied, calm and unshaken, as though it were a truth too obvious to be argued. "And you'll do it better than anyone else could."

A sound left her, caught between a laugh and a sob. "That almost sounded like faith."

His eyes were molten black. "It is, Ella. And it's only a

gamble if there's doubt," he said. "Only a fucking fool would dare to doubt you."

Her breath stalled, surprise cutting through the grief.

Gods, this man might yet be my undoing.

Sleep didn't come easily. She lay staring at the branches above her while the fire dwindled to embers, grief growing heavier with every hour she tried to shoulder it alone, until at last, she rolled toward him and found Jakobav already watching her, as if he'd been waiting.

"Ella," he said, her name low and rough in his mouth, as though it carried a question she wasn't ready to answer.

"I just...don't want to think for a while."

What she really meant was that she didn't want the distance between their bedrolls and didn't want silence echoing back at her without the anchor of him close at her side.

He searched her face for a long moment then, without a word, opened his blanket. She moved closer and slipped into his bedroll, the heat of him closing around her at once.

"Are you always this warm?" she murmured, reaching for lightness.

"Are you always this cold?" His arm came around her waist, his hand splaying across her stomach.

"Careful, Prince. People might think you're being kind to me."

"Careful, Princess. People might think I care about their opinions."

The sound that left her was almost a laugh. "You're insufferable."

"You're shivering," he said, drawing her back until her spine fit to the curve of him. "Sleep."

She didn't, not for a long time, but when her eyes finally

closed, it was to the rise and fall of his chest steady against her back.

They rose before dawn, packed, mounted, and were back on the road by the time the sun cleared the horizon, hooves hitting the ground in a relentless cadence. Jakobav said nothing, though his gaze flicked to her again and again, clouded with an emotion that looked too much like unease.

By late afternoon, the border markers rose from the grass, stone obelisks carved with Orchid's sigil. The air sweetened, warmer and buzzing with life, as if the soil sensed her return.

A pulse of warmth struck beneath her collarbone. Ella's breath caught as her royal Orchid tattoo unfurled across her chest in black ink, no longer faded and no longer lost. Her mark had claimed her the moment she crossed the border, settling permanently against her skin.

Jakobav had watched her discover the reappearance. His gaze dropped to the mark and went utterly still, a low sound breaking from him, nearly torn from his chest.

He reached out slowly, as if fighting the impulse, and his knuckles brushed the edge of the ink, the touch no more than a ghost—but it felt like a vow.

"Good," he murmured. "Let the world see who you are."

THEY MADE camp that night in a sheltered clearing just inside Orchid territory, and Ella had barely dropped her pack before Jakobav knelt by his saddlebag and drew out a dark glass bottle sealed in crimson wax.

Her brows lifted. "Is that—?"

"Fae wine."

"Really?" Her tone was unreadable. "You know that's a punishable crime in Orchid, right?"

His brows drew together. "Who enforces that law? They patrol this far from the capital?"

She met his gaze without blinking. "I could have you arrested right now."

One dark brow arched, suspicion and curiosity alighting there as he dragged a hand slowly through his hair, his eyes never leaving hers. "I can't tell if you're being serious right now."

"I am," she said, leaning in as if she meant every word.

Then, with a softening smile, "But I'll only punish you if you don't share it."

He blinked once, and then the laugh that rumbled from him was unrestrained, his eyes glinting in the firelight with amusement—the first true smile she'd seen from him since the news.

His smile faded, gaze darkening as though something far less harmless crept beneath its surface. "I don't like to share," he said, voice dropping. "But I suppose I could be convinced."

An ache pulsed low in her belly, sudden and startling. He wasn't talking about her...but gods, her body didn't seem to care.

Minutes later, they were sitting close by the fire on a fallen log, passing the bottle between them, the wine sweet on her tongue, like berries steeped in smoke, settling into every part of her. Each time she took the bottle, her fingers brushed his. The contact lingered long after it was gone, his touch not easily forgotten.

"You've gone quiet," he said after a while, watching her over the flames.

She traced her thumb along the neck of the bottle, the glass already warm from both of their hands. "I've been thinking about my mother."

They sat in silence for a few breaths before she continued, the words spilling, fragments of memory both fragile and indelible: the way her mother's hair never stayed in its braid, the way she could end a council meeting with a single look, and how she had smelled of rosewater and sandalwood.

Jakobav listened, and she could tell he wasn't just pretending, his attention hanging on every word, the firelight painting his face in gold and shadow. When she finished, he didn't offer empty condolences, but only waited as though he knew she needed a moment to just be.

She tipped the bottle and drank deep, her gaze lingering on the intricate etching along its glass, the way the firelight caught in its patterns until she found herself staring at it as if it might hold the answers to the questions circling through her mind.

"You're opening up to me," he said with a faint smirk. "Must be the wine loosening your tongue."

Maybe it was being back on Orchid soil, or maybe it was simply irritating to have her overindulgence called out; either way, the words struck a nerve.

She narrowed her eyes at him. "Caelen Verelith used to point that out every time I had too much Fae wine. Ruined the fun before it started."

A low, dangerous chuckle rumbled from him. "And who is Caelen Verelith?"

She hesitated only a beat. "Just a man from court who never stopped trying to convince me that we were a match."

Jakobav's mouth curved, slow and knowing. "Caelen," he repeated, dismissive. "Unfortunate name."

He took the bottle from her hand, his thumb grazing her knuckles. "Drink as much as you want, Princess. I'll match you."

He tipped the bottle back and drank deep, his other hand

settling on her thigh, fingers squeezing just enough to make her pulse spike.

She let the smallest smile tug at her mouth. "Match me if you like, Prince. Just don't cry about it when you can't keep up."

Hours blurred as they traded stories, his about growing up in the shadow of a crown, hers about her parents and the girl she used to be, until at some point, the fire dwindled to embers.

"Rekindle it," he said, nodding toward the embers. "Show me what this Orchid soil does for you." A sensual confidence laced his voice, and gods, it was doing something wicked to her.

She accepted the challenge without breaking eye contact, lifting her hand with the barest motion. Flame surged, bursting upward in a rush of fire that roared into a bonfire licking at the sky.

"Shit." He moved fast, dragging her against him to shield the blaze as he pulled her into his lap.

They froze, breaths tangled, and then the tension snapped. Laughter spilled free, reckless and wine-loosened, until it shook through them both.

"Well," he said, still holding her there, "now I'm intoxicated, and we just sent up a giant smoke signal, announcing our presence." His mouth lifted with dry humor. "Maybe we should snuff it out and call it a night before I start a war."

"I'd say that's wise," she teased, still catching her breath.

The risk was small; this stretch near Thirelle's border was never patrolled. The alliance had always kept it unchallenged, at least before she left.

When the moment ebbed, she pushed to her feet, slipping from his lap and turning slightly away, but his hand caught her arm and pulled her back down, steady beside him on the log.

His hand remained on her arm, and when he spoke again, the change in his voice was stark, cutting clean through the levity. "Ella, my father's never waking up. He's not sick or recovering. He's in a coma. Before you, the plan was to survive the Claiming, announce the truth, take the crown, and throw everything into fortifying Dravaryn against the breaches."

Ella's gaze snapped to his. "And now?"

"Now it's on hold." His voice didn't waver. "And I'm not one bit upset about it."

Her chest tightened.

"You can't put your life on hold for me."

He leaned in, the firelight catching on the line of his jaw. "I can damn well do as I please."

She shook her head, overwhelmed by the force of him, and found the only words that made sense. "Jake. Don't. You've already made me your friend. Please don't make me the villain."

He went still, studying her for a long, burning moment. Then, "I'll take you as a friend or villain," he said, his voice deep enough to shiver through her. "I'll take you any way you let me."

The words hit low, molten and dangerous, her body recognizing the promise within.

37

FLAMES AND MERCY

The second bedroll hit the ground with a heavy thud, and Ella blinked at it, then at him, disbelief catching in her voice as she said, "Seriously?"

Jakobav didn't answer. He crouched with a slow intensity, dark hair sliding forward as he worked at the leather strap, loosening it until the roll spilled open across the ground.

The fire cracked between them.

She crossed her arms and tried to hold her ground. "After all that...the wine, the stories, the..." She faltered, suddenly flustered, unable to summon a third thing. "You're going to make me sleep over there?"

He stood and walked back to her as one corner of his mouth curved, but there was nothing kind in it. She huffed a breath, then rolled her shoulders back.

He glanced past her to the fire and then back down at her, his voice low and certain. "Will you move?"

Her jaw dropped. "Excuse me?"

Before she could find words, he was already working. He bent and grabbed the first bedroll in one smooth motion, slinging it over his shoulder as he crossed in front of her with a slow, unhurried stride, shadows rippling over the broad planes of his back and shoulders.

"Jake..." Her voice broke on his name, hovering somewhere between warning and plea.

He didn't answer or explain. He simply held the bedroll over the fire, and for a heartbeat nothing happened, the cloth unrolled and hanging there as if waiting for judgment and execution. The seams surrendered with a sudden whoosh and flames leapt greedily upward.

Ella's mouth fell open. "What the—"

"You're not sleeping apart from me tonight," he said, his voice rough enough to kindle warmth deep in her stomach. "Or ever again if I can help it."

The burning cloth curled inward on itself, ash breaking apart and drifting into the night air as he stepped back toward her, a current following him like a tide. Firelight ran up the black ink etched along his corded forearms, muscles shifting beneath skin as his hands dropped loosely to his sides, danger in every measured movement.

Her pulse stumbled, and she swayed, unsure if it was the wine or just him. "That's...one way to say it."

"That's the only way to say it."

He stopped in front of her, so close she had to tilt her head back to meet his eyes. His hungry gaze held her captive, heat rolling off him until the very air felt as if it might ignite.

"Take off your clothes, Princess," he said, radiating dominance, smooth enough to ruin her. Her breath caught hard in her throat.

"Fuck." Her lips trembled around the word, her voice more prayer than curse, slipping from her before she even realized, Jakobav's command still hanging in the air.

He didn't blink. He only watched her from his full height,

dark eyes catching every flicker of firelight, waiting to see if she would obey.

She did.

The wine that still coursed through her blood, the hours of sharing stories, the bedroll he'd burned to ash, and the vow he'd spoken—to never sleep apart from her again, all of it had her standing taller instead of shrinking back.

Her fingers found the laces at her bodice, and she pulled at them slowly, intentionally, as though each loosened knot was a promise she meant only him to hear.

She wasn't nervous, not tonight.

Piece by piece, she let the fabric fall away, and his gaze never wavered; he tracked every inch she revealed with relentless fixation, like a man engraving her into memory.

The last barrier slipped from her body, her undergarments pooling at her feet. She looked at him through lowered lashes, her stomach tightening at the sight that met her.

He wasn't even trying to hide it, his fingers flexing at his sides—restrained movements belonging to a predator holding himself back from a strike.

The firelight revealed the hard, unmistakable shape straining against his pants, and memory crashed into her; she'd felt him before, wanted all of him before they were interrupted. But now? No one knew where she was, no one to interrupt. The thought, equal parts terrifying and intoxicating, sparked a need she could no longer quiet.

Ella's tongue brushed her bottom lip before she could stop it, and his jaw tightened in response.

The size of him was impossible to ignore, every shift a reminder of the strength she'd felt when he'd pinned her before, the sheer force he could use now if he wanted.

His cedar-and-amber scent wove into the night air, rich

and intoxicating, flooding her senses until she swore she could taste it on her tongue.

Jakobav moved then—not closing the space between them but stepping past her instead, his arm grazing her bare skin in a brush that left a fevered trail. He lowered himself onto the waiting bedroll with the casual grace of a man who owned the moment entirely, leaning back slightly on his palms, shadows playing across the ridges of his shoulders.

"Well?" His voice came smooth and steady, eyes glinting in the half-dark as he tipped his head toward the bedroll. "Or are you planning to sleep standing up?"

She crossed the space toward him, her chin lifted in defiance, but before she could sit beside him, he caught her wrist, and with one effortless pull, he drew her between his legs, placing her upright on her knees, close enough to feel the heat of his desire. He sat back on his palms, his knees bent and spread, relaxed yet radiating control.

Fuck.

She was naked before him, every inch of her exposed to the firelight and to him, her skin alive with tingling anticipation, her pulse racing so hard she could feel it in her fingertips.

And he hadn't even touched her yet.

Jakobav shifted forward, breaking his lazy sprawl as his hands found the backs of her thighs, tracing upward in a slow, possessive sweep, his thumbs pressing into her skin just enough to make her shiver. He looked up at her then, gaze burning like she was a prize he'd fought for and would never give back.

Ella leaned toward him, drawn by instinct, her lips parting in the faintest invitation, but his palm came to rest firm against her stomach, holding her upright, keeping her exactly where he wanted her.

"Not yet," he said, his voice a low command that left no room for argument.

Her breath caught, the denial only fanning the ache inside her.

"Tell me you want to be here," he said.

"Yes," she breathed, the word falling from her without hesitation, despite the faint tremble of her thighs.

He didn't break eye contact or rush. His grip only tightened, the unspoken message thrumming through her: she wasn't leaving this space without knowing exactly what they were to each other.

He still didn't kiss her. His mouth found the inside of her wrist instead, brushing a single warm line there, right over the black rose mark, barely enough to count as a touch yet enough to set every nerve alight.

She swayed closer without meaning to, evidence of the want pooling between her thighs, the wine still humming in her blood and dissolving the boundaries she never thought they'd cross.

"Good," Jakobav murmured, his voice threaded with approval that sent a shiver racing through her. "Now spread your legs wider for me."

Her breath stuttered.

His grip guided her knees apart, forcing her open before him, and she realized with a jolt of shock that she'd never obeyed a command so quickly, so eagerly. She prayed he might show her mercy and touch her soon, because the ache between her legs was already unbearable.

His fingers gripped higher on her thighs, anchoring her there, and then, without warning, one hand skimmed over the slope of her hip while the other slid between her legs. Heat seared through her at his touch, unhurried, exploratory, until at last he pressed one finger inside her, then two, finding a rhythm that tore a gasp from her lips. His other hand slid around and cupped her backside, but he didn't let her go or let her escape that deep, relentless pressure building inside her.

The feeling was exquisite in a way that felt almost unbearable.

"You're drenched for me already. The memory of that scent has been torturing me. I've thought of little else besides the need to taste it again," he said, his voice pitched low and dangerous.

Gods, the way he said it had her rocking against his hand, fucking his fingers while he tightened his hold on her ass. His rhythm was steady and consuming, his thumb brushing the point of pleasure that made her shudder.

"Good girl." His lips brushed her throat, his teeth grazing her skin. "That's it. Bounce for me." Then he bit her, just hard enough to make her shiver. He wasn't rushing. Every movement was intentional, meant to keep her straining on the edge, as if he found satisfaction in the very act of denying her the release she begged for without words.

"Keep going. Just like that." Jakobav's tongue pushed against the inside of his cheek in a way that could have wrecked Ella forever.

"Let me feel you. Every drop of wetness, every tremor, just for me. I want to drown in your arousal."

Before she could fall apart entirely, he pulled his fingers free and guided her onto his lap, her knees bracketing his hips as she faced him. She ground her hips against his hard length, desperate for more friction. As if sensing where her mind had gone, he freed himself, fisting his cock lazily. Her lips parted without permission, a moan slipping free.

He watched her reaction like he could live on it.

One of his palms slid to her waist, then up to cup her breast, his thumb brushing a slow circle over the peaked center. His other hand dropped between her thighs, fingers sliding through her heat before pressing back inside her, deep, the movement coaxing a gasp straight from her chest. Then he leaned in, taking one nipple into his mouth, slow and savoring.

Ella's boldness sparked hot, and she reached for his cock, desperate to feel him inside her, but he caught her hand with the one that was cupping her breast, guiding it away with unerring control. His other hand never faltered—his fingers kept moving inside her, steady and devastating, as if nothing could break his focus.

Gods, this man can multitask.

"Not so fast, Ella. I want you dripping and so desperate you can't stand another second without me taking you."

She shook her hand free and gripped him in defiance, sliding her palm along his full length, her breath catching at the sheer weight of him. "Fuck," she murmured, half in awe, the word slipping from her lips as she tried to take in what seemed impossibly beyond her grasp.

Before she could go further, Jakobav caught her wrist again and guided her hand up behind his neck. "Leave it here. Don't make me tell you again."

Another shiver coursed through her with a reckless thrill of temptation. For a heartbeat, she considered testing him. Instead, she curled her fingers into his hair right as he brushed her over her clit, circling the spot with unwavering friction, the combination so overwhelming her body chose obedience for her.

"Better. You will not come until I tell you to." His voice was low and unyielding. "Keep your eyes on me while I push you to the edge. I want you to see exactly what you're doing to me." A groan escaped him. His touch deepened, driving harder—punishingly perfect—as he continued. "How your very essence has melted into my bones, ingrained so deep in my soul, that I would endure anything for you and anything from you, my merciless Ella."

Gods, how can his words be so eloquent and intentional when his hands move with nothing but instinct and hunger?

He praised her as he pulled his fingers out, quickly tugging his shirt over his head, and pushed them right back inside her, the motion sparking a wave of pleasure. She didn't know how much longer she could hold back her release. So she focused instead on his body, the firelight gilding the hard planes of his abdomen, each defined ridge a reminder that he was dangerously, stupidly beautiful.

She bent and bit gently at his neck, savoring the heat of his skin, before pulling back just far enough to meet his gaze, his hand moving faster between her legs. He leaned in and kissed her, hard, his low groan rumbled against her lips, vibrating through her as though he wanted her to feel his approval as much as hear it.

"Yes, Ellandria," he murmured, his voice almost reverent.

He freed his fingers and raised them to his mouth, tasting her arousal in one long pull. Then his hands clamped around her hips, fingers locking like iron, tilting her forward with the ease of a man who knew he had complete control. The sight of his determined jaw, lips set with concentration as though nothing else in the world existed, made her dizzy with want, and in one brutal, fluid motion, he pulled her down onto him. The solid length of him filled her so completely she couldn't breathe for a heartbeat, the force of it reverberating up her spine until every nerve blazed alive, her body instinctively tightening around him as if she meant to hold him there forever.

Her gasp tore loose, almost a cry, but there was no hesitation. She moved with him, fast and determined, the fire crackling at her back and the man beneath her making the rest of the world disappear. His breath struck the side of her face, warm and rich, his scent wrapping around her like smoke.

"Ride me until you can't remember your own name," he growled, as he kissed her neck tenderly. Once again, his words and actions were at war with one another, reminding her that this man was a constant contradiction, and fuck, she loved it.

"Gods," she breathed, moving against him as if they had been made to fit together, every thrust pulling a sound from her throat, every grind of his hips threatening to break her open. Release built inside her with relentless urgency, each wave cresting higher than the last, until moans slipped from her without her permission, wild and unrestrained.

"Not yet," Jakobav said, his voice commanding even as his body strained with hers. "You can come apart when I say so."

His feral words only heightened her hunger.

She bit down on her lip, riding him harder, desperate, every spasm inside him making her dizzy with pleasure, every heartbeat a reminder that she was on the verge of ruin. She thought she might die from the force of it when the first wave nearly broke her.

"Now," he growled, his voice tearing ragged from his throat. "Fall apart with me."

Her release hit the moment he gave permission, ripping her name from his mouth in a rough growl as she shattered around him.

Then, with effortless strength, he flipped her, pressing her forward onto her hands, driving into her from behind with a force that left her trembling. His fingers found her clit, drawing endless circles, his other hand cupping her breast as his thrusts drove her higher, closer, breaking her all over again.

"Fuck, Ella. I will never get enough of you."

"Please," she gasped, the word slipping raw from her

throat, though she didn't know what she begged for, only that she couldn't bear for him to stop.

She didn't want mercy.

She needed *more.*

The fire popped, sparks scattering into the night, and the world beyond them had ceased to exist. There was only the press of his body, the sound of his breath, the low rasp of her name as if it was the only word he'd ever known. She came undone again, body bowing to the onslaught of him, their bodies collapsing onto the bedroll. They stayed tangled together, her cheek against his chest, his hand tracing patterns over the curve of her spine.

She knew this would complicate everything. It might even cost her. And still, she would never take it back. She could never un-hear what he'd confessed—that he would endure anything from her and anything for her. It was the most reckless, romantic threat she'd ever received.

This man.

Dawn would come soon, and Orchid's capital would be waiting. But for now, she wasn't a princess or a warrior or a pillar of prophecy.

For now, she was only his.

38

BETWEEN WAKING AND THE WORLD

She slept harder than she had in months. No restless tossing, no half-waking to count his breaths, no jerking upright at every whisper of wind—only the steady warmth of his arms banded around her, one palm curved over her spine. His scent wrapped around her, cedar and amber and smoke, grounding her in a way she'd needed.

At some point in the night, his hand moved to cradle the back of her head, fingers buried in her hair. His breathing stayed deep and even against her ear, and she felt his mouth brush her temple once before he leaned his forehead to hers, leaving their heads resting together. She stayed like that until just before dawn, drifting in and out, until she wasn't sure if she was asleep or not.

It began with light, not the pale blue-gray that bleeds into Orchid mornings, but a pulse that seemed to gather beneath her ribs, a soft tug that was not wind or breath, a pull she recognized from the night she had first Threadwalked into a realm that was not her own. She felt it before she saw anything at all, the draw tight-

ening nearer, and when she opened her eyes, the camp was gone, the fire gone, the bedroll gone, and Jakobav gone with them.

She stood barefoot on wet stone, rain-slick and glimmering beneath a sky so drowned in stars it seemed enchanted. A terrace stretched outward into that sky, its ledge framed in winding silver vines with unfamiliar flowers whose pale petals released a scent of frost, night-blooming jasmine, and rain. Rain tapped softly against the stone, a quiet rhythm under the starlit silence.

She blinked hard, and he was there, the man from the painting, closer than she expected, close enough for the light to catch on the fine silver threads woven through the dark of his coat. The pendant at his throat pulsed once in a muted violet, like the echo of a second heart. His face was all cool elegance and impossible symmetry, the kind of beauty that appears sculpted rather than born. His black hair, cut short on the sides and slightly longer on top, lay damp and lifted in the faintest curl at his temples. He stood with practiced confidence, as if every angle of his body had been rehearsed for centuries.

"You have lost someone," he said, his voice smooth and resonant, the undertone of it making the air feel charged.

"My mother," she said, unsure what had compelled her to answer. Her throat closed around the words.

"I am deeply sorry." He stepped toward her, his gaze an icy emerald, a shade of green that would haunt her. With a touch that was entirely sure of itself, he brushed a strand of hair behind her ear.

Ella flinched before she could stop herself.

His smile sharpened, delighted by the reaction.

"You will see her again, Ellandria."

The words should have sounded hollow; instead they sank into her like hope, and the tightness in her chest loosened enough for breath to move again. She should've felt fear from the way he used her name, like they were old friends, but the sincerity in his words had thrown her.

She let herself look at him fully then, as if only now daring to take measure. He was built with fervent grace, enough to both entice and intimidate. Ink wrapped his throat in intricate lines, black threaded with a faint silver shimmer, runes she didn't recognize yet felt familiar nonetheless.

He smiled, almost to himself, as though he were glad she'd come. Like he'd been waiting. Then something shifted. He inhaled once, sharply. The smallest flare of his nostrils erased all warmth from his face, sincerity gone as if it had never lived there, and in its place, an intensity that was unnerving.

"Another man's scent clings to you," he said, velvet-dark, disdain threading through his tone like conviction. It left no room for protest or denial.

Her pulse stumbled in answer.

His mouth curved, not with kindness, but with accusation. "The last time I scented you marked with betrayal like this, you nearly cost lives, Ellandria. And in the Sacred Fae Garden, no less. Reckless little princess. Save that for someone who deserves you."

Heat knifed up her throat, shame rising unbidden, yet a traitorous stir simmered low at the sound of his voice, like seduction wrapping around judgment; fury surged to drown it, but the betrayal of her own body made her want to bare her teeth.

He clicked his tongue once, the softest tsk, *and stepped back as though the scent itself offended him.*

"You were reckless then. Defiant now. Defy me again, and you will learn what it means to bleed for your choices."

Ella swallowed, thoughts churning.

Fuck.

The ripple of wrath in the garden had been his. The creature that burst through the breach near the castle gate had been sent by him.

And now he dragged truth into the light from under her skin as if she were made of glass. Fury and humiliation warred behind her ribs, yet she forced herself not to react.

"Tell me your name," she said, the demand out before she could pull it back. "If you know so much of me, I should at least know yours."

His smile deepened and became a knife. "One day you will. One day my name will be all you think about. And you will earn the right to speak it."

Her heart kicked hard. Heat crawled under her skin; sweat pricked her palms. She took a step back. "I do not know who you—"

"You know enough," he said, his jaw tightening, something like hurt flashing so quickly across his face she couldn't be certain she'd seen it. "And yet you came to me. Again."

She was about to say she hadn't meant to, that she needed to leave. The thought had barely taken shape when his hand closed around her wrist. The speed stole her breath. No human moved like that, not even close, but she'd known from the first time she laid eyes on him that he wasn't human.

His grip on her wrist was unyielding—not crushing at first, then tightening until pain lanced up her arm, a cry splitting from her throat before she could stop it. She tried to wrench her arm away, but he was impossibly strong.

"Please do not go," he said, silk-smooth, his fingers biting deep enough to leave their claim behind.

She gasped, not only at the pressure but at the sudden flare of heat under her skin as her Orchid sigil roared to life; black lines changing to crimson and gold as she looked down in horror. Bright lines spilled down her shoulder, her mark growing and climbing along her arm to the place where his hold bound her, the tattoo writhing like living fire and glowing against his pale hand.

She stared, and two truths landed at once. The last time she'd seen the full mark blaze like this was the night she Threadwalked for the first time, and second, she hadn't spoken her intent to leave aloud, not even in a whisper.

Echobinder. The Fae was a fucking Echobinder.

His gaze fell to the crimson and gold mark shifting along her arm and her hand. For the first time, his composure cracked. His eyes widened by the smallest measure, and what lived there was a grim, quiet triumph.

"Threadwalker," he breathed, reverent and dangerous, like a word he'd waited centuries to name.

His grip didn't loosen immediately; instead he leaned close enough that the cold of his breath stirred the air against her cheek, his voice dropping to a whisper. "There is more in you than even you understand, little Threadwalker, and one day you will beg me to be the one who shows you how deep it runs."

Her pulse thundered. This man was volatile, and she had a feeling he wasn't some low-bred Fae with a diluted bloodline, but older and darker, a thing wrought from a court that did not bend, elite and ancient and quite possibly the most powerful being she'd ever encountered.

Then, as suddenly as he'd taken her, he released her, the pain vanishing.

Her sigil dimmed and retreated along her arm until only her Orchid tattoo remained—black ink settling once more beneath her collarbone. She staggered and clutched her wrist, now marked by his hand; she was left with the echo of his strength and the memory of her magic answering his touch.

"You will understand in time," he said, the smile returning, softer yet no less perilous. "The only question is if you will welcome it...or even survive it."

His gaze lingered as if he meant to memorize the fear and fury etched there. His expression was cold, utterly unforgiving.

Then, the terrace and the stars fell away, an illusion shattering like glass. The smell of jasmine disappeared along with it, like smoke in the wind.

She woke with her cheek pressed to Jakobav's chest and the steady drum of his heart beneath her ear.

That didn't happen. It was just a dream. The Fae man isn't real.

The words looped like an old charm that she didn't believe. Despite repeating them in her mind, the smell of frost and jasmine still clung to her skin where no Orchid night would have left it. Her hair felt cool and slightly damp, as if the drizzle had followed her back. The red grip mark around her wrist was still warm under her fingers.

A cold, animalistic fear rippled through her. No dream leaves marks, no dream presses bruises into living flesh. That wrongness clung to her even as she turned toward the man who held her now. She shut her eyes and forced a breath in, then another, and another.

He's not here. He can't reach me here.

The terror ebbed by inches, trembling as her heartbeat steadied.

Her pulse spiked again when she remembered he'd known she was about to leave; he'd told her not to go before she even voiced it.

Echobinder.

A name she'd only ever heard whispered about with fear and disgust. She'd never seen one, and had never thought she would. Jakobav had said himself there were none in Dravaryn. That man was the first she'd ever encountered—both the first Echobinder and the first Fae, for that matter—terrifying and unpredictable, and yet he had made a crucial mistake. He showed her what he was. The knowledge of his true nature meant she carried a weapon of her own if their paths ever crossed again.

Ella tried to push all thoughts of him aside. Still, wrongness clung to her skin like frost that refused to melt, a reminder that the mark of him lingered, no matter how deeply she tried to bury it. But when she turned toward Jakobav, the comfort of their connection, and of his steady faith in her, anchored her in a way nothing else could. Jakobav was here, solid and warm at her side, and after all she'd been through in the past weeks, the night she'd spent with him was one of the best of her life.

She lifted her head and looked at his sleep-mussed hair and shadowed jaw. Her twisting insides had nothing to do with politics or fear. She bent and pressed her mouth to his, as if kissing him would banish all thoughts of that Fae.

His eyes opened, slow and alert at once, and before she could pull away, his hands slid to her hips as he rolled her over him with effortless ease, kissing her deep enough to pull an unguarded sound from her throat. She kissed him back harder.

"Careful," he murmured against her lips. "Keep that up, and I'll forget we have a road to ride."

She smiled, already half tempted to find out how serious he was, but he broke the kiss and glanced at the light spilling across their bedroll. "As much as I'd love a repeat of last night, the sun is already hunting us. We have ground to cover, and we're one day from your castle."

"We really have to go?" Her voice dropped, soft but daring. "Because I can think of at least one very persuasive reason to stay." She was only half joking.

"Your kingdom waits. And I doubt they'll welcome their lost princess showing up with the future King of Dravaryn as her sole protector. But, the sooner we ride, the sooner we face it. Together."

39

THE CROWN OF ASHES

They broke camp before the first birds found their courage. Jakobav moved with quiet efficiency, every gesture controlled and unmistakably his.

Ella crouched to tighten the laces on her boots, fingers working through the knots. When she glanced up, Jakobav was already standing over her—hand extended to her, palm up, as though he'd done this a hundred times before. She pretended not to notice the subtle lift at his mouth when she placed her hand in his and let him pull her to her feet.

Her wrist still ached from the Fae holding her in place on the rainy terrace, his strength bruising, furious at the scent of Jakobav on her. She remembered his mocking disdain, the way his anger had branded her.

Now, in the pale light, that red welt had faded, but something else had taken shape. A faint silver crescent lived on the inside of her pulse point, like a sigil etched into permanence. A souvenir from her Threadwalking. A Thread-burn.

Ella's stomach dropped.

She lifted her wrist closer, rubbing her thumb over the

mark as if pressure alone could erase it, but the silver sheen stayed.

The crescent appearing on the wrist opposite her black rose felt more fated than coincidental. Had the Fae man seen the rose mark on her? No. Surely not. If he'd been that enraged by the scent of Jakobav on her, he would've unleashed something terrifying at the sight of a permanent brand tying her to him.

She was grateful he hadn't seen the rose at her wrist.

How fucking absurd.

She owed him nothing. She didn't even know his name.

Her gaze returned to the crescent, and she longed for the moment before she'd known it was real, but there was no more pretending. She had Threadwalked in her sleep, and her skin carried back the proof. Instinct told her to hide it, so she tugged her sleeve down over the mark before Jakobav could see.

He had swung into the saddle first and drew her up after him, settling her against him as if that position was their natural state. He adjusted the reins, his voice low, edged with suggestion. "Sleep well?"

She gave him a sidelong look, her cheek brushing the line of his jaw. "You're a distraction, even in your sleep."

She wasn't ready for Jakobav to know yet. She wasn't even sure what to make of it herself. And he hadn't exactly been thrilled by her reaction to the Fae's portrait in the Dravaryn library. He'd already been furious that she recognized the man from her dream.

What would he think of her Threadwalking straight to him in her sleep? And worse—right after the night she and Jakobav had shared?

Her cheeks flushed at the thought. No, that would not be

good at all. She forced the haunted look from her eyes before he could catch it.

His gaze flicked to her mouth before turning back to the road ahead. "We should get moving."

With the heat of him at her back and his arm firm around her waist, it was impossible not to feel his attention. Or maybe it was the guilt tugging at her. She went back and forth for hours about how and when to tell him about the man with the emerald eyes.

They continued south, and by midday, the wind grew heavy and warm, laced with fruit and rain. The trail spilled them onto a high ridge, and Orchid unfurled below as though a story had been poured across the land and left to bloom.

Dravaryn had its own feral beauty, all iron cliffs and shadowed pines. Orchid answered with excess.

Hills swelled in greens of every shade: deep moss, bright fern, and pale mint layered until the eye almost drowned. Rivers braided through the land like veins of light, slow and golden in the shallows, dark where the jungle pressed close. Towering trees spread, bases so wide they rose like walls of living wood, their roots climbing high above the ground before plunging back into the soil. From their branches, vines stitched the canopy into a single, breathing roof.

Orchids blanketed spots of the earth as though the kingdom had named itself into being. Some glowed like spilled ink, others burned scarlet from volcanic soil, their petals speckled like embers cooling in the dark. Ella had studied sketches of her kingdom's flora in school, but the drawings had been polite. Seeing it now at its peak was longing rendered into light, and Jakobav looked equally mesmerized.

A bird like a living jewel flashed by and vanished. Butterflies with glassy wings drifted overhead, their shadows flickering like ghosts. On a sun-warmed stone, a copper lizard blinked at them with the arrogance of royalty.

Jakobav's arm tightened firmly around her as the horse descended down a small ridge. The humidity curled his hair, and beads of moisture gleamed across the ink that coiled down his arms. On most men, sweat looked unkempt, but on Jake, gods, it looked like even the weather obeyed him.

"Did you get to venture out this far from the capital very often when you were growing up?" he asked at last.

She exhaled, her gaze sweeping across the endless green. "I did, but it never fails to take my breath away. The castle walls kept me safe, but they never kept me in. My friends and I were always sneaking out to explore. My best friend, Nira, especially loved these forests. Probably because she has never met an animal she doesn't adore. And her hair never frizzes in this humidity, unlike mine." A small smile touched her lips, then faltered as her throat tightened. "I hope you get to meet her."

"I would like that."

His words caught in her chest. The truth was, Ella had no idea if Nira was safe. She hadn't been home in years, not since the breaches had begun multiplying, not since the Veil had started to split. A deep sadness threatened to consume her.

"I don't really know how my people have endured the Threadshifting. Or if Nira is alive."

Jakobav's reply was quiet and certain. "If she's anything like you, she'll have survived."

Her chest lifted, eased by the comfort of his words as they descended into the green, the path narrowing until it dissolved altogether. What passed for a road here was little more than a memory and a slight dip in vegetation. Ferns brushed their knees, and a creature with bright eyes watched from the hollow of a strangler fig while flowers threw their perfume in fistfuls, the sweetness clinging to her skin until it was dizzying. No wonder Jakobav had known her instantly. Flowers and smoke ran thick in her blood, her kingdom itself betraying her.

They crossed a creek by a tumble of slick stones, the horse stepping careful and sure-footed, and on the far bank, a thin snake hung from a branch like a strand of new silk, leaf-green with a white belly and a little arrow of a head. It tasted the air as it slithered toward Ella, her pulse spiking as the serpent nosed closer, its tongue flickering at her ear before it vanished back into the leaves without a sound.

"So that's normal," Jakobav said dryly.

"If you were raised on tales of Orchid spirits, yes." She glanced to the spot the serpent had disappeared. "The stories say the river-witches send their scouts ahead of the travelers they favor. The snakes send messages and listen for lies."

"Should I be nervous?"

"Oh, definitely."

He gave her a look that hovered between amusement and concern, an expression she liked on him.

Animals presented themselves as if by appointment. A cloud of tiny bats slept like a cluster of fruit, wrapped in their own wings beneath a palm frond, while high above a pair of long-tailed parrots argued with righteous outrage.

"I didn't realize the beasts of Orchid would be so loud," Jakobav said.

"Careful," she replied. "They prefer to be called citizens."

He made a sound that might have been a laugh.

The heat deepened, and the light took on a yellow-green cast as it passed through the leaves. The humidity felt dense, even in the shade, and Ella loosened her cloak and let the air reach her skin.

The path curved, and Ella slowed. That tug she'd felt since crossing back into Orchid sharpened now, low and insistent, pulling at her ribs like a thread wound too tight. The horse balked once, then settled again, as though it felt it too.

Jakobav noticed. "Why are we stopping?"

She squinted through the dense green. A break in the trees revealed faint smoke curling above the canopy. "Because something is telling me to."

His jaw flexed. "That is not reassuring."

Ella smiled faintly. "Relax. Worst case, you get to keep playing protector."

He gave her a long look but nudged the horse forward anyway.

When the smoke thickened and the trees began to open, they dismounted and tied the reins to a low branch, leaving the animal to graze while they went on foot.

"Ella," he said quietly, scanning the trees. "I don't think there's anything out here. You sure that instinct of yours isn't saying turn around and head straight to the castle?" He laughed, as if his joke was funny. It wasn't.

She huffed out a breath and ignored him, pushing farther down the narrow trail.

Finally, they came across a cottage where the jungle thinned and the soil changed from brown to black. The trunk of a massive tree split and wove around a one-room house, its roots forming ribs and its branches holding up a roof thick with living thatch and bright flowers. Chimes sang in the breeze, feathers and teeth hung from a line like a string of weathered prayers, and the front steps were laid in mosaic, little chips of glazed tile in blues and greens and a streak of gold. The air smelled faintly of crushed herbs and rain-soaked earth.

The door stood open.

A woman leaned in the doorway as though she'd been waiting since the first seed had sprouted here. Her skirt was forest green with ruffles. She had white stockings that climbed to her knees in a froth of lace, and a matching corset cupped unapologetic cleavage that probably made men forget their own names. Her midriff was a ribbon of warm skin, and strawberry curls fell in glossy ringlets past her hips. When she smiled, it was like a handful of sugar dropped into tea.

Ella took one look at her and snorted. "Too bad Thane isn't here. He could finally put that world-renowned flirting of his to good use."

Jakobav's mouth twitched, though his jaw set before he replied. "Actually, I think he likes blondes."

Ella blinked at him, surprised.

The woman clapped her hands together, her gaze fixing on Ella with a smile that carried recognition.

"There you are," she said warmly. "I was beginning to think you'd ignore the whisper and make me send more snakes."

Ella's mouth went dry. "Have we met?"

"Not properly," the woman said. "You were in my head and I was in yours, and then I woke up on the roof of a bakery with a pigeon sitting on my stomach. It was very affectionate, but I do not recommend it." She stepped aside and made a sweeping courtly gesture that somehow involved only wrists and hair. "I'm Octavia. Come in, dearies."

Jakobav and Ella traded a look. He nodded once toward the doorway as if to say, "after you."

Ella hesitated just long enough to shoot Jakobav a dark glare. Then she leaned in, close enough that her breath stirred the dark hair at his ear.

"If I die in here," she whispered, "I'm haunting you for eternity."

His mouth curved then shrugged, raising one hand as if questioning her and whispered back, "Hey, I followed you here. You just had to trust your instincts." He gestured her forward with infuriating calm and then walked behind Ella into the cottage.

Inside, it smelled like flowers and honey, every surface holding something: jars with careful labels, dried bundles of leaves, a bowl of shells sorted by color, and stones with holes through their centers. There were teacups that didn't match, and on the far wall, a string was hung with little squares of paper, each painted with a symbol in black ink. Ella didn't recognize all of them, but she knew how it felt to stand near words that meant more than the ink they were made of.

Octavia poured tea the color of fresh dirt. "I'm sorry if the vision startled you," she said, all contrition and dimples.

Ella went still.

She remembered where she'd heard "Octavia."

That name had lived at the root of her choices for years. Octavia was the voice she'd heard in the dream that drove her from Orchid, the vision that told her to follow the prophecy's pull north. To search for the relic.

"You're the one," Ella whispered. "The vision was yours."

"When they come that strong, I tend to fall right out of myself. Full blackout. It's very inconvenient. Once, I woke up spinning on a windmill. Another time in a fisherman's net, quite frightening actually. It was rank with the scent of disappointing men. Oh and once, in a duchess's wardrobe. We had a very honest talk about her taste in hats."

A sound broke the air; Jakobav's laugh sounded more like a bark. His hand went to his mouth at once, turning it into a cough as if the sound had betrayed him.

What a bizarre moment for him to develop a sense of humor.

She shot him a glare, then turned back to Octavia. "You projected it?" she said slowly. "Into my mind?"

Octavia's curls bounced. "A courtesy when the thread

insists. The future is a fickle animal, dearie. Sometimes it drags you by the hem until you agree to look."

Jakobav settled by the window, not touching anything, and his eyes seemed to be counting exits out of habit. Octavia noticed and smiled.

He looked like a large, polite wolf trying to sit in a tea chair.

Suddenly, Octavia's brightness shifted, and a sorrow passed over her features that made her look older by a century. She set the teapot down with care and took Ella's hand, warmth moving up Ella's arm with the contact as if someone had poured sunlight into her veins.

"Your mother," Octavia said very softly. "Queen Serenya."

The name struck like a blade. For an instant, Ella couldn't breathe, her chest hollowing, the air shattering in her throat, and the world tilting as though the floor had given way beneath her. She'd been holding herself together with mission and duty, but that name unstitched her in a single stroke.

Jakobav was there before she could unravel into the depths of it, one hand firm at the small of her back and the other braced against her arm as if he would not let her fall even an inch. His touch steadied her, yet it was his presence at her side that pulled her back from the edge. He didn't speak, but everything in him told her she wasn't alone.

"She was light," Octavia continued. "A brave light. She chose to spend it."

Ella folded in on the ache, her vision blurring as grief consumed her. She'd known grief would come like this, sudden and crushing, but still worse was knowing she had not been there. She'd been running across strange soil, bleeding on borders, sleeping in borrowed bedrolls, chasing a path the fates had carved for her. That path might save more than her own kingdom, but at the cost of never saying goodbye.

Jakobav's hand remained on her back, a wordless anchor

holding her upright. Octavia clasped her free hand and hovered until her strength returned. The strangeness of their combined presence was not unwelcome, and when Ella's eyes finally cleared, Octavia's were kind and bright, shining with far less pity.

"The land loves you," Octavia said, squeezing her fingers. "It called you home for a reason."

A little current prickled Ella's wrist where the Thread-burned crescent lay.

Octavia's eyes went white like a storm erasing a horizon, the chimes at the door ringing despite the lack of wind.

Her voice, when it came, belonged to a mouth of ancient riddles.

"*When ash is a crown and green is a throne, the daughter of embers will claim what is sown. A queen lays down, and the river runs wide. Blood writes a bridge where the realms used to divide.*

Seek where the roots drink fire and the orchids wear night. The key that you chase is a mirror turned right. Not iron, not stone, not the bone of a king. The lock lives in flesh, and the door is a wing.

One path is storm, and one path is sky. One bears a taste that the earth will deny. Choose with your marrow when the Veil begins to thin. The oath that you keep is the war that you win."

The words vibrated in the air, very calm and very terrible.

Octavia blinked and came back into herself like someone surfacing from deep water. She swayed, then laughed, breathless and looking pleased.

"I adore when they rhyme," she chirped happily.

Jakobav hadn't moved. His knuckles were white where he gripped the window frame; he was listening with his whole body.

Ella was listening with the weight of her past and the fear of her future, attempting to hide the chill her body betrayed.

Octavia looked between them, mischief returning. "Now,

that is enough doom before my second cup of tea. Let me see your hand, dear."

Ella hesitated, then held out her hand, a voice inside her that wasn't entirely her own mind told her to listen. Octavia pushed her sleeve up, exposing her wrist, then traced the crescent with a fingertip, and warmth flared again, then steadied.

Ella looked at Jakobav in that moment and saw him clock the mark on the inside of her wrist. His eyes widened, then his gaze cut toward Ella with suspicion.

Ella met his gaze, pleading silently, a tiny shake of her head asking him to save the questions for later.

Octavia was oblivious to the shift in the room; Ella looked away from Jakobav, avoiding his silent inquiry by focusing on Octavia.

"Threadwalker," she murmured. "Yes. You step where doors should not open. Be careful, little ember. Threads can knot as well as guide."

Her gaze snapped up, pupils wide as another vision took her. This one seemed lighter, or perhaps she was enjoying it more.

"Tall," she said, absolutely delighted. "And handsome. Foreign to this soil in the old way. The fated pair will taste of elsewhere. And the children will be gorgeous, of course."

Ella's stomach turned. "Excuse me?"

Out of the corner of her eye Ella caught movement; Jakobav had gone rigid, then shifted as if he could no longer be still, crossing to the wall of shelves and lifting a glass jar with deliberate care, pretending to study the dried leaves within. Octavia kept speaking, untroubled, while Ella tracked him in her periphery, every line of him tight enough to snap.

Octavia sighed like a poet, emphasizing each word with enthusiasm and longing. "A riot of curls and eyes like stormwater. Clever little hands, eager to push boundaries. Oh, do say you will bring them to visit. I make the best spice cake. Convinces even toddlers to behave."

Jakobav choked on nothing, and the jar slipped from his hand. Glass shattered against the floor. He swore under his breath. "Shit. Sorry."

Octavia only waved a hand, unconcerned. "Don't trouble yourself, dearie. A lot gets broken in here whenever my visions knock me out. Comes with the territory."

Then his eyes narrowed, the air thickening as though the mention of children had set his blood on edge. "I'd say that's enough vision talk for one day. She's heard enough about her future even without your help."

Ella stared at him, then away, then at him again, which did nothing to keep her mind from fixating on a select few of Octavia's words: tall, handsome, and foreign in an old way. She knew of exactly two men that both fit that description.

Ella's stomach churned as she tried to shove the words away, as though refusing them would make them less true. She told herself Octavia's visions were nonsense, nothing but riddles draped in honey. But denial held only so long. The images pressed back against her, unwanted yet undeniable, and suddenly she was picturing faces despite struggling not to. Jakobav, steady and infuriating and far too close. And the Fae man of silver and shadow, whose presence unsettled her in a way she couldn't quite smother—a draw she didn't want, didn't understand, and absolutely would not admit aloud.

Octavia clapped once, untroubled by anyone's existential crisis. "More tea?"

"I think we'd better be on our way. It was interesting to meet you. Thank you for the kind words about my mother," Ella said, very carefully, as if the floor might buckle if she were too loud.

Ella squirmed under Octavia's bright stare, tugging her

sleeve back down. Jakobav's gaze caught the motion and slid to her wrist. He stilled, appearing to be putting something together that didn't quite make sense. For a heartbeat he didn't move, then his hand flexed once against his thigh, tendons sharp beneath the ink. His gaze hardened, the kind of look that said more than words ever could, and the line that cut between his brows warned her exactly how furious he was.

Her mind was spinning. Did he have any idea what the Thread-burn meant? Or was he just upset that she hadn't told him about it? Ella was dying to ask him.

He drew a slow breath through his nose, controlled, almost too quiet, and when he finally looked away toward Octavia, the movement was clipped, as though every inch of him had been locked into restraint.

"We appreciate your time," he said, the words even but carrying none of the ease of politeness.

Ella's pulse tripped. He'd seen. He knew. And if not for the other woman watching them, she had no doubt he would've demanded answers right then and there. Answers she didn't have.

Jakobav was the first to move. He turned on his heel and strode for the door without another word, his shoulders squared, his silence a wall she was forced to follow. Ella dipped her head once to Octavia, though her throat was too tight for speech, and trailed after him into the humid afternoon.

The air outside was dense, the forest waiting for them like a living thing. Jakobav didn't slow, his steps cutting a path through the overgrowth. Ella kept close, the skirt of her dress snagging on bushes and brushing leaves still damp from an earlier rain. The jungle noise swelled and hushed in waves, a tide rising and falling, and beneath it, the taut thread between them was drawn tighter with each step.

The silence became unbearable. Panic rose in her chest, her

face going pale. She stopped walking and folded her arms tight across her body. "So what, you're just going to give me the silent treatment all the way back to Orchid? Or are we going to act like adults and talk about it? Ask me what you want to know. Say it, Jake."

He halted so abruptly she nearly stumbled.

Slowly, he turned, his shadow falling over her as he closed the distance in two strides. Icy anger radiated from him, prickling her skin. "Oh, so you're going to open up to me now? Suddenly you are feeling forthright, Ella?" His voice was low and dangerous, and when he leaned in impossibly close, her lips parted before she could stop them, traitorous and wanting. It seemed he might kiss her, but he drew back, cold and distant.

"I guess opening up and letting me in was only in the physical sense," he said, and hurt flickered across his face before the mask of indifference slid back into place.

Fuck. What if this isn't just a fight? What if I pushed him past the point of return?

"Jake—" Her voice cracked, stuttering against the thought of it. "It's not like that. I haven't figured out how to tell you what I need to tell you. I haven't had a chance to breathe since I met you. I want to open up, I want to tell you everything, but I wasn't sure I was ready. I'm—"

He cut her off, his tone final. "Then let me know when you are. Until then, I have no interest in being lied to."

Her temper snapped. "I haven't lied to you."

"You've left me in the dark," he shot back without hesitation, the words striking harder than any shout.

She faltered, realizing he wasn't wrong, the truth hanging heavy between them. He turned with a scoff, his cloak brushing leaves aside as he strode back toward the horse.

"Let's get you to your castle, Princess," he called over his shoulder, not bothering to face her.

At last the path bent, and the horse came into view where they'd tied it among the ferns. The animal lifted its head at their approach, ears twitching in the thick heat. Jakobav didn't reach for her hand this time, nor even look at her. He stood waiting, his expression unreadable, until she hauled herself into the saddle alone. Only when she was seated did he mount, the leather groaning as he settled behind her, his arm brushing hers as he gathered the reins in a brisk motion.

She looked straight ahead, but the words fell out, quiet and urgent. "Just give me some time. Time to figure everything out." She almost left it there, almost swallowing the rest, but the thought of losing what they'd built forced her to say it with unguarded truth. "Let me deal with the return to my kingdom, and the fallout of my mother's death. Then I'll tell you everything."

She knew it was a low blow to invoke her grief to soften his fury, but he'd changed so much since the night she first met him, and she couldn't let everything unravel here.

Jakobav exhaled, the sound half sigh and half surrender, and wrapped one arm protectively around her waist. His other hand gripped the reins as he steered the horse toward her homecoming, the quietude now less punishment and more like a promise held in check.

The jungle closed in on either side, the canopy muting the light. Heat radiated up from under the leaves, and the kingdom that was already hers, whether she was ready for it or not, breathed steady beneath her feet.

Octavia's words clung like burrs: *Tall. Foreign. Two paths. One crown.*

The horse carried them forward, hooves thudding in rhythm with her heart, and each step twisted tighter in her chest. Either terror or relief, both seemed to war inside her. Behind them, Octavia's soft laughter returned like a bell struck in an empty room, an eerie lullaby following them into the trees.

By the time the jungle thinned and the salt wind found them again, Ella's pulse still hadn't steadied. The closer they drew to the castle gates, the heavier the crown of Orchid seemed to settle on her shoulders, though she hadn't yet touched it.

40

COURT OF RUMORS

The gates of Orchid Castle opened with a sound like old stone sighing, and she sat straighter in her saddle as the view unfolded before her. The castle stood at the northern edge of Aradessa, Orchid's capital city, its high terraces carved along the rise of a cliff that overlooked both the bustling streets below and, in the distance, the glimmering outline of the southern sea.

Garlands of blossoms arched above the entrance, scarlet hibiscus and gold-petaled fronds, flowers so large they looked conjured from a painter's brush. Their perfume drifted on the salt-tinged breeze rolling up from the coast, mingling with the warm air until the entire courtyard felt lush enough to drown in color and scent.

A crowd gathered in a bright blur of color. Ella searched every face she could see, her pulse climbing as each familiar stranger lifted their eyes toward her. Her throat tightened.

Then the crowd parted.

Nira pushed through at a run, skirts gathered in her hands, her hair glossy and dark and elegant as ever, not a strand out of place despite the heat. Relief punched the breath from Ella's chest. She barely had time to dismount before her oldest friend collided with her, arms wrapped tight around her shoulders. Ella laughed into her hair, sudden and shaky, tears stinging in her eyes.

"You're late," Nira whispered, fierce and trembling.

Ella pulled back enough to see her face, brushing at her damp lashes with the heel of her hand. "And you're exactly the same. Gods, Nira, I missed you."

Nira wiped her cheeks, then glanced past Ella's shoulder. Her smile turned sly. She leaned in, voice dropping as she gestured with a subtle tilt of her chin toward the massive brooding prince still seated on the horse.

"Tell me he came with the horse," she murmured, trying and failing to hide her grin. "And where can I get one?"

"Nira," Ella hissed, scandalized and delighted in equal measure, "behave."

Nira giggled behind her hand. "I am behaving. I'm also admiring."

Behind them, Jakobav lifted an eyebrow as if he somehow knew exactly what had been said.

Behind her, Marisol, the castle's chief steward, the woman who had smuggled sweets into Ella's bed as a child and taught her the difference between herbals and poisons, wrapped her in an embrace that smelled like cinnamon and home. Ella's knees nearly gave out.

"Marisol," she breathed, her voice breaking around the name. "I'm so happy to see you. I have so many questions I need to ask you."

Marisol smiled, warm and knowing, and held her tighter. "Of course, but I might have more questions for you, Ellandria." She glanced over at Jakobav. Marisol laughed softly, lifting a hand to her mouth as if to contain it, and Ella felt her cheeks warm in response.

This was going better than she'd dared to hope.

The crowd gathered in the courtyard was a mix of familiar faces and newcomers—castle staff in their formal attire, members of the royal court in embroidered silks, and even a scattering of citizens from Aradessa who must have rushed uphill at the news of her return. She'd worried they would take one look at the brute from Dravaryn and recoil, whisper treason or demand answers she wasn't ready to give.

But instead, the welcome rose around her in a warm, swelling chorus—servants and courtiers, childhood friends and strangers alike—calling her name, cheering as though she'd returned from a long voyage rather than the brink of war. For one fragile moment, it felt as though she'd simply come home.

Then King Eryndor of Orchid stepped forward.

Her father had aged since she last saw him, his dark hair streaked with silver, his shoulders thinner beneath the ceremonial mantle, but his eyes, pale blue as sea-glass, were as sharp as ever.

"Ellandria," he said, his voice carrying through the courtyard like judgment.

"Father!"

His arms went around her, sudden and strong, crushing the breath from her chest. She froze, then clung back, breathing cedar oil and the remembered scent of the old throne room where she'd spent many days at his feet.

When he drew away rigidly, the shift was immediate; the warmth fell away, and the authority of the king settled over him again, cold and uncompromising. His gaze cut past her to the man she'd brought to her kingdom's gates.

Jakobav was already dismounting, boots striking the

pavers with a sound that stilled the noise of the courtyard. He stepped forward, massive and inked, every inch of him exuding power, a warlord from their enemy kingdom. Courtiers shrank back at the sight of their standoff, and Ella could imagine what they were thinking: Was he the reason she'd gone missing? Why had she brought him here?

Jakobav stopped just beyond her father's reach, steady as a drawn blade, and inclined his head a fraction. "King Eryndor."

He might have spoken more, but before the next step was taken, the air snapped brittle. Every torch along the walls guttered and then roared higher, flames stretching toward the sky as though yanked by invisible strings. Heat fell over the courtyard stones. Sparks hissed from her father's fingertips, and then fire spidered across the ground in molten veins, racing toward Jakobav's boots.

And above it all, a fiery crown burst from her father's shoulders and formed over his head, a burning coronet that made him seem less man than god. Courtiers gasped, garlands ignited into ash, and the crowd stumbled back in terror as Orchid answered its king's fury.

Ella's body moved before her mind could stop it. She stepped between them, palms raised. The wildfire surged at her feet, the crownfire burning overhead, and she pulled the two raging currents together, twisting them into a single roaring column that shot skyward and burst like a comet above the city, scattering embers harmlessly into the humid air.

She lowered her hands, her palms tingling with power, faintly glowing as though it hadn't entirely released her. The courtyard had gone completely still, the kingdom pausing to witness what she'd done.

Manipulating fire like this was not soldier's magic, nor even the refined craft taught to Orchid's nobles. Only women born into the royal line could bend another's flame into obedience, and even then it demanded focus, discipline, and years of training. It was the reason Orchid passed its Crown through its daughters—the kingdom's strength lived in its queens. But this...this had been different.

The sacred waters of the Claiming still lived in her veins, amplifying the Orchid fire she carried from birth until the flames answered her as if she were their source. She'd pulled two warring currents together with barely a thought, and the ease of it unsettled her almost as much as the display itself. The thought sent a tremor through her even as she lifted her chin to the silence.

Gods, she hadn't meant to put on a show. But the Court had seen one now, and before the welcome banquet even began.

She looked between her father and Jakobav, her voice cutting clean through the hush.

"Anyone I invite into Orchid answers to me. I answer to no one but the Crown."

Ella said nothing more. If her father wished to challenge her authority, he would have to do so in front of all of Orchid. She would not back down.

Her father's expression changed from anger to grief and then pride, the storm shifting behind his eyes, until at last it fully softened when he looked back at her. "Ellandria," he said again, his voice quieter now, a thread of weariness woven through it.

Jakobav hadn't moved. He watched, eyes narrowed.

Ella stepped forward before the courtyard could draw its next breath, her hand closing around her father's arm as if the gesture had been planned all along. She knew what she was doing, knew she had to put on a show strong enough to steady the court and bend the moment back in her favor.

Eryndor's gaze slid past her to Jakobav, his words carefully selected. "I assume you mean for your...guest...to stay for dinner, then?"

"I do," Ella said before Jakobav could answer, her voice carrying clear and even. "And considering he was brought here by the future queen, I didn't think I would need to ask for an invitation. Or your permission."

Her father studied her for a long moment, pale eyes fixed unblinking on hers as though searching for the child he'd raised and finding instead the woman who had returned. When he finally spoke, his tone was measured, the challenge unmistakable. "Then you take full responsibility for his presence. And for his actions?"

Ella held his gaze without flinching. "I do."

Her father inclined his head once, a gesture so slight it could barely be called a nod. "Very well. He may remain as your guest."

Relief drifted through her like a sudden breeze, and she could feel it ripple through the gathered crowd as well, courtiers and servants murmuring to one another, as if the king's words had unlocked them and they'd been given permission to move again.

"Thank you, Father," she said softly.

He shook his head, the stern lines of his face easing into something warmer, almost tender. At last, a half-smile touched his mouth. "I've missed you, Ellandria. Come. Let's go inside and celebrate your return."

She rose on her toes and pressed a kiss to his cheek, her smile sweet and practiced, the very image of a dutiful daughter guiding her father toward the castle while signaling the others to follow.

The cheers swelled again, bright and eager, yet beneath the noise, Jakobav's gaze burned against her skin. He said nothing, but she was positive that he knew exactly what she was doing.

Appearances were another kind of blade, and tonight she would wield them for her kingdom and the foreign heir walking at her back, shadowed by Orchid guards.

The banquet that followed was lavish, the long tables stacked with tropical fruits, roasted meats, and sweet delicacies Ella had nearly forgotten. The walls were lit with torchlight that reflected off the tiled mosaics. Courtiers spoke in hushed tones that weren't hushed at all.

Her father raised his goblet, eyes never leaving her. "Imagine our surprise," he said evenly, "when we received a letter from Dravaryn—the last kingdom we ever expected to hear from. And to announce that our missing daughter would be returning home, accompanied by the prince of our oldest enemy. Imagine the pure shock I felt at the plea for asylum, for the safe passage for this man."

Ella blinked, questions rising as quickly as her irritation. "If you knew he was coming, then why did you try to torch him on arrival? And what letter? Who sent it?"

He leaned forward, studying her face with an intensity that made the whole hall seem to lean in. "Good to know your demand for truth still lives. I was beginning to wonder." His mouth softened into the barest smile before he went on. "Yes, we received the letter yesterday, from a young man on horseback, terribly nervous. Nearly fell off the beast at the gates."

"Kerris?" she murmured, glancing at Jakobav for confirmation. He gave a subtle shake of his head. Right—not the time. The collision of her two worlds knocked her off balance.

Eryndor continued as though she hadn't spoken. "The letter was long, elegant, and carefully worded. And then, at the end, there was a note in a different hand."

He set the goblet down with more force than likely intended, wine sloshing across the mosaic tiles. His voice cracked with more than anger. "It said: 'Tell Ella that Bryn wants his feather back. Don't lose it.'"

Shit. Where is his purple feather?

The entire hall went still, every gaze snapping toward her.

"What in the hell is that supposed to mean, Ellandria?" His words rang through the banquet, making courtiers flinch. Yet beneath the fury, his voice was nearly broken and raw, his fingers braced on the table as if steadying himself. "Why did I have to hear of my daughter's return from a courier of Dravaryn?"

His jaw worked once, his lashes rimmed with tears, and his voice dropped lower, hushed and trembling. "We prayed to the gods for your safe return. When years passed, I began to lose hope. But your mother never lost faith that you'd come home."

Around them, the banquet carried on—dishes clattering, servants weaving between tables—too loud for anyone to catch more than the shape of their expressions.

His hand shook as it reached across the table, rough as it closed around hers. "And now you're here. You're truly here."

A soft, disbelieving smile lifted the corners of his mouth. He didn't hide the sheen in his eyes. As a few nobles glanced their way, he straightened and cleared his throat, the mask of the king settling over him once more. But it didn't hide everything.

Her throat burned, the words tearing free in little more than a whisper. "I'm here now. And I wish she was too." A single tear fell down her face, and she wiped it away quickly.

Her father had always held himself rigid in public, every emotion tucked behind duty and crown. Yet here he was, letting grief and joy sit openly on his face, however briefly. It struck her that she wasn't the only one who'd changed over these past years. He'd changed, too.

For this moment, family shone brighter than the kingdom.

Guilt slammed through her, brutal and immediate. She wanted to tell him everything, explain the prophecy and the stakes, but she couldn't do it here. Instead, she hugged him briefly and said, "I'm so sorry, Father. I should've been here."

He hugged her back fiercely, and for the first time since she'd ridden through the gates, it actually hit her that she was really back in Orchid. She was home.

Eryndor drew a steadying breath, then frowned, his brows knitting as he looked at her. "And how in the world did you come to have his feather? Sounds like Bryn hasn't changed at all."

Ella's throat closed. "You know Bryn?"

She and Jakobav said it at the same time, both half-rising from their chairs.

Her father turned his gaze on Jakobav. Cold. Measuring. "Of course I know him. Do you even know how old he is, boy?"

Jakobav's jaw clenched, the ink along his forearm stark against the strain as his hand balled into a fist against the table. For a moment, he said nothing, collecting himself before his expression smoothed into something controlled. But Ella knew better.

His voice, when it came, was steady and ironclad. "I know exactly how old he is."

The two men locked eyes, steel meeting steel, and the tension stretched so taut across the table she worried it might snap.

Ella broke it, her voice measured. "We're really doing this at dinner?"

Her father's gaze softened, the fight in his shoulders loosening as he exhaled. "Of course not, sweetheart. Forgive me. Your return has stirred emotions I thought I'd long buried. We will welcome your guest. He may stay as long as you wish. And with the Veil being tested as it is, perhaps it is time to consider all potential allies."

The hall exhaled with him, the tension spilling out in a collective rush. Murmurs rolled through the chamber like distant thunder.

"Dravaryn's heir at her side."

"Many years gone, and she returns with him?"

"Is this her coronation or her wedding?"

"He looks more like a warlord than a guest."

"Gods, he's beautiful."

"Beautiful? He's a weapon. Look at those arms."

Ella forced herself to keep calm, her gaze fixing on her plate, though heat prickled at her cheeks. The Court of Rumors had earned its name long before tonight, but never had it grated at her like this. She searched for a distraction, anything to break the tide.

Jakobav straightened his shoulders, slow and confident, with a half-smile on his face. She was certain he'd heard every word. He let them look, let them call him beautiful, let them call him a weapon, and his smile told them he was both, and more besides.

The tales spread faster than servants could refill goblets, speculation knotting through the air with greedy hands. Was this a celebration, an alliance, or a scandal turned marriage negotiation? Courtiers leaned closer to one another, eyes gleaming as though every rumor was a coin to be traded. Ella straightened her spine and tried to let none of it touch her.

Across the table, her father's gaze found hers once more. The steel in his eyes had dulled to sorrow, and his expression made her stomach turn.

"How has Orchid fared since I left?" Ella asked quietly. She already feared the answer.

"For a long while, things remained steady, the Threadshifting kept our forces busy but not overwhelmed," Eryndor said, his voice quieting the table around him. "But recently... that has changed. The breaches are worsening. Threadshifting accelerating. Magic unraveling just when we need it most."

He drew a slow breath, lines deepening at the corners of his eyes.

"An entire village was lost two weeks ago. A creature slipped the Veil before anyone could reach them. My council fears Orchid won't last much longer without reinforcements."

His hand trembled faintly as he lifted his goblet, the wine trembling with it. "At the very least, I will see my daughter wear the crown of Orchid, no matter how brief that reign may be."

A jolt of panic cut through her—but she forced it down, clinging to the one sliver of hope she had left. The prophecy had spoken of a red sun. And the red sun was still a week away.

Surely that meant she still had time.

Time to understand the relic—Jakobav.

Time to figure out how he might be the key.

Time to stop the Veil from shattering.

She repeated it like a prayer she didn't quite believe: *I still have time.*

She tried to cling to faith and fates and prophecy, even as her father sat across from her already resigned, accepting the acceleration of gloom and the inevitability of doom.

However brief her reign might be.

Her fire surged at his words, clawing at her ribs as if it longed to burst free and set the table to ash. Ella dug her nails into her palms beneath the cloth to remain still, forcing her magic back into its cage. Not here. She swallowed hard.

Across the table, Nira met her eyes and mouthed one word for her alone: *breathe.*

Ella clung to it like a rope thrown into stormwaters, her

best friend's gaze anchoring her even as the news her father had shared threatened to drag her under.

The room clattered with cutlery and wine and rumor, yet all she could hear was the grief hidden in her father's voice. She'd come home to warmth, to laughter, even to Bryn's ridiculous inside joke echoing across kingdoms, and within an hour, politics had stripped it bare, leaving only duty and loss. Her mother's shadow lingered in every corner.

Ella folded her hands in her lap, spine unyielding. She wouldn't cry.

There would be time to grieve later.

If the fates allowed her that much.

41

BLOOD WITHIN THE VEIN

Her father leaned close, his voice pitched low enough that only she could hear. "Ellandria... I have to announce it tonight," he murmured, the words tinged with worry. "Your coronation will be in two days. The people need something to hold on to."

Panic swelled in her chest, despite knowing this moment would come. The prophecy rose in her memory, no longer distant lines cast by the fates but a relentless drumbeat beneath her ribs:

A queen will fall, her time undone,
The daughter crowned beneath red sun.
She'll thread the Veil that none may cross,
Restore what kingdoms thought was lost.

Her fingers clenched tighter around her goblet, the rim cooling her skin even as the words burned through her. She was the daughter. She was the crown. But was she the path forward for every kingdom trembling beneath the unraveling Veil?

Eryndor turned fully toward her, his hand brushing her

arm. "You look beautiful tonight, Ellandria." His eyes glimmered with years and grief and pride. "When I heard whispers you were tangled in a Dravaryn Claiming, I was terrified. We all were. I still have questions, gods know I do. When I learned you were returning, I braced myself to see a ghost of your former self. But you"—his gaze held hers steady, unwavering—"ran away a girl and returned a woman. Strong, powerful, and full of purpose."

Her vision blurred as she threw her arms around him, clinging tightly. Her father was here, alive, and back in her life. The ache she'd carried for years cracked open, flooding her with a relief she'd never dared let herself feel.

She glanced down the table, searching for Jakobav. He wasn't watching, though he must've heard every word. His attention was fixed elsewhere, too carefully, the avoidance louder than a stare. She tried to smooth her expression, unwilling to let him see her this raw. "Technically," she managed, "I have the same purpose I did when I left. But now I feel capable of achieving it."

A soft chuckle rumbled in her father's chest as he held her tighter. "Your stubbornness hasn't gone anywhere."

He straightened, lifting his goblet, and the hall hushed. "In two days' time," he declared, his voice striking the vaulted ceiling like a bell, "Orchid will crown its queen."

A cheer surged through the chamber. Goblets lifted, feet stomped, voices rose in celebration. Ella lifted her chin high, though grief burned her hollow, and refused to falter.

Marisol approached with a fresh decanter, her steps light but certain. She bent to refill their goblets.

"You don't have to do that. Sit with us," Ella said warmly.

Her father's mouth curved faintly. "Marisol is no longer the castle's chief steward. She's just helping with the banquet tonight."

Ella turned to Marisol and said, "Really? What are you doing now?"

Marisol's smile deepened, soft but with purpose. "Helping where I'm needed. I stepped away from stewardship some time ago. I've been working under the castle's defense council." She lowered her voice as she refilled Ella's goblet. "Most of my time is spent restoring the old archives. Translating what remains of the ancient texts. Some of them...are becoming relevant again."

The shift in Marisol's tone told Ella more than the words themselves. The Veil. Maybe even restoring lost Fae scripts. Secrets waiting in dust.

Ella set down her cup. The Crown loomed closer with every minute, a responsibility she could feel gathering around her like stormlight. There was so much she didn't know. So much she'd missed.

"I'll need to be caught up on everything that's happened," she said quietly, more to herself than to either of them.

"Don't worry about that now. Tonight, we're celebrating." Her father nudged the goblet toward her. "Drink. It might help."

Jakobav leaned back in his chair, the faintest smirk cutting across his face. "I'm not sure that's wise. I've seen what happens when Ellandria drinks Fae wine."

Ella sputtered into her drink, coughing, then smacked him squarely in the chest. He didn't even flinch, only raised his brows with infuriating calm.

Marisol giggled behind the decanter.

Eryndor's smile faltered, eyes widening as his posture stiffened.

"Forgive me," he said after a beat, steadying his voice. "Your...friendship...may take time to get used to. Last I knew, striking the heir of Dravaryn could start a war."

Ella laughed, reckless and unguarded.

Jakobav's smile looked real this time. And it was devastating.

A tall, dark-skinned man with rolled sleeves paused beside her, coaxing a hibiscus into a harmless ember-bloom with a flick of his fingers. A soft rush of warmth brushed her arm, carrying the sweet-sharp scent of singed petals before fading.

"Say the word, and I'll light his boots," he murmured.

Ella's grin widened, sudden and fond, as she recognized her childhood friend despite how much he'd changed—still handsome, somehow even more magnetic. She leaned to clasp him in a quick half-hug. "Permission to stand down, Demetrius."

He tipped two fingers in salute and vanished back into the crowd.

From the corner of her eye, Ella caught Jakobav's raised brow, the question in it impossible to miss. She pursed her lips and gave the faintest shake of her head—a silent promise of "don't worry."

Music rose, jubilant, filling the hall with the churn of silk skirts, stomping boots, and laughter. Ella's heart twisted. Her mother had loved dancing—so had she—but tonight the sound scraped raw. Their joy felt like a betrayal of Queen Serenya. Ella sat straighter, forcing her face into what the court needed most: hope.

"I know it's difficult, but your return brings them light," her father murmured, his hand warm and heavy over hers.

The musicians played louder, couples whirled faster, and Ella forced herself to watch. Surely nothing could feel worse than this performance while her bones still rattled with sorrow.

And then the doors opened.

Caelen Verelith entered the great hall with a glide of silk, his expression holding the same golden arrogance she remembered all too well. He walked straight toward her and paused, offering a deep, unnecessary bow. This was another childhood friend, once almost something more. Why the formality? And gods, he looked different. He'd grown into his features, carried himself with a style that finally fit.

"Ellandria," he murmured, voice meant for her alone—smooth, gentle. "You look radiant tonight."

Then he turned toward her father with the smile that courtiers used to climb thrones. "Your Majesty. What a triumph tonight is. Orchid is blessed by your leadership, truly."

Eryndor offered a small smile, wary but gracious.

Caelen shifted back to Ella, lowering his voice until only she could hear. "When I heard the news of your return...I was so relieved. Orchid needs stability. And you need someone... who understands what you've been raised for."

Ella's spine stiffened. Jakobav drifted behind her, his demeanor stoic, as unmovable as a guard refusing to leave his post.

Caelen glanced at him, polite curiosity masking what looked a little bit like contempt. "And you brought a guest," he said pleasantly. "Dravaryn's heir, no less. How diplomatic of you, Ellandria."

Jakobav took a step forward and smiled without warmth. "Diplomacy isn't what brought me here."

"Mm," Caelen hummed, still casual, still smiling. "So I gathered."

He smoothed a hand through his light brown, slicked-back hair and, with a slow inhale, stepped closer—too close—his breath brushing her jaw as if he had a right to be there. The sour trace of wine clung to him.

"You and I have unfinished plans we need to discuss," he murmured. "Your mother agreed that Orchid needed a united front. A mating ceremony to solidify it. You at my side."

Ella's blood chilled.

He lifted her hand to kiss it, but she tugged free, ducking as if to retrieve something from the floor. She smoothed her dress, and he coughed into his hand, covering what he clearly viewed as a breach of etiquette.

"When did you speak to my mother, Caelen?" Her voice was even but her skin prickled with alarm.

She looked toward her father, wanting to ask if he knew anything about it, but he was deep in conversation with a nobleman she recognized by face, though his name escaped her.

"I'm so very sorry for your loss, Ellandria. If you need someone to speak with, I am yours, whenever you're ready. I'm always around."

She couldn't do this. It was too much. Caelen had been one of her closest friends when they were little. But something about him no longer matched the boy she remembered.

She offered a noncommittal reply, and she wasn't even sure what she'd said.

"Congratulations on the upcoming coronation, by the way," he added, composure neatly restored.

Ella met his eyes but couldn't bring herself to smile. She would give anything not to have an impending coronation, for her mother to remain on the throne, yet she still found herself offering the mannered response. "Thank you. It... means a great deal to Orchid." She tipped her chin, polite but distant. "And as you can imagine, there is much I need to review. Decisions that must be made. I've been gone longer than I should have, and I intend to understand everything that has happened in my absence."

It was the most diplomatic way she could say "I don't have

time for you" without igniting even more gossip than she already had.

Bringing the enemy home to meet the family and all that.

Caelen's lips curled. "Ah, yes...of course. I can't tell you how pleased I am with your return." He leaned in slightly, voice softening into something that tried to sound intimate. "I would love to schedule a meeting tomorrow. I can fill you in on all that has happened, and you can tell me everything in return." His gaze sharpened. "It seems you've come back with stories," he murmured. "And with...attachments."

His gaze dipped, lingering where Jakobav stood, a presence hewn from night. "But attachments can be undone."

She didn't breathe.

Ella knew he was ambitious, but she didn't remember him being this forward. Not with her.

His next words brushed her ear, quiet enough to be mistaken for affection.

"But do be careful, Ellandria. You wouldn't want the wrong man to think he has any claim on you."

Jakobav moved with a quiet, lethal restraint, and Caelen's smile faltered.

Only then did Caelen raise his voice enough for the nearby courtiers to hear.

"Prince Jakobav," he said, bowing with razor-edged elegance. "Orchid welcomes you. Do enjoy the evening. This night is important for us all."

Jakobav's jaw flexed. "Oh, I intend to."

Ella felt the tension draw tight as a bowstring.

Caelen's hand lifted before she could step back, his knuckles brushing her cheek. "Ellandria, be sure to save a dance for me." He said her name like he owned it. Then he strode to the far corner of the hall and leaned against a pillar as though the place belonged to him, his tunic gleaming with gold and self-importance.

Ella swallowed and turned toward Jakobav. "Would you like to go outside for a moment? I need some air."

His expression eased by a fraction. "Thought you'd never ask."

They stepped onto the balcony. A faint sea breeze moved across the terrace, reaching her beneath the stone arches. Ella inhaled deeply.

Jakobav rested a hand against the railing, watching her. "Tell me the truth. Are you alright?"

Ella gave a small, tired exhale. "I should be asking you that. Not everyone has been...friendly."

"Friendly is generous," he said, though his tone stayed even. "I expected worse."

"Not all of them were that bad," she said.

His gaze flicked back to the hall. "One was."

Ella didn't deny it.

Jakobav angled his head toward her. "I'll get us two goblets of wine. We can stay out here as long as you want." His mouth pulled into a slow, unexpected smile. "Forever, if you like."

Something in her chest softened. "Thank you."

He gave a brief nod and disappeared inside.

For the first time since stepping into the hall, the air moved through her freely. The balcony was quiet. Open. Real. A place untouched by expectations or watching eyes.

She wasn't alone for long.

Unsteady footsteps approached.

Caelen emerged from the shadows at the far end of the terrace, the polite façade he'd worn inside nowhere in sight. The lanternlight caught the faint flush along his cheekbones; the wine had settled deep.

"So this is where you're hiding," he said.

Ella straightened. "I came out for air."

"You came out here to avoid him." Caelen stepped closer, his eyes unfocused but intent. "Interesting."

She kept her voice level. "Go back inside, Caelen. You're drunk."

He laughed—quiet, humorless. "And you're naïve if you think that matters anymore."

His expression tightened. Gone was the polished boy she'd once trusted. So was the pleasant courtier. What stood before her now was someone adulterated by ambition and bitterness and too much power left unchecked.

"I waited for you," he said, stopping a breath away. "Years. And you return with him?"

"Jakobav is—"

"Not the point." Caelen's voice dropped lower. "You were promised to Orchid. Promised to me. That is how this kingdom will survive." His gaze hardened, voice gaining a new severity. "But if you refuse me...Eryndor will be the next to die."

The world narrowed.

"What did you just say?" Ella whispered.

Caelen leaned in, the wine on his breath harsh and overwhelming now. "I said your father is a liability. And I don't let liabilities stand in the way of what must be done. Besides—he knows too much."

Her hand moved toward her blade on instinct, but Caelen was faster, fingers closing around her wrist.

Heat surged instantly beneath his grip. A rising burn that dug into her skin and climbed with dangerous intensity.

Pain surged up her arm. She tried to pull free. His grip only tightened.

"Don't," he murmured. "You'll make this worse."

Heat pressed deeper, steady and relentless, weakening her knees.

Gods. He might actually kill me.

She'd sensed something different about him, not just his appearance. His Veinfire had grown stronger. That shouldn't have been possible.

The burn dug past skin and into an agonizing pain. She didn't know how long she could withstand it before her body gave out.

Behind them, the balcony door opened.

Two goblets slipped from Jakobav's hands and hit the stone, wine spilling across the floor.

His entire body went still.

"Touch her for another fucking second," Jakobav said, voice low and clear, "and you won't leave this balcony alive."

Caelen didn't release her.

He didn't flinch.

"Jake—wait. You don't know what he's capable of."

Caelen turned his head slightly, his grip still locked around Ella's wrist. "You can go back inside now," he said calmly. "We have catching up to do. I apologize if I worried you, but she's taken care of."

"Ella," Jakobav said, his eyes fixed on Caelen's hand, "come here."

She tried to step back; Caelen's hold didn't budge.

"How bold of you to bring your leash into Orchid, Ellandria," Caelen murmured.

Jakobav bared his teeth, releasing a low warning growl. "Careful," he said softly. "You're confusing which one of us is on a leash."

Caelen straightened, color climbing his cheekbones. "You don't realize who you're up against, brute. No matter. You'll learn. Ellandria was always meant to stand beside me. That was the plan before she ran off to"—his gaze dragged slowly over Ella, voice dropping low—"play in enemy beds."

Jakobav's hand twitched toward his blade, and Ella's chest tightened.

"Jakobav," she hissed under her breath.

But Caelen only smiled wider. "Tell me, Ellandria—does he touch you the way I will? Does he know everything you're destined to become? Everything that was promised to me." His eyes gleamed as he leaned closer, his voice barely above a whisper now. "Think of it. The power we would wield as a mated pair."

The last tether snapped. Jakobav reacted, closing the distance, a cold fury radiating from him.

The sword sang free of its sheath, slicing through the air.

Caelen's grip didn't lessen. Fire bloomed across his arms, crawling like molten veins until his skin glowed from within. The heat rippled outward, piercing and metallic, like iron left in the forge too long. Sweat prickled at her brow, her silk skirt clinging damp against her legs. He flexed his fingers, and flame snaked down them in dark-orange threads, eager to ignite.

"Veinfire," Ella whispered to Jakobav, knowing a warning wouldn't save him from it.

Caelen's grin turned venomous, and his other hand closed around her forearm before she could twist away, power licking across her skin, her veins flaring with sudden light. Ella gasped and yanked back, a thin scorch streaking across her arm like venom. Veinfire behaved differently than any other Orchid flame. It couldn't burn cloth. It was hungry only for flesh, eager to sear deeply, devouring its victim from inside out, from soul to skin.

It was the only fire Ella couldn't bend to her will.

Jakobav moved. His sword slammed down between them, sparks flaring as metal met flame. The smell of scorched skin permeated the air. His gaze snapped to her arm, to the faint glow beneath her skin, and something inside him seemed to lock into place. His voice came out low and very calm.

"You should never touch a woman who wants nothing from you," Jakobav said, each word slow and lethal. "You are nothing."

His sword hit Caelen hard, driving him back a full step and ripping his hand off her. Ella stumbled free, scrambling behind Jakobav as he stepped forward, placing himself squarely between them.

Caelen's hand shot toward Jakobav's throat.

If he got a grip, those deadly veins would blaze under Jakobav's skin—and strength wouldn't matter. Veinfire would kill him.

But Jakobav moved faster.

Steel clashed against fire, sparks flying. Caelen swung again, and this time, the Veinfire latched onto Jakobav, searing across his knuckles and spreading up his arm. He didn't pull his arm back.

Why wasn't he moving?

Fuck.

Ella's stomach plunged.

Gods, he was letting the Veinfire take him, devouring him from the inside out. She could already see the blaze climbing.

He's going to burn for me.

"Jake!" she screamed, the name tearing from her throat like it could drag him back from the fire.

Caelen braced wide, both arms outstretched, fingers clawed as if he could rip Jakobav open with sheer force. Veinfire poured from him in a torrent, veins glowing like molten ore, the blaze lashing straight into Jakobav.

Ella held her breath, waiting for grief and devastation, for Jakobav to scream, to fall.

"No!" she yelled, the plea echoing through the night air.

The balcony doors slammed open.

Light and voices spilled out as King Eryndor stepped onto the terrace, half the council crowding behind him. Their laughter died instantly at the sight—Caelen stood wreathed in Veinfire, Jakobav staggering under the force of it, Ella scorched and pinned helplessly against the railing.

"Caelen, stop!" Eryndor roared. "Stand down at once!"

Caelen didn't turn.

He ignored the king entirely, the veins in his arms burning brighter as he poured more power into Jakobav.

Jakobav raised one hand as though to ward it off, his body rigid, jaw clenched, the fire searing across his skin until Ella swore she could smell ash.

Her stomach dropped.

Jakobav's head snapped up, teeth bared in a feral smile, and then he struck. His other hand flashed, steel gleaming as a second, smaller blade—one he must have kept hidden—arced swiftly, scoring a shallow line across Caelen's forearm. Not deep, but just enough to open him, and blood welled bright against the heat. Jakobav angled the blade, letting a single drop roll toward its tip. His tongue flicked against the steel, and the moment the blood touched him, his veins lit like fire catching oil.

Caelen froze at the horrific sight.

His nostrils flared, his body tightening as though the blood itself was singing through him, power thrumming in his bones. Veinfire radiated from him, alive, his skin glowing with stolen flame.

Jakobav smiled wider, and Caelen looked both stunned and disgusted.

He wielded it with devastation, flaring bigger and brighter than it had on Caelen, the result of years of practice with borrowed powers and necessary brutality.

Caelen staggered back, his own veins flaring in response, his voice breaking into a snarl. "Mine!"

Jakobav's grin was pure ruin. "It's mine now. Just like she never was, and never will be, yours."

He raised his hand, and flame erupted under Caelen's skin, crawling up his neck, illuminating every vein in his body splitting apart in branching red fissures.

A court member gasped just before Caelen screamed, his arrogance melting into raw panic. His own magic betrayed him, burning through him where everyone could see.

Jakobav stepped close, his voice a growl meant for Caelen's ears alone. "This is what you are. Hollow fire in hollow veins."

Then he slammed the hilt of his sword into Caelen's jaw, and he crumpled to the floor, unconscious, his glowing veins dimming to nothing.

Silence swallowed the court.

Jakobav stood over him, chest heaving, dark eyes sweeping the stunned faces watching him. His mouth was stained red at the corner—a smear of blood he didn't bother to wipe. He looked less like a guest, less like a prince, and more like a weapon forged for nights exactly like this.

No one stepped forward. No one dared.

Jakobav turned, his gaze finding the scorch mark on her arm. His jaw hardened. Without a word, he closed the distance, lifted her, and swung her over his shoulder.

A murmur of shock, courtiers parting in a wave. Her hair spilled down his back, and her fists beat once against him before she went limp.

Jake is alive.

The balcony tilted, her view reduced to Jakobav's back, the hard line of muscle beneath black leather. Heat radiated from him, every step jolting, her stomach flipping as much from the position as from the way he carried her—like she was his prize, his proof, his fury.

"Put me down," she hissed, too low for anyone else to hear.

His grip only tightened around her thighs. "Not a chance."

The court's whispers chased them.

Warlord. Weapon. Beautiful. Dangerous.

And gods help her, part of her didn't care. Suspended over his shoulder, Ella's pulse hammered, torn between outrage and a wild, treacherous thrill.

As they passed the crowd, she caught her father's gaze upside down and muttered through clenched teeth, "Don't look at me."

Eryndor did anyway, his expression unreadable, somewhere between fear and a terrible sort of pride. His voice reached her, low enough that only those nearest could hear.

"So much like your mother."

Nira and Marisol stood beside him, smiling. Ella watched, mortified, as they exchanged a quick glance, both of them blushing and barely hiding their giggles as she was carried past.

Jakobav didn't slow. He carried her through the doorway and into the castle as if nothing were amiss—as if he'd simply grown tired of the banquet and chosen to leave. Behind them, the Court of Rumors fell into a stunned silence.

Her return to Orchid wasn't off to a great start. She felt less like a graceful queen-to-be and more like a sack of potatoes.

42

EDGE OF THE BREAK

He carried her through the castle as if she weighed nothing, his stride long and unbothered despite the spiraling hallways and high-arched corridors he'd never set foot in before.

"Put me down," Ella hissed.

He didn't.

She glared up at him even though he couldn't see it.

"Jake, put me the fuck down."

He stopped and set her on her feet, though he didn't look remotely sorry about it. His hands lingered at her waist, as if letting go might undo everything he'd just fought for. Finally, he let go and took a single step back.

"You don't even know where you're going," she said, brushing her hands over her dress.

Jakobav's mouth twitched. "Fair point."

"So maybe let the person who actually lived here lead."

She took the front, and he fell into step behind her. They crossed two long galleries, past pillars and tall windows spilling moonlight across the floor, until she turned into a quiet wing lined with closed doors.

"Marisol said they kept my room exactly as it was. Only attendants entered to clean. No one else has stepped inside since I left." Her fingers hovered near her skirts, restless. "In case I came home." Her chest tightened, a small pang of guilt stirring before she shoved it down.

They stopped in front of a familiar door.

Ella swallowed hard.

The hall outside Ella's chambers glowed golden, torchlight painting restless shadows across marble while the faint perfume of jungle flowers drifted through the open lattice at the end of the hall. The silence in the corridor hung thick, humming with the aftermath of the evening.

"Where am I supposed to sleep?" His voice was rough, pitched low, the battlefield still clinging to it.

Ella's lips curved. "With me, obviously."

Something feral lit behind his eyes, barely leashed, and he caught her wrist, drawing her forearm into the torchlight. The faint scorch from Caelen's Veinfire traced itself like ink across her skin, and his jaw clenched, a muscle ticking hard. Then his other hand closed around her opposite wrist, pulling it into the light as well. The silver half-moon Thread-burn gleamed faintly against her pulse, etched into her like an unhealed secret.

Jakobav's eyes darkened as if the sight struck him deep. His grip tightened just enough to anchor her in place, his gaze locked on the twin marks carved into her skin.

"If anyone else ever lays flame or fate on you again, I'll end them."

The words sat between them, too full of truth.

He drew in a slow breath, looking like he was trying to

push the violence back behind his teeth. "Does it hurt?" His voice was quiet.

"The Veinfire still stings," Ella replied honestly.

He slid a square of linen from his coat, but instead of tending to her right there in the corridor, he nudged her door open with his boot and guided her inside.

The chamber held a faint floral scent, the basin gleaming on the table as though waiting for this moment. He poured water over her arm, the touch cold against the burn, and bound her forearm with careful hands. When he finished, he bent and pressed his mouth to the skin just above the bandage, sending a shiver through her despite the warm night.

She couldn't believe he was there with her, in her chambers, a place she'd thought she would never see again. Ella's thoughts slipped back to the banquet, to the way women had leaned forward when he entered, their gazes drinking him in.

Vultures.

"Half the hall would've dropped their goblets to be the one you noticed. And yet here you are, tending to my injury."

His jaw flexed, but instead of the smirk she expected, he only stilled. His steady gaze locked on hers.

"I didn't come here for politics. I walked into enemy territory not knowing if I'd be met with an army. I came for you, Ella." His voice roughened, conviction burning low and fierce. "I'll follow you anywhere. Into whatever hell the fates unleash. Not because you're a prize to be won, but because you're the only choice I'll ever make."

Her chest tightened, the jealousy dissolving into something hungrier, something that pinned her in place.

"Now, no more touching you until you say so," he murmured.

Liquid heat pooled low in her belly at his words.

This man would kill anyone who dared touch her without

permission, and gods, the dark promise of it throbbed through her, desire gathering between her thighs.

"I'm saying so," she breathed.

The corner of his mouth lifted. "Then say it again."

Her fingers fisted in his collar. "Stay."

Jakobav pushed the door shut with his shoulder, sealing off the empty corridor. Her back hit the wood as he crowded into her space, his hands cupping her jaw and sliding to the nape of her neck.

"Tell me no," he rasped against her mouth.

"No...I won't. Please, Jake. Stop holding back," she breathed.

Cloth tore between them, tugged impatiently as though every barrier had become an offense. He stripped her bare, and for a heartbeat, he only looked, his eyes dark and reverent, worship and feral hunger tangled together. "Fuck," he growled, his voice breaking with truth. "You're beautiful, Ellandria."

His gaze traveled over her. "Now get on the bed. On your knees. Face me."

Heat scalded her cheeks, but her body obeyed. She turned toward the mattress, the sway of her hips intentional, aware and unashamed of her nakedness before him.

She climbed onto the bed, knees sinking into the furs as a sound broke from him, a half-groan, half-growl, primal and ragged. He followed her onto the mattress in one fluid motion, closing the distance in a swift blur. One hand gripped her hip with bruising strength while the other skimmed along her spine. His palm landed hard on the curve of her ass, anchoring her, then his mouth brushed her ear—almost tender—a contradiction so sharp it made her shiver.

Jakobav pressed her into the mattress, braced above her on his forearms. Their mouths found each other again and again, desperate, as if kissing were the only language left to them. Her fingers slid into his hair, tugging him closer until his forehead pressed to hers, his breath uneven, rough velvet against her lips.

"Tell me what you want," he rasped.

"I want you to fuck me, Jake. Now," she shot back, voice breaking like a challenge and a plea.

His control snapped, and the kiss turned deeper, hungrier. She met every thrust of his tongue with hers, her thirst turning carnal and hands roaming over his chest, his abdomen, and then lower. Fuck, this man was unacceptably hot. And ridiculously hard.

She pressed herself against him, body arching with need.

He held her face in both hands, as though she were the only one he desired in this world. Her legs wrapped around him, pulling him flush against her, and he answered with a groan that sounded closer to prayer than sin. She rocked her hips, knowing he could feel her wetness and scent the want dripping off her.

He pressed his cock into her slickened core, slow at first, teasing her. She gasped from the fullness of it. She would never get over how completely he filled her, each thrust driving deeper.

"Fuck, Jakobav," she breathed.

Her fingernails bit into his back, clutching him as if begging not to stop. A moan tumbled from her lips, and was answered by his hips thrusting deeper, quickening the pace in a delicious, relentless torture.

His mouth brushed her jaw, her cheek, the corner of her lips. The worship in his eyes, the maddening softness of his kisses, made her entire body tense with anticipation of sweet release.

She whimpered against his mouth, wanting him to come apart for her just like she was unraveling for him.

"You're so fucking perfect, Ella," he murmured, guiding her hand between their bodies and placing it on her clit, his hand on top of hers, working over her sensitive spot, demanding the rhythm he wanted from her before removing his hand.

"Keep going until I tell you to stop."

Her breath shuddered. A moan escaped, and he swallowed it with another kiss, deep and unguarded.

When his mouth grazed her throat, she whispered, "Don't bite me this time. Don't draw blood. Please." Her own words startled her. Desire warred with dread—the memory of the Fae's fury never far from her mind. If Jake tasted her again, a ripple could tear open in the middle of Orchid's castle.

He moaned against her throat, teeth grazing. "Tell me what you're hiding."

She said nothing, her mind going to the crescent on her wrist, hidden by the bandage. The green-eyed Fae had all but admitted to punishing her and sending that creature through the breach near the Dravaryn gate. He'd scented her and Jake through the ripple, and worse, he called it the Sacred Fae Garden.

Gods...what does that even mean?

She moved her palms flat to Jakobav's back, grounding herself in the present moment. She realized she hadn't actually answered his question. She'd given him only silence.

He searched her eyes, then exhaled roughly, like a man surrendering to a choice he'd already made. He shook his head once. "Fuck it," he growled. "I told you I'll take you any way you let me."

He returned to her neck, placing kisses down the column of her throat, hungry and careful at once. His hands slid lower, found her ankles, then swept them into his grip, tugging her down the bed like drawing a thread through a needle. He eased her knees higher, folding her open to the torchlight, then drove into her, unyielding, each thrust a promise hammered into rhythm.

The wood creaked, the headboard shuddered, and her voice shattered on his name. He found the beat beneath her skin and followed it, his breath ragged against her mouth as he moved faster.

Jakobav tore his mouth from hers long enough to growl against her ear, "Fuck. We fit so perfectly. You're mine."

Ella clutched him hard, nails dragging down his chest, her head thrown back against the furs. The tension coiled inside her, tightening into something unbearable. But before she could sink into the feeling, he caught both her wrists and lifted them above her head, pinning them gently. Ella's pulse kicked hard.

Gods, after the fight, after watching him nearly burn, after hearing him claim her in front of half the court, how was she supposed to ever come down? How was she supposed to want anything but this?

He slammed into her, thrusting with a relentless rhythm as the world narrowed to the drag of his breath against her throat. Her need to release was all-consuming and daring her to surrender.

Gods, she wanted to.

She lifted her hips to meet him thrust for thrust. With her wrists still pinned in one of his hands, his other hand slid down to the sensitive spot just above where their bodies slammed together, skilled fingers circling and bringing her to the cusp.

"Please, Jake, fall apart with me." She didn't recognize her own voice, aching, trembling, sounding dangerously close to begging.

He refused to slow down, driving into her again and again. The feel of him between her thighs made her widen her legs to take in every exquisite inch. Her legs began to shake.

"I'll never stop falling for you," he replied.

It stole her breath.

Pleasure shot up her spine. Words crumbled into sound—hers, his, tangled like smoke and wildfire.

He fought for me.

He burned for me.

He would die for me.

And gods help her—

She wanted him with an ache that bordered on salvation.

Pleasure hit like surf over rock, again and again, wild and somehow sublime.

He might be her damnation instead.

When it finally ebbed, Ella lay beneath him, breathless, every nerve alight. The banquet, the coronation, the whispers—they all drifted to the edges of her mind like distant noise. She would face them soon enough. For now, she held to the only truth that mattered.

He'd chosen her.

And she'd chosen him.

The torches hissed, steady and low, as though the castle had suspended itself in the moment with them.

DAWN FOUND them in a tangle of sheets that smelled of amber and rose, pale gold from the lattice spilling across the floor while the jungle's slow hymn rose beyond the open window. Ella woke to his arm at her waist and the steady beat of his heart beneath her palm, and she let herself float there—small and infinite at once, held between warmth and light.

At least she hadn't Threadwalked in her sleep this time.

The glaring truth of all she'd kept from him started to creep in; Jakobav was likely wondering why she'd asked him not to draw blood. She hadn't explained last night.

She was afraid.

Afraid of what might happen if the Fae man scented amber on her skin again. Especially after his warning that the consequences would be far worse. And this time, her kingdom would've paid the price. She shivered as guilt encroached upon her.

She hadn't told Jakobav that she knew who'd sent the Tracker through the breach. Not when he bled for her, nor after he stood against Veinfire for her, and not even now.

Instinct warned her that speaking about the Fae—telling Jake the exact words the green-eyed man had said to her—would bring catastrophe down on both their kingdoms.

His lips pressed against the back of her head.

"You're awake," she whispered.

"I don't sleep much, remember?" His smile was lazy, and his voice still carried last night's heat.

She turned within the circle of his arm. The blood smear may have been long gone from his mouth, but the look in his eyes was not. "They all saw," she said softly. "What you did to Caelen. Blood-Scenting magic." She drew a breath. "Jakobav... should you even be able to do that in Orchid?"

"It's not power born of Dravaryn soil. It's never been limited to the borders of my own kingdom," he said. "But his Veinfire came to me faster and stronger than any ability from blood has before. Didn't think much about it at the moment. Been distracted ever since."

"It was quite a spectacle. You need to prepare for knowledge of your power to be widespread. Word travels fast here in Orchid. And the council will likely call a meeting to decide—"

"If the court decides I'm to be feared, we'll be surrounded before a crown ever touches your head."

"They already decided you're terrifying," she said, a wry light in her voice. "They watched you take him down without even blinking."

His mouth tilted. "You weren't blinking either."

"I was busy," Ella answered. "And why didn't you use your shield? You could've stopped him before he touched me."

Jakobav's jaw tightened. "I haven't had nearly as much practice with that ability as with my others. I almost killed Soren with my shield. I would never forgive myself if—" He broke off, jaw flexing. "And some things I don't reveal unless I must."

His admission settled between them.

She recognized herself in it more than she wanted to, her thoughts tormenting her with all she still held secret.

A tingle raked over the small silver crescent at her pulse, and memory uncoiled—wet stone and a terrace of stars, jasmine in the air, a pendant beating violet, and eyes like ice-cut green answering a thought she hadn't spoken. Echobinder. Stalking. Waiting.

She wondered if she should tell Jake right then, the confession pressing against her tongue until she bit it back.

"I understand better than most," she said, her frown softening as she chose to ease rather than burden.

He raised a brow. Clearly waiting for her to elaborate.

"What happens today," she said, "happens with you at my side and we face it together."

His hand stroked her temple, a gesture of comfort and protection. "I'll follow your lead in your hall," he said, quiet and sure. "But if something reaches for you, I'll end it. Quickly."

"I'd expect nothing less, Commander," she replied with a smirk.

He smiled back, breath drawing for a response—then a brisk knock came at the door.

"Your Highness?" Marisol's voice carried through the wood. "Crown fittings in a few minutes. Breakfast first. Then the council meeting at second bell."

Ella closed her eyes and opened them again, the world waiting while the crown called. "Come in," she called as she eased out of bed and reached for her robe. Then, lower to Jakobav, she murmured, "Try not to look like death incarnate in my sitting room."

He lay back on her pillow like a storm pretending to be a man. "I can't help how I look," he said, smiling with his eyes.

The day began with Marisol sweeping in, carrying a tray piled high with sugared fruit, dark bread, and a small pot of tea. Nira followed, hair pinned and dress immaculate, and—because he had never learned the meaning of a dignified entrance—Demetrius breezed in on a current of his own making.

"Good morning to royalty and whatever he is," Demetrius announced, tossing Jakobav a salute before striding straight to him and catching his hand in a firm shake. "Demetrius. Floral arsonist. Terrible influence. For the record, never had a crush on Ellandria, don't plan to mate her, and have no delusions about destiny. Clear?"

Jakobav's mouth actually twitched. "Clear."

"Excellent," Demetrius said, satisfied. "I like your terrifying face. Very inspiring."

"Demetrius," Marisol warned, half-laughing as she set the tray on Ella's desk. "Manners."

"I have so many," he said solemnly. "I just rarely bring them all at once."

Warmth loosened something tight in Ella's chest and held for exactly three heartbeats before the glass vase by the window cracked with a sound like ice under a boot and burst into a scatter of bright shards across the floor, the orchids on the sill slumping over.

Demetrius's hands went up at once. "Not me."

Ella's gaze cut to Marisol. "Was that you?"

"Absolutely not," Marisol said, eyes wide.

The candles on the mantel answered as if to argue, thin flames leaping into spears and climbing to lick the carved edge. Heat rushed across the room, the nearest curtain blackening at the hem. Before Ella could move, Nira stepped forward, her palm lifting as the fire collapsed into smoke with a soft, shocked sound, the air going gray as she waved her fingers and coaxed the smoke to twist and coil and sift into a neat spill of ash on the hearth.

"Bad candle," she told it, dusting her hands. "We do not eat drapery."

Demetrius let out a low whistle. "Show-off."

Nira arched her brow without missing a beat. "Says the one who lights roses on fire for applause."

"Art," he corrected, and to prove his point he flicked two fingers toward the wilted orchids. Flame shimmered delicately along their petals until the flowers rose on their stems and rebloomed in leafed tongues of fire that did not consume but only burned beautiful, living cinders that glowed against the dim chamber.

Ella stared despite herself, her throat tight as the room seemed to thin around her, stretched taut like a drumskin drawn too far. "Marisol?"

Marisol lifted her hand over the mantel, and the nearest flame leapt half a length taller. "I might be able to amplify a small flame," she said carefully, her eyes fixed on the blaze-touched orchids. "But I didn't touch those."

A cold thought sliced through her. What if the Fae man had somehow sensed Jake on her again, and these were the first signs of his retaliation? What if she'd brought devastation home to her people without meaning to?

Fuck. This can't be happening.

Jakobav was watching her closely, as if he could see every direction her mind was spiraling, a look of concern written on his face.

"This isn't from you," Jakobav said quietly. "Or from me. Magic was already unraveling. Whatever's happening...it's accelerating."

"Then it's the Veil," Ella murmured, her voice almost lost to the dread—and the faint, guilty relief of knowing the danger might not be her doing.

Jakobav had remained a silent figure by the bedpost, but now he moved to the window, his shoulders squared and soldier-straight. "Your kingdom is bracing," he said. "Thread-shifting might yet shatter the realm unless it's met with equal force."

"Then we brace for it. We find a solution," Demetrius answered far too lightly. His wink at Ella carried its own kind of defiance. "Starting with you, Your Highness. Coronation fittings demand their victim. Also, I brought pastries."

"You didn't bring pastries," Marisol countered.

"I brought enthusiasm," Demetrius said solemnly, "and that is almost as filling."

As if conjured by Demetrius's nonsense, a trio of seam-stresses swept in, wrists bristling with glittering pins. Behind them came goldsmiths. Another team followed with a long coat of deep black for Jakobav, Orchid silk lined in storm-gray, the collar embroidered with the smallest pattern of vine and flame that was still tasteful.

They measured Ella first. Marisol hummed soft approvals while Nira kept one eye on the restless candles. Demetrius, predictably, had claimed a chair and provided commentary.

"Turn," one seamstress said.

"She was born for turning," Demetrius intoned with reverence. "Look at that queen posture. Frightening. Ten out of ten."

"Get out," Nira told him, fond exasperation threaded through her voice.

"Leaving by choice before I'm thrown," he replied, rising with exaggerated dignity. He clasped Jakobav's forearm in parting, quick and sure. "Try to smile during the ceremony. Or don't. Either way, I'd like to live long enough to see the after-party."

"I'll consider it," Jakobav said, which for him sounded dangerously close to friendly.

Demetrius grinned at Ella. "Don't fret your coronation. You're a natural. And if you break anything, I'll grow you a new one out of fire." He swept a bow so theatrical it almost passed for elegant and slipped out just as the seamstresses demanded privacy.

By the time they were finished, Ella's coronation whites lay across a stand like a promise: silk that caught the light and gentled it, a sash stitched with gold thread, the crown fittings ready beside it like petals of metal waiting for dawn.

Jakobav endured his fitting with the patience of a man tolerating ritual, though the result suited him indecently well. Orchid silk clinging to his shoulders, narrowing through the waist, and falling in a lethal line to his boots. The storm-gray lining flashed when he moved. Ink climbed his forearms where the cuffs rode back, barbed knots and ash-dark sigils ghosting tendon and vein before disappearing again beneath fabric. The top toggle lay undone, showing a narrow V of throat and the barest glimpse of more ink at his collarbone. Muscle lived under all that polish, and nothing about him looked soft. His mouth was a straight, unforgiving line that suggested he could topple a capital before breakfast and be bored by dessert.

Nira exhaled, not even pretending to be unimpressed. “Unfair,” she muttered.

Ella didn’t trust her voice at first. “You look...” She searched for a word that would not betray how affected she was. “Prepared.”

His gaze locked on hers. “For whatever comes.”

The shutters gave a faint rattle, as though agreeing.

Somewhere deep in the castle, a bell tolled twice, the sound reverberating. Marisol glanced at the door. “Second bell.”

Ella adjusted her braid until her hands felt steady. “Then we start with the council.”

Jakobav offered his arm, but she stepped past him, letting him fall half a pace behind, exactly where the court would notice.

They left the hush of silk and pins, traveled quickly through the castle, and entered the council chamber, into the heat of an argument.

Orchid’s oldest hall had been built like a temple pretending to be a war room. A river of mosaic tile ran the length of the floor: blue glass for water, gold for sandbars, green for jungle, all bisecting a long table.

The council chamber was crowded when Ella stepped inside. Orchid lords and ladies crowded the table, rings flashing as ink-stained ledgers snapped open. Wax and too many opinions thickened the air.

Representatives from every corner of Orchid had been summoned: river merchants in travel-stained coats, coastal envoys still smelling of salt, and highland stewards wrapped in their formal sashes. Generals stood along the right wall in lacquered armor, helms tucked under their arms.

At the long table, several noblemen and senior members of the court had already taken their seats, their ledgers open, quills poised over parchment. A few scholars hovered behind them, ready with records and reports.

At the head of it all sat King Eryndor. Her father smiled when Ella took her place at his right hand, a smile and a wink that instilled more confidence than any speech. Jakobav positioned himself behind her chair, a shadow that made other shadows wary.

Nira and Marisol waited near the braziers, steady and alert. Two guards flanked the door with spears crossed, the tension in their stance unmistakable.

Then the King rose, and the room obeyed.

"Be seated," he said, and the command rippled outward.

Lord Verron Verelith did not sit. Caelen's father wore mourning black as though it were armor, his ruby ring, large as a knuckle, throwing firelight as he leaned forward, his gaze honing on Jakobav like a blade finding its mark.

"Majesty," he said, his voice smooth and poisonous, "must we conduct this council with that savage standing behind your daughter's chair? My son lies in the infirmary because of him."

The flames hissed in their iron bowls, and high above, a chime tolled, hollow as bone.

Eryndor's mouth thinned. "Your son is grievously wounded," he said evenly, "but he will live."

"Live to be humiliated in his own hall?" Verron snapped. "To watch a foreign warlord plant himself like a pillar behind Orchid's queen?"

Jakobav didn't move, his stillness carrying more weight than any gesture, silence radiating from him like a threat.

"Lord Verron," her father said, iron beneath the calm, "this chamber will not be a battlefield."

Lady Isola of the Estuary, with her silver-and-coral braided hair and her tide-bright eyes, tapped one fingertip against the table. "With respect," she said coolly, "this is theater. The breaches are not. Boats have gone dark on calm waters, farmers have vanished, and fish wash ashore with their eyes turned wrong. What is Orchid doing, beyond rehearsing speeches and pinning gowns?"

Murmurs frothed along the table's length.

"The Veil thins by the day," said a scholar, his voice papery with sleeplessness. "We require decisive doctrine."

"We require a queen who can command more than a room and a smile," another voice added. "One who hasn't been absent for so many years."

The words landed between Ella's ribs. She set her palms on the table, its coolness seeping into her skin, and she lifted her chin. "I went where I was pulled," she said steadily. "I learned what Orchid would need. I returned because the kingdom called me home."

"Pretty," Lord Verron sneered, his lip curling. "But pretty doesn't close a breach."

Voices rose in overlapping waves until the chamber felt smaller than its walls, recommendations tangling into recriminations, fear curdling into anger. Ella opened her mouth to speak, but three men cut across her, their words colliding until the torches guttered and flared, unsure which way to go.

Jakobav slowly walked to the front of the room.

He didn't raise his voice though the chamber re-aligned around him as if pulled by a tide.

"Dravaryn stands with Orchid," he said, each word steady. "You will have our alliance, our steel, our armies, and the full support of a nation that does not break or falter. Ever."

Her father's brows lifted a fraction.

The scholars didn't blink.

For the first time, Lord Verron seemed exquisitely at a loss.

Ella knew Dravaryn would not take this pledge lightly. Jakobav had just rewritten diplomacy, and possibly the fate of the realm, with barely more than a sentence.

Shock and gratitude sank into her chest.

He'd just offered up a kingdom as though it were nothing, as though she were everything. The danger was not in his armies or his steel, but in the certainty with which he chose her.

She rose and moved to stand beside him. Her hand slid into his, steady, unshaken. The torchlight flickered once and then steadied.

"Tomorrow," she said, and her voice did not waver, "I will be crowned your queen. We will restore Orchid. Together we will heal the Veil."

For the first time all night, no one dared to interrupt her. Even the candles seemed to listen. The marble floor seemed to vibrate as though something deep in the castle had shifted, like a beast before it runs.

Her father looked at her and didn't hide the pride in his face.

"You heard our future queen. Ellandria has secured a better alliance than we could've hoped for. Council adjourned." He said it quietly. "Prepare."

The chairs scraped back, and the lords rose. Lord Verron's gaze lingered on Ella a shade too long before he bowed to the king and swept from the room.

As the chamber emptied, Jakobav didn't release her hand.

"Bold," he murmured, his eyes still fixed forward.

"You started it," she murmured back.

43

BETWEEN ORCHID AND THE ROSE

The throne room of Orchid had been remade into a myth. Vines and blossoms hung in garlands from the rafters, dense as constellations, while torches in carved orchid sconces burned along the walls, their petals cradling flame. At the far end, the coronation dais rose in black marble veined with gold. Upon it waited a pedestal and the crown, hammered thin as leaf, gleaming for a brow not yet claimed.

The court swelled close, a sea of silk and rumor, while beyond the balconies, the jungle exhaled its breath into the hall. The air carried salt and florals, and beneath it, something harsher, like the first strike of a storm.

Ella's coronation whites clung too tightly, each pin and seam calculated to make her gleam like a symbol, though she'd never felt less like one. The silk bore the burden of promises she wasn't certain she could keep. A queen's gown ought to have been a sort of armor; instead it was a confession, pale as bone against a body etched with secrets.

Her heartbeat quickened beneath the sigil she now understood was bound to more than fire alone. Jakobav stood behind her, his presence as charged as it was necessary. Her kingdom had no knowledge of her Threadwalking, nor of the Echobinder who haunted her memory. And her mother's death closed in like a prophecy fulfilled too soon. Too many truths lay buried beneath this coronation, threads pulled taut in too many directions at once.

She faced a room of expectant lords and ladies who believed they saw a princess flaunting a warlord at her shoulder. Did they believe she was the queen Orchid needed? Her mother had been loved by all; Ella feared she would never measure up—not on the first day of her reign, perhaps not ever. But maybe, with time. Except time was not on her side... The Veil was slipping by the minute. And she was afraid the crowd could somehow sense her deepest fear: that she wouldn't be enough.

I've spent my whole life trying to prove I'm good enough—strong, fast, smart, brave enough. That I don't need anyone. That I can do it all on my own.

She told herself to keep moving, to play the part. But she didn't have to do it alone. She could lean on her father's wary pride, Marisol's steady kindness, Nira's warmth, Demetrius's confident humor, and Jakobav himself close by her side.

Enough to survive her coronation, perhaps, but not nearly enough to brace for a world on the verge of splitting open.

Then the great doors boomed.

The sound rolled through the garland-hung rafters and shook petals loose from their stems. Courtiers startled, and voices cut short. Heads turned in unison toward the entrance, toward the war that arrived along with the scent of obsidian stone.

Gods, she missed that smell.

Four figures crossed Orchid's marble floor as if it belonged to them. Dust clung to their boots, travel and battle written into the set of their shoulders. They didn't enter; they invaded.

A muscle jumped in Jakobav's jaw, the only betrayal of how hard his control slipped at the sight of them. He didn't move toward them, but something eased in his stance, a tension she'd seen him carry for days.

The crowd recoiled, and a whisper surged through the chamber, catching and spreading like fire through dry grass.

"Dravaryns."

"First Guard."

Thane approached first, shoulders broad as fortress gates, tattoos coiled down his muscled arms like serpents that might strike if provoked. His grin was unrepentant, as though arriving late to her coronation were a private joke and Ella herself the punchline. His gaze landed directly on her, and he lifted his brows in a silent question. Without hesitation, Ella nodded, her fingers slipping to the slit of her gown as she tugged the silk aside and pale fabric parted to reveal the emerald-jeweled hilt of Thane's blade strapped high on her thigh, gleaming keener still against the whiteness of her coronation dress.

Thane's smile broke wide open, feral delight flashing across his face.

Jakobav noticed, his jaw set, his expression turning storm-dark.

Thane blew him a kiss. "Happy to see you too, Prince," he drawled, laughter undercutting every syllable.

Maeren followed, iron contained in flesh, every step measured as though she carried an army in her shadow. She moved like a commander who'd already walked through brimstone and would do it again if the kingdom dared her to falter.

Soren drifted next, sliding to the dais edge before tilting his head sideways and going utterly still. A sentinel carved from dusk, he unsettled the torches until their flames guttered, as though the fire itself feared him.

Savina came last. Long blonde waves gleamed like burnished light as she shed her hood, beauty so terrible and exacting that Orchid nobles stared in open awe. Ella startled herself by blurting, "Sav!" with warmth, excitement in her voice before she could school it. Savina returned her smile, genuine and devastating in its rarity.

A few noblemen's gazes lingered too long on Savina, and Ella rolled her eyes. Savina cut the chamber a glance sharper than any blade, and the entire court seemed to look elsewhere as if remembering who she was.

The hall braced, Orchid's banners straining as though pulled by an unseen wind. Ella's chest tightened. Reinforcements had arrived. Not only Jakobav, but every piece of him.

And now the court would see the truth: Dravaryn stood with her.

The chamber had barely steadied when Maeren stepped toward Jakobav, her voice pitched low. "The rest of the Guard was left on breach detail."

Before Jakobav could respond, King Eryndor cleared his throat, the sound loud enough to still half the court. His brows rose a fraction. "Perhaps Dravaryn business can wait until after my daughter is crowned."

A ripple of uneasy laughter stirred, breaking tension like glass.

Maeren inclined her head, poised as ever, but instead of retreating, she crossed to Ella. From her cloak, she drew a single black rose, its black-violet petals glimmering faintly. The chamber hushed as Maeren fastened the bloom against Ella's gown. It sat against her chest, a stark bloom on white silk, Dravaryn's mark in a hall of Orchid.

Maeren bent low, her voice meant for Ella alone. "You were

meant to wear a crown," she murmured. "I'm honored to witness it."

Ella's throat tightened, but before she found words, Maeren had already stepped back.

"Don't trip on that gown," Thane called cheerfully, his grin wicked as he moved across the throne room. "I would hate to catch you and make every Orchid girl fall for me instead."

Several ladies tried to hide their smiles, while a few noblemen looked scandalized. Ella stifled a laugh of her own, heat rising traitorously to her cheeks.

Jakobav clenched his fist, his glare fixed on Thane, who only looked more delighted.

The ceremonial horns sounded, and the murmurs fell away like a curtain.

Ella stepped forward in her coronation whites, the silk catching the light and softening it, the gold-stitched sash curving over her ribs. Her hair had been delicately pinned, Marisol's hands steady and Nira's eyes bright.

The court watched her, their collective stare almost suffocating. Nerves stirred low in her stomach, bright and uneasy.

Jakobav took his place behind her, his tailored black coat transforming restraint into quiet ferocity.

Her father rose from the throne, his voice carrying without effort. "Let Orchid bear witness."

The coronation ceremony began with old words, and Ella repeated them, each vow falling steady from her tongue. To guard the flame. To hold the river of this people. To stand between Orchid and all that would unmake it. To keep the Veil as law.

When she spoke the final vow, the sigil over her heart flared, bright as noon, glowing crimson and gold, no longer black.

A murmur rippled through the crowd, part fear and part

awe. The court probably thought it was the ceremony—emotion, sanctity, the weight of the vow—stirring the royal Orchid mark on her chest.

But Ella knew better.

She knew what that glow meant. Something was coming.

Oh gods.

Her father lifted the crown.

The throne room held its silence.

He set it upon her head.

Ellandria stood in her coronation whites, crowned and unraveling, her sigil threatening to burn straight through her skin as she did all she could to hide the pain on her face. Throughout the chamber, nobles bent to their knees, a ripple of obedience moving like tidewater through silk. For the space of a single heartbeat, Orchid was whole.

Then the Veil tore.

44

THE VEIL BETWEEN THE REALMS

Light imploded before sound arrived. The air split down its center with a sickening crack. Above, the oculus blazed white as wind poured down from nowhere and everywhere at once, tearing garlands from the rafters and ripping ceremonial flowers, their petals scattering like ash. Torches flared, flames clawing the air in wild arcs.

The marble pedestal shrieked as it split apart, a jagged seam opening in the center of the throne room—a wound in the fabric of the realm. The tear did not stop at the dais. It carved straight through the central aisle, slicing between benches, rending a path out the throne room doors and into the courtyard beyond, as if the very land itself were being unstitched.

Ella's breath seized.

Hysteria swept through the throne room. Bodies surged toward the doors in a crush of silk and terror. Lords shoved past their own attendants, ladies lifted their skirts and ran, and guards fought to guide the spiraling crowd toward the outer halls. Someone screamed for the gods.

But a small knot of Orchid soldiers held their ground. She saw her father across the room shouting orders to the guards who hadn't fled.

Demetrius reached Ella first, still standing on the dais. Nira stumbled up behind him, smoke coiling from her palms in thin gray ribbons. Marisol arrived at Ella's other side, eyes wide but steady.

"We're with you, Your Majesty," Demetrius said. None of his usual flourish colored the words. His voice was tight with determination.

Ella swallowed hard. "No. Not all of you."

Their heads snapped toward her.

"Demetrius, Nira, go. Get the courtiers out. Your magic will not hold against this." She touched Demetrius's shoulder and then Nira's trembling hand. "Your gifts will not help against creatures of the Veil. I have seen them. Save our people. That is an order."

Demetrius hesitated, anguish flickering across his face. But he bowed and dragged Nira toward the fleeing crowd, smoke trailing behind them as they disappeared into the chaos.

Marisol stayed rooted beside Ella, flame flickering between her fingers like an instinct she could not suppress.

Jakobav appeared at Ella's side in a rush of cold air and steel. His voice was low and certain. "You sure?"

Ella met his gaze. "Marisol can amplify flame. That could turn the tide. She stays."

Marisol straightened, shoulders lifting with quiet pride.

Around them, Dravaryn steel answered the call. Maeren stepped in with her jaw set for war. Thane positioned himself at Ella's left, blade drawn. She didn't see Soren or Savina, but her gut told her they weren't far.

They formed an imperfect half-circle around the split in the marble just as the wind bent inward and the seam pulsed.

The dais was wide enough to hold their line, yet suddenly it felt too narrow, too fragile, with the Veil's wound carved straight through its heart. Ella leaned forward and peered into the tear, revealing depths so dark they seemed to swallow the torchlight whole.

A howl rose from the darkness. Not a sound but a violation, a shriek she had heard once before and prayed never to hear again. It split the air like a blade. Every person standing stumbled back from the seam, instincts driven by terror older than reason.

A creature slid through.

Towering. Twisted. Human only in the cruel suggestion of its outline. Black sinew clung to ridged bone, a vertical seam glowing like an unhealed wound where a face should have been. It moved with a predator's grace broken by the spasms of a marionette.

"Veil Leach," Ella whispered—the word slipping out before the court could blink.

"Raise the flame shields!" her father roared, his voice cutting through the wind from across the throne room.

The guards obeyed, fire lifting in a unified wave, yet the blaze faltered even as it formed, their shields paling before the darkness that surged against them from the tear in the Veil.

The Leach moved sideways in a blur, faster than eyes could follow, and struck. One guard collapsed with a wet, gurgling sound as the creature latched and drank, pulling not only blood but heat and color and the very spark of life, until nothing remained but a heap of fine ash crumbling over scorched marble.

Panic fractured the room. Screams filled the air as the remaining courtiers stumbled over toppled benches and fleeing guards. She spotted her father pushing through the chaos, crossing the hall instead of fleeing, driving the remaining Orchid guards into a tight defensive line at the foot of the dais.

"Ella." Jakobav's voice was steady, an anchor in the chaos.

"I don't understand," she said, breath catching. "The red sun is still days away—we should've had more time."

"Time's gone," Jakobav snapped. "Stay behind me."

She stepped down from the dais. Her crown didn't shift, as if it knew this was the hour it had been set for. Fire leapt to her hands from where it always waited. She cast it in a clean, blinding line, and the flame struck the Leach, burning white. The creature swelled, then came again with a renewed hunger.

Fuck. Did it just get bigger?

Jakobav spun around her and met it head-on, blade flashing, a single vicious strike that carved through its lunge and forced it sideways.

Another scream split the air. A second Leach spilled out, taller than the first, its claws gouging the stone as it righted itself.

Something echoed down the length of the seam, a distant shriek carried from far beyond the courtyard as if answering the one inside the hall.

Fuck. How many other creatures are crawling out of this tear across the realm?

"Savina!" Jakobav commanded without turning.

Savina appeared next to him and lifted her hands. The floor didn't just respond. It bowed to her. The marble convulsed, heaving upward with a force Ella felt in her teeth. Black pillars of stone erupted from the ground like the jaws of the gods. One Leach was caught mid-lunge, trapped before thought could even form behind its faceless skull.

The black pillars slammed shut with a sound like mountains grinding, like the realm itself snapping its teeth. When they tore apart again, nothing was left—only a smear of shadow and a rain of crushed stone dust drifting down like black snow.

Ella's breath punched out of her.

The shockwave rippled outward, cracking the marble into a spiderweb that raced across the room. Savina stood at the center of it all, jaw clenched, chest heaving, the floor still trembling beneath her boots. Guards stumbled back with strangled cries, as though the ground might rise again and devour them.

Shit. No one here has ever seen Dravaryn stone power.

The Veil truly had cracked—Savina was able to use her soil-forged magic here in Orchid.

Gods. Ella had watched breaches tear through the world like paper. But she'd never seen a mortal woman command the ground with that kind of strength.

More Leaches climbed from the tear, dragging themselves over the broken marble. Fights erupted everywhere at once, Orchid guards and Dravaryns locked against the creatures in a dozen frantic clashes. One broke free of the chaos and lunged for Ella, its glowing seam splitting open as it came for her.

She didn't think. She only moved.

Her hand closed on the hilt of the blade Thane had gifted her. The serpent-carved handle fit her grip with unnerving perfection—still far too regal to have ever belonged to Thane.

She slashed upward in a clean arc. Steel sang, and when the Leach met the Velmirian edge, its shadowed form split apart—riven into two staggering halves that twitched and tried to knit back together, only to fail and collapse into ash. A spray of black ichor struck her cheek, hot and foul, stinging where it touched her skin.

"Damn," Thane muttered, appearing beside her, awe softening his grin. "I always suspected you two would get along."

The Leach's death scream funneled back into the breach,

and the seam yawned wider as though dragged open by its echo.

Jakobav had moved to the far end of the dais, pushing her father back from the tear. His sword was drawn, his commands cutting through the chaos as he forced the remaining guards into a line to shield the throne—to protect her father.

Her breath caught. The man destined to rule her kingdom's oldest rival was now standing between her father and death.

Another creature came, and the breach convulsed, tearing wider as something immense forced its way through. The whole hall seemed to hold its breath. A sound rose from the depths, a layered shriek that raked across the stone. For a moment it sounded like one monstrous thing clawing its way upward.

Then the darkness broke apart.

Not one creature. Many. A cluster of Leaches crawled over each other, their limbs tangled, their seams glowing as they dragged themselves toward the surface in a single heaving mass.

Screams tore through what remained of the crowd. Orchid guards rushed forward, forming a line at the base of the dais. The moment the first Leach broke free of the tangle, they struck, flames surging from their palms in a unified blast.

Ella moved before she could think. She threw out her hands and poured her fire into theirs, forcing the line higher, hotter, brighter. Heat surged across the marble in a blinding wave.

At first, it seemed to work.

Then the Leaches began to swell.

Their bodies expanded as if filling from within, black sinew stretching over bulging ridges. Their seams brightened, glowing a sickly, pulsing gold. The creatures shuddered, drinking in the flame like starving animals.

One of them lifted its head, distended and glistening, and let out a wet, gorging hiss.

They were feeding.

They were growing.

And Ella realized with dawning horror that the Orchid fire was making them stronger.

"Get back!" she barked. She tore her hands away, flame retreating into her palms. "All fire-wielders, fall back! No more fire—GO!"

Jakobav's voice cut through the chaos a heartbeat later. "If you can't fight hand-to-hand, MOVE! Get to the outer halls!"

Marisol hesitated only a second, flame still flickering between her fingers.

"Marisol—go!" Ella shouted. "You'll only make them stronger."

Soren appeared at her flank, rising from the dust like he'd pulled himself out of the floor. Earth streaked his cloak, his expression grim.

"I'll take her," he said, voice rough with urgency. "I'll get Marisol out and anyone else I can reach. Then I'll be back."

Ella nodded once—there was no time for more.

The Leaches began to swarm.

"Get back!" Maeren barked. She stepped forward and drove her palm out; stone rippled up her forearm, forming a solid spear that jutted straight from her hand. She rammed it through the first Leach, tore it free, and pivoted to stab another.

A larger one surged toward her—bloated from ingested flame, its whole body heaving with that awful shriek. It slammed into her with such force it lifted her clean off her feet and hurled her into a bench. Wood and marble cracked under the impact.

She didn't rise right away, bracing on one elbow, breath snagging.

"Maeren!"

Another Leach slipped from the swarm. It skittered across the shattered dais, hugging the shadows, and lunged straight for the king. A young soldier threw himself into its path and missed. Eryndor staggered back, his heel catching on broken marble as he tried to regain footing.

Savina moved before Ella could breathe.

She thrust out both hands. The floor jolted and black spikes shot upward, locking together in a sudden wall between the Leach and the king. The creature hit the stone and burst into dark ichor that hissed on the tiles. Savina's teeth flashed, not in triumph but in the grim set of someone already calculating what the next strike would cost.

Another massive Leach dragged itself free of the breach, ichor dripping from its limbs as it bellowed. It charged straight at Thane while he was still pulling his blade from the body of another. He turned in time to see it, tried to spring clear, but the blow caught him full in the ribs and sent him crashing into a pillar. He slid down the veined marble and didn't rise.

Someone screamed. Ella couldn't tell who.

She ran to Thane's side, her blade raised, ready if the Leach circled back.

Jakobav reached him an instant later. He dropped to his knees and caught Thane beneath the shoulders. Blood seeped between Jakobav's fingers, soaking his sleeve and spreading fast across the floor.

"Too many," she said, voice low and urgent. "More by the second. Fire doesn't work, and blades aren't going to hold them back for long."

Jakobav looked up, snapping, "It's barely working now."

She looked around—every remaining guard locked in

desperate combat, bodies on the ground, Savina alone holding an entire line of Leaches at bay, and several creatures hunched over the fallen, feeding.

Ella gripped her blade tighter. "We need a way to push them back into the seam—and hold them there."

Jakobav shook his head once. "My shield won't do it. If it rebounds like last time, it'll take us out before the Leaches."

A rough breath escaped Thane. He blinked hard, dazed but conscious, pain twisting his features. "I know what could push them back..."

Jakobav whipped toward him. "Thane—"

"Use it," Thane rasped, a thin line of red sliding from the corner of his mouth. "It's our only chance. Do it."

"No." Jakobav's voice cracked with the force of it. His jaw locked, as if refusing could hold the world in place.

Thane coughed, breath hitching, and managed a bloodied half-smile. He grabbed Jakobav's wrist. "Jake... you and I both know I'm not powerless. I haven't been near my own soil long enough—but the Windforce is in me."

Jakobav shook his head once, and it seemed to be his final answer.

Thane's face contorted with pain, his breath hitching, but he pressed on. "You're the only bastard I'd let use it before I ever get to see it myself. So take it—before more Leaches come, before that tear opens wider, and before the realm implodes—taking every last one of us with it."

"No!" Jakobav shouted, composure long gone.

"Including Ella."

Jakobav flinched at her name. His gaze snapped to her—raw, torn, his refusal breaking in his eyes.

Ella watched as Jakobav bent with the grim resolve of a man who had run out of refusals. He pressed his thumb to the blood at the corner of Thane's mouth and brought it to his own lips.

Thane's mouth twitched, a shadow of his usual grin. "Knew that would do it."

The effect was instant. Jakobav's body jolted, muscles tightening as if something struck from within. His eyes went wide and strange, and for a moment he looked as though he were staring past the hall into some unreachable place. Then he wrenched himself back, chest heaving once, shoulders squaring.

The air changed direction.

45

CROWNED BENEATH RED SUN

It wasn't a draft or the erratic pull of the breach.

Jakobav stood with his hands thrust out as the wind answered him.

The force of it seized the room as if it had finally found its master, snatching at torchlight, banners, hair—at the very smoke twisting through the rafters. Everything bent to his will. His gaze locked on the glowing seam splitting the dais.

And the Leaches reacted.

A wave of wind crashed downward, hard as a hammer. The nearest Leach skidded across the cracked marble, claws tearing grooves as it was shoved toward the tear. Another was flung sideways, dragged screaming toward the breach as Jakobav forced the current deeper, pushing them back into the darkness below.

Ella braced herself as the wind tore past her.

She watched him turn and walk straight to Savina, who was holding back a swarm of Leaches by force, her stone spikes trembling. Jakobav thrust out his hands. The wind slammed forward in a single brutal surge, ripping every creature off the stones and hurling them into the open seam.

Yes. It's working. Thank the gods.

She watched as more were forced into the tear in the marble. Their cries vanished down the darkness as the wind drove them deeper. Jakobav stood over the seam, wind surging down into it to hold the creatures at bay.

She'd seen him do this before. But not this much and not this long.

Power that wasn't his always burned through him fast. Minutes, sometimes less. The longer he held it, the more she saw it draining him—his shoulders trembled under the strain. His breath was ragged, his arms rigid as the wind pinned them there.

The shadows in the tear shifted.

The Leaches were still deep in the darkness—but the moment the current faltered, the shadows surged upward again.

The Leaches were climbing back up. And his strength was waning.

"Shit," she said.

Jakobav couldn't hold that wind forever. And when it finally slipped, every Leach below would claw its way back up.

A cold certainty slid through her. This wasn't over.

Beneath the roar of the wind, she felt it thread-deep—the breach didn't stop in this hall. It ran farther. Beyond Orchid. Across the world.

She swallowed hard.

She'd closed a breach once before—the small tear by the castle gate. Maybe she could force this one shut long enough to figure out her next move.

Reckless.

Stupid.

Necessary.

Her body moved before doubt caught her. She stepped toward the seam and lifted her hands, reaching not for her flame but for the trembling threads within the split.

I have to patch it. Just long enough.

The breach surged toward her, darkness and smoke leaching out of the seam and slamming into her with enough force to drive her to the ground. Sprawled across the broken marble, she realized the threads were fighting her, forcing her back. She rose to her knees, searching for a tighter hold. The threads shimmered, tugging against the breach. She begged them to let her seize them, but every tug scraped her own flesh raw.

"Hold," she whispered, to herself or to the tear in the Veil. She couldn't tell.

Her father's voice rang out across the chaos, barking orders as he drove the last of the guards from the hall, forcing them to flee for their own lives while he stayed behind. He was utterly exposed now.

Fuck. She couldn't lose her father too.

The dais buckled beneath her knees. The breach widened.

If she could hold a little longer, reinforcements might reach the hall. But if she kept pushing herself like this, she'd reach burnout, fatal if pushed past the breaking point. If she died here, it would be an honorable death—queen for less than an hour and yet trying to save Orchid with all the strength she had left.

She poured everything into the threads that scraped her hollow from the inside. Heat built behind her eyes until her vision blurred. Something wet slipped from the corner of her eye down to her jaw. Sound thinned into a high, needling ring over the widening tear. Bitter smoke coated her tongue—resin, ash, and iron.

Jakobav turned. His eyes found Ella and stilled, and whatever he saw there made him move.

"Ella!" His voice thundered across the space between them, raw and absolute as he ran.

Ella's body shook with effort. Her Threadwalking power wasn't working—her sigil tattoo flared weakly and guttered out.

Then her power fizzled out entirely, her body collapsing.

Fuck. I burned myself out. All for nothing. I'm going to die here.

Her knees slid on grit. Jakobav reached her as the hall doubled and blurred, her father's face wavering through heat and tears.

"I can't hold on," she rasped, the words tearing the sore place in her throat.

She sagged into Jakobav's arms, a small, brittle laugh catching on the way out.

"The prophecy," she whispered, half-mocking and half-broken. "Crowned under the red sun. What a joke. All of this, and nothing to show for it."

With each breath, she was letting go.

His arms tightened around her and refused to yield.

"Do not let go. That is an order."

Her tears came harder, burning down her cheeks.

"I cannot," she sobbed.

She wiped her face and stared at the liquid on her hand—bright scarlet, not clear like water.

Blood tears.

Fuck, this is not good.

"I'm sorry. Jake, I didn't—"

"Don't do that." His voice broke, stopping the words.

He framed her face in both hands, desperate, as if the pressure alone could keep her from fading.

His brow pressed to hers, and she felt the steady heat of

him instead of the cold pull of the breach tugging at her like it meant to strip her lifeforce away.

"Do not let go of the prophecy," he said.

"I can't access my Threadwalking power—I burned through it all. The prophecy was wrong, Jake. My fire is useless. So am I. I've spent my whole life afraid I'm not enough—and I never will be."

Jake's breath hitched, a sound too close to a choke. "No."

His grip tightened on her hand, desperation breaking through the steel of his voice. "Fuck. Don't you dare give up on me."

He lifted her hand to his mouth and kissed her knuckles—hard, almost frantic. "Listen to me," he said, the words tumbling out fast and uneven. "The prophecy... it can't be wrong."

His thumb brushed her jaw. "The red sun must mean something else. The sun—it has to be you," he said, fierce and certain. "And the red—"

His gaze locked on what she guessed had to be the blood sliding from her lashes.

Gods, I must look disturbing.

He bent and closed his mouth over the track of tears. The tip of his tongue followed the line of blood, and she shuddered.

Power surged from him in a rippling shock wave, quick and bright.

Ella thought she'd imagined it—her body fading fast, hallucinating as it went.

"Picture the Veil," he said, voice rough. He lifted her against his chest as the Leaches' cries closed in. "I'll take us to it."

She pictured the threads of the Veil and reached for them with all she had left. But this time she felt something she never had before: Jakobav in the threads with her. They were Threadwalking together.

Her magic surged again; his blood magic was calling to her flame. She felt the pull toward him like she had that first night in the castle—the pull toward the relic.

The two magics met like opposing stars caught in the same orbit. Around them, the threads arranged themselves like constellations, each strand lit, spanning into a thousand radiant paths between ripples and realms.

Their combined magic wove itself through the fraying lattice of what used to be the Veil. Her fire mapped all the places it had fractured, its threads pulsing faster until the vibrations felt like the Veil was screaming at her.

And suddenly she understood.

The Veil wasn't broken because of its cracks. It was broken because it had been forced into place to seal the realms closed—twisted against its nature until every thread strained past breaking. It didn't need repair. It needed release.

"Jake," she whispered through the threads, her voice trembling with the knowledge settling into her bones, "we're not supposed to restore it. We have to burn what's left—free it."

His power flared in answer, steady as a vow, as he gripped her tighter.

She reached for the frayed lattice, her fire gathering. She saw her flame change color—not orange from Orchid, not white from the Claiming, but a brilliant, impossible red.

His blood and her flame merged into a single burning force—a red sun.

Together they unleashed it into the shattered fabric until each thread blistered and finally began to unravel.

The Veil burned bright as a dying star.

The threads burned, glowing with that red flame before disintegrating one by one into brilliant dust.

The Veil disappeared, unmade and free at last.

Jakobav's voice reached her. "Hold on to me."

She did.

A figure formed in the light ahead of her: tall, luminous, features shifting like memory.

"At last," the figure said, voice layered with ages. "The realms were never meant to be sealed. You bring the balance we have waited for."

A hand lifted in benediction, something in the motion achingly familiar.

"Be proud, Ellandria. And go home."

The figure dissolved into radiance, and the threads snapped with a sound like breaking dawn. Light rose in a single note, brighter than starlight, searing until suddenly, they were back on the dais.

Jakobav staggered and fell back with her in his arms. The hall lay in wreckage—pillars broken, marble cracked, the air full of settling dust. No new creatures pushed through the seam. The wound in the world had gone still.

She knew the realms now lay open, no longer straining against the ancient enchantment that had sealed them apart.

Jakobav lowered her to her feet, keeping one steadying arm around her waist as she found her balance. The crown sat slightly askew in her tangled hair, her coronation whites reduced to torn silk streaked with soot.

She reached for his hand without hesitation. Their fingers met amid dust and ruin, anchoring them to the world they had remade. Ash drifted in slow spirals, bright as snow in torchlight.

Maeren dragged herself upright with a grimace and a crooked smile. Soren lifted from a crack in the marble floor like a man climbing from a river, shoulders streaked with grit. Savina lowered her hand, and the pillars she'd called settled back into the dais, leaving scars the stone would no doubt remember.

She heard a gasp from one of the few who remained—guards, the injured, the inner circle still standing. And there, watching from the steps of the dais, was her father.

She had just disappeared and returned—she could only imagine the shock and confusion he must have been feeling.

Instead, her father looked at her like he'd witnessed a miracle. His gaze went to Jakobav and then returned to Ella.

"Gods, Ellandria... you're alive," he breathed.

Her father crossed the distance in two staggering steps and pulled her into his arms, holding her tightly as if afraid she might vanish again.

The Veil was gone, but the air still trembled with what it had cost.

Gods. They'd actually done it.

The realms were open. The prophecy was real.

The red sun had never been a star in the sky.

Red was his blood magic. Sun was her fire.

And Jakobav truly was the relic.

A sob rose unbidden as she looked across the shattered hall at the faces that had once been her enemies—Maeren's battered but unyielding stance, Savina's jaw set with exhaustion, Soren's eyes dark with quiet pride, Thane leaning bloody but grinning against the broken marble.

They'd come for her.

They'd fought for Orchid. For her father. For every kingdom still clinging to light.

She'd been so wrong about the Dravaryns. Of course they'd crash her coronation uninvited—and by doing so, save the fucking world.

She let out a half-laugh, half-sob.

The enormity of it hit her all at once, leaving her swaying but unbroken. Her hands were raw, her skin streaked with soot. She looked up to the oculus where stars burned in daylight, and warmth bloomed inside her in answer.

Tears cut tracks through the debris on her face. She touched one with the tip of her finger, half afraid it would still be blood, but it fell clear and warm.

The realms hadn't ended.

They'd only just begun to breathe.

46

ROOTS AND REUNIONS

Two months later, Orchid gleamed.

The entire castle had been scrubbed of ash and grief, the mosaics reset, the garlands replanted until they spilled from balconies in thick jeweled ropes, and the jungle unfurled around the castle, lush and watchful, its green tide lapping at the fringes of the grounds.

When the Veil vanished, the massive split in the marble did not disappear. In those first chaotic hours, Savina had used the last of her stone power—before gifts forged from Dravaryn's soil stopped answering her on Orchid ground—to drag the fractured floor back into place. In the weeks that followed, Orchid's best masons smoothed and polished the repaired stone until, from the oculus above the throne, light fell through warm air and gleamed on unbroken marble.

The courtyards and markets filled again with people whose laughter stitched itself to the drumbeat of work. They bowed to their queen with eyes that shone not only with respect but with relief; the ground had steadied beneath them and Thread-shifting was finally behind them.

Power had settled back into the natural order. The court scholars agreed that magic answered its own soil once again: Dravaryn's stone and earth in Dravaryn, Orchid's flame on Orchid ground, Thirelle's water magic held within its borders, and Velmire's windcraft bound to the heights that claimed it once more. Jakobav, seeking to mend what hatred had divided, insisted that Velmire would prove an ally to Orchid once he'd spoken with Thane's father.

The realization still burned in Ella's chest. When Jakobav had tasted Thane's blood, the memory it carried was never meant to see the light of day. He told her what he'd seen in that instant: a sky city where wind harps sang between white towers, and streets lay cut clean as bone; a boy sparring in a training court, laughter lifted on the gale as sunlit hair snapped loose; a king above with serpents chased in gold at his cuffs, citrine eyes cruel and calculating as they tracked every strike; the bow the boy offered; the smile the king returned. Later, behind closed doors, came the punishment that followed for not striking fast enough, brutal enough that Jakobav had spared her most of the details.

The vision had torn away for him, leaving two truths behind: Velmire had tried to force Thane toward a future he'd refused, and the wind Jakobav wielded to hold the Veil Leaches at bay had been exceptionally strong because of its inheritance —a power Thane had carried all his life from his royal bloodline without ever wielding. And with that truth came another secret for her to bear: Thane Ironfell was the rightful heir to the Velmire throne. At least this secret she shared with Jakobav.

Thane and the rest of the inner circle were back patrolling Dravaryn, but she hoped they would visit soon. If not, she would be tracking them down herself before long. She missed them all, even Bryn, and especially Savina and Thane. The knowledge of what Thane had endured as a child would haunt her forever.

Ella shivered and forced her thoughts elsewhere.

In the quiet that followed the Veil shattering, it was almost a comfort to have magic tied to soil as law again.

Jakobav had returned north to steady his kingdom and then come back just a week later, moving through the castle as if space had been made for him, through the Orchid court as if he'd been born to it, and through her rooms like a man who had stopped asking permission.

Ella didn't ask whether his Claiming gift still held or whether his Blood-Scenting still reached beyond Dravaryn. She thought she'd seen a shield flicker once, instinct more than proof, but too much else demanded her hands: rebuilding and oaths, bread and borders.

He surprised her with one more gift. He had become a better mentor than many men twice his age. All that time beside the King of Dravaryn had left him rich with knowledge, even though the king could no longer speak. Ella drank in every lesson. He didn't talk over her or soften the work. He showed her the price of command along with the possibilities and stood steady while she chose her path through it.

Thirelle's queen sailed in blue and silver to thank Queen Ellandria of Orchid for opening the realms and preventing the Veil's shatter from destroying the mortal world. Ella traveled in return with a guard of Orchid steel to stand with the monarch and further reassure their alliance. She was met with adoration from the Thirelle people and an overflow of warm hospitality from their royalty. Water rose to a lifted hand and poured into a glass as they cheered to good health and pledged support for one another. The devotion there, the way a whole people bowed to tide and lake, was familiar. It wasn't the same as her homeland's fire, but it was kin to it, something living that honored an element both purifying and essential.

Spies from every kingdom had been posted along the continent's far horizon since the day the Veil shattered. Orchid skiffs kept to the currents, Dravaryn watchers guarded the stormlines, Thirelle listened through water, and Velmire's commanders kept watch in the high wind. The land across the sea, once belonging to the Fae, lay quiet as bone. No lights. No voices. No proof of life at all. Yet with the realms now open, and those with the ability to travel between them free to do so, it had never been more vital to know where each mortal kingdom placed its loyalties.

Ella sat on the throne that afternoon and, for the first time, did not feel crushed by it. It had taken weeks of practice, pretending, before turning into something she could bear.

Petitioners from Orchid's capital, Aradessa, arrived in waves. They came and went, speaking of food and bridges and borders that were mostly old grudges in new clothes. At her right stood Jakobav, silent and immovable: she felt the comfort of his protection even when she didn't look his way. Some petitioners faltered at the sight of him, their words stumbling, but none dared to question aloud why the prince of Dravaryn stood so near their queen.

Ella gave orders when orders might move the world, coin where coin could do honest work, and silence when silence proved wiser than speech. Out of the corner of her eye, she kept catching the clean shine of marble and the small markers of a home that had endured. She smiled at the familiar faces in the throne room, at Nira's mix of warmth and humor and Demetrius's chaos and loyalty, reminders that Orchid remained hers in more ways than lineage.

Her father entered without ceremony.

Eryndor moved differently now, lighter around the eyes as if grief had sanded him down to his best parts.

He paused at the foot of the dais until she inclined her head. At his gesture, the chamber emptied, voices dimming as the doors thudded closed. Marisol was the last to walk out and, just before leaving, she turned and met Ella's gaze, bright with curiosity, as if she were trying to say something without words.

Jakobav didn't move at first. His gaze found hers, and she wanted nothing more than to hold it. Eryndor looked from the man at her side back to Ella.

"May I speak with you alone?" he asked, the words both a question and a father pulling rank.

She inclined her head.

Jakobav stepped closer before he left, brushing his fingers along hers where they rested on the arm of the throne. The touch was brief, but it left her pulse unsteady. His mouth bent close enough that only she could hear.

"I need to return to Dravaryn," he said. "Something has called my attention back, and it can't wait. I shouldn't be gone more than a couple weeks."

Ella's brows drew together. "What calls you away?"

He shook his head once. "I've been in Orchid too long without checking on my own kingdom. You know I can't neglect it forever." His voice gentled, warm enough to melt her unease. "Every second I'm gone, I'll wish I wasn't."

She couldn't even argue. He'd been at her side day and night for weeks, present in every council meeting.

Before she could speak, he bent and pressed his lips to hers, restrained but certain. The heat of it lingered on her lips as he pulled back, his eyes locked on hers for a final moment. Then he turned and left.

The doors closed, and the room felt too large, too quiet, without him.

Eryndor stepped forward, his voice steady. "I'm so proud of you, Ellandria. Your mother would be too."

Her throat tightened as he stepped closer and cupped her cheek as if she had never left. "She always said you were just like an orchid yourself, quite a fitting flower for the girl who would grow into a great ruler. You grew in every direction, you took to heat and made it home, and your roots were patient and strong, waiting for the day they would need more room."

He studied her for a long moment and gave an almost-smile. "But now that I've seen you bloom, I don't think the metaphor fits anymore. You've come into yourself too quickly and too brilliantly, as if you struck a match to a field and set it blazing, burning through every expectation, leaving only ash where the world thought it knew you. From that ash, a new path has taken root."

Her eyes began to water. He had never spoken to her like this—gentle, unguarded, proud, stripped of politics and duty, speaking only as her father. The words settled, warm and heavy beneath her ribs, and he let them rest there before his hand fell away. "But the real reason I need to talk to you, Ellandria," he said, his voice steadying, "is that there is something you need to know about who you are and what you are."

Ella let out a quiet chuckle, a small smile breaking through even as tears pricked her eyes. "If this is another speech about orchids, I swear..."

Her father's hand lingered on her cheek, and she let it, because his words had cut straight through her. It was the most beautiful orchid metaphor she had ever heard, and she'd grown up in a court that lived and breathed them.

Her father's tone shifted. He drew a slow breath, as if bracing himself.

"You are part-Fae."

The color drained from her cheeks.

A laugh rose unbidden, sharp and absurd, as if he'd just said the most ridiculous thing imaginable. She choked it down when she saw his face.

"You have Fae blood," he continued. "Your mother did too. It's in your blood."

Ella stared at him.

"We hid it to protect you," Eryndor said. "To keep you safe. To keep you alive, Ella."

Her heart struck once, hard, and she couldn't move. Her breath stilled, as if even her lungs weren't prepared for it.

Ella's instinct to deflect with sarcasm died in her throat, replaced by brutal honesty. "How could that be possible? I don't know if I believe it."

His face hardened. "Claiming ceremonies were never meant for mortals alone. They are Fae rituals. They draw on Fae magic to steady the body, to birth a chosen power into blood and bone. When the realms were sealed, that current was cut off. Many who attempted the Rite died. So many were lost, Ella. Only mortals with extraordinary strength survived, or those with Fae blood."

His voice carried the devastation of tragic loss. "That is the real reason Claimings were banned all those years ago."

She shook her head slowly, hands curling tight around the carved wood of the throne.

"We had to hide what you are, what your mother was," he pressed, "because if anyone guessed...they would have hunted you for it. The rest of the mortal world would have rejected our kingdom, slaughtering thousands of innocents who had no knowledge of the secrets behind Orchid's royal line."

Ella could barely form words, trying to piece it all together before she fell apart. "So ignorance was protection."

Eryndor's mouth thinned. "Not ignorance. It was just protection. And your mother chose it too. She never underwent her Claiming. We found a way to hold her Fae side quiet, to keep her from Threadwalking and burning herself out while the realms were locked. For years, it worked."

Ella's head snapped up.

"What did you just say?" Her voice cracked against the marble, disbelief burning in every word. She shoved back against the throne as if the wood had lied to her. "My mother was a Threadwalker? Like me?" Her tone was full of shock and bitterness.

"You're telling me she had it in her blood and you just kept it chained, locked away?" She shook her head, hard enough to sting her temples. "I stepped into another realm without even trying. There's no stopping it." She closed her eyes, inhaled deeply, and attempted to collect herself. "It's not a choice. It's instinct. So how did you keep her from Threadwalking?"

Her father's voice was steady, but there was gravity behind it. "Your mother wanted a family. Without the ability to fully awaken her Fae gift, to cross into other realms, to undergo the Claiming, she was destined for an early death, just like those before her. Just like your grandmother. But she wanted to live long enough to get to know you, Ellandria. So we searched far and wide, across all four kingdoms, desperate for an answer. For scraps of knowledge that had not been sealed or destroyed when the Fae were exiled." Her father brushed his hand across his forehead, where beads of sweat had begun to form.

"We found it in the most unlikely place—Dravaryn—lying deep within our enemy kingdom. There we met an even more unlikely, yet thank the gods, willing, person to help us. A healer. Quirky. Unpredictable. I believe you have come to trust and care about him yourself."

Ella froze. "Bryn?"

"Bryn," Eryndor confirmed. His mouth twisted. "Don't get me started on his ancestry. One revelation is enough for today."

Her jaw clenched until it ached. She stared at the polished floor until her vision blurred. "I knew there was more to the mischief in his eyes," she whispered, voice thick with disbelief. "He stood at my side, took care of me, bled with me, laughed with me...and the whole time he was helping keep this secret? Helping her hide it?" She bit off the rest, nails digging into her palms until they stung.

Eryndor's tone softened. "He swore to protect your mother. Protecting her meant keeping you from the truth. He did it to help us. Saving many others in the process."

Her voice was filled with hurt and betrayal. "I trusted him."

"So did we. I still do," her father said quietly.

He let the silence hold for a moment, then went on. "When you were Claimed, the current returned. To you. To your bloodline. We felt it here even before word reached us. Your mother felt it most. The seal we had kept on her failed, and once your true power woke, hers stirred. She began to decline almost at once."

Ella's throat burned as if she'd swallowed glass. "So my Claiming killed her."

"No." Eryndor's answer was firm. "Your Claiming freed what could not be bound forever. The Veil would have burst one day with or without you. Your mother knew this. She chose the path that gave you life and gave the rest of the realm centuries."

"Don't dress it up." Ella's voice snapped like a whip. "If I hadn't gone through the Claiming, she might've had more time."

His eyes closed for a beat. "Months, perhaps. But never years. She would have chosen the same outcome again and again. What you did saved more than just the mortal realm, Ella. And it wouldn't have been possible. Without your Claiming, you wouldn't have survived."

Ella pushed herself to her feet to head for the doors, but the room tilted and spun. She caught herself on the rail, then forced her way down to the lowest step. Her knees buckled, so she sat hard, pressing her thumb into the marble until the sting anchored her.

Her father followed and lowered himself beside her. He put his arm around her shoulders, and this time she didn't shake it off.

He inhaled a long, slow breath, then said, "There is more you need to hear. Not all the magic in you answers Orchid soil. Some of it ignores the natural order, crosses borders."

Ella gave a harsh, bitter laugh. "Yeah, I noticed."

"Then you know this too," he said. "You need to be careful who you trust; you have an entire kingdom looking to you for protection now. And there are others in the mortal realm who possess powers not born of this soil."

Her head snapped toward him.

Ella only stared. Then the words left her mouth at the exact time the thought formed. "Fuck. Jakobav's bloodline is part-Fae." The words tasted wrong in her mouth. She leaned forward, pressing her palms flat to her knees. "Does he know? Has he been hiding it from me this whole time?"

"I cannot answer that," her father said. "Dravaryn guards its blood histories as tightly as its borders. What I do know is this." Eryndor rose off the bottom step and started pacing, as if worried about how she would take what he was going to say next, making Ella's stomach drop.

"Jakobav carries Fae blood; his Blood-Scenting ability is not mortal, nor is it from Dravaryn soil. It is a Fae inheritance, one passed down for generations. His grandfather had it. His father had it. He has it."

Ella thought she might be about to get sick. Jake hadn't told her that.

Does he know I'm part-Fae? Is that why he pulled me into his fucking Claiming?

A tight wave of dizziness hit her, thank the gods she was already sitting. Her pulse stuttered, hard and uneven. Was this why he'd left so quickly? Did he somehow know what her father was going to tell her? She had half a mind to grab a horse and chase him down herself just to drag the truth out of him.

But her father continued on as if he had to get it all out before he lost his nerve.

"They kept performing Claimings even after the realms were sealed. Half of their mortals who attempted it died. But they kept doing it anyway. I will say this; it weeded out the weak and left only the most powerful standing, leading to a fearsome military force. Now you know why your mother and I worked tirelessly toward maintaining the peace. Starting another war would not end well for any kingdom beside Dravaryn."

Ella let out a dry, scornful sound. "So the honorable Rite they value so highly is a fucking gamble, a deadly game, one where those playing aren't even fully informed of the rules?"

"They would not call it that," he said. "They view it as an honor to be claimed and bestowed with ancient gifts. And before you ask, I doubt Jakobav knows the full cost. Secrets that size stay locked above a prince as long as a king can hold them."

Eryndor's voice dropped, steady but grim. "There is more. The King of Dravaryn can't survive without using his Blood-Scent magic, just as your mother couldn't survive without using her Fae ability. But the difference is this: Blood-Scent magic may work on mortals, but it requires Fae blood from a bloodline not their own. He can manage for some time without, but eventually the price must be paid. Even a small amount of Fae blood sustains the king when his own strength fails."

Ella jerked upright. "What?" The word snapped out, loud and flat.

"I need to ask you questions, and I need the truth. Did Jakobav ever ask for your blood?"

"No."

"Did he ever drink from you?"

Her head whipped toward him. "Absolutely not."

The lie slipped out before she could stop it.

Though it wasn't entirely a lie. Jakobav had tasted a drop a few times, yes, but he had never fully drunk her blood—not that she was aware of. Her father had seen Jake take a drop of Caelen's blood from his blade, and he'd watched him take a drop from Thane to wield his wind magic. It dawned on her then that when Jake had licked the blood tear from her face as she was losing the battle, it must have looked like nothing more than a final kiss goodbye.

"Good. Do you have any reason to believe he might have taken blood from you to give to his father?"

Her jaw clenched so hard it hurt. "If someone touched me like that, I would know. So no."

He studied her face, then nodded once. "Did you ever meet the king in private?"

"No."

"Did anyone else from Dravaryn take your blood for any reason?"

Her stomach churned. "Bryn took a sample for healing, with my permission, but that's it."

"Then we must keep our guard high," her father said. "If the king has gone too long without Fae blood, then someone near him is surely looking for it."

Ella barked out a scoff. This was unbelievable; her anger started to rise, suspicions climbing along with it. "And you think that someone would use me if they were to find out my lineage?"

"I think power creates need," he said, "and need breeds ugly choices." He exhaled. "There's more I could say—mostly rumors not yet confirmed. When I know the truth, you'll hear it from me first."

Ella shoved herself upright. Heat rushed her face and drained just as quickly, leaving her skin cold. She somehow remained standing and started pacing as she dragged her hands down her face. Her voice was rough, low. "Why would Bryn help the king and queen of Orchid at all? He's loyal to Jakobav and his kingdom. I've seen it."

Her father's eyes narrowed. "Bryn worships survival. He cares for Dravaryn, yes, but he also cared about keeping the mortal realm intact. When we asked him, all those years ago, why he would agree to help us, he said it was the key to keeping the world from breaking. I think both can be true, Ellandria."

"It sounds like you're asking me to forgive him. Maybe Bryn didn't lie directly, considering he almost always speaks in riddles, but there's some shit he left out."

"I am asking you to see the board before you move a piece."

Her gaze dropped to her wrist. She turned it so the inside caught the light, the skin pale around the black rose mark. "So if all of this was caused by my Claiming...and if I'm to believe that I'm part-Fae, then explain to me why I was marked with this." She thrust it toward him. "The Dravaryn rose. Why did the High Vexari grab me during the Rite, and why did she look at it like she wanted to tear my skin off? She went from curious to enraged in a blink. Tell me what that means."

Her father leaned forward. His eyes fixed on the mark, and his face changed.

"She touched you?" he asked, voice gone hard.

Ella barked out a laugh. "Touched me? She dug her nails in. She was not gentle."

His shoulders stiffened. "Then she suspects what you are. Or she already knew and wanted proof."

Ella's mouth twisted. "So the High Vexari of Dravaryn has a personal interest in my bloodline? Fantastic."

"You will not be alone with her again," her father said.

Ella's head tipped back, a harsh laugh echoing up into the rafters. "No argument from me there. She was godsdamned terrifying."

Eryndor exhaled slowly, his gaze fixed on her as if he could see the implications of everything he'd just told her settling on her shoulders. "There is one last thing you need to understand. The moment you first Threadwalked, we felt it here in Orchid. We knew you were alive and moving somewhere in the mortal realm. It was like a flare shot into the dark. From that moment on, there was no doubt. You weren't just surviving. You were awakening."

Ella's stomach twisted. She pressed her nails into her palm until her skin stung. "And no one thought to get a message to me? Give me some sort of heads up about my own bloodline or my own gift stirring beneath my own skin?"

"We wanted to. Gods know we wanted to. But if word had spread that the heir of Orchid was alive and vulnerable in a foreign kingdom, you would have been hunted and unable to follow your fate. The less who knew, the longer you lived. And when word arrived that you had undergone the Claiming in Dravaryn, hand in hand with Jakobav..." His mouth tightened.

"We knew the seal on your mother would fail. We knew she had days left. We were in shock for days ourselves. And then we prepared for what came next."

"So everyone else knew my life was fate and tragedy waiting to happen. Everyone but me."

"You should have been told," he admitted. "I carry that failure."

Her voice was flat. "Don't expect thanks. Don't expect forgiveness either."

"I expect you to use it," he said. "What you carry now is truth. And truth is power."

Ella shoved her hair back from her face, rough and quick. "So let me line this up. I am part-Fae. My mother was also part-Fae. She needed to Threadwalk to survive but her power was bound by magic supplied by Bryn. My Claiming woke the bloodline. Dravaryn's Rite kills mortals for glory. Their king needs Fae blood to keep breathing. Jakobav's bloodline is as tangled in this as mine, and I've been the last godsdamned person to know, in every way that matters."

"Yes."

"Fuck every secret that got us here."

"You're right to feel that way. And I regret not telling you sooner, Ellandria," her father replied. He paused, gathering himself before he continued. "With the realms open, ignorance is no longer protection—it's a weapon someone could turn against us. Marisol has been invaluable in gathering information about Fae bloodlines and Blood-Scenting. We've been piecing together truths that others would rather keep buried."

"From now on, you tell me everything," she said quietly, but her voice held. "Hide another truth from me, and I'll appoint someone else to guide this court. I won't rule beside anyone who would allow me to lead blindly."

She was done holding back. It hit her, all of it at once—the devastation, the lies, the not knowing if she'd been betrayed or if Jakobav was as much in the dark as she was.

"*Why didn't you tell me sooner? Why today?*" Anger poured through every word she screamed at him.

"One of our court seers had a vision that something is stirring within the realms, though she was unable to see the source. Similar reports have come from Thirelle, which means the other kingdoms are aware of it too. We must prepare ourselves and our people. I suspect that's the reason Jakobav returned to his own in such a hurry."

He hesitated for a moment, scanning Ella's face before continuing on. "And I couldn't help but notice he didn't give you details when you asked what had called him away. I'm sorry, Ellandria." Eryndor looked utterly gutted, as if he was the one who had possibly been betrayed.

Before Ella could press him further, the doors blasted open. Guards stumbled in, pale and sweating, their boots slipping on polished stone.

"Your Majesty," one gasped, dropping to his knees. "The far coast. The entire continent—"

"Speak," Ella snapped.

"It is inhabited," the guard blurted. "All at once. Thousands, maybe more. Lights where there were none, towers where there was mist. The Fae have returned."

The hall, even empty, seemed to pull back from the words.

Another guard stepped forward with a scroll sealed in obsidian wax, the sigil pressed so deep the stamp had cracked at the edges. No one in this lifetime had seen that seal with their own eyes, and yet every royal knew it from their earliest teachings. Her father snatched it from his hand.

He broke the seal and read in a voice that did not waver:

"To the rulers of the four kingdoms of this mortal realm: You are hereby summoned to a council. We will speak of our return and the

balance of the realms. Attend at once. The stability of your world demands it."

Not a request. A command.

"When did this arrive?" Eryndor asked, holding the summons away from his body as if it were venom.

"Mere minutes ago," the guard said.

He lowered his voice, as if afraid the word itself might bloom in his mouth. "It arrived by...Rose Magic."

A murmur rippled through the guards before the chamber stilled. Even her father's breath seemed to catch, sweat beading on his forehead and upper lip.

The man swallowed and spoke lower, as if afraid a more sinister force of Fae magic might punish him for speaking on it. "It opened in the council room," he said. "From the mosaics. A crack first...then a stem forcing through, green and wet as if it carried its own rain. It climbed fast. Thorns split from it. And then—" He swallowed. "It flowered. A single rose, large as a fist, right on the table."

The guard's hands shook. "The petals shimmered with every color. When we reached for the bloom, it loosened its hold and left the scroll in its place. The moment the parchment lifted free, the stem blackened, and the rose turned to smoke."

A silence followed that was louder than the scream the messenger seemed to be holding back.

Ella's skin prickled. The word her tutors had whispered in restricted stacks came back to her. It was the courier craft of the Fae, roses that could root in dust, in wood, in water, in stone. A bloom that could appear anywhere, in the middle of a meal or in the center of a bed, each color carrying a meaning no mortal record had preserved.

As he folded the parchment, a smaller slip slid free, tucked beneath the wax. No sigil. Only her name written in a hand that looked alive on the page.

Ellandria.

She didn't ask for her father to leave, although she probably should have.

Her nightmares were taking shape right before her eyes.

She took the note.

The paper was warm. The ink shifted when she turned it, as if light and shadow disagreed about the letters.

Dearest Ellandria,

Now, I already know what you're thinking: why would the devastatingly handsome King of Fae want to meet you alone?

Her pulse hammered so hard she thought the guards must hear it. Heat crawled along her throat, shameful and sharp, because part of her recognized the voice on the page as though it were speaking from inside her skull.

She knew without a shadow of a doubt—it was him. The man from her vision, then again in a painting, once more in Jakobav's room when he had scared her so badly she stumbled onto the bed, and then most recently when she'd Threadwalked straight to him in her sleep.

The Fae man with the pendant, icy green eyes, and wrath disguised as elegant strength.

He was the fucking King of Fae.

Ella's hands trembled, and she hoped no one noticed. She wanted to crush the paper, burn it, hurl it into the nearest torch, but her focus wouldn't leave the words. They pulled her on, dread twining with a fascination she couldn't smother. Her intrigue was disgraceful.

Worst of all, no one else would know what the words on that parchment truly meant. He probably thought himself cunning when he slipped in the words: *Now, I already know what you're thinking.* But she knew exactly how deceptively accurate that was.

He had once heard loud and clear what she hadn't said aloud.

Which meant the King of Fae was a fucking Echobinder.

They were undoubtedly and irrevocably fucked.

He'd been inside her head. He'd marked her wrist with his grip. And now he was toying with her.

Shame came crawling up her spine once more. She loathed the part of her that leaned closer, itching to continue reading.

The answer, of course, is because you fascinate me.

I know what you are. I know what you've done. And I am not in the habit of waiting.

Attend the council. Smile for your court.

Let Dravaryn's prince stand too close.

When it ends, you and I will meet.

Privately. I insist.

Until then, think of me.

Yours,

Zavrik

Remember, Ellandria, not all roots are buried.

Her heart stopped.

Her hands were shaking.

A cool, clammy touch pressed against her ankle. She looked down and saw a green snake coiled there, Octavia's familiar. Its tongue flicking at the air as if tasting the faint sweetness that had bloomed from the letter.

Ella couldn't believe the serpent was there, in her throne room, summoned by her suffering. "Godsdammit, Octavia. Not now," she muttered, though her voice trembled.

Its scales pressed cool against her skin, steadying her even as her heart began to race again. As if it was sent to remind her of the two paths predicted by Octavia. As if the snake had been sent solely to gloat.

A flare tightened beneath her ribs, anger rising raw.

She was getting fucking tired of others finding her fate before she did.

Her Orchid sigil burned as she lowered her eyes and saw it glowing violet, the ink threaded with living light, a color her tattoo had never taken before. It pulsed once, twice, then steadied, a promise she didn't understand, but had a feeling she would soon find out.

She looked back down at the letter, gripping it so tightly her knuckles went white. The scent of jasmine clung to the page, cloying and lush, and it didn't fade when she closed her fist around it, crushing it beneath her fury.

My father doesn't get to read this. He can sit on the wrong side of a secret for once.

Deep within her, a whisper began to stir.

It was a promise to uncover every last truth, to set ablaze anyone who would dare stand in the way of the reckoning she would bring. It was time to protect her kingdom, claim the path that had always been hers, and step out of the dark she'd been held in.

Ella vowed she would rise into the light. She would show the world the queen she was—or burn everything to the fucking ground as the Orchid On Fire.

ACKNOWLEDGMENTS

Thank you to my husband for supporting me through every late night and every moment I needed space to write. Your steady encouragement made this possible.

To my children, who brought joy into even the most exhausting days, thank you for grounding me and reminding me why stories matter.

Thank you to the friends, early readers, and supporters who cheered for this world long before it was finished. Your belief carried me through.

And to every reader who steps into the magic of these realms, I am grateful for you. Some stories insist on being written, and this one poured out of my soul. I am honored to share it with you.

ABOUT THE AUTHOR

L. R. Mirelle writes slow-burn romantic fantasy filled with danger, spice, and ancient magic. Her debut novel, *Orchid on Fire*, Book One of *The Path Between Realms*, introduces readers to a world of lethal heirs, realm-shifting power, and a romance that could ignite the end of an age.

When she is not weaving worlds or rewriting prophecy, Mirelle works in the healthcare industry, balancing leadership, family life, and the quiet chaos of creativity. She lives in the Midwest with her husband and three young children, who inspire her to chase every story that refuses to stay quiet.

You can find her sharing behind-the-scenes peeks, bookish humor, and release news on TikTok (@orchidonfire) and Instagram (@lrmirelleauthor). To stay updated on future books and exclusive content, visit **lrmirelle.com** to join her newsletter.

ALSO BY L. R. MIRELLE

The Path Between Realms Series

Book Two: Coming Soon

Follow updates at lrmirelle.com

www.ingramcontent.com/pod-product-compliance
Lightning Source LLC
Chambersburg PA
CBHW060758310726
48980CB00002B/147

* 9 7 9 8 9 9 4 2 3 2 1 2 5 *